The HENNA ARTIST

Praise for *The Henna Artist*

"Eloquent and moving… Joshi masterfully balances a yearning for self-discovery with the need for familial love."

—*Publishers Weekly*

"Reading *The Henna Artist* is like travelling in a car that is going at just the right speed. At times, author Alka Joshi stops to point out sights and scenes on the way. At other times, she revs up the story and you find yourself on a thrilling ride to an unknown destination."

—*The Week*

"Rich in detail and bright with tastes and textures, *The Henna Artist* is a fabulous glimpse into Indian culture of the 1950s."

—*BookPage*, starred review

"Lakshmi Shastri… empowers me."

—Freida Pinto, Actor

"Joshi has constructed a bewitching glimpse into the past with a tough heroine well worth cheering on."

—*Booklist*

"An entertaining debut about an important theme—balancing family with personal ambition—that allows readers to escape into a fantasy teeming with sensory pleasure."

—*San Francisco Chronicle*

"Vibrant characters, evocative imagery, and sumptuous prose create an unforgettable tale."

—*Christian Science Monitor*

"Romantic, old-time Rajasthan leaps to life... I can hardly wait for Alka Joshi's next masterpiece."

—Sujata Massey, internationally bestselling author of *The Widows of Malabar Hill*

"Fantastic, so evocative and beautiful and full of life and light... and deeply satisfying in its storytelling."

—Leah Franqui, author of *America for Beginners*

"Read this book slowly and savor it: Every page is rich with intricate pleasures for both the mind and the heart."

—Anita Amirrezvani, author of *The Blood of Flowers*

"Bold, ambitious, beautifully written... The broad cast of characters will etch themselves into your psyche."

—Tom Barbash, author of *Stay Up with Me*

Also by Alka Joshi

The Secret-Keeper of Jaipur

The HENNA ARTIST

A NOVEL

ALKA JOSHI

HarperCollins *Publishers* India

First published in the US in 2021 by Mira
by arrangement with Harlequin Books S.A.

First published in India by
HarperCollins *Publishers* 2021

HarperCollins Publishers India, Cyber City, Building 10-A, Gurugram,
Haryana-122002, India

www.harpercollins.co.in

2 4 6 8 10 9 7 5 3 1

P-ISBN: 978-93-5422-652-6
E-ISBN: 978-93-5422-693-9

Printed and bound at
MicroPrints India, New Delhi

MIX
Paper
FSC FSC™ C218906

This product is made of FSC®-certified and other controlled material.

HarperCollins Publishers, Macken House, 39/40 Mayor Street
Upper, Dublin 1, D01 C9W8, Ireland

For my mother, Sudha Latika Joshi, who championed my independence
For my father, Ramesh Chandra Joshi, who sang me the sweetest lullaby

The traveler has to knock
at every alien door to come to his own,
and one has to wander through all the outer worlds
to reach the innermost shrine at the end.

—From the poem *Journey Home* by Rabindranath Tagore

When the Goddess of Wealth comes to give you her blessing,
you shouldn't leave the room to wash your face.

—Hindu Proverb

CHARACTERS WHO APPEAR

Lakshmi Shastri: 30-year-old henna artist, living in the city of Jaipur

Radha: Lakshmi's 13-year-old sister, born after Lakshmi left her village

Malik: Lakshmi's servant boy, 7 or 8 years old (he does not know which), lives in the crowded inner city with his Muslim auntie and cousins

Parvati Singh: 35-year-old society matron, wife of Samir Singh, mother of Ravi and Govind Singh, distant cousin of the Jaipur royal family

Samir Singh: renowned architect from a high-caste Rajput family, husband of Parvati Singh and father of Ravi and Govind Singh

Ravi Singh: 17-year-old son of Parvati and Samir Singh, in boarding school at Mayo College (a few hours from Jaipur)

Lala: long-serving spinster servant in the Singh household

Sheela Sharma: 15-year-old daughter of Mr. and Mrs. V. M. Sharma, a wealthy Brahmin couple of humble origins

Mr. V. M. Sharma: official building contractor of the Jaipur royal family, husband of Mrs. Sharma, father of four, including his youngest daughter Sheela Sharma

Jay Kumar: bachelor school chum of Samir Singh from Oxford days, practicing physician in Shimla (at the foothills of the Himalayas, an 11-hour drive from Jaipur)

Mrs. Iyengar: Lakshmi's landlady in Jaipur

Mr. Pandey: Lakshmi's neighbor and another tenant of Mrs. Iyengar, Sheela Sharma's music tutor

Hari Shastri: Lakshmi's estranged husband

Mrs. Joyce Harris: young Englishwoman, wife of a British army officer who is part of the transition team in Jaipur for the handover of the British Raj

Mrs. Jeremy Harris: Joyce Harris's mother-in-law

Munchi: old man from Lakshmi's village who taught her how to draw and taught Radha how to mix paints

Kanta Agarwal: 26-year-old wife of Manu Agarwal, educated in England, originally from a literary Calcutta family

Manu Agarwal: Director of Facilities for the Jaipur royal family, husband of Kanta, educated in England, related to the Sharma family

Baju: an old family servant of Kanta and Manu Agarwal

Maharaja of Jaipur: a figurehead post-independence, the highest ranking royal in the city, wealthy in land and money, possessing multiple palaces in Jaipur

Naraya: the builder of Lakshmi's new house in Jaipur

Maharani Indira: the maharaja's stepmother, married to the late Maharaja of Jaipur, childless, also referred to as the dowager queen

Maharani Latika: the current maharaja's wife, 31 years old, educated in Switzerland

Madho Singh: Maharani Indira's parakeet

Geeta: widow, Samir Singh's current mistress

Mrs. Patel: one of Lakshmi's loyal henna clients, proprietress of a hotel

PROLOGUE

Ajar, State of Uttar Pradesh, India
September 1955

Her feet step lightly on the hard earth, calloused soles insensible to the tiny pebbles and caked mud along the riverbank. On her head she balances a *mutki*, the same earthenware jug she uses to carry water from the well every day. Today, instead of water, the girl is carrying everything she owns: a second petticoat and blouse, her mother's wedding sari, *The Tales of Krishna* her father used to read to her—the pages fabric-soft from years of handling—and the letter that arrived from Jaipur earlier this morning.

When she hears the voices of the village women in the distance, the girl hesitates. The gossip-eaters are chatting, telling stories, laughing, as they wash saris, vests, petticoats and *dhotis*. But when they spot her, she knows they will stop to stare or spit at the ground, imploring God to protect them from the Bad Luck Girl. She reminds herself of the letter, safe inside the *mutki*, and thinks, *Let them. It will be the last time.*

Yesterday, the women were haranguing the headman: *Why is the Bad Luck Girl still living in the schoolteacher's hut when we need it for the new schoolmaster?* Afraid to make a sound for fear they would come inside and pull her out by her hair, the girl had remained perfectly still within the four mud walls. There was no one to protect her now. Last week, her mother's body had been burned along with the bones of other dead animals, the funeral pyre of the poor. Her father, the former schoolteacher, had abandoned them six months ago, and shortly after, he drowned in a shallow pool of water along the riverbank, so drunk he likely hadn't felt the sting of death.

Every day for the past week, the girl had lain in wait on the outskirts of the village for the postman, who cycled in sporadically from the neighboring village. This morning, as soon as she spotted him, she darted out from her hiding place, startling him, and asked if there were any letters for her family. He had frowned and bit his cheek, his rheumy eyes considering her through his thick glasses. She could tell he felt sorry for her, but he was also peeved—she was asking for something only the headman should receive. But she held his gaze without blinking. When he finally handed over the thick onionskin envelope addressed to her parents, he did so hastily, avoiding her eyes and pedaling away as quickly as he could.

Now, standing tall, her shoulders back, she strolls past the women at the riverbank. They glare at her. She can feel her heart flutter wildly in her breast, but she passes, straight as sugarcane, *mutki* on her head, as if she is going to the farmers well, two miles farther from the village, the only well she is allowed to use.

The gossip-eaters no longer whisper but shout to one another: *There goes the Bad Luck Girl! The year she was born, lo-*

custs ate the wheat! Her older sister deserted her husband, never to be seen again! Shameless! That same year her mother went blind! And her father turned to drink! Disgraceful! Even the girl's coloring is suspect. Only Angreji-walli *have blue eyes. Does she even belong to us? To this village?*

The girl has often wondered about this older sister they talk about. The one whose face she sees only as a shadow in her dreams, whose existence her parents have never acknowledged. The gossip-eaters say she left the village thirteen years ago. Why? Where did she go? How did she escape a place where the gossip-eaters watch your every move? Did she leave in the dead of night when the cows and goats were asleep? They say she stole money, but no one in the village has any money. How did she feed herself? Some say she dressed as a man so she wouldn't be stopped on the road. Others say she ran off with a circus boy and was living as a *nautch* girl, dancing in the Pleasure District miles away in Agra.

Three days ago, old man Munchi with the game leg—her only friend in the village—warned her that if she didn't vacate her hut, the headman would insist she marry a widowed farmer or demand she leave the village.

"There is nothing here for you now," Munchi-*ji* had said. But how could she leave—a thirteen-year-old orphan girl with no family or money?

Munchi-*ji* said, "Have courage, *bheti*." He told her where to find her brother-in-law, the husband her older sister had abandoned all those years ago, in a nearby village. Perhaps he could help her find her sister.

"Why can't I stay with you?" she had asked.

"It would not be proper," the old man replied gently. He made his living painting images on the skeletons of *peepal* leaves. To console her, he'd given her a painting. Angry, she'd almost thrown it back at him until she saw that the image was of Lord Krishna, feeding a mango to his consort, Radha, her namesake. It was the most beautiful gift she had ever received.

Radha slows as she approaches the village threshing ground. Four yoked bulls walk in circles around a large flat stone, grinding wheat. Prem, who cares for the bulls, is sitting with his back against the hut, asleep. Quietly, she hurries past him to the narrow path that leads to Ganesh-*ji*'s temple. The shrine has a slender opening and, inside, a statue of Lord Ganesh. Gifts are arranged around the Elephant God's feet: a young coconut, marigolds, a small pot of *ghee*, slices of mango. A cone of sandalwood incense releases a languid curl of smoke.

The girl lays Munchi-*ji*'s painting of Krishna in front of Ganesh-*ji*, the Remover of All Obstacles, and begs him to remove the curse of the Bad Luck Girl.

By the time she reaches her brother-in-law's village ten miles to the west, it is late afternoon and the sun has moved closer to the horizon. She is sweating through her cotton blouse. Her feet and ankles are dusty, her mouth dry.

She is cautious, entering the village. She crouches in shrubs and hides behind trees. She knows an alone girl will not be treated kindly. She searches for a man who looks like the one Munchi-*ji* described.

She sees him. There. Squatting under the banyan tree, facing her. Her brother-in-law.

He has thick, oily, coal-black hair. A long, bumpy scar snakes from his bottom lip to his chin. He is not young but neither is he old. His bush-shirt is spotted with curry and his *dhoti* is stained with dust.

Then she notices the woman squatting in the dirt in front of the man. She is supporting her elbow with one hand, her forearm dangling at an unnatural angle. Her head is completely covered with her *pallu*, and she is talking to the man in a quiet whisper. Radha watches, wondering if her brother-in-law has taken another wife.

She picks up a small stone and throws it at him. She misses. The second time, she hits him in the thigh, but he merely flicks his hand, as if swatting away an insect. He is listening intently to the woman. Radha throws more pebbles, managing to hit him several times. At last, he lifts his head and looks around him.

Radha steps into the clearing so he can see her.

His eyes widen, as if he is looking at a ghost. He says, "Lakshmi?"

PART ONE

ONE

Jaipur, State of Rajasthan, India
November 15, 1955

Independence changed everything. Independence changed nothing. Eight years after the British left, we now had free government schools, running water and paved roads. But Jaipur still felt the same to me as it had ten years ago, the first time I stepped foot on its dusty soil. On the way to our first appointment of the morning, Malik and I nearly collided with a man carrying cement bags on his head when a bicycle cut between us. The cyclist, hugging a six-foot ladder under his arm, caused a horse carriage to sideswipe a pig, who ran squealing into a narrow alley. At one point, we stepped aside and waited for a raucous band of *hijras* to pass. The sari-clad, lipstick-wearing men were singing and dancing in front of a house to bless the birth of a baby boy. So accustomed were we to the odors of the city—cow dung, cooking fires, coconut hair oil, sandalwood incense and urine—that we barely noticed them.

What independence *had* changed was our people. You could see it in the way they stood, chests puffed, as if they could finally allow themselves to breathe. You saw it in the way they walked—purposefully, pridefully—to their temples. The way they haggled—more boldly than before—with the vendors in the bazaar.

Malik whistled for a *tonga*. He was a small boy, thin as a reed. His whistle, loud enough to be heard as far away as Bombay, always took me by surprise. He lifted our heavy tiffins into the horse carriage, and the *tonga-walla* begrudgingly took us the short five blocks to the Singh estate. The gateman watched as we stepped off the *tonga*.

Before independence, most Jaipur families lived in cramped family compounds inside the old Pink City. But generations of Singhs had always lived on an expansive estate outside the city walls. They were from the ruling class—rajas and minor princes, commissioned army officers—long used to privilege before, during and even after British rule. The Singh estate was on a wide boulevard lined with *peepal* trees. Eight-foot-high walls spiked with glass shards protected the two-story mansion from view. A marble veranda, overhung with bougainvillea and jasmine vines, extended along the front and sides of each story, and cooled the house in summer, when Jaipur could get as hot as a tandoori oven.

After the Singhs' *chowkidar* had witnessed our arrival by *tonga*, we unloaded our cargo. Malik stayed behind to gossip with the gateman while I walked down the paved stone path flanked by a wide manicured lawn and up the stone steps to Parvati Singh's veranda.

On this November afternoon, the air was crisp but humid. Lala, Parvati Singh's longest-serving help and nanny to her sons, greeted me at the door. She pulled her sari over her hair as a sign of respect.

I smiled and brought my hands together in a *namaste*. "Have you been using the magnolia oil, Lala?" On my last visit, I had slipped her a bottle of my remedy for calloused soles.

She hid a smile behind her *pallu* as she thrust one bare foot forward and twisted it around to show off her smooth heel. *"Hahn-ji,"* she laughed lightly.

"Shabash," I congratulated her. "And how is your niece?" Lala had brought her fifteen-year-old niece to work at the Singh household six months ago.

The old woman's brow creased and her smile disappeared. But as she opened her mouth to answer, her mistress called from inside. "Lakshmi, is that you?"

Quickly, Lala rearranged her features, smiled tightly and indicated with a tilt of her head: *she's fine.* Turning toward the kitchen, she left me to find my own way to Parvati's bedroom, where I had been many times before.

Parvati was at her rosewood desk. She checked her slim gold wristwatch before returning to the letter she was writing. A stickler for punctuality, she hated tardiness in others. I, however, was used to waiting while she dashed off a note to Nehruji or finished a phone call with a member of the Indo-Soviet League.

I set down my tiffins and arranged the cushions on Parvati's cream silk divan while she sealed her letter and called for Lala.

Instead of the old servant, Lala's niece appeared. She kept her large, dark eyes on the floor and her hands clasped in front of her.

Parvati's eyebrows gathered in a frown. She considered the girl and, after the briefest of pauses, said, "There will be a guest for lunch. Make sure we have *boondi raita*."

The girl blanched and looked as if she might be sick. "There's no fresh yogurt, MemSahib."

"Why not?"

The girl shifted uneasily. Her eyes searched for an answer in the Turkish carpet, the framed photo of the prime minister, the mirrored cocktail cabinet.

When Parvati spoke, her words were glass, clear and sharp. "Make sure there is *boondi raita* for lunch."

The girl's lower lip trembled. She looked imploringly at me.

I moved to the windows overlooking the back garden. Parvati was my mistress, too, and I could no more help the girl than could the tiger skin mounted on the wall.

"Today, have Lala bring the tea." Parvati dismissed the girl and eased herself onto the divan. Now I could begin her henna. I took my customary seat on the other end of the chaise and took her hands in mine.

Before I came to Jaipur, my ladies relied on women of the Shudra caste to henna their hands and feet. But the low-caste Shudra women painted what their mothers had before them: simple dots, dashes, triangles. Just enough to earn their meager income. My patterns were more intricate; they told stories of the women I served. My henna paste was finer and silkier than the mixture the Shudra women used. I took care to rub a lemon and sugar lotion into my ladies' skin before applying the henna so the imprint would last for weeks. The darker the henna, the more a woman was loved by her husband—or so my clients believed—and my rich, cinnamon designs never disappointed. Over time, my clients had come to believe that my henna could bring wayward husbands back to their beds or coax a baby from their wombs. Because of this, I could name a price ten times higher than the Shudra women. And receive it.

Even Parvati credited her younger son's birth to my henna skills. She had been my first client in Jaipur. When she conceived, I saw the pages of my appointment book fill up with the ladies of her acquaintance—the elite of Jaipur.

Now, as the henna on her hands was drying and I began

drawing on her feet, Parvati bent forward to observe until our heads were almost touching, her breath sweet with the scent of betel nut. Her warm sigh grazed my cheek. "You tell me you've never been outside India, but I've only seen this fig leaf in Istanbul."

My breath caught and, for an instant, the old fear came over me. On Parvati's feet, I had drawn the leaves of the Turkish fig tree—so different from its Rajasthani cousin, the banyan, the miserly fruit of which was fit only for birds. On her soles, intended for a husband's eyes alone, I was painting a large fig, plump and sensual, split in half.

I smiled as I met her eyes and pressed her shoulder back, gently, onto the cushions of the divan. Arching a brow, I said, "Is that what your husband will notice? That the figs are Turkish?"

I pulled a mirror from my satchel, and held it to the arch of her right foot so she could see the tiny wasp I'd painted next to the fig. "Your husband surely knows that every fig requires a special wasp to fertilize the flower deep inside."

Her brows rose in surprise. Her lips, stained a deep plum, parted. She laughed, a lusty roar that shook the divan. Parvati was a handsome woman with shapely eyes and a generous mouth, the top lip plumper than the bottom. Her jewel-colored saris, like the fuchsia silk she wore today, brightened her complexion.

She wiped the corners of her eyes with the end of her sari. "*Shabash*, Lakshmi!" she said. "Always on the days you've done my henna, Samir can't stay away from my bed." Her voice carried the hint of an afternoon spent on cool cotton sheets, her husband's thighs warm against hers.

With an effort, I banished the image from my mind. "As it should be," I murmured before resuming my work on her arch, a sensitive spot on most women. But she was used to my ministrations and managed never to shake my reed.

She chuckled. "So the Turkish fig leaves remain a mystery, as do your blue eyes and fair skin."

In the ten years I'd been serving her, Parvati had not let this matter rest. India was a land of coal-black irises. Blue eyes demanded an explanation. Did I have a sordid past? A European father? Or, even worse, an Anglo-Indian mother? I was thirty years old, born during British rule and used to aspersions being cast on my parentage. I never let Parvati's comments provoke me.

I draped a wet cloth over the henna paste and poured some clove oil from a bottle onto my palm. I rubbed my palms together to warm the oil, then reached for her hands to rub off the dried henna paste. "Consider, *Ji*, that an ancestor of mine might have been seduced by Marco Polo. Or Alexander the Great." As I massaged her fingers, flakes of dried henna paste fell onto the towel below. The design I'd painted on her hands began to emerge. "Like you, I may have warrior blood running through my veins."

"Oh, Lakshmi, be serious!" Her bell-shaped gold-and-pearl earrings danced merrily as she let out another laugh. Parvati and I were both born to the two highest Hindu castes, she a Kshatriya and me a Brahmin. But she could never bring herself to treat me as an equal because I touched the feet of ladies as I painted their henna. Feet were considered unclean, only to be handled by the low-caste Shudras. So even though her caste had relied on mine for centuries to educate their children and perform spiritual rites, in the eyes of Jaipur's elite, I was now a fallen Brahmin.

But women like Parvati paid well. I gave no attention to her needling as I removed the last of the paste from her hands. Over time, I had saved a great deal and was so close to getting what I wanted—a house of my own. It would have marble floors to cool my feet after a day of crisscrossing the city on foot. As much running water as I wanted instead of begging my landlady to fill my *mutki*. A front door to which only I had the key. A house no one could force me to leave. At fifteen, I'd been turned out from my village to marry when my parents could no longer afford to feed me. Now *I* could afford to feed *them*, take care of them. They hadn't responded to any of the letters or gifts of money I'd sent over the years, but surely they would change their minds and come to Jaipur now that I was offering them a bed in my very own home? My parents would finally see that everything had turned out all right. Until we were reunited, I would keep my pride in check. Hadn't Gandhi-*ji* said, *An eye for an eye makes the whole world blind*?

The sound of breaking glass startled us. I watched a cricket ball roll across the carpet and come to rest in front of the divan. A moment later, Ravi, Parvati's older son, walked through the veranda doors, bringing with him the November chill.

"*Bheta!* Close that door at once!"

Ravi grinned. "I pitched a burner and Govind wasn't ready for it." He spotted the ball near the divan and scooped it up.

"He's so much younger than you are, Ravi." Parvati was indulgent with her sons, especially with the younger boy, Govind, the child who in her opinion was surely the product of my henna applications (I had done nothing to discourage that notion).

Since I'd last seen him, Ravi had grown taller and broader across the shoulders. His square chin and jaw, so much like his father's, were now shadowed. He must have started shaving. With the rosy complexion and long eyelashes he had inherited from his mother, he was almost pretty.

He tossed the ball in the air, and caught it, with one hand behind his back. "Is there tea?" It could have been his father speaking—so alike was their boarding-school English.

Parvati rang the silver bell she kept next to the divan. "You and Govind take yours on the lawn. And tell the *chowkidar* we need a glass-*walla* to replace the pane."

Ravi grinned at us, winking at me on his way out. He closed the door so carelessly another shard of glass fell out. I watched him jog gracefully across the lawn. Three gardeners, their heads wrapped in mufflers, were weeding, watering and trimming hibiscus shrubs and sweet honeysuckle vines in the back garden.

Ravi's appearance was the perfect segue to what I'd come here to accomplish. Still, I needed to move forward cautiously.

"Home from boarding school?"

"*Hahn.* I wanted Ravi to help me cut the ribbon on the new *gymkhana.* You know Nehru-*ji*—how he wants to modernize India." She sighed and laid her head against the cushion, as if she were besieged by daily calls from the prime minister. For all I knew, she was.

Lala entered with a silver tea tray. While I took out the savories I had cooked especially for Parvati from a tiffin, I heard her say to the older woman, "Did I not tell you to send her away?" Her voice was reproachful.

The servant put her hands together in prayer, touching them to her lips. "My niece has nowhere to go. I am her only family now. Please, *Ji.* We are at your mercy. Won't you reconsider?"

I had never seen Lala so distressed. I turned away, afraid she was about to drop to her knees. A shrine for Lord Ganesh sat on a small table beside the four-poster bed. A garland of gardenias and another of *tulsi* leaves were draped around the statue, in front of which a *diya* burned. As modern as she liked to portray herself, Parvati spent every morning praying to the gods. I used to pray to my namesake, Lakshmi, the Goddess of Beauty and Wealth. Maa loved reciting the story of the Brahmin farmer who offered his scythe, his sole possession, to the goddess. In gratitude, she gave the farmer a magic basket that produced food any time he desired. But that was only a story, as true as any other Maa told and, at seventeen, I turned my back on the gods, just as now I turned away from Ganesh's shrine.

Parvati was still addressing Lala. "I wouldn't want to lose you, too, Lala. See that the girl is gone today." She glared at Lala until the servant dropped her gaze, her shoulders drooping.

I watched Lala leave the room, She did not look up. I wondered what Lala's niece had done to make her mistress so angry.

Parvati reached for her cup and saucer, a signal for me to pick up my own. The tea set was the kind the English loved, depicting women in corseted gowns, men in pantaloons, curly-haired girls in frocks. Before independence, these objects had signified my ladies' admiration for the British. Now, they signified their scorn. My ladies had changed nothing but the reasons for their pretense. If I had learned anything from them, it was this: only a fool lives in water and remains an enemy of the crocodile.

I took a sip of tea and raised my eyebrows. "Your son has grown into a handsome young man."

"Unlike the Rao boy who thinks he's the Rajasthani *Devdas*."

Parvati, like my other ladies, said things to me she would never have said to one of her peers. I was childless and, therefore, a subject of pity, someone to whom my ladies could feel superior. At thirty, I was neither a foolish girl nor a gossipy matron. My ladies had long assumed my husband had abandoned me—an assumption I'd taken no trouble to contradict. I still wore the vermillion *bindi* on my forehead, announcing to the world that I was married. Without this assortment of credentials, I would never have been allowed into the confidence of my ladies, or into bedrooms like the one I found myself in now, my feet resting on pink Salumbar marble, my mistress seated next to me on a rosewood divan.

I took another sip of my chai. "Finding a perfect match for such a perfect son! I certainly don't envy you."

"He's only seventeen. At twelve, I lost him to the Mayo School. A year from now, I'll lose him once again to Oxford. Losing him to a wife? I can't bear to think about that now."

I adjusted my sari. "That's smart of you. The Dutts, I fear, may have been in too much of a hurry."

I caught the sparkle in her eye.

"Meaning?"

"Well," I continued. "They've only just arranged for their son to marry the Kumar girl. You know the one—with the beauty spot on her cheek? Of course, the marriage will be put off until he's completed his degree." I looked out the window at her sons in their cricket whites. "The good ones are going like hot *jalebis*. Once a son is off to Britain or America, parents worry he'll come home with a wife who doesn't speak a word of Hindi."

"Quite. The happiest marriages are when parents choose the girl. Just look at Samir and me."

I could have said something, but I didn't. Instead, I made a show of blowing on my tea. "I also heard the Akbar girl has been promised to Muhammad Ismail's boy. One of Ravi's classmates, isn't he?"

I took another sip while holding Parvati's gaze.

She sat a little straighter and looked out the window. On the lawn, Lala's niece was serving the boys their tea. Ravi spoke to the girl and tapped her nose once, playfully, which brought a fit of giggles from her.

Parvati frowned. Without taking her eyes off the scene outside, she leaned toward me, slowly, like a baby bird, a sign for me to feed her. I placed a *namkeen* in her mouth, the one I'd made this morning, seasoned with parsley. Like all my ladies, she never suspected that the ingredients in my treats, combined with what I drew on her hands and feet, fueled her desire and her husband's lust.

After a moment, she turned from the window and set her teacup delicately on the table.

"*If* I wanted a match—and I'm not saying I do..." She dabbed her mouth with a napkin. "Would you have anyone in mind?"

"There are many eligible girls in Jaipur, as you know." I smiled at her over the rim of my cup. "But Ravi is not just any boy."

When she turned to look at her sons again, Lala's niece was gone. Parvati's face relaxed. "When I ask him to, Ravi always comes down from school. What's the good of sending him away, Samir says." She laughed lightly. "But I miss him. Govind misses him, too. He was only three when Ravi went to boarding school."

She lifted the teapot and poured herself another cup of chai. "Have you heard anything of Rai Singh's daughter? They say she's quite striking."

"Pity. Only yesterday she was snatched up for Mrs. Rathore's son." I let out a sigh. It was delicate, this conversation we were having, one where neither Parvati nor I could tip our hand.

She searched my face with narrowed eyes. "Something tells me you have a girl in mind."

"Oh, I fear you'll think my choice unsuitable."

"How so?"

"Well...unconventional, perhaps."

"Unconventional? You know me better than that, Lakshmi. I went not once, but twice, to the Soviet Union last year. Nehru-*ji* insisted I go with the Indo-Soviet League. Come now, let's hear it."

"Well..." I pretended to tuck a strand of hair back into my bun. "The girl's not Rajput."

She raised one tweezed brow, but would not look away. I held her gaze. "She's Brahmin."

Parvati blinked. She may have thought herself a woman of the times, but the possibility of Ravi marrying outside his caste was something she hadn't entertained. For centuries, each of the four Hindu castes—even the merchant and laborer castes—married largely within their own group.

I fed Parvati another snack.

"I can't imagine a better match for the Singh family," I continued. "The girl is beautiful. Fair. Well-educated. High-spirited. The sort Ravi would appreciate. And her family's well connected. Oh, has your tea gone cold? I fear mine has."

"Do we know the girl?"

"Since she was a child, in fact. Shall I call for more?" I set my cup down and reached for the silver bell, but Parvati caught me by the forearm.

"Forget the tea, Lakshmi! Tell me about the girl or I'll wipe my feet on this towel and ruin the last hour's work."

Instead of meeting her eyes, I tapped the henna on her feet to test for dryness. "The girl's name is Sheela Sharma. Mr. V. M. Sharma's daughter."

Parvati knew the Sharmas, of course. The two families often moved in the same business circles. Mr. Sharma's construction company, the largest in Rajasthan, had just won the contract to remodel the maharaja's Rambagh Palace. Parvati's husband owned an architectural firm that designed many of the residential and commercial buildings in the city. It would be an unexpected union of two prominent families. If I could pull it off, Jaipur's elite would be clamoring for my services as a matchmaker, a far more lucrative prospect than being a henna artist.

She cocked her head. "But...Sheela's still a child."

Over the past year, rice puddings and extra helpings of *chapatti* with *ghee* had added a layer of soft flesh to Sheela's body. Now, she looked less like a girl and more like a young woman.

"Sheela's fifteen," I said. "And quite lovely. She attends the Maharani School for Girls. Just last week her music master told me her singing reminded him of Lata Mangeshkar."

I picked up my teacup. I could imagine the list Parvati was making in her head, the same one I had made in mine the previous week. On the plus side: the two businesses—Sharma Construction and Singh Architects—once allied, would be more profitable than either were on their own; and Parvati would have an English-speaking daughter-in-law to entertain politicians and *nawabs*. The only minus: Sheela was of high caste—but the wrong one. There was more I wouldn't disclose: the ugly twist of Sheela's mouth before she yanked her cousin's pigtails, the way she ordered her nanny about and the laziness her music tutor despaired of. I had spent years in the homes of my ladies, watching their progeny mature. I knew their children's personalities, the tics that even a professional matchmaker wouldn't catch. But these were flaws for a husband to discover, not for me to reveal.

Parvati was quiet. She toyed with the fringe on one of the small bolsters.

"Remember the Gupta wedding?"

I smiled in acknowledgment.

"The moment I saw your maiden-in-the-garden design for the bridal henna, I knew she would deliver a baby boy before the year was up. And so she did."

The Gupta girl's marriage had been a love match, but I didn't share that with Parvati.

"Your work does perform miracles." Her smile was coy. "I think you could help someone very dear to us."

I tilted my head politely, not sure where she was headed.

"Last night, Samir and I were at the Rambagh Palace. A

fundraising event for the final portion of the *gymkhana*," she said pointedly. She wanted me to know she was progressive, after all. "The maharaja told us he was turning his palace into a hotel. Can you imagine? We fought for independence and threw the English out, only to have them move back into our palaces?" She shook her head, annoyed.

I understood: only wealthy Europeans, mostly Britishers, would be able to afford the rates.

"The maharani wasn't at the function last night, which was highly unusual. Latika loves parties." Parvati lowered her voice. "I heard she has been...out of sorts."

I waited.

She rubbed her palms together and inhaled the fragrance of the henna. "Might your talents put her right?"

I had waited so long for Parvati to make an introduction to the palace! At the thought of it, I set my cup down, afraid my hand might shake. A commission with the maharani would inevitably lead to others. I would have my house paid off before I knew it! Already I was doing the calculations in my head, barely listening to what Parvati was saying.

She leaned forward for another savory, and I placed one on her tongue, careful not to meet her eyes. I was afraid she would see the eagerness in mine. She might already have seen my fingers tremble.

"I told His Highness how your henna helped me conceive my Govind. Discreetly, of course. If I were to recommend you to the palace..."

I could see where she was going now. Parvati wanted me to make the match for Ravi, but she didn't want to pay for it. What cheek! A marriage arrangement took both skill and effort. She would easily have paid a man of high caste and a title two or three times what she might pay me. Even if I had agreed to take a mere ten thousand rupees, my services would still be a bargain. I could expect to put in weeks, even months, of work before all parties were satisfied. And it was not unheard of for a match to be rejected—for all that work to come to nothing.

Here was Parvati, hoping I would make the match *in exchange for* an introduction to the palace. Before I countered, I needed to think. Her blood relation to the royal family (her father was a cousin of one of the maharanis) would guarantee me, at the very least, an appointment with the palace. But what Indian woman, no matter how wealthy, wouldn't try to bargain? If she didn't, she'd come off as a fool, easy prey. So if I accepted, outright, what Parvati was offering, I would seal my reputation as a woman who could be easily outmaneuvered. The risk to me was that I might—or might not—end up working for the palace at all. An appointment didn't guarantee me anything.

Sensing my hesitation, Parvati leaned forward and looked at me until I was forced to meet her gaze. "If I had the talent for drawing you have, Lakshmi, I might have gone into your profession." To my ladies, the word *profession* was a slander, not a compliment.

I swallowed. "Oh, *Ji*, your life was meant for grander things. Who else could throw such lavish parties for politicians? Someone has to do the work of making them feel welcome."

She chuckled in appreciation of my retort. And now we settled back into a comfortable footing: me, the underling; she, the MemSahib.

But I meant to play my final hand. "Your confidence is well-placed, but I must warn you: Her Highness will probably expect the very best supplies."

Parvati pursed her lips. She looked thoughtful. "Would six thousand rupees cover it?"

I straightened the velvet cloth under Parvati's feet and tested the paste, then reached for the clove oil to remove the dried henna. "Some of the products may have to come from far away. The Kaffir lime leaves, for example. The most potent ones come from Thailand."

She was quiet. Had I overplayed my hand? I could feel the pulse at my temples as I massaged her feet.

She squinted at the Pan Am calendar on the far wall. "Our holiday party is coming up," she said finally. "December 20. That same afternoon I could give a special henna party for the girls in Ravi's circle." Parvati tapped her rosy cheek. "I'm thinking I might get that Shakespeareana Group to come. The kids are mad for their performances." This would be her opportunity to scrutinize the girls who would be suitable for Ravi. Sheela Sharma was sure to be among them.

She stretched her feet and turned them one way and then the other as she examined my work. "But perhaps your calendar is already full? Would you check?"

A henna party would be a lot of work, but it would be well worth the promise of an introduction to the palace.

I gave her my most gracious smile. "For you, MemSahib, my calendar is always open."

She grinned, showing her small, even teeth, her bright eyes. "It's settled, then. Nine thousand for the Maharani Latika's supplies?"

I released the breath I'd been holding. I had secured my first marriage commission, and while it wasn't as lucrative as I'd hoped, it would help me take another step toward finishing, and paying for, the house I would share with my parents—my apology for all I had put them through. Now all I had to do was make the match happen.

As I replaced her heavy gold anklets, I said, "And you must let the henna party be my gift to you."

On the Singh veranda, I slipped into my sandals. I spotted Malik laughing with the head gardener on the front lawn, under the enormous apple tree, its bare branches spiky against the cloudless sky.

I called out to him.

He ran to me on his stick legs. He could have been six or ten. How many meals had he missed before I'd finally noticed him, a half-naked street urchin in dirty shorts, following me around the city? I'd handed him a few tiffins to carry, and he'd smiled, a gap where his front two teeth would have been. Since that day three years ago, we'd worked together, mostly in silence. I'd never asked where he lived or whether he slept on hard ground.

"Any news?" I asked. While I worked on my ladies, Malik often ran errands. Every day for the past few months, he had checked the train station to see if my parents had arrived. By now they would have received the money for the train tickets I'd sent them in my last letter. But so far, there had been no word.

He shook his head and frowned; he hated disappointing me.

I sighed. "Please get the *tonga*."

He ran off in the direction of the front gate. Today, he was wearing the yellow cotton shirt I'd given him to replace the bush-shirt he used to wear. His navy blue knickers were new, too. He refused to wear shoes, however, preferring cheap rubber sandals, which were often stolen by the other children in his neighborhood. The sandals were easier to replace; he could always steal someone else's. Today's pair, I noticed, were a size too big.

Malik would have to get to a busy street to hail a rickshaw, so I sat on the veranda wall to wait, soothed by the fragrance of frangipani. I plucked two blossoms from the vine and tucked them behind my ear. Tonight, I would put them in a glass of water and wash my blouse with the scented water in the morning.

I removed a tiny notebook from a pouch I'd sewn inside

my petticoat. My father, the village schoolteacher, would rap his students' knuckles with a ruler if they failed to provide the correct answers. To avoid such a punishment, I'd started keeping notebooks, in which I diligently recorded (and memorized) multiplication tables, names of British viceroys and Hindi verbs. It became a habit, and later, I used notebooks for appointment dates and times, summaries of conversations, supplies I needed to purchase.

On the page labeled *Parvati Singh*, I wrote *November 15: 40 rupees for hands/feet.* Next, I wrote the date for the henna party at Parvati's house and noted the nine thousand rupees I would receive for the marriage commission. I knew that Mrs. Sharma, another client of mine, was clever enough to grasp the benefits of a Singh-Sharma union. She was blind to her daughter's petulant nature, but I had no doubts that Ravi Singh's charms could overcome it.

I turned to a blank page. With a shaking hand I wrote *Maharaja Sawai Mohinder Singh and Maharani Latika—palace commission?* My mind was full of possibilities. Such an engagement would have every woman in Jaipur demanding my services. I might, perhaps, retire that henna reed sooner than I'd planned. Just then, my mother's words echoed in my head: *stretch your legs only as far as your bed.* I was getting too far ahead of myself.

I closed the notebook and shut my eyes. Thirteen years ago, my only desire was to get as far as possible from the husband my parents had relinquished me to. I would never have imagined that I would, one day, be free to come and go as I pleased, to negotiate the terms of my life. How would my parents react when they saw all that I'd accomplished? How often had I thought about the day I would take them to my house, show them the beautiful terrazzo floor I had designed, the electric ceiling fan, the courtyard where I would grow my herbs, the Western privy no one in their village could afford? I'd hoped the builder would have finished everything by the time they arrived, but I kept adding little luxuries. And once my parents saw what I had designed, surely they wouldn't mind sleeping at my lodgings until the house was complete?

I pictured the astonishment on my parents' faces when they took it all in. I could hear my father saying, Bheti, *all this is yours?* How proud they would be at the life I had made for myself. I would feed them rich *kheers* and *subji* and tandoori *rotis* till their stomachs were full to bursting. I would buy them sleeping cots so new the jute strings would squeak under their weight. I would hire a *malish* to massage Pitaji's tired feet. I could see Maa, now, lounging on a rosewood settee like Parvati's! And—why not—silk cushions! Stuffed with feathers! I was getting so carried away—of course, I couldn't afford all this just yet—that I couldn't help laughing at myself.

"Am I *that* funny looking, Lakshmi?"

When I opened my eyes, I saw Samir Singh coming up the steps, and my world suddenly felt lighter. Where Parvati was round, her husband was angular: sharp nose, bony chin, jutting cheekbones. It was his eyes I found the most appealing: a rich brown with the striations of a glass marble, alive with curiosity, ready to be amused. Even when his face was still, his eyes could flirt, coax, tease. In the ten years I'd known him, the hollows underneath his eyelids had deepened and his hairline had receded, but he'd never lost his restless energy.

"The one-eyed man is king among the blind," I replied, smiling.

He laughed as he stepped out of his shoes. Samir was that curious blend of the new India and the old; he wore tailored English suits but followed Indian customs. *"Arré! What does a silly monkey know of the taste of ginger?"*

"One who cannot dance blames the floor."

This was a game we often played, trading proverbs. I'd learned mine from my mother's prudent tongue; his had come from years at boarding school and Oxford.

I stood, tucked the pencil in my bun and slipped the notebook in the pocket of my petticoat.

He arched one eyebrow as he walked toward me. "Are you hiding the Singh silver in there?"

I smiled coyly. "Among other things."

"I see you've already helped yourself to my flora?" His eyes were on the frangipani tucked behind my ear. He leaned in, close, and inhaled. "*Bilkul* intoxicating," he whispered, his breath warm on my earlobe, shaking something loose inside of me, just below my belly.

Thirteen years had passed since I'd last felt the heat of a man against my skin, the weight against my breasts. If I turned my head just slightly, my lips might have grazed Samir's; I could have let my own breath warm the hollow space between his neck and collar. But Samir was a natural flirt. And I was still a married woman. One wrong move and I could lose my livelihood, my independence, my plans for the future. I was alert to the sound of servants approaching—the swish of a broom, the slap of bare feet on stone. Reluctantly, I took a step back.

"You have an intoxicating wife, as you'll soon see for yourself."

Samir grinned. "On the days when Lakshmi Shastri has attended her, Mrs. Singh is always feeling very…amorous. Speaking of which…" He held out his hand.

"Ah." I removed three muslin sachets from the folds of my sari and set them in his palm. "You're a lucky man, Sahib. A wife waiting in the bedroom and freedom outside of it."

He weighed the sachets in his hand, as if weighing rubies. "Freedom is relative, Lakshmi." With one deft move, he laid several hundred-rupee notes and a piece of paper in my hand. "At one time the British were over us. Now they're just under our feet."

I unfolded the paper and read the note inside. "An *Angrezi* woman?"

"Even the English need your services. She's expecting you tomorrow. She'll be home." He put the sachets in his pocket and said, "How's the house coming?"

Now would be the time to tell him how the builder had suggested, rudely, that I settle up my debt. I still owed four thousand rupees. But that excess was no one's fault but mine. I was greedy for the kinds of things my ladies had: an inlaid stone floor, a Western toilet, double thick walls to repel the noonday heat. The problem was my own creation and I alone would solve it. A successful marriage commission would help put me in good standing. I said, "Tomorrow they will seal the terrazzo with goat milk. You should see it."

His eyes dropped to my lips. "Are you offering me a private tour?"

I laughed. "You've already thrown my schedule off, and you think I should reward you?"

From behind me came another voice. *"He deserves paradise who makes his companions laugh!"*

Samir and I both turned to see who had just spoken. A tall man, dressed neatly in a gray wool suit and red tie, bounded up the steps of the veranda. Only his dark curls were in disarray.

Samir stepped aside to embrace the newcomer. "Kumar!" he said. "Glad to see you, old chum! You made it out to Jaipur. Finally!"

"I didn't trust the Shimla railway to get me here in time for lunch—or even dinner," Kumar said, glancing at me with a bashful smile, revealing two overlapping front teeth. "Pleased to meet you, Mrs. Singh."

Had Samir and I been standing *that* close to one another?

Samir patted Kumar's back heartily. "*Nahee-nahee.* Allow me to present Mrs. Lakshmi Shastri, purveyor of beauty to all of Jaipur."

"I see she hasn't started on you yet, Sammy."

Samir chuckled. Kumar looked at me, at Samir, at the veranda, his shoes, then back at me. Eyes like these belonged to the cautious.

"Lakshmi, meet an old friend from Oxford. Jay Kumar. *Dr.* Kumar."

I folded my hands in a *namaste* just as the doctor extended his hand to shake mine, jabbing me on the wrist.

Samir laughed. "Forgive him, Lakshmi. Too much time abroad. No wife to teach him Indian ways."

The color rose in Dr. Kumar's face, his eyes darting from Samir to me. "My apologies, Mrs. Shastri."

"No bother, Doctor." Over his shoulder, I could see Malik watching us from the veranda steps. *"Tonga?"* I asked him.

Malik wagged his head back and forth in confirmation. A few blocks from the Singh house, we would abandon the horse carriage and continue in a cheaper rickshaw to our next henna appointment.

"Pleased to meet you, Dr. Kumar. Till next time, *Sammy.*" Coming from me, the old nickname must have sounded as ridiculous to their ears as it did to mine. They both laughed.

I picked up the tiffins and my vinyl carrier and reminded Malik to fetch the other two holdalls under the apple tree. As I nodded my goodbye to the two men, I was thinking that I must remember to note Samir's payment for the sachets in my notebook.

I went down the steps and heard Samir say, "Let's go in. Parvati is very much looking forward to meeting you!" On the last step, my sandal caught, and I turned to replace it on my foot. I glanced up just in time to see the doctor watching me as the front door closed.

At the corner of the veranda stood Lala, biting her lip, her hands nervously twisting the ends of her *pallu*. I thought I saw a plea in her eyes and almost went back up the steps to meet her, but she turned quickly and was gone.

A busy day of henna appointments had stretched into evening once again, and Malik and I were both exhausted. We stopped just outside the Pink City Bazaar, which was coming to life at this late hour—women in patterned saris selecting hairpins, men in *kurthas* munching spicy *chaat*, old men killing time, their glowing *beedis* cutting orange arcs through the dusky night. I envied them their easy camaraderie, the freedom with which the laborer and merchant castes moved about at night.

Since Partition, the pedestrian walkways of the old Pink City streets had become narrower, crowded as they were on both sides with tiny, makeshift shops, sometimes with nothing more than an old sari or canvas cloth tenting them. The old bazaar vendors had made room for the Punjabi and Sindhi refugees from West Pakistan to set up stalls that sold everything from spices to bangles. After all, the Jaipuri merchants joked, the Pink City was painted the color of hospitality for a reason.

Malik lived somewhere inside one of the many buildings that made up the Pink City. I had never asked whether he had a sibling, a mother or a father. It was enough that he and I were together ten hours a day and that he hauled my tiffins, flagged down rickshaws and *tongas*, haggled with suppliers. We shared confidences, of course, like the look of impatience he'd given me today when our last client kept us waiting an hour.

I placed three rupee coins in his palm, after making him promise he would buy real food for his dinner instead of greasy snacks. "You're a growing boy," I reminded him, as if he weren't aware of it.

He grinned and took off like a top, winding his way between shoppers toward the bright lights.

I called out after him, "*Chapatti* and *subji*, agreed?"

He turned around, waving his free hand in the air. "And

chaat. You can't expect a growing boy to starve," he said quickly, and disappeared into the thick crowd.

As I climbed into a waiting rickshaw, I thought about visiting my house—so close to being finished—to check the progress. If I failed to inspect it every other day, the builder, Naraya, was quick to cut corners, which meant I would then have to quarrel with him, insist that he tear things apart and start over (I'd had to do this more than once). But it was late, and I was too tired to bicker. I told the rickshaw-*walla* to take me to my lodgings.

By the time I locked the gate behind me and hurried across Mrs. Iyengar's interior courtyard, it was eight o'clock. My stomach rumbled with hunger. I set my empty tiffins next to the waterspout. I would scrub them tonight as soon as Mrs. Iyengar's servant had finished washing her dishes. I was about to head up the stairs to my rented room when my landlady called to me from an open doorway.

"Good evening, *Ji*." I brought my hands together in a *namaste*.

"Good evening, Mrs. Shastri."

Mrs. Iyengar wiped her hands on a small towel. Hot *mirch* threatened to make me sneeze. The Iyengars were from the South, and they liked their food so spicy it burned my throat just to smell it.

A short, squat woman, Mrs. Iyengar gazed up at me. Her eyes were stern. "You had a visitor today."

No one visited me here except Malik, whom Mrs. Iyengar referred to as "that ruffian."

Her gold bracelets tinkled as she rubbed dried *atta* off her fingers. "He asked to wait in your room. But you know I don't allow that sort of thing here." She shot a warning glance at me.

In a soothing voice, I assured her, "You did quite right, Mrs. Iyengar. Did he say what he wanted?"

"He asked if you were the lady from Ajar village. I told him I didn't know." She searched my face to see if I would add to the sparse details of my past. "He had a big-big scar." She ran a finger from the corner of her mouth to her chin. "From here to here." Wagging that same finger at me, she frowned. "Not a sign of good character, in my opinion."

My heart thumped against my ribs as I reached for her hand—as much to calm myself as to placate her. "Cooking can make the hands so dry, don't you think? If you'd like, I can rub some geranium oil on them tomorrow."

A crease formed between her brows, and she looked down at her hands, as if she had never seen them before. "I wouldn't want to trouble you."

"It's no bother. And the next time your husband reaches for you, he will remember you as his young bride." I laughed airily, turning to go. Keeping my tone light, I said, "I don't suppose this visitor said when he'd be back?"

Mrs. Iyengar was busy clearing sticky batter from under her fingernails. "He didn't say," she said.

Her servant, who had started cleaning pots in the courtyard, said, "I just saw him across the street when I went to throw the vegetable scraps out for the cows."

As Mrs. Iyengar scolded her servant for not minding her own business, I made my escape to the second-floor landing and into my room, bolting the door behind me. My heart was beating wildly, and I tried to calm my breathing. Hadn't I expected Hari to turn up one day? Always, I had kept an eye out for the heavy eyebrows and that awful scar. Then, as the years passed without incident, I fooled myself into thinking my husband would never find me.

How had he tracked me here? In my letters to Maa and Pitaji, begging their forgiveness for my desertion, I had been careful never to reveal my address. Even when I'd sent them money for the train tickets to Jaipur, I had instructed them to ask for Malik at the train station, and he would lead them to me. But so far, Malik had reported that no one had asked for him at the station. Had my parents sent Hari to fetch me back home instead? Did they resent me so much, still? Would they never forgive me?

Without turning on the overhead light, I walked to my window and looked out. There, almost hidden by the mango tree across the street, was the bottom half of a white *dhoti*, glowing in the darkness. Then the red arc of a *beedi*. No one loitered in this residential neighborhood this late at night. Mrs. Iyengar's servant said she'd seen him a few minutes ago. It had to be Hari. I had to think—to figure out a way to meet him away from here.

I heard the soft footfalls of Mrs. Iyengar's other tenant, Mr. Pandey, on the stairs, and opened my door. He was lost in his own thoughts, and looked up, startled.

"Mrs. Shastri, good evening." His full lips parted in a slow smile that built up gradually. His eyes drooped at the ends, making him seem kind and patient, a desirable trait for a music master. He kept his hair long; the ends curled neatly around his shoulders. Sometimes I pictured him in bed with his wife, his hair intertwined with hers on the pillows.

"*Namaste*, Sahib." I clasped my hands together in greeting, to keep them from trembling. "How goes the teaching?"

"Only as well as the student." He smiled.

"Sheela Sharma sang beautifully at the women's gathering for the Gupta wedding. Thanks to you."

"Nahee-nahee," he laughed softly, touching his earlobes to ward off jealous spirits. "We have far to go before we turn Sheela into Lata Mangeshkar." He had been tutoring Sheela Sharma since she was a young girl, and from the little he'd told me, I gathered Sheela's natural talent had made her arrogant and not a little lazy. Unless she applied herself, it seemed

unlikely she would ever equal the musical prowess of the legendary singer—quite the opposite of what I'd told Parvati.

"And Mrs. Pandey's health?"

"Excellent. Thank you for asking."

"Mr. Pandey, would you kindly do me a favor?" I was talking so softly he moved closer to hear. I pulled my notebook from inside my petticoat, tore off a page and wrote quickly. I folded the note and held it out to him. He took it, without moving his eyes from mine.

"There's a man across the road. He's smoking a *beedi.* Would you please give this to him? It would not be proper for me to meet him alone…" I let my voice trail off, dropping my eyes and stepping backward.

He cleared his throat. "Of course, of course. Now?"

"If you wouldn't mind."

He held up a hand and wagged his head. "It's no bother." He set off down the stairs.

I rushed to my bedroom window. My lights were still off, so I could look outside without being seen. I recognized Mr. Pandey's white *kurtha pyjama.* He crossed the street, then hesitated. A few paces to his left, a match flared, and he turned toward it. I let out the breath I'd been holding.

TWO

Wet plaster, cement, stone. My new home smelled of these. Earlier this evening, I had resisted the urge to come here and check the builder's progress. At ten o'clock at night, when I should have been doing my accounts and preparing for the next day, I stood in my unfinished home waiting for Hari, my hand gripping the knife I used for cutting plants and splitting seeds.

Outside, the light from the streetlamp fell across my beautiful floor, revealing a mosaic of saffron flowers in the round, spiraling *boteh* leaves and vases with feminine curves. I thought of Hazi and Nasreen and the other courtesans in the city of Agra who had first introduced me to the designs of their native lands—Isfahan, Marrakech, Kabul, Calcutta, Madras, Cairo. In the city of the Taj Mahal, where I worked for three years after leaving Hari and before coming to Jaipur, I decorated the arms, hips and backs of the pleasure women with henna. My patterns became more fanciful with time. I would place a Persian peacock inside a Turkish clamshell, turn an Afghan mountain bird into a Moroccan fan. So when it came time to design the floor of my house, I created a pattern as complex as the henna I had painted on those women's bodies, delighting in the knowledge that its meaning was known only to me.

The saffron flowers represented sterility. Incapable of producing seed as I had proved incapable of producing children. The Ashoka lion, like the icon of our new Republic, a symbol of my ambition. I wanted more, always, for what my hands could accomplish, what my wits could achieve—more than my parents had thought possible. The fine work beneath my feet required the skill of artisans who worked exclusively for the palace. All financed by the painstaking preparations of my charmed oils, lotions, henna paste and, most importantly, the herb sachets I supplied Samir.

Had Hari come to take all this away from me?

Crunch, crunch. Footsteps on the gravel outside. I slid my thumb gingerly along the sharp edge of the knife.

There was a pause. Then the footsteps continued, stopping at my front door. I stood to one side of that door now, in the dark, taking shallow breaths.

The door opened, and Hari entered the room. He stood illuminated in the streetlight, as if he were onstage. His hair was still thick and wavy, falling into his eyes. His profile, sharp, but his jawline, soft. The high cheekbones made him almost handsome. I watched his eyes circle the room until they came to rest on me.

For a long moment, we regarded one another. His eyes traveled—slowly—from my face, down the length of my fine cotton sari to my silver sandals. I resisted the urge to pull my sari tighter around me.

His mouth opened. He attempted a smile, a shy one. "You're keeping well."

Did he mean it? Or would he follow a kind remark with a cutting one, as he used to do?

His shirt was torn under one armpit and spotted with curry stains. His *dhoti* was covered with dust. Loose flesh gathered under his chin. He was thinner than I remembered. The smell of his sweat and cheap cigarettes filled the space between us.

When I didn't answer, he walked to the plastered wall, rubbed his palm flat against it. He looked impressed. I flinched; I didn't want him touching what was mine.

He considered the mosaic on the floor. "Is this...? Who lives here? I thought—don't you live at the other place? With the South Indians?"

"It's mine. I built it." I heard the pride in my own voice.

He frowned and tilted his head, as if trying to understand. We had once lived in a one-room hut, his mother sleeping in the front half with the kitchen utensils, he and I in the back. A curtain between the two areas.

He covered his mouth with his hand and left it there, as if deep in thought. "*You* built this?"

This was the Hari I knew. The one who never believed me worthy of anything but rooting and minding children.

"I earned it. All of it." And then, before I could help myself, "More than *you* ever did."

A hard light came into his eyes. His mouth twisted. "*I...? You* deserted *me*, remember?" He closed his eyes and shook his head quickly, as if to shake off his anger. "I don't want to get off to a bad start, Lakshmi. What's done is done, right? I forgive you. We'll start over."

At first, looking at his clothes and the ragged state of him, I had been tempted to feel sympathy. How foolish of me! Granted, he had earned his bitterness: a barren wife is a thing of shame. A burden that justifies returning her to her family.

At fifteen, I'd been too timid, too naive, to navigate Hari's rough ways. In the intervening years, I had learned not to be cowed easily. I would make no apologies.

"You forgive me? After the way *you* treated *me*?"

He looked confused. "But your sister said..."

"Sister?" What was he talking about? "I don't have a sister."

His brows drew together as he turned his head to the door. "Did you lie to me?"

I followed his gaze. A girl, skinny as a *neem* twig, was standing in the shadows just inside the doorway. How had I not noticed her?

As if in a trance, she walked to the center of the room, her eyes locked on mine. She was half a head shorter than me. Her dark brown hair, dusty and loose, parted on the side and plaited down her back, hung almost to her waist. An orange cotton wrap covered half her ragged petticoat and wound up her back and around her shoulders. She wore a dull blue blouse. No jewelry, no shoes.

She lifted a hand as if to touch my shoulder. "Jiji?" she said.

I was nobody's older sister! I took a step back. The knife in my hand glinted in the streetlight. She gasped.

Hari stepped between us. He pointed a finger at her. "Answer me!"

The girl jumped and wrapped her arms around her stomach.

I looked at Hari, at the girl, at Hari again. "What's going on?"

Hari fished a matchbox out of his pocket and tossed it at my feet. "See for yourself."

Was this a trick? To light a match, I had to set the knife down. I moved slowly, keeping an eye on Hari. His fists clenched and unclenched, but he remained where he was. I struck a match and held it to the girl's face. Her green-blue eyes, the color of peacock feathers, iridescent, were enormous. Her nose was thin and straight, with a small bump in the middle. She had rosebud lips, round and pink. I lifted the match to her eyes again, which hadn't blinked once.

Blood pounded in my ears. I shook my head. "How could—? After me, Maa carried two girls, but neither survived her first year."

Hari seemed confused, too. "She told me she was born the year you left me. She said you knew."

Maa was pregnant when I left Hari? With another baby girl? And I hadn't even known? So many thoughts whirled around my brain. The expense of another dowry must have exasperated her! Like many poor women, my mother had felt burdened by girl children. But why hadn't my parents come with her to Jaipur when I had sent them money to do so? Why hadn't she come with Hari?

I looked at the girl's body, using the light of the flame. I saw bruises on her arms. "What's your name?"

She glanced at Hari before replying. "Radha."

The match burned my fingers. I dropped it on the floor and struck another. My hands shook. "Where is Maa?" I asked.

Her eyes filled. "She's gone, Jiji." Her voice was small.

The words sank in. My legs felt rubbery. "And Pitaji?"

The girl moved her head to let me know my father had died, as well.

Both dead? "When?"

"Pitaji, eight months ago. Our Maa, two months."

I felt as if I'd had the wind knocked out of me. All this time I'd been dreaming of a reunion with my parents, never once considering that I might never see them again. Had my mother and father gone to their pyres shrouded in shame? Surrounded by gossip about the undutiful daughter who had abandoned her husband?

My parents would never know how often I had considered leaving Hari in the two years I was married to him. The only thing that held me back was fear of what my desertion would do to their reputation—until the day I could no longer endure my husband's beatings, the wounds that made me bleed, the words that cut me open. The mornings I could barely get up off the floor. And all for what? For the child I couldn't give him. In the first year of our marriage, his mother, that dear woman, hoped that teas of wild yam and brews of red clover and peppermint would encourage my body to produce a baby. She made tonics from nettle leaves to strengthen my organs. I chewed pumpkin seeds to moisten my women's parts until the inside of my mouth was covered in blisters.

My mother-in-law tended my body as diligently as I tended her medicinal garden—nurturing the soil, planting seeds, feeding the fragile plants. But all my *saas*'s patient ministering did not give her son what he craved most. To an Indian man, a son—or daughter—was proof of his virility. It meant he could take his proud and rightful place in the legions of men who would carry the next generation forward. Hari felt—as many men in his position would have—that I had robbed him of that right.

I could have explained it—all of it—to Maa and Pitaji if they had come to Jaipur. They might then have agreed that I was right to leave Hari, to build the shiny new life I had created. But they never came.

I didn't want to ask him, but I had to know. "And your mother? Is she…still with us?"

Hari swallowed. He looked away.

My eyes teared. His mother, my *saas*, was also gone? I had loved that gentle woman as much as my own mother. She spent hours showing me how to harvest the flowers from a Flame of the Forest tree to regulate menses, how to grind snakeweed just fine enough to soothe a blister without burning the skin. I had turned her teachings into my life's work.

She was the reason I'd survived. She would never know, now, that I had.

When I found my voice again, I said, "But if Maa has been gone two months...why has it taken you so long to get here?"

The girl snuck a peek at Hari and lowered her eyes.

He rubbed the scar on his chin with his hand. "We needed to prepare. For the journey."

I knew he was lying by the way he hid his scar. He'd done the same when he told my father that he could support me by pulling a rickshaw.

Again, I held the match's flame up to the girl's face. Was that a bruise on her throat or merely a shadow? She smelled of cow manure. So did Hari. They certainly hadn't used the money I'd sent to my parents on train tickets.

I looked at Hari. "What did you do with the money I sent?"

Hari pressed his lips together and stared at me, defiant now.

The match went out, and I lit another, turning to the girl again. My breathing was ragged as I said, *"Rundo Rani?"*

The girl wrung her hands.

I tried again. *"Rundo Rani?"*

Her lips parted.

"Rundo Rani," I repeated, louder this time.

Her words came out in a rush. *"Rundo Rani, burri sayani. Peethi tunda, tunda pani. Lakin kurthi heh munmani."* She clapped a hand over her mouth to hide a smile.

My father had made up that nursery rhyme and sang it to all his baby girls, including me. *Little queen, thinks herself so grand. Drinks only cold, cold water. But does so much mischief!*

I held my breath for an instant and let it out slowly. She confirmed what I'd already seen: my mother's eyes in Radha's face.

The girl lowered her hand. She was smiling openly now, her face transformed—a woman's face in a girl's body.

I had a *sister*—and she was growing up all the while I'd

been running from my past. But why hadn't my parents let me know? *But how could they have done that without an address on the letters I sent?*

I'd forgotten Hari was there until he said, "We're still married. You are still my wife."

My shoulders twitched.

"We can try again, Lakshmi."

No! I threw the box of matches back at his feet. "We will divorce."

His nostrils flared in anger. This was the Hari I knew. "I see now." He jerked his head at Radha. "You two really are sisters. You *both* lie."

What did he mean by that? I looked at Radha for the answer, but she was staring at the floor.

Hari's jaw clenched as he turned back to me. Through gritted teeth, he said, "Even your name is a lie, Lakshmi. Not a Goddess of Wealth, are you? You could never have earned this by yourself." He waved his arm to indicate the house. His eyes narrowed. "Whose keep are you?"

Of course he would think I was a rich man's mistress. Leave it to him to think a woman could never do this on her own!

With an effort, I kept my voice under control. "They passed a law this year, Hari. We can divorce now."

He bit his lip and picked up the matchbox. He looked around the room again, at my floor, my sari. For a few moments, we stood in silence.

Then it came to me. "You want money," I said. Of course he did! Instead of going to the bigger cities to pull a rickshaw for a week and coming home to give me what he'd earned, Hari had spent most of his time in the village sleeping, eating or trying to bed me. If his mother hadn't earned a small income from her medicinal herbs and treatments, we wouldn't have had enough to eat.

Suddenly, his features softened. "Just until..." He sounded contrite.

"How much?" I snapped.

He scratched his forehead, shifted on his feet. "How much can you spare?"

"I work hard, Hari. Everything you see here came from years of work. And it's not even mine yet." I narrowed my eyes. "I have debts, and unlike you, I honor them."

He was working his jaw again. "You want me to tell people the truth about you? What would your MemSahibs say if they knew?"

My heartbeat quickened. In his current state, no *chowkidar* would let him past the front gates of the grand houses they protected. But he knew as well as I did that the gatemen—like everybody else with mouths to feed and dowries to arrange—could be bribed.

Radha was watching us closely.

I said to Hari, "How long will you stay in Jaipur?"

He shrugged.

I inhaled deeply once, twice, three times. I pulled the roll of rupees from my petticoat. Rupees I'd been saving to pay my next installment to the builder. I tossed the bills onto the terrazzo floor—the way he had tossed his meager earnings on the floor of our hut all those years ago.

He stared at the bills. It was probably more money than he had ever seen. After a pause, he moved forward to pick up the rupees.

He rubbed the bristles on his chin. He lifted his eyes to meet mine. He opened his mouth, as if he wanted to say more.

I waited.

But his mouth clamped shut. His eyes shifted to Radha, who would not meet his eyes. He shook his head and walked out the door.

I stood, unsettled, without knowing why. For years, I had

imagined what I would do if I saw Hari again. I would beat him with my fists. I would slap him with the flat of my hands. I would kick him with my feet. For all the times he had hurt me, made me feel small. Yet, when I faced him for the first time in thirteen years, I felt more pity than anger.

Radha's voice cut through my thoughts. "Jiji, have you been in Jaipur the whole time? Your clothes—"

I silenced her with a motion of my hand. I ran to the window and watched Hari move down the street. When he was out of sight, I put my fingers to my mouth and whistled. Within seconds, Malik was at the window, two young men twice his height behind him, all there to protect me.

"Gone, Auntie-Boss. Rickshaw waiting for you around the corner."

I counted out five rupees. Malik gave his pals one coin each, pocketing the other three. He was a born businessman.

On the rickshaw ride home, I felt Radha studying my clothes, my hair, my sandals. I imagined her questions, the ones I hadn't allowed her to ask. *Where have you been all these years? Why did you run away? How did you come to be in Jaipur?* I was still trying to recover from the shock of seeing Hari, of learning that the three people who were once so dear to me were no more. And I was getting used to the idea of having a sister, who was sitting next to me, as solid as the headache at my temples.

Slowly, deliberately, I rearranged the sari over my shoulder and cleared my throat. "First thing—it is not polite to stare."

She looked away, but, as if she couldn't help herself, turned her head to me again. "Jiji—"

I held up a hand between us. "Second thing—we talk at home." Like birds that sowed the land with the seeds they ate, rickshaw and *tonga-wallas* spread the gossip they consumed. I made it a point not to feed them.

I felt Radha's gaze again, and I closed my eyes to shut her out. The pressure on my temples was worse now. Could this girl really be my sister? How filthy she was! As dirty as a Brahma bull that had been in the pasture for a week. At her age, I was fixing my own hair, wringing my wet petticoats clean by the river, washing my feet before lying down on my mat. Had Maa not taught her anything? She smelled like a hay bale, which meant Hari had roped passing farmers into giving them a ride to Jaipur. And pocketed the money I had sent home.

I glanced sideways at her clasped hands. Her blackened fingernails looked no cleaner than a beggar's. How was I to explain a sister I never knew I had? It wasn't as if my clients knew any details of my family life, but Mrs. Iyengar—what would I tell her? I added to the list in earnest. *Third thing: never mention Hari to anyone.* Judging by the looks of him, he still wasn't able to rub more than a few rupees together. It was possible he intended to stay in Jaipur and live off my money for a while. Why, at a time when I was finally reaping the efforts of my labors, had I been given two more mouths to feed?

But how unfair I was being! I would happily have accepted responsibility for feeding the two people I had been expecting: my mother and father. Maybe Radha was my penance for the disgrace I had brought upon them. My parents, my mother-in-law and Hari—they would all have been ostracized and ignored after my desertion. Kept away from holy ceremonies, weddings, births, funerals, even spat upon. I felt my face grow warm with guilt.

Radha's head nodded forward, and I realized she had fallen asleep to the rhythmic movement of the rickshaw. She was starting to lean toward me, and I found the closeness uncomfortable. I shifted on my side of the seat, and her body tilted to the other, her head resting against the battered canvas roof of the carriage.

Now I was free to study her face, which was the shape of Maa's, more oval than mine. Mine was heart-shaped, the chin coming to a point, like Pitaji's. If she'd been born the year I left, Radha must now be thirteen, but she looked older. For such a young girl, she already had a deep crease between her brows. And worry lines along the corners of her mouth.

I examined the dark, round indentations on her arms where I imagined Hari's hands had been. Had I escaped Hari's cruelty only to have him inflict it on Radha? The thought made me shudder.

As if in response, Radha shivered. I removed my woolen shawl and tucked it around her thin body. I doubted she owned a sweater. She must have frozen on the trip here!

The color of her skin was a shade darker than mine. No doubt she had spent more time in the sun, pulling water from the village well or collecting cow dung in the midday sun, as I had done all those years ago. The soles of her feet were cracked. A bath would have to wait till early morning. I couldn't risk waking all of Mrs. Iyengar's household as well as Mr. Pandey's family.

If she was thirteen, she must be in sixth form now. I would need to look into a government school for her. I knew from the daughters of my ladies that the next school session would start in January. Until then, what? I couldn't leave Radha home in our lodgings while I attended to my ladies. Mrs. Iyengar was nosy and would ask her a hundred questions. Could I take Radha with me to henna appointments? Clothes! She would need new clothes before I could present her to society.

My head felt too small to contain all the thoughts swirling around. I didn't dare think beyond tonight. If I did, I might never sleep again.

I shook Radha's shoulder to wake her. There was much I had to teach her, and soon.

THREE

November 16, 1955

Mrs. Iyengar charged me a small sum for the rental of her *almirah.* On one shelf of the cupboard, I kept folded saris in pastel hues. The prints were delicate—tiny dots, thin stripes or embroidered flowers no larger than a ladybug. The next shelf held my blouses, arranged in columns according to color: light blues, leafy greens, candy pinks, spotless whites and ivories. The *salwaar-kameez* sets, which I used to wear more often when I was younger, sat on the bottom shelf with their matching *chunnis.*

"These are all yours, Jiji?" Radha, her body wrapped in a towel, fresh from her bath, peered inside the *almirah.* She rubbed her fingers together, as if she were longing to touch the fine cottons, the silks. Last night in the rickshaw I'd told her about the women I worked for and warned her, "Fourth thing—do not touch anything that is not yours. The ladies will accuse you of stealing faster than you can deny it."

I chose a rose pink sari bordered in small fuchsia flowers and, with practiced fingers, pleated the folds before tucking them into my petticoat. "Most of my ladies don't wear cottons, only silks so fine you can pull them through a ring. For special occasions, they wear saris heavy with embroidery. Mostly gold and silver threads." I looked at my sister. "I did the henna of a bride recently. There was so much gold on her sari that three of the bride's sisters had to help her up the steps to the *mandap*."

"How did she manage to walk around the fire?"

I raised one eyebrow. "Very, very slowly."

Radha's laugh was surprisingly deep. It fluttered like the sound of playing cards that boys wove into the spokes of their bicycle wheels.

Slapping a pair of brown sandals on the stone floor, I urged her to slip them on. The heel was flat, the straps plain. From her calloused soles, I could tell she was used to walking in bare feet. These would ease her transition into shoes.

As she unwrapped the towel, my eyes went to her bruises again. Their color had faded from the angry red of yesterday. When our eyes met, she crossed her arms across her chest to hide them. "A sheep on the truck—she butted me in the ribs. The marks will be gone by tomorrow."

So much remained unspoken between us. It had been the same on the roof when I'd bathed her this morning, at dawn—before the female street sweepers made their rounds and before Mrs. Iyengar's servant girl took yesterday's saris off the clotheslines. Radha refused to talk about some things while I stayed mum about others. I was torn: part of me wanted to know if Hari had hurt her (as he had hurt me), but another part of me was afraid to find out. Whatever her answer, I was sure it would have been my fault. He would have done it to get back at me.

I pulled a tunic in leaf green cotton over her head and smoothed the fabric over her thin shoulders. The *kameez* was loose through her small chest, and I gathered the extra fabric to see how much needed to be taken in. The white cotton *salwaar* also needed to be hemmed a few inches; the pants were pooling around her feet and the waist was five inches too loose. Finally, I draped a white chiffon *chunni* loosely around her shoulders. I stepped back to inspect my work.

The green of the tunic intensified the pond-green of her irises and made her hair appear blacker. My zealous scrubbing had made her skin rosy and the coconut oil had given her arms a lovely sheen. With her hair piled high on her head, a jewel or two around her neck and a little more flesh on her bones, she could have been mistaken for one of the daughters of my ladies.

She could tell the effect pleased me and she pressed her lips in a shy smile. "Jiji, do you have something in a brighter color?"

"Gaudy colors will mark you as a village girl," I said. "The only way to wear bold colors is on silk, like my ladies do. And forget those ticky-tacky mirrors sewn into your clothes like a common washerwoman."

Her mouth fell open and her lips trembled.

Had I sounded too harsh?

Her gaze fell on the *mutki* she had carried all the way from our village. From the mouth of the vessel, the hundreds of tiny mirrors on Maa's wedding sari twinkled at us.

Too late, I realized I had hurt her feelings, just as I had on the roof when I was picking ticks out of her hair.

"Don't you ever wash?" I had asked.

"For ten days we rode a sugarcane cart, and then we were picked up by a truck carrying sheep to Jaipur."

Her voice had been small, apologetic, and I'd instantly regretted my tone. If Hari had wanted to spend my money in other ways, what could she have done? Besides, hadn't ticks also latched on to me back in Ajar when I'd wandered among goats and mangy dogs? I would have to be gentler with her.

Clang-clang. The jostling of metal canisters announced the arrival of the milkman in Mrs. Iyengar's courtyard. Relieved by the distraction, I hurried into my sandals. "I have to catch the *doodh-walla.* We'll need another liter to make *burfi.*"

I opened the door just as Malik was about to knock. His thick hair was uncombed, but his shirt and knickers looked clean. His jaws were working on something.

"*Arré*, Malik! You're early."

He jutted his chin at Radha. "Who's she?"

"That is Radha, my sister. She has come to stay."

No further explanation would I give and, with Malik, none was required. "Chewing *paan* will make your teeth black, you know."

Unfazed, the boy replied, "Today's market day, Auntie-Boss. No ladies to swoon over me." He grinned, his teeth stained with tobacco paste.

From my petticoat, I pulled out a shopping list and handed it to him. Malik scanned it. "Anything else?"

I glanced at the row of bottles on my worktable. "Lavender oil." We'd used the last of it on Radha's bruises this morning. "And magnolia extract." Radha's feet had been far drier than Lala's. I wondered if Radha had ever worn shoes in her life.

Malik nodded. He was staring at my sister again.

From the floor, I picked up Radha's dirty traveling clothes. "When you come back from the market, burn these."

Radha let out a small cry.

I turned to look at her. Perhaps they were her only clothes. "They're infested, Radha. We'll get you something new."

She blushed, glanced at Malik and quickly dropped her

gaze. Had I embarrassed her by saying such a thing in front of him? I glanced at him to see his reaction, but his face was a blank. I ushered him out the door, and we walked down the stairs to our separate errands.

When I returned to my room with the steel milk jug, I stopped at the threshold, aware that something had changed. Radha stood to one side of the long table where I kept my herbs, her hands clasped behind her. Her eyes had the wariness of a wild animal. What had she done? Whatever it was, she must have thought I was going to punish her. My eyes scanned the bottles of oils and lotions, my mortar and pestle, the marble board where I spliced my plants and seeds—all were slightly askew and not in the order I had left them. The jar of fresh herbs had also been moved. Then I saw it. In the bowl where I'd submerged my blouse with frangipani blossoms, one blossom was missing. I looked at Radha, whose hands flew up to her hair. There, on top of the bun I had arranged on her head, was the other flower.

Her smile was sly. "Tenth thing—always smell of flowers if you want ladies to invite you into their homes."

Last night, after the first, second, third and fourth thing, I taught her the fifth thing: *sit up straight* (she was hunched, as if she were used to squatting on the ground over the laundry or the cooking); sixth thing: *don't let your mouth hang open* (she stared at scooters as if she were seeing monkeys singing in Hindi); seventh thing: *eat with your mouth closed* (she barely finished one bite of *chapatti* before starting another, as if she hadn't eaten in weeks); and eighth thing: *smile when I introduce you to Mrs. Iyengar in the morning* (Radha's usual expression seemed to be a worried scowl). When I was up to the ninth thing, Radha had finished her dinner, and her eyelids were starting to droop. I spread a bedsheet in front of the *almirah*. She'd been scratching her head, and I told her once we got the *juey* out of her hair, she could sleep on the cot with me.

She didn't argue. Either she was used to sleeping on the floor or she was too exhausted to fuss.

I had been on my own for so long and had no experience raising a child. Should I remind her to ask instead of just taking something, or should I indulge her, a village girl enchanted with the everyday niceties I took for granted? A flower was such a small thing, after all.

I moved into the room and set the milk jug on the table. I smiled at her. Pointing to the bowl with the remaining blossom and my blouse, I said, "Would you hang my blouse to dry on the roof while I fix my hair?"

Her body relaxed, as if she had been holding her breath. She picked up one of the bottles on the table and asked, "Jiji, what is this one for?"

"That's *bawchi* oil," I said. "It makes your hair grow. You don't need it. Yours is thick enough."

She pointed to a clay bowl sitting atop a square of red velvet. Its rim was stained a dark cinnamon. "Is there something special about that pot?"

Before she could lay her hands on my *saas*'s old mixing bowl, I steered her away from the table. "I mix henna paste in it. Now hurry with the blouse." Checking my wristwatch, I said, "We're going to the seamstress. If we catch her early, she'll be bargaining on an empty stomach."

The seamstress's sparse hair was parted in the middle and pulled into a straggly bun. Parts of her yellow-brown scalp showed through. After she had pinned the three pairs of *salwaar-kameez* we'd brought with us, she leaned out her second-story window and called for tea. Five minutes later, a boy entered, carrying three tiny glasses of steaming chai. I accepted a glass, but the layer of oil floating on top kept me from taking a sip. Radha, on the other hand, had gulped hers down in less than a minute. She did the same to mine when

I handed it to her. I would have to teach her how to drink without seeming thirsty.

"How much?" I asked the tailor.

The woman removed a large tin of Scorpion Brand Snuff from a shelf and pinched the tobacco between her thumb and forefinger. She inhaled it, sharply, first through one nostril, then the other, the way Maa used to, then snorted, with her mouth open.

"You never told me you had a sister," she said.

I said, "You never told me you had the raw silk in orange when I asked for it. Imagine my surprise when I saw Parvati Singh wearing a blouse you'd made from the same fabric."

Her lips flattened.

I noticed Radha watching us, eyes darting from the tailor to me.

Making enemies was not my way, and certainly not with one of Jaipur's best seamstresses. I pulled a small bottle out of my carrier. "Let me give you this before I forget."

She grabbed the bottle, and we watched it disappear in the folds of her sari. "It will take two days," she said.

I stood. "Tomorrow."

As soon as we left the tailor's house, Radha asked me what was in the bottle.

"You can't guess?"

We walked in silence. Suddenly, she stopped. "*Bawchi* oil?"

Smiling, I took her arm to get her moving again. "Before she started using my oil, the poor woman was almost bald on one side."

Radha laughed.

"Auntie-Boss!"

A rickshaw pulled up beside us, Malik on the running board.

I squinted up at him. "You're wasting my money on a rickshaw?"

He held a hand to his heart and tilted his head. "Auntie-

Boss, I'm taking care of my ladies." He pulled me up by the hand, then turned to help Radha. His mouth was busy sucking a tamarind candy, and he offered one to Radha, who hungrily popped it into her mouth.

Thirteenth thing: *eating sweets will ruin your teeth*, I added mentally to Radha's list. Busying myself with the purchases, I began unwrapping the newspaper bundles. "Did you get the Moonstar brand of lavender oil?"

Malik, who had squeezed in next to Radha, leaned forward to look at me. "*A wise man to the rest of the world is a nobody at home.* Madam, not *only* Moonstar but a discount on the best brand money can buy."

"So I should be getting money back?"

He held his hands out, palms up, toward the rickshaw driver. "Does the driver work for free?"

This made me want to laugh, but I stopped when I saw him lift his brows and *salaam* Radha formally, his cupped palm rolling gracefully from his forehead to his mouth to his heart, making her smile. I turned my attention back to the packages.

"Jiji! Look! Just like the crown of Krishna!" Radha shouted, pointing across the street.

Gently, I pulled her arm down. "Sixth thing, Radha?"

Radha frowned, thinking. "Don't let my mouth hang open?"

"Very good. That building is the Hawa Mahal. It has almost a thousand windows. The ladies of the palace may be looking out those windows, and they do not wish to be seen."

As we left the Palace of Wind behind, I knew Radha was fighting the urge to turn around and see if the ladies were watching us. I would have to keep an eye on her. My younger sister was lively and curious, which was good, but she was also untamed—and that could be a dangerous combination.

Twenty minutes later, I asked the rickshaw-*walla* to stop. "I need to run an errand, so I'm getting off here. When you get home, Malik, show Radha how I make the *laddus*. But don't let Mrs. Iyengar catch you at her hearth."

"Certainly, Auntie-Boss. But…"

"What?"

He shrugged exaggeratedly. "*Laddus* are not food, as you so often tell me, Madam."

My cheeks felt hot. Of course! I'd completely forgotten that aside from tea at the seamstress's and a tamarind candy, Radha had had nothing to eat. Malik had noticed. I hadn't eaten anything, either, but I was used to it. Radha, on the other hand, was a growing girl. I should have known better. "At home there's *aloo, gobi, piyaj*. Radha, can you make the *subji* and *chappati*?"

She moved her head from side to side, looking serious. *Yes*.

"Good." Stepping off the rickshaw, I warned them, "Wash your hands first. And this time, Malik, be sure to use soap."

Ten years ago, I was earning my living in Agra by making contraceptive teas for the courtesans to keep them childless, and they paid me well. Madams like Hazi and Nasreen were especially kind to me, offering me lodging in properties they owned in return for my teas. In their spare time, they taught me the art of henna. Skimming a reed across skin was only slightly different than brushing paint across a *peepal* leaf skeleton as I had done with Munchi-*ji* back in my village. I took to henna painting quickly. Before long, I was decorating the arms, legs, bellies, backs and breasts of pleasure women with designs they taught me from each of their native lands—Isfahan, Marrakech, Kabul, Calcutta, Madras, Cairo.

Samir Singh frequented the pleasure houses of Hazi and Nasreen whenever he had business in Agra. There, Muslim noblemen, Bengali businessmen and Hindu doctors and lawyers smoked hookahs, and ate and drank as the courtesans recited ancient poetry, sang sweet, nostalgic *ghazals* and performed classical *kathak* dances to the beat of skilled musicians. When Samir heard of my henna skills, he sought me out. "There are many gentlemen in Jaipur who would like to start digging a well before their houses catch fire, if you know what I mean. And they'll pay triple what the pleasure houses pay you." What Samir proposed was a move to Jaipur and more money than I could have imagined, preventing unwanted pregnancies for men like him, men who dabbled outside their marriages. He explained that while he liked visiting the pleasure houses, he personally preferred young, childless widows. These women, no matter how young they had been when they lost their husbands, were often doomed to a life of loneliness; that was how society preferred it. (Not so for widowers, who could marry without repercussion.) Samir lavished widows with compliments, presents and his considerable charm, and they responded gratefully.

It was the respectable cover Samir offered me that cinched the deal. I could offer my henna to high-caste women like his wife *while* I discreetly sold my contraceptive tea sachets to his friends and acquaintances. When Parvati lamented her inability to conceive, I fed her what my *saas* would have—red clover, primrose oil and wild yam in the form of sweets or savories—until she became pregnant with Govind. Pleased, Parvati introduced me to the ladies whose names now graced my appointment book.

By the time I met Samir in 1945, I had already created my own life of independence. I could pay for my lodging, eat well and send a little money home to my parents. What Samir did was offer me a chance to grow my business, and I grabbed it, the way a child grabs a firefly: snatch the air—quick!—before it disappears.

Now, standing in front of a neat row of bungalows, I checked Samir's note from yesterday: *Mrs. J. Harris. 30-N Tulsi Marg.* The woman with the gray victory rolls on either side of her head, who was snipping spent flowers off a climbing rose on the front terrace, looked past her childbearing years. I looked at the address again, puzzled. In all the time I'd been making my herb sachets, I hadn't encountered a woman on the far side of fifty who needed them. Still, with English women, you never knew. The Jaipur sun was as merciless on their freckled skin as it was on the hands of my Indian ladies.

"Mrs. J. Harris?" I asked.

The Englishwoman turned and flashed a smile crowded with gray teeth. "You've found her! The gardener never gets this right. If I want it done properly, I have to do it myself. You must be the governess come to interview. Good with babies, are you? Well, I must say you look a mite cleaner than the ones the army's sent. But then, my husband, Jeremy, used to say, how can they clean the dust off when they haven't any proper place to bathe?

"Major in the British Army, he was. After he died, I stayed on. Couldn't very well afford a Bristol cottage on his army pension, could I? I'll call for tea, shall I? I warn you—none of that spicy chai you all like so much…bad for the stomach. Good old-fashioned English tea for me, thank you. Come inside. You must be freezing, dear. Twenty-one Celsius is glorious as far as I'm concerned, but you Indians pull out your woolies the instant there's the slightest breeze. Never understood it. Fresh air's the stuff for me!" Her busy English swallowed the *r* and softened the *d*—consonants we Indians took such care to pronounce. Army came off as *aamy.* Indians became *Injuns.*

Murmuring apologies, I turned, ready to make a hasty departure, when a younger woman rushed through the front door to rescue me.

"Ah, there you are, Mrs. Shastri. I believe you have some products to show me? My friends have been raving about your hand creams!"

★ ★ ★

We sat in the young Englishwoman's bedroom with the door locked, our voices low.

"I apologize for my mother-in-law, Mrs. Shastri," she whispered.

I had a feeling she was apologizing for more than her *saas*'s presence.

"*She* is Mrs. Jeremy Harris. I'm also Mrs. Harris but my first name is Joyce." The young woman's cheeks pinked. "My mother-in-law had a bridge game scheduled today but it was canceled. I'd assumed we'd be alone."

"Mrs. Harris, I don't wish to pry, but your mother-in-law seemed to think I was applying to be a governess. You have another child?"

Joyce Harris shook her head, lowering her eyes to her belly.

"But you are pregnant? And your pregnancy is not a secret?"

She shook her head again.

"I need to know how far along you are," I said gently.

Her eyes filled. Two tears dropped onto the bodice of her cheerful nylon dress. She watched the water travel down the length of the flowered fabric but made no move to wipe it away.

"Mrs. Harris?"

She hesitated. "F-four months."

It wasn't safe for women to eliminate babies too far into their pregnancy; four months was the upper limit. When women came to my mother-in-law for help, she would tell me: *we must leave the women as healthy as we found them.* "You're sure?"

A beat, and then she nodded.

"At this stage it would be risky—both for you and for the baby. And my main concern is for your safety. I need you to be sure it's no longer than four—"

She interrupted me with an urgent whisper. "I want this baby with all my heart. But if I'm thrown out on the street..."

The women I helped always wanted to confess their guilt, but it would have been easier for me and for them not to take me into their confidence. I wet my lips. I had to be sure she was telling me the truth.

"If you can tell me with absolute certainty that you aren't more than four months along, and if you follow my instructions precisely as I give them to you, then you should be fine, but—"

"I can't sleep. My headache is constant. If I could have this baby, I would. But I don't know if it's...my husband's."

Many of the women I handled at Samir's request were having an affair.

"Madam, there is no need to explain."

Joyce Harris leaned toward me and clasped my hand, startling me. I stared at the pale skin stretched across her knuckles, the loose wedding band, her bright red nail polish. She expected from me what wasn't mine to give. Forgiveness. Absolution. I was a stranger.

I looked at her face—wet, blotched, streaked with pink. The whites of her eyes were bloodshot.

"He plays squash at the club with John—my husband. That's where I met him. At the club. He's married, too. The baby may be John's but it could be...his." She released my hand and removed a handkerchief from her belt to wipe her eyes. "He's Indian."

For the briefest of moments I wondered if her Indian lover was Samir. But Samir was far too cautious; he made sure to supply each of his mistresses with my tea sachets so he could move on to the next woman with a clear conscience. If Joyce Harris were one of his lovers, he would have told me. He'd never made a secret of the others. Besides, he favored widows, and Joyce Harris was clearly married.

"What would my husband say if I handed him an Indian baby? I don't have to wonder what Mother Letty would say. I couldn't bring a brown baby back home to Surrey. There's no place in English society for such a child. There's no p-place my baby would be safe."

I waited until her sobs had subsided.

"Mrs. Harris, I'm sure you're doing what's best for your circumstances and for...those around you. But again, I must warn you not to delay. Boil one herb sachet for a half hour in one quart of water. Drink a cup of the liquid every hour until it's finished. It will taste bitter. You can put honey in the mixture to make it more palatable. Repeat the process once more. Within a few hours, you will develop cramps. Be sure to put some cotton padding in your underwear to catch the flow of blood when it starts. At your stage of pregnancy, your body will expel large clots of tissue, as well. It will be painful, but do not panic. Let the herb do its work."

Joyce Harris closed her eyes, letting more tears fall. I paused to let her absorb the instructions.

"I will leave three sachets with you, but you should not need more than two. To help with the pain, you can keep a hot water bottle on your belly or soak towels in warm water and apply them to your female parts. Only after it's over should you call your doctor. He'll think you've had a miscarriage. If you call him too soon, he'll try to save the baby, which, I believe, is not what you want."

I patted her pale arm. "It works most of the time, but there is no guarantee. If you're losing too much blood, you must call the doctor immediately. Again, I need to warn you there will be a lot of pain." I set a small vial on the tea table and told her to apply the lotion I'd prepared to soothe her female parts, which would feel raw after her body had expelled the fetus. "Do you understand everything I've told you?"

She nodded. We sat a little while longer in silence.

"Do you have any more questions?"

"Only the ones neither of us can answer," she told me in a voice I had to strain to hear.

As soon as I entered my lodgings, Radha sprang up from the floor, where Malik was gathering pebbles from a game of fivestones. She ran to the cooking pots and came back with a steel plate of food, relieving me of my carryall. "For you, Jiji."

Something was amiss. My eyes circled the room.

Malik stood and pocketed the pebbles. He stared at the floor sullenly, not meeting my eye. Radha ran to the water jug and returned with a full glass.

Now I was standing with a plate of fried dough and a glass of water, two anxious faces watching me.

"*Dal batti?* I thought I told you to make *laddus*."

She offered a nervous smile. "Malik said *dal batti* is a Rajasthani specialty. I took off the burned pieces. Taste, Jiji." She was anxious to please.

I ignored her. "Malik?"

Radha took a step forward, as if to shield him. "It's not his fault, Jiji. He was only putting out the fire. Then Mrs. Iyengar started screaming—"

Fire? Mrs. Iyengar screaming? *"Chup-chup!"* Putting the plate and tumbler on my worktable, I took a deep breath. "Start from the beginning."

She told me she was making *dal baati* when her *chunni* caught fire. Malik rushed down the stairs to help, and Mrs. Iyengar yelled at him for polluting her hearth.

Malik made circles on the floor with his big toe. "Sorry, Auntie-Boss."

Radha frowned and looked from him to me. "Malik has nothing to be sorry for. He saved me from burning! That mean old crow—"

Had it not been for her insolence, I might have been more

sympathetic. But her attitude must be curbed now or it would color my relationship with the landlady.

I held up a finger. "That old crow is our landlady." I held up another finger. "This is her home, not ours. She has the right to tell us what to do."

"That's not fair! Why don't we just move now to your new house? Get away from her?"

The vein on my temple throbbed. I pressed it gently with my fingers, resisted the urge to raise my voice. "I told you, Radha. We'll move into our house when it's ready. Not before."

I looked at Malik. "Did it happen as she says?"

He nodded.

I placed my hand on his head. "Thank you for keeping Radha from burning the house down."

He gave me a small smile.

"As for you, Radha, you must be more careful from now on—"

"But—"

"Especially when it comes to Mrs. Iyengar's hearth."

"Jiji—"

I reached for Radha's shoulder to calm her. She flinched, as if I were about to slap her. Is that what Maa used to do? Or what Hari did?

I dropped my hand. She wouldn't meet my eyes.

I let out a sigh. Appeasing the pious Mrs. Iyengar would cost me plenty. The last (and only other) time Malik had unknowingly walked across her hearth, she had insisted on a Brahmin *pandit* to purify it. (Muslims like Malik ate meat; the Iyengars didn't. They would have objected even if the Singhs had crossed their hearth. Rajputs ate meat also.) The first purification had cost me forty rupees. First my debt to the builder, then Hari. Now, this.

I tucked the end of my sari in my petticoat, steeling myself for a chat with my landlady. "I will go see what our punishment is."

Malik ran to the herb table, picked up two bottles and handed them to me. "I've already mixed them."

I looked at the labels: a hair tonic and a skin lotion. I smiled at him. "Good man." He knew as I did that bribery was the way to the landlady's heart. Mrs. Iyengar had us dangling over a well: we couldn't cook treats for tomorrow's clients until the *pandit* had finished his purifying ceremony, which could take from one to three hours. It was going to be a long night.

As if he'd read my thoughts, Malik said, "Pandit-*ji* is coming in one hour."

It was midnight, finally. My favorite hour. The moon was at the window. A *koyal* cried out its love song; the spotted dove joined in. The day's heat and dust were at rest, as were the people of Jaipur. The room was fragrant with the savories and sweets we had cooked (dandelion leaf *pakoras* for Mrs. Patel's arthritis, sweet almond *laddus* for Mrs. Gupta's headaches) and the lotions we had made (fresh sandalwood oil for Mrs. Rai's aching feet).

Malik had gone home hours ago. Radha was sleeping on the cot. I sat at my herb table with a small *diya* burning to give me light. I opened my notebook, licked the tip of my pencil.

The pandit's ablutions (he'd taken an hour to purify Mrs. Iyengar's hearth): debit.
The lavender and clove oils, turmeric and saffron that Malik bought today: debit.
Money I'd received from Samir for his tea sachets: credit.
Money paid by Joyce Harris for her sachets: credit.
The builder's invoice: debit.
Payment to Hari: debit.

Overall, a loss. I closed the notebook and began taking the pins out of my hair. I wondered how long it would take to finalize the Singh-Sharma union. And if the builder would give me an extension on what I owed him. How much more would Hari demand for his silence? I really needed the palace commission, but how long would I have to wait for Parvati to talk to the maharani?

I sifted through my hair with my fingers. Saasuji once told me there were three kinds of karma: the accumulated karma from all our past lives; the karma we created in this life; and the karma we stored to ripen in our future lives. I asked myself which karma had led to my marriage with Hari. And deserting my family—was that a new karma I had created or was it a karma from a previous life that had ripened in this one?

In her sleep, Radha cried out, as if she were shouting for help through a closed mouth. I rushed to the cot before she woke up the entire household.

"Radha. It's only a dream." I rubbed her shoulder.

But she would not wake up. She was curled on her side the way a baby lays in a womb. Her fists were balled tightly under her chin. Her tears dripped on the pillow. She looked so fragile. A flash of memory came to me: crying myself to sleep every night of my married life with Hari.

I lay down behind her and pressed my chest against her back, my cheek against her cheek, my leg against her leg. I wrapped my body around hers until there was no space left between us. I touched the skin of my ladies daily in my work, but being *this* close to another body was a new sensation.

"Shh. There now. Shh," I whispered.

With my free hand, I stroked her hair, still scented with the frangipani from this morning. *"Rundo Rani, burri sayani. Peethi tunda, tunda pani. Lakin kurthi heh munmani,"* I sang softly at the edge of her lip, my father's voice guiding me.

Her breath relaxed. Her muscles softened. She was awake

now. She reached for my hand and hugged it to her breast. I felt her ribs rise against my chest, then fall as they settled, with each breath.

I wiped her face and neck with the edge of my sari. "Tell me. About the dream, Radha."

She sniffed. "It was dark. Pitaji was in a well. And he only had me to hold on to. The gossip-eaters had gone home a long time ago. I was trying to help him. But he was so much heavier than me." She released a racked cry. "And I let go. Jiji, I let go. I couldn't help it. I couldn't. I looked for you but you weren't there!" She took a great gulp of air. "So many times I wished you would come and help me. One time, I started off from Ajar to find you, but Mala, our neighbor, saw me and sent me home again." A fresh wave of tears flooded my hand, the one she was holding. "When Maa died, I didn't tell anyone. For two days. I let her lay there. On the cot. I was so scared. I didn't know what would happen to me. I was so alone. Where were you all this time, Jiji? Why did you leave us? Leave *him*?"

I loosened my grip on her. Of course she wanted to know. For thirteen years I had kept the answer to myself.

I swallowed. "I would have died if I'd stayed. Hari would have made sure of it. I couldn't go back to Maa and Pitaji." She knew as well as I did that, once married, a woman was her husband's property. Unhappy wives couldn't just go back home to their parents, expecting sympathy. Some families even changed their daughter-in-law's first name as soon as she came to their household, as if her previous self had never existed.

I told Radha about the one good thing in my marriage, Hari's mother. How she taught me to heal women who came to her from surrounding villages. Mostly, they complained of stomach upsets, cooking burns, female pains and barren wombs. I didn't tell Radha about the wombs they wanted to empty without their husbands' knowledge.

I told her about Hari's beatings and the day I walked out of his hut one afternoon, making my way to Agra on foot, hiding behind a bush or in a trench whenever I saw anyone. It took me a week. I ate whatever I could forage along the way, often at night, when no one could see me, making sure there were no wild boars around. In the city of the Taj Mahal, I told her I helped women in much the way my mother-in-law had. What I left out were the details, that most of my income had come from wrapping a few tablespoons of ground cotton root bark in muslin pouches—as my *saas* had done for the village women—and selling them. It wasn't that I was ashamed of my work; if not for me, many courtesans and dancing girls would have sought cruder, and more harmful, means to keep pregnancies at bay—douching with detergents, throwing themselves down stairs or piercing the fetus with a knitting needle. But the ears of a thirteen-year-old village girl were too tender to hear such things.

I explained to her that Agra was where I learned to paint henna. I smiled as I thought of Hazi and Nasreen teaching me to paint a woman's body to inflame desire, but I didn't share that with Radha. I told her about the offer I'd received to paint henna for more money in Jaipur, and how I had jumped at the chance. "It allowed me to send more money back home."

"But henna work is for Shudras, not Brahmins," she said. "Pitaji would never have allowed you to touch other people's feet."

I let go of her hand then, and rolled over on my back. "It was better than being a whore, Radha." I had intended to sound harsh, and I had.

We lay quietly for a while.

"How did Pitaji die?" I asked.

"He drowned. But he was sick, too. In his stomach."

"What do you mean?"

"He liked his *sharab*," she whispered. "He thought he was hiding it from us, but by nightfall, he was too drunk to walk. The next day, I would have to go and teach school for him."

I knew Pitaji had started drinking around the time we came to live in Ajar, but he'd never been so drunk that I had to take over the school. "Did Maa ever forgive him?"

Radha turned her face to look at me. "For what?"

Just then, she looked so much like Maa that it was almost as if I were lying next to my mother the night I asked where her gold bangles were. I was just a little girl then, and as long as I could remember she'd never taken them off, even as she bathed, cooked and slept. I loved playing with them when we lay together like this. Maa's eyes filled with tears at my question, and I felt fear for the first time in my life.

I stroked Radha's cheek. "We didn't always live in Ajar. Didn't Maa tell you? We came from Lucknow. Pitaji had become obsessed with the independence movement. He would skip work to join the freedom marches. He spoke out against British rule at rallies. Then, when the movement needed more money, he sold Maa's gold, the jewelry from her dowry—wedding bangles, necklaces, earrings—against her wishes. Maa was furious.

"The British, who ran the school system, hadn't approved of his freedom fighting. So they demoted him to Ajar, this tiny, backwater place. I must have been about ten. In one fell swoop, they cut his salary and his pride."

"But Pitaji was right, wasn't he? India won in the end." Radha wanted to believe in our father, to defend him, as I had.

"Of course he was right," I said. It was people like our father, millions of them, who had made it clear to the British that Indians would no longer be held hostage in their own country.

But I could also see why Maa disapproved. So many Indians had been hurt or imprisoned for standing up against the British. She pleaded with our father: Why couldn't he keep quiet, just take care of his family, and let others fight? But our father was fervent in his beliefs; I admired him for that. He was committed to his ideals. Unfortunately, high ideals came with a price.

Once he had depleted his savings, he sold the remainder of Maa's only possessions, the gold that could have saved us from poverty, that was supposed to keep Maa secure in widowhood, that might have kept me from having to marry at fifteen. In a country where a woman's gold was her security against the unforeseen, Maa's naked earlobes and bare wrists were a constant reminder that my father had put politics before his family.

And so, we were forced to move to Ajar, where my mother buried her disappointment and my father buried his pride. Independence wouldn't come for another twelve years, but by then, he was already broken.

Radha said, "Maa never talked about you. Never spoke your name. I didn't even know you existed until the gossip-eaters told me you disappeared the same year I was born. As soon as I learned to read, I realized it was your letters Maa was burning whenever they arrived. The only letter of yours I read was the one you sent about the train tickets to Jaipur. You didn't mention me in the letter at all. I knew then that you didn't know I existed, either."

I closed my eyes. *Oh, Maa, how angry I must have made you. Your husband betrayed you. I betrayed you. If only you had opened those letters!*

As soon as I was able to earn enough, I'd sent money in every envelope for my parents to spend on their needs. I'd begged their forgiveness for leaving my marriage and told them I would send for them as soon as I could. If the money had been destroyed along with my letters, no wonder Radha's clothes had looked so threadbare when she arrived in Jaipur.

I curved my body around hers again, as if I were hugging my mother, as I longed to do.

Radha squeezed my hand, bringing me back to the present, reminding me that I had a living, breathing sister. She may not be my penance for the wrong I had committed, but my salvation. I could no longer make anything right with my parents, could no longer humble myself before them, could no longer restore their good reputation. But I could take care of my sister, guide Radha into maturity, into womanhood. Make sure she became someone my parents would be proud of—unlike me.

Radha stirred. "Jiji, remember Munchi-*ji*?"

I remembered the old man in Ajar, hunched over a tiny leaf skeleton, painting a *gopi* and cow no larger than my thumb, dotting the milkmaid's sari with his camelhair brush. He'd been the one I'd run to when my parents argued about money. I escaped my mother's bitter silences and my father's drinking by losing myself in my painting. Old man Munchi taught me to see, to really notice, every tiny detail of what I was about to paint before ever handing me a brush. It was this practice that made it easy for me to pick up a henna reed years later and paint designs etched intricately in my memory.

"Is he still painting?" I asked.

"*Hahn.* He always said you were his best student."

I found myself smiling. "Did you paint with him, too?"

"I don't have your gift, Lakshmi. Mostly, I made the skeletons for him out of *peepal* leaves. I also ground his paints." She turned to look at me again, a mischievous smile playing at her lips. "Do you know what you get when you feed a cow mango leaves, then mix the cow patty with urine and clay?"

"What?"

"Orange paint!" She grinned. "Munchi-*ji* said my paint was smooth as silk."

"I can show you how to grind henna leaves to make my paste if you'd like."

"Accha." Yes. She closed her eyes, yawning loudly.

"You should cover your mouth when you yawn, Radha."

Her eyes slid upward, coyly, to meet mine, her lips curving. "Twentieth thing?"

I'd always been a light sleeper, so when I heard the rattle of the doorknob, I was immediately awake and off the cot. It was still dark outside. Radha was fast asleep. Samir burst through the door, and my first thought was that he'd had too much to drink at his club and lost his head—until I noticed the woman in his arms. She was bundled in a quilt. Eyes closed, moaning softly. Samir's friend, Dr. Kumar, stood beside him. As I sprang out of bed, I glanced at the wall clock. It was two in the morning. I ushered them inside the room before Mrs. Iyengar woke up.

When I flipped the light switch, Samir's expression was grim.

"Something's wrong with Mrs. Harris," Samir whispered. "Kumar has some questions for you." Then his eyes darted around the room until he spotted my cot, where Radha was propped on one elbow, rubbing her eyes.

I rushed to her. "Radha, please get up."

She scampered off, her eyes growing wider, as Samir laid his charge carefully on the cot, on the sheet where she and I slept. As he did, the quilt fell open and I saw the congealed blood shining in the weak light of the ceiling bulb. Joyce Harris's eyelids, flushed and blue-veined, fluttered, and her knees rose toward her chest. She was clutching her stomach. Her teeth were chattering so loudly I was surprised Mrs. Iyengar wasn't already pounding at my door, telling me to be quiet.

"Why are you bringing her—"

"No time. Kumar will explain."

I noticed the doctor's black medicine bag. He pulled a stethoscope from it.

Samir grasped my hands. "Thank you, Lakshmi. Please do as Dr. Kumar says," he begged. Then he was gone, pulling the door closed quietly behind him. The whole exchange had taken less than a minute. The air in the room was close, thick with the Englishwoman's moans.

Dr. Kumar, whose eyes hadn't yet found a place to rest, kept his voice low. "She's taken something. I need to know what she took and how much."

"I don't understand—"

"What's to understand?" He frowned. "She's taken a dangerous herb to kill her baby, and she'll die unless I know what she took."

"But I only—" I felt my face flush. "Hasn't Samir explained to you what I—"

"Do you know how risky it is to abort a baby at five months?" His gray eyes flashed.

"Five months?" My mouth hung open.

Kumar nodded and placed his stethoscope on Mrs. Harris's abdomen. She let out a cry. "I'm picking up the baby's heartbeat, so it's eighteen weeks at least. But the heartbeat is faint. The woman has lost a lot of blood. She needs a transfusion. Samir is calling in favors to get her to a private hospital." As he talked, his eyes wandered from Joyce Harris to me. "I don't think the baby will survive." He glanced at my hands, which were clasped in front of my sari.

Finally, he removed the stethoscope. "What did you give her?" His words were measured, as if he were trying to contain his anger.

I tore my eyes from the woman writhing on the cot. "I gave her cotton root bark in the form of a tea. If she had followed my directions, she would have boiled one tea sachet in a quart of hot water. She was supposed to sip it every hour until she had finished the quart. Then repeat the process. That's usually all it takes to expel fully. But I left an extra sachet with her just in case."

Dr. Kumar put two fingers on the woman's wrist and checked his watch. "Her pulse is very faint. She may have taken all three doses at once or mixed less water to make it more potent."

"But she swore she was no more than *four* months along. I asked her twice and told her it was dangerous if she were any further along. I had no reason not to believe her."

He stared at me. Did he think I was lying?

"I've never given this herb to any woman who is more than four months pregnant. Either Mrs. Harris didn't know, or she was desperate and lied to me."

I watched him saturate a cotton ball in alcohol and rub the crook of her arm with it.

"How did you and Samir…find her?"

He removed a vial and syringe from his bag. "A friend of hers phoned Samir at the club where we were having dinner. He said she needed help." He tapped the Englishwoman's arm to raise a vein and plunged the needle into it. Joyce Harris flinched. "We picked her up. Her husband and mother-in-law left for Jodhpur today so no one was at home. Hold this here, will you?"

I pressed a ball of cotton firmly on the woman's arm. Dr. Kumar capped the syringe and put his implements back in his bag. Then he picked up the woman's wrist and looked at his watch for a long moment. His fingers were long, his nails immaculate. He laid her wrist back on the quilt.

"I've given her a tiny bit of morphine for the pain—but I

need her conscious. The morphine shouldn't interfere with what you gave her. But we'll need antibiotics to fight the infection." Dr. Kumar's cautious eyes explored my hands, my face, my hair. I noticed threads of silver in his dark curls, a freckle above his upper lip. "Do you really think, Mrs. Shastri, that you can cure a woman's...problems...with *herbs*?"

"When a woman has no other options, yes."

"This woman would have had options."

"She didn't think so."

"How is that possible? She's English. She has all the options in the world. A hospital for whites, for one."

"And if the baby's father is Indian?"

The doctor's fine eyebrows rose and he regarded his patient with new curiosity.

"Samir didn't tell you, then?"

From the corner of my eye, I saw Radha move. All at once, I remembered she was still in the room. She had heard everything. I stole a glance at her as I said to the doctor, "Mrs. Harris doesn't know if the baby is her husband's." *Please, Radha, try to understand.*

Radha covered her mouth with her hand.

The doctor's fine eyebrows rose. "Still, with herbs, it's risky. For all you know, you may have given her poison."

I clenched my jaw. "I have done no such thing, Dr. Kumar. I've given her an herb that makes the womb slippery. Within a six- to eight-hour period, the fetal material will slide out, along with any sustenance the mother's been creating for the baby." To my own ears, my words sounded defensive.

"And how exactly does your herb make the womb slippery, as you put it?"

"It stops the woman's body from producing a substance that helps attach the egg to her womb."

He studied me for a long moment. "Progesterone," he said. "What you're referring to is called progesterone." The doctor checked his patient's pulse. "Have you ever had a woman experience adverse side effects from your herb?"

"Never."

Dr. Kumar opened his mouth, as if to ask another question, when a loud knock at the door startled us all. Joyce Harris let out a small yelp, and for the briefest of seconds, her eyes circled the room wildly before she collapsed again into quiet delirium. The doctor and I stared at each other.

Mrs. Iyengar's loud whisper could be heard from the other side of the door. "*Kya ho gya?* Mrs. Shastri, what's all the noise and fuss about?"

Quickly, Radha climbed into bed next to the sick woman and pulled the quilt over them both, hiding Mrs. Harris from sight.

"It's two o'clock in the morning!" Mrs. Iyengar began to open the door.

I rushed to block her entry. "I'm sorry, *Ji*. My sister—she's not well."

Mrs. Iyengar craned her neck to peer around me. Radha let out a moan, feigning pain, to cover the soft cries of the Englishwoman.

"I called for the doctor, Mrs. Iyengar," I indicated Dr. Kumar with my eyes. "I'm so very sorry for waking you."

Joyce Harris began to murmur, and Radha groaned louder. Dr. Kumar reached for my sister's wrist, pressing it with his thumb as he looked at his watch. "She needs rest, Mrs. Shastri," he said, as if annoyed by the landlady's intrusion.

Radha closed her eyes and cried out, "Jiji."

"Perhaps she's eaten something—"

"I must go, Mrs. Iyengar—" I moved to close the door.

But the landlady didn't want to leave. "Sour and salty in the winter, my husband always says, sweet and mild in the summer—"

"Yes, yes, thank you. I'll take that advice and add to it the doctor's. So sorry to have awakened you."

I shut the door firmly and braced my back against it. I stared at Radha in amazement. How had she known what to do? Her actions had been swift and *clever.*

Mrs. Harris whimpered now. Radha eased out of the bed and tucked the quilt around her.

The doctor was eyeing me warily.

I pushed myself away from the door and wound my hair into a bun. "Radha, pluck the pollen from the chamomile flowers."

"No more herbs, Mrs. Shastri." Dr. Kumar's voice sounded tired.

"She trusted me to help her, Dr. Kumar." I walked to the table of herbs. "Radha, quickly!" I said, waking the girl out of her daze.

Radha hurried to join me and began separating the chamomile petals and stems from the pregnant pollen centers, which she handed to me. I ground them in the mortar along with two leaves of peppermint and a few drops of water. As I worked the paste, a scent sweet and sharp, fruity and floral, filled the small room.

"Wet a rag," I told Radha.

Radha dampened a fresh scrap of cloth. I placed the paste in the middle, folded the cloth and knotted the two ends closed to form a poultice.

I sat opposite Dr. Kumar on the narrow cot, tenderly blotting the woman's feverish forehead with the poultice. For a second her eyes opened, and I saw a flicker of recognition before she closed them again.

"Breathe, Mrs. Harris," I told her. "You will be fine. Breathe." Like a priest's incantation or a templegoer's plea to Ganesh, I repeated the mantra steadily, until her forehead relaxed.

I pulled the quilt down. The Englishwoman's hands were still gripping her stomach. I pressed a point just below her sweaty wrist until her fingers uncurled, releasing their hold. Then I placed the poultice on her stomach. After a minute, her limbs stopped twitching. Her breathing became more regular.

Dr. Kumar stared, incredulous.

"It draws out the infection," I told him, handing him the pouch.

"It's hot." He held it gingerly, as if it burned his fingers.

I smiled. "My *saas* taught me how to make it."

The door latch clicked. We turned to see Samir rushing toward us. He lifted the patient from the cot. "We're taking her to Gola's private hospital. Remember him from school, Kumar?"

Dr. Kumar nodded.

"Is she doing any better?"

"She's in less pain. But she will lose the baby." The doctor looked at me as he said it. He sounded resigned; he wasn't accusing me. He picked up his black bag.

"Can't be helped." Samir was halfway to the door. He seemed eager to let the matter drop. "Let's go, Kumar!"

I followed them to the door. "You'll let me know how she fares?"

"I'll send word in a few days," Samir whispered as he carried Joyce Harris down the stairs.

Dr. Kumar looked around the room, his gaze alighting on various objects before settling on me. He tilted his head to one side in farewell and hurried out.

I shut the door behind him and rested my forehead against it. The silence in the room was as noisy as cicadas on a hot summer day. I waited for Radha's questions.

After a while, she said, "That woman—the *Angrezi*—she *wanted* to lose her baby?"

"Yes."

"And you helped her?"

"Yes." My shoulders slumped. I hadn't thought I'd have to tell her for a few more years. How naive I'd been.

"But earlier you said the henna is how you make money..."

I pressed my lips together. I looked away.

Radha frowned, considering. "The beggar woman we saw yesterday. With her baby. You said she shouldn't have any more children. She couldn't afford to feed them."

"Yes."

"But tonight. The *Angrezi* woman. She must be rich."

"Women have their own reasons for needing to do difficult things." I flattened my lips. "I don't ask why. I don't need to know."

She looked at the cot. "How do they find you?"

I shrugged. "I'm known."

"And those two men? Who were they?"

"Samir Singh is a friend. Someone I've known a long time. The other one, Dr. Kumar—all I know is he's an old friend of Samir's."

Another pause. "Does Malik know?"

I made the slightest movement with my head. *Yes*. "One more question, Radha. Then we must start cleaning up."

"Why?"

"Because you'll have to give me more time to explain things. It's complicated."

"No, I mean why do you do it? Help the women rid themselves of babies?"

Radha had seen and heard so much tonight that was new to her. I could tell by the quiver in her legs, the way her eyes couldn't tear themselves away from the bloodstain on the cot.

How could I explain men who knocked on the door in the middle of the night? Or women who had lovers outside their marriage?

I remembered what my mother-in-law said when she taught

me how to make the contraceptive sachets. I'd been fifteen, a new bride in her home. "How can I say no to these women, *bheti*? Their land is dry. Their granaries are committed to the *zamindar* for taxes. They cannot feed the little ones waiting for them at home. They have no one else to turn to."

My sister was only thirteen. Simple explanations wouldn't be enough. But I was too exhausted to find the right words, to help her understand.

In the end, I repeated my *saas*'s words. "They have no one else to turn to."

After a full minute of silence, each of us lost in our own thoughts, I said quietly, "Let's go up to the roof to clean up." I whipped the stained sheet off the cot. Joyce Harris's blood had seeped into the jute below. I would have to scrub it with a mixture of *ghee* and ash. "Radha?"

She looked up from the soiled charpoy. Her eyes were troubled.

"You did well tonight. But we must keep this to ourselves, *accha*?"

I hated having to ask this of her, but keeping this secret was too important to my livelihood. One word of Mrs. Harris's misfortune would put a full stop to my business.

At first, I thought Radha would argue with me. Then, so quietly that I almost didn't hear, she said, *"Hahn-ji."*

FOUR

November 17, 1955

The next day I woke Radha at dawn, even though neither of us had slept very long, or very well. I showed her how to grind the henna, and to my surprise, she created a finer henna paste than I ever had. Apparently, old man Munchi had not been exaggerating. My sister even suggested adding more lemon juice to make the color stronger. When I complimented her, she looked alarmed, as if she weren't used to praise.

I couldn't enroll her in school until January, so I was taking her with me and Malik to my henna appointments.

My first appointment that day was with Kanta, one of a handful of clients who treated me as an equal. Perhaps it was because I was a little older than her—Kanta had just turned twenty-six. Perhaps it was because, like me, she was a transplant to Jaipur, having been raised in Calcutta and educated in England. Or perhaps it was because she was also childless, although, more than anything, she wanted to be a mother.

Kanta came from a long line of Bengali poets and writers; her father and grandfather had passed their time composing sonnets and organizing literary salons. "The only thing Jaipur women read is *Readers Digest*," she'd once complained.

Now, before I'd even stepped foot on her veranda, Kanta herself opened the door, edging her seventy-year-old servant, Baju, out of the way. He straightened his Marwari turban and stroked his long mustache. "Really, Madam!"

She was tingling with anticipation. "Lakshmi! I can't wait to hear what happened at Parvati's. Baju, don't just stand there! Take Malik into the kitchen and feed him a snack." Finally, she noticed Radha standing behind me. Looking from my eyes to Radha's, she cried, "*Arré!* I'm seeing double?"

I introduced Kanta to my sister, telling her that Radha had come to Jaipur to study at the government school here. I glanced at Radha to see how the explanation sat with her. I needn't have worried. She was staring at Kanta, fascinated. She was studying Kanta's shoulder-length bob, her slim capri pants, the sleeveless shirt tied across her exposed midriff. (Traditional women, like Parvati, who covered their plump midsections alluringly with saris, would sooner have joined a brothel than bare their stomachs.)

Kanta's lipsticked mouth stretched wide. She grinned at Radha. "I heartily approve of education for women!" Kanta's Brahmin family had always prized its daughters, never raising them as the lesser gender. They had sent her to England for her graduate studies.

While Kanta led the way to her bedroom, I kept an eye on Radha, who was soaking up her surroundings like a parched gazelle. The airy bungalow, with its squared settees and bare floors, not one painting of a raja or rani or a god or goddess on the walls, might have been common in Calcutta or Bombay, but not in Jaipur.

Radha slowed down to study the framed photos on the walls: a large one of Gandhi-*ji*, one of Kanta and her husband, Manu, in front of their college, one of Rabindranath Tagore—a distant relative of Kanta's and one of India's most famous literary figures.

When Radha came to the photo of two men standing together, one in a splendid headdress, she tapped my shoulder. I stopped to look.

Kanta, who had been watching us, said, "That's Manu on the left. And his boss, the Maharaja of Jaipur. Handsome, aren't they?" She chuckled merrily, on the move again toward her bedroom.

Kanta's husband worked for the palace as the Director of Facilities. It was because of his elevated position that the Agarwals lived rent free in one of the impressive colonials where a British family had once lived. The original six-bedroom house and grounds had been divided down the middle into two dwellings to accommodate two families.

As we entered her bedroom, Kanta asked, "Well, Lakshmi? Will Manu get his wish?" She was closing the door as she said it, but her mother-in-law pushed the door from the other side, barging in.

"Yes, Lakshmi, will Manu get his wish for a baby boy?" She shot a pointed glance at Kanta. It was customary for widowed mothers to live with their oldest son, and since Manu was her eldest, his mother lived with them. Kanta rolled her eyes at me over her *saas*'s head.

I smiled. "I'm working on it."

Kanta's *saas* pointed her sandalwood rosary at her daughter-in-law's stomach. "If there's a baby in there, he's probably afraid to come out. Just look at her. She doesn't cover her head when elders enter the room. She lets strange men see her buttocks in trousers. If my husband were still alive—"

"He would have picked out a girl Manu would have rejected," Kanta teased, smiling.

Manu and Kanta had met while studying at Cambridge. Theirs had been a love marriage, much to her *saas*'s chagrin. Kanta had often joked how, emboldened by the freer Western atmosphere in England, they had started holding hands, which led to many stolen kisses, and had they not married, they wouldn't have stopped there.

Her mother-in-law scoffed. Lowering herself and her voluminous white muslin sari onto the bedroom divan, she said to no one in particular, "Kanta is going to see me to my funeral pyre without the grandchildren I am owed."

Kanta looked stricken. I was used to their affectionate bickering, but today, her mother-in-law's words had a sharp edge. I knew the old woman felt the competition among her cronies, grandmothers twice, three times over. Most wives would have given birth to several babies by Kanta's age. I felt the pressure, too; to date, all my herbal remedies to help Kanta conceive had ended in miscarriage.

"Now, you two," I scolded them gently. "Saasuji, when you see this design, you will feel the baby is already here. And if I am to succeed, I need peace and quiet."

The older woman placed a hand on each knee and heaved herself to standing. "Baju! Where is my buttermilk?" she called to the servant on her way out. "That old man moves slower than a dead elephant. All day he steals our *ghee* and eats our *chapatti*."

When the door closed, I turned to Kanta with a chuckle, but she was staring at the ceiling, trying to blink away the tears in her eyes. "She's at me night and day about grandchildren."

I took Kanta's hands in mine and led her to the divan. Sitting down next to her, I used a corner of my sari to wipe her eyes.

She turned to me with a haunted look. "It's just—we have tried and tried..." Her desperation was palpable.

I grieved for my friend. "You and Manu have spent the last five years getting to know each other. You know whether he likes *chapatti* more than rice. Whether he prefers poems to prose. If he favors starch in his *kurtas*. And that's so important because when the children come, you'll be too busy asking him, '*Arré, arra-garra-nathu-kara!* Manu, you *char-sobeece*! Where have you hidden my girlish figure?'" My voice had risen in imitation of village women selling bitter melon in the market.

Kanta bit her lower lip and started to laugh. She looked at Radha, who was also giggling.

I was ready to begin. I told Kanta to lay down on the divan and lower her capris. We were covering her stomach with henna today, and she would need to be absolutely still. I dribbled some clove oil on my hands. "Radha, why don't you read to Kanta while I work?"

"Splendid!" Kanta said. Restored to her cheerful self, she said, "Radha, choose a book from my bedside."

Radha's face brightened. She had told me last night that she had read and reread all of Pitaji's books that the rats hadn't chewed: Dickens, Austen, Hardy, Narayan, Tagore, Shakespeare. (I remembered those books fondly, too.) When Pitaji died, she said she began teaching the village children their letters and maths so she and Maa could go on living in the hut. Of course, after Maa died, the villagers would no longer allow a young girl to live in the schoolteacher's house by herself.

I watched Radha examine the books on Kanta's bedside table. *"Jane Eyre. Bahagvad Gita. Lady Chatterley's Lover?"* As she read the last title, Radha looked at us; she was blushing.

Kanta laughed at the expression on her face. "If you haven't already read *Jane Eyre*, let's start with that. I read it every few years. I love how the orphan girl gets everything she wants at the end."

I rubbed the clove oil on Kanta's stomach while Radha started. Faltering at first, Radha gained confidence as she read aloud. The big words took her a little time, but her command of English was impressive. "'There was no possibility of taking a walk that day. We had been wandering, indeed, in the leafless shrubbery an hour in the morning; but since dinner…'"

I began painting with henna. With a slim reed I drew a large circle around Kanta's navel. Next, I painted six lines from the navel to the edges of the circle, like the spokes of a wheel. In each of the resulting triangles, I drew a baby eating, a baby sleeping. Reading. Playing with a ball. Putting on a shoe. Crying.

As Radha read about Jane Eyre's isolation, I thought about Kanta's loneliness. Jaipur was not as cosmopolitan as Calcutta, Bombay or New Delhi. The ideas here were far more traditional, the people more entrenched in the old India, less given to change. She felt separate from my ladies and longed for friendship. Motherhood, she felt, would be her entrée into a world of cozy chats, shared intimacies. She had faith that I could help her get there. And I was loath to disappoint her. I was continually trying different recipes for treats that might help strengthen the eggs in her womb. Today, I'd brought *burfi*: sweetened with yam and coated in sesame seeds. I didn't let her sit up for tea but fed her lying down so the henna could dry properly. All the while, Radha read aloud, inflecting her voice with emotion and drama. Where had she learned to do that?

When it was time, I rubbed my hands vigorously with geranium oil and massaged Kanta's belly to remove the dried henna. After I finished, she jumped off the divan and walked to the mirrored doors of her *almirah*. She turned left and right to admire the design, framing her flat stomach with her hands.

"Oh, Lakshmi! My very own baby. Six of them! I can't wait to show Manu!" She turned to look at me. "But why is one of them crying?"

I shrugged. "In real life, babies cry."

There was mischief in Kanta's eyes. "Only if they have my *saas* for a grandmother."

Her gaze landed on Radha. "You are welcome to borrow my books anytime. You read beautifully. Be careful when my *saas* is around, though. Always leave *Lady Chatterley's Lover* at the bottom of the pile and the *Bahagvad Gita* on top!"

Radha looked happier than I'd seen her since she arrived in Jaipur.

Kanta put a finger on her lip. "Lakshmi, have you ever taken Radha to the Minerva?"

I balked at telling her I had no idea if Radha had ever been to the cinema.

Misunderstanding my silence, Kanta laughed. "It's all right, Lakshmi. My treat. There's a Marilyn Monroe film that I've been dying to see. I can take Radha."

The suggestion made my stomach flutter. My ladies fretted about the influence of these movies—and the behavior of men at the cinemas—on their impressionable daughters. Indians were crazy for films, and the sight of American stars like Elizabeth Taylor and Marilyn Monroe in tight skirts drove the rickshaw drivers and *charannas* so wild they threw coins at the screen. (At some point, the manager would always come out to scold them.)

"Is it wise to expose her to—to—" I felt my face grow hot. I sounded just like my matronly clients!

"To Western women? Scary, aren't they?" Kanta's cackles made my words seem priggish. I was being too protective. If Radha was going to live in a big city, she *needed* to experience it. If wouldn't do any good to shield her excessively. And who better than Kanta—so worldly and sophisticated—to guide her? Besides, it was only a film!

Clapping her hands, Kanta smiled at Radha, "Oh, we'll have such fun!" She raised her brows at me. "It's very naughty of you not to tell me you had a sister. Look at those eyes! Men will be falling all over her."

I smiled, uneasy. It pleased me that my sister's beauty had not gone unnoticed by one of my favorite customers. But I worried. Would her curiosity go unchecked? Her impulsiveness? I shook my head; I was being far too Victorian.

Outside Kanta's house, I jotted a few lines in my notebook. Radha leaned against a pillar on the veranda. We were waiting for Malik to return with a rickshaw.

"Kanta Auntie is sad."

"Hmm."

"Why can't she have babies?"

"I don't know, Radha. Her bleeding has always been irregular. She may not be able to produce enough eggs. You know the *burfi* I fed her? I'm hoping the wild yam in them will help regulate her cycles." I frowned, realizing how little I knew about my own sister. "Have you started your menses yet?"

Her cheeks colored and she lowered her chin. "Two months ago. Just before we came to Jaipur."

"Well, it means you're a woman now, you know. You can… have babies." I stopped, not sure how to explain it to her. "You must be careful of men at the cinema. And on buses. And don't walk on the street unless Malik or I are with you."

Her eyes flickered, glazed with doubt.

There were probably a thousand other things I needed to warn her about, but this was new territory for me. When was the right time to tell her about what husbands do in bed? My reticence surprised me. Women told me intimacies all day long; why did it embarrass me to talk to my sister about sex?

But Radha's mind seemed to be elsewhere. She asked, "What was Kanta Auntie so excited about when we first came to the house?"

I tucked the notebook into my petticoat. "Ah. The Maharaja of Jaipur is converting one of his palaces into a hotel. He wants Samir Singh to design the remodel. But Mr. Sharma, who is the official contractor for the palace, has another architect picked out. So Kanta's husband wants to figure out a way to get Mr. Sharma to hire Samir."

"Can't the maharaja hire anyone he pleases?"

"Of course. But it's not his way to order people around. He wants Mr. Sharma to think it was his idea."

"How can *you* help?"

"You'll see." I smiled.

When Kanta first confided Manu's problem to me, I knew the answer straightaway. The best way to seal the fate of the Sharmas and the Singhs was through an arranged marriage, which would make the business partnership an afterthought. I wanted to wait until both parties had agreed to the marriage before telling Kanta.

We turned at the sound of Malik's high-pitched whistle. He stood off to the side of Kanta's veranda, gesturing for us to step down. His clothes, which had been spotless when we left the house this morning, were splattered with mud. A trail of blood was on one shoulder, and his ear on that side of his head was red, oozing. I ran to him, removing a cloth from my carryall. Radha ran after me, the tiffins clanging in her hands.

"Malik! *Kya ho gya?*"

Before I could reach him, he turned away, walking quickly toward the front gate and leaving us to catch up.

When we were safely out of the *chowkidar*'s earshot, he said, "That *maderchod* builder! I paid him the two hundred rupees you gave me, and he threw it back at me! *'You're putting a cumin seed in a camel's mouth,'* he said. He boxed my ear and told me not to return unless I had the entire amount we owed." He pivoted to a stop. "Here." Malik reached in his pocket. He handed me the two hundred rupees I'd given him.

I pressed the cloth to Malik's bleeding ear. He yelped and then took over, flattening the fabric against his head. Instantly, the cloth turned pink. I stared at it.

I didn't want Malik paying for my mistakes. But how could I pay the builder the thousands of rupees I owed him? I hadn't heard from Parvati yet about an audience with the palace. I would have to go around her.

"Malik, you need to get word to Samir that I must see him. But first, Radha, let me have the lavender oil for Malik's ear."

After attending to Malik, I told Radha to go home and launder his clothes. When Malik was presentable again, they were to join me for our afternoon appointment at Mrs. Sharma's house.

In the front courtyard of the Sharma residence, Radha, Malik and I set down our bags. Malik had changed into a clean shirt and the swelling on his ear had gone down.

We had come to create a courtyard *mandala*, which was usually designed by the women of the family using colored chalk and rice. But Sheela, Mrs. Sharma's youngest and only girl child, was singing tonight at a big family gathering, and Mrs. Sharma wanted something far more elaborate. She'd commissioned a design similar to my henna work. In addition to white rice, we had brought bags of turquoise and coral chalk we'd ground to a fine powder, red brick we'd crushed into the size of tiny pebbles, mustard seeds and dried marigold petals.

We were waiting for the grocery-*walla* to clear out of the courtyard. His camel chewed placidly on dry grass as the storekeeper pulled tins of sugar biscuits and sesame oil from his cart. Mrs. Sharma was checking the delivery before signing off on the receipt. When she noticed us, she plodded down the veranda steps, her homespun cotton sari rustling in her wake. Where Parvati was vain, Mrs. Sharma was practical. She saw no reason to fuss with her appearance when she had a large household to manage—her own three children and Mr. Sharma's five younger brothers. Even though she could afford better, her habitual garb was a *khadi* sari, an ode to Gandhi-*ji*, and a simple ruby and diamond nose stud.

"Lakshmi, if you'll be patient, we'll have these folks out of your way shortly. I want to make sure you have enough time to create your magic before the musicians start arriving." She smiled broadly, the large mole on her right cheek lifting. "Everything must be perfect for Sheela's performance at the *sangeet* tonight."

"I'm sure Sheela will be wonderful, Mrs. Sharma."

The matron laughed. A *mandala* welcomed the bounties of Goddess Lakshmi. "With a *mandala* created by you," she said, "we can welcome the entire pantheon!" She extended her arms wide, the wedding bangles on each pudgy arm tinkling, the soft gold misshapen and dented after thirty years of wear.

At last the area was cleared, and Radha and Malik began sweeping a ten-foot square area with long-whiskered *jharus*.

I took a handful of rice from one of the sacks and released a steady stream of grains from my palm to create the inner circle. A small fire would be lit here in the evening. Around this circle, I drew a lotus flower with eight enormous petals. Radha followed me with the tiny red pebbles, filling in the outlines.

Suddenly, she cried out. *"Waa!"*

I looked at her. Radha was staring at the veranda, where Sheela Sharma stood in a satin frock the color of a sunset after rain. The half-sleeves were puffy—the current rage—and the empire waist sat just under her growing bosom. She looked like the princess of a miniature kingdom. All she lacked was a tiara to crown her blue-black hair, curled at the ends, Madhubala-style. She was striking.

I smiled at her. "I hear you're the star of tonight's show."

She flipped her hair over one shoulder. "It's only family. I'll perform for a *real* audience at Mrs. Singh's party next month. The maharaja will be there, you know."

So Parvati was taking my proposal seriously. She knew that any daughter-in-law of hers would have to entertain heads of state, and she'd decided to test Sheela's poise in front of royalty. I would need to do my part to ensure that Sheela caught Ravi Singh's eye. It was clever of Parvati to let her son fall for Sheela on his own; she wanted to choose his mate, but she didn't want him to know it.

I looked to my left to indicate Radha, who stood agog. "Sheela, this is my sister, Radha." I tilted my head toward Malik, who was sweeping at the edge of the courtyard. "I believe you've seen Malik before?"

He nodded at Sheela.

I turned to look at Sheela, whose gaze flitted from Radha to Malik. Radha also looked at Malik. Sheela pursed her lips and lifted her chin, scanning him from head to toe—his rough hair, his pink ear, his soiled feet, his too-small *chappals*. He, too, looked down at himself to see what she found offensive.

"Lakshmi, I only want you to work on the *mandala*," Sheela said. She was used to getting her way.

I allowed her an indulgent smile. "Without help, Sheela, the design will take twice as long, and I still have all the ladies inside to henna. We want your party to be a big success, don't we?"

But Sheela didn't smile back. Pivoting smartly on her black patent heels, she marched inside the house. Malik shrugged at Radha.

I decided to ignore Sheela's mood. She was a spoiled child,

but she ruled her mother's heart. It didn't do any good to make an enemy of her. "Radha, the brick pebbles, please."

"Lakshmi?"

I looked up to see Mrs. Sharma standing in the front door, Sheela behind her. I poured the rice from my palm back into the sack and walked up the steps.

"My daughter is not comfortable with the boy here. Perhaps you have an errand for him?" Mrs. Sharma asked the question in a voice both commanding and apologetic. Her eyes skittered around the front garden, distressed. Over her shoulder, I saw the satisfied face of Sheela Sharma.

"Has he done something, Madam?"

"Sheela is...particular...about who works on our *mandala*."

I glanced at Sheela. "Of course."

I went back down the steps and made a show of looking through my cloth carrier. "Malik, I need you to grind more henna for tonight and bring it back. I don't think we mixed this batch well enough."

But Malik was looking at my lie: two large earthenware bowls of rich henna paste wrapped in damp cloth—enough for twenty hands—sitting inside a carryall. This morning, I had even praised the smooth texture of Radha's paste within Malik's hearing.

He gazed at the veranda, at Sheela, who was staring at him defiantly. I could see him rubbing his thumb and forefinger together, something he did when he was angry. I didn't know if she was singling him out because he was male (the *mandala* was, after all, a woman's chore) or because she didn't like his appearance.

Malik dropped his sack on the ground.

I took two rupees from my waistband. "Hire a *tonga*."

It was a small consolation. I forced the money into his shirt pocket and put my hands on his shoulders until he nodded.

As I was returning to the circle, I saw Radha plunge her

hand into the sack of brick pebbles, then draw her arm behind her head. She was aiming for Sheela's retreating back. *Hai Ram!*

"Radha!" I called, loudly, as I placed my body in front of her to hide her gesture from Sheela. I seized her arm, forcing her hand back into the sack, and held it there. She was stronger than I'd realized. I pinched the inside of her wrist, hard. She loosened her grip and released the pebbles.

I could feel Sheela's eyes on my back. Making sure my voice carried to the veranda, I said, "Remember not to pour so much into each circle. The *mandala* will come out uneven, and we need it to be perfect for Sheela, don't we?" My eyes pleaded with Radha to behave. "Let's get started on the turquoise chalk."

My sister blinked, stared into my eyes, blinked some more. She lowered her gaze, and I let go of her arm.

From the corner of my eye, I saw Sheela go back inside the house. My knees were shaking, and I squatted, sitting back on my heels to steady myself.

I licked the sweat off my upper lip. Had any of the household servants seen anything? Who knew what damage they could cause!

My hands trembled as I grabbed a fistful of turquoise powder to fill the interior. What could Radha have been thinking? *We* could so easily be replaced, but Sheela would always be the princess of this kingdom. I'd never had to teach Malik that; he understood the nuances of class and caste instinctively. He would never have compromised us.

For the rest of the afternoon, Radha and I worked in silence. I would point to a sack, and she would bring it to me. I was too upset by what she'd done to say anything.

The farther out I went from the center circle, the more detail I added to the lotus flower. Finally, I stood back to inspect my work. In the middle of each petal were the things associated with the goddess: a conch shell, an owl, an elephant, gold coins, pearl necklaces. My back would suffer tomorrow from hunching over the *mandala*, but Mrs. Sharma would be pleased with the result.

I handed Radha the empty sacks. "Go home. Have Malik help you with the ladies' treats for tomorrow."

She left without a word.

Dusting my palms, I made my way to the kitchen. I needed to make sure the servants weren't aware of what happened this afternoon and to see if they had anything to tell me about Sheela Sharma's marriage prospects.

Several burners were in use and the heady fragrance of fried cumin, garlic and onions filled the kitchen. Mrs. Sharma's cook, a broad woman with coarse hands, was separating the *atta* into tiny balls that she would roll later into *samosa* pastry. A younger woman sat cross-legged on the floor. She cradled a stainless steel bowl in which she was mixing boiled potatoes with peas and *masala* for the mixture that would go inside the samosas. The back door had been propped open to let the cooking heat out.

I smiled at the cook and asked for water. She filled a glass for me and went back to her task. If anyone in the household had seen Radha throwing rocks at Sheela, the cook would have let me know as she saw me.

I lifted the glass and drank without touching my lips to the rim.

"Are you making your famous drumstick *dal* for tonight's *sangeet*?" I asked. The Sharmas' cook was from Bengal. She was famous for flavoring her lentils with the flowers and fruit of the *sajna* tree. She would chop the drumstick-like vegetable finely and sauté it with poppy and mustard seeds before adding it to the cooked lentils.

She lifted her arms in a shrug and opened her palms to the ceiling, a piece of dough resting in one hand. "When am I not making my *dal, Ji*? It's *these* people I must make it for one day, *those* people the next."

"It's because your skills are so refined."

"What can I do? I was born with this gift." She sprinkled a little dry flour on a round wooden board and slapped the ball of dough onto it. "Lately, everyone wants to see the little miss. Last week, we had many *Pukkah* Sahibs here." She flattened the ball with a rolling pin, pressing left, then right, back to the left, until she had created a perfect circle for the pastry.

"Really?"

"*Hahn-ji*. The Mariwars. Lal Chandras."

"Mathur Sahib and his wife." The cook and I turned to look at her assistant, who had contributed this information without looking up from her task.

"Are you mashing the potatoes fine enough? I don't want to see lumps in the *samosas* like last time!" The cook scowled at the other woman, and the assistant lowered her head closer to the bowl.

I hid a smile. "Did I hear a rumor about the Prashads, as well?"

"They are coming next week." The cook wiped the glistening skin above her upper lip with the end of her sari. "After all, there is only one of me." She jerked her head at her assistant. "That one over there, I have to watch every minute. How much time does that leave me to cook?" she asked as one of the lids began clattering on its pot, steam trying to muscle its way out. She turned to the other woman and shouted, "What? I have to watch all the pots, too? Can't you see the *kofta* is done?"

Her assistant scrambled to her feet and wrapped the end of her sari around the handle of the pot to lift it off the burner. For good measure, the cook directed more insults her way.

As I'd suspected, the competition for Sheela Sharma was keen; the Sharmas were entertaining offers. Parvati would have to make a move soon. An offer from the Singhs, one of the most prominent and among the wealthiest families in Jaipur, would give the Sharmas what their humble background lacked—an official tie to the royal family. Parvati was smart to drive home the point by inviting Jaipur's royal family, along with the Sharmas, to her holiday party.

The sooner the marriage was settled, the sooner I could clear my accounts. Until then, I would keep the arrangement to myself lest any other matchmakers picked up the scent.

I set my glass on the counter and left the two cooks to their work.

FIVE

November 18, 1955

I waited for Samir at my Rajnagar house, having finished another inspection with Naraya, the builder. (I'd had to request another coat of plaster on the walls to make sure it was skin-smooth.) I was sitting on the floor, my arms wrapped around my knees, gazing at the patterned terrazzo.

It's better to have a petticoat be too tight rather than too loose or your sari will sag and the pleats will come out.

Place a compress soaked in cold tea on each eye daily to diminish under-eye circles.

Never wear common rubber chappals, *only sandals or shoes.*

How foolish I'd been to think advice like this was enough to prepare Radha for city life! I couldn't even say, with certainty, how *I* had learned to manage challenges like the Mrs. Iyengars and Parvatis and Sheelas of this world. Radha would have to learn not only patience, but also the necessity of moving indirectly toward her goal. Like I did. Like Malik did.

But how could I keep vigil over her and still meet with clients, negotiate with suppliers and solicit new commissions?

When I returned home exhausted from the Sharmas the evening before, I asked Radha if she made a habit of throwing stones at people.

Her face crumpled. "It's the only way the gossip-eaters would stop taunting me, Jiji," she said. "They always called me the Bad Luck Girl. *Saali kutti. Ghasti ki behen.* All kinds of curses. Little boys would trip me when I carried well water on my head. Everything was my fault. If the cow's milk wasn't sweet, the gossip-eaters said it was because I'd walked in front of it. If insects ate the grain, the farmers said it was because I'd called them in the night. When the headman's son died of fever, they came looking for me, carrying sticks. Maa couldn't stop them. I ran to the riverbank and climbed up a *peepal* tree. I stayed there for two days until the traveling doctor told them the baby had died of malaria."

Radha wiped her wet eyes and nose on the sleeve of her *kameez*, a habit I was trying to break. "It's been like that since I was born. The gossip-eaters have long memories."

In India, individual shame did not exist. Humiliation spread, as easily as oil on wax paper, to the entire family, even to distant cousins, uncles, aunts, nieces and nephews. The rumormongers made sure of that. Blame lay heavily in my chest. Had I not deserted my marriage, Radha would not have suffered so much, and Maa and Pitaji would not have been so powerless against an entire village. Today, when she saw how unfairly Malik was being cast off, she reacted as she always had—like a defenseless animal. She knew no better because no one had taught her any better.

She dropped to her knees in front of me. "Jiji. Please don't send me back. I have no one else. I won't do it again. I won't. I promise." Her thin body was shaking.

Embarrassed and ashamed, I helped her to standing and wiped her tears. I wanted to say, *Why do you think I would send you back? You're my sister. My responsibility.* But all that came out was, "I promise I'll do better, too."

Someone was nudging my hand. "Beauty, wake up."

My eyes fluttered open; I knew it was Samir's voice, but in the dark, I couldn't make out his face. I looked around to get my bearings. At some point, I'd stretched out on the terrazzo and fallen asleep.

"Joyce Harris is recovering." His white shirt glowed in the dark above me. He smelled of cigarettes, English whiskey and sandalwood, scents I recognized from the houses of the courtesans. "Her husband has returned from Jodhpur. He thinks she miscarried naturally."

I rubbed my eyes. "You know I did nothing wrong, Samir, don't you?"

"I know." With a sigh, he lowered himself to the floor and lay down beside me. He pulled a pack of Red and Whites from his suit pocket and lit a cigarette. "But we have to go easy on the sachets for a while. What happened to Mrs. Harris has made people nervous."

I swallowed.

"So what's going on? Malik said you needed to talk," he said.

"I owe a great deal of money."

"That doesn't sound like you."

"And I've run into some…unexpected expenses."

"Like?"

I cleared my throat. "A sister."

"The girl who was in your bed?"

"Yes."

"She lives here in Jaipur?"

"She does now. As of a month ago." I turned to look at him.

He studied my face. He knew our rules: we only revealed what the other needed to know. He turned back to the ceiling.

For a while, he was quiet, now and then taking a puff from his cigarette. A man of business, he thought before he spoke. "To whom do you owe money?"

"The builder, for one."

"How much does he want?"

"Doesn't matter. I just need more time to pay him."

"Why not let me—"

"No," I said, perhaps too forcefully. "It's my debt. I'll take care of it."

He blew out cigarette smoke noisily. We'd had this discussion before. The only time I'd borrowed money from him was during my first week in Jaipur, when I needed to pay for henna supplies and my herbs. I had paid him back within a week and never asked for another *paisa*.

I reached for his hand and shook it lightly. "Sorry to take you away from cards."

Samir chuckled. "How did you know I'd been playing?"

"You haven't been playing. You've been losing." I looked at his profile. "You drink more when you lose. You start buying rounds for everyone so they won't feel sorry for you."

He squeezed my hand. "I have one wife already, Beauty."

I turned my eyes back to the ceiling. He smoked.

"Who's your builder?"

"Naraya."

Samir groaned. "He's third-rate. If you weren't so stubborn, you could have let me hire mine."

"And it would have cost me twice as much. This is what I could afford, Samir. It's my house. And Naraya has been fine."

He'd been difficult, yes, but I was too stubborn to admit I could have done better.

He sighed.

"Do you know Mr. Gupta?" he asked after a pause.

"I did his daughter's bridal henna."

"Gupta wants to build a hostel near the Pink Bazaar. I think your builder is just the man for the job."

Puzzled, I looked at him. "How will that get him off my back?"

"Gupta's loaded." Samir sucked on his cigarette. "He'll keep Naraya busy for a few months and pay him well."

"To do what?"

He smiled at me. "Install WCs—hundreds of them. *To a clerk a bribe; to a Brahmin a gift.*"

I laughed. The irony was not lost on me. Naraya was willing to build toilets, which the Shudra caste normally did, for the handsome profit to be made. Like me, he, too, was a fallen Brahmin.

My hand, loosely knotted with Samir's, rose and fell in rhythm with his breath. I could have stayed like this forever. He turned his head toward me. I turned mine, too, until our noses almost touched and his warm breath floated over my cheek.

We were alone, our bodies touching. It was late. *It would be so easy.* I felt myself yearning to press my body against his. As if in response, he turned on his side to face me, one arm supporting his head. He lifted his free hand and smoothed my hair away from my forehead, the touch as delicate as a feather.

"So beautiful," he said in a voice so soft I barely heard him.

I didn't realize I was holding my breath until I released it.

I forced myself to look away. I heard him sigh. He lay on his back again but he didn't let go of my hand.

I'd already decided not to tell him about Hari. My husband was my problem, a problem I had created by running away.

Samir didn't need to know about him, didn't need to know more about my past than I was willing to share.

"How are the courtesans of Agra, Samir?"

"They were asking about you just last month. It's been ten years, and Hazi and Nasreen have never let up. I *stole* you, their best-kept secret, they always claim. They finally imported a girl from Tehran. They say her henna is almost as beautiful as yours."

"Liars!" I laughed.

Samir blew smoke at the ceiling and pointed to it with his cigarette. "You should do one of your designs on the ceiling. Bloody spectacular that would be."

"I've already designed a floor I can't afford." I unwound my hand from his and sat up to fix my hair. "Once I pay that off, I'll think about the ceiling."

He stood and reached down with his hands to help me up. As he pulled me, I lost my balance and tumbled toward him. He twirled me, pinning me to the wall. His lips, so close to mine, were wet. If I put my mouth on his, would his lips part softly, gently, or would they crush mine, eagerly, hungrily? Then, as always, I remembered his wife, Parvati, my other benefactor.

I fastened one hand on his chin and eased it downward toward the floor. "You haven't admired my work yet."

Samir groaned and pushed himself off the wall, then felt his pockets for his silver lighter. Using its flame, he looked more closely at the spot where we had lain.

He snapped his fingers. "You hid your name in this!"

I suppressed a smile. Of course he would know. He'd been around *nautch* girls who concealed their names within the henna design on their body. If a man found it, he won a free night in their bed. If he didn't, the women were paid double rate.

"What if I find it?" he asked.

"You don't have to do me the second favor."

"Is there no end to your demands?"

"I'll make it worth your while."

The cigarette glowed orange and red as he drew in the smoke, surveying the floor. "I give up." He scratched behind his ear.

"Word has it the palace might need my services."

"Whose word?" Smoke curled up from both sides of Samir's mouth.

"Your wife's. Something about the Maharani Latika not feeling well. Parvati thinks I could help her."

He raised his eyebrows.

"Could you whisper my name in the right ears there? *Two echoes in a well are louder than one.*"

He blinked, and I knew he wasn't thinking whether he would do it but how and when. With his cigarette, he pointed at the floor. "This was worth whatever you paid for it."

"Or haven't yet paid." I wrapped my shawl around my shoulders. "In return, I have something for you."

One corner of his mouth lifted—a half smile.

"The Rambagh Palace remodel. Swallow your pride and meet with Mr. Sharma. Convince him you're the architect for the project."

He squinted. "Sharma already has architects." He made a face. "Second-rate ones."

"But the maharaja wants only you."

He released a stream of smoke. "Really?"

I smiled and drew my shawl tighter around me. "You'll make sure Parvati knows that information came from me?" I walked into the moonlit courtyard. "Come. I have to get a rickshaw."

"That's all the thanks I get?"

"You don't need thanks. You've got a driver."

SIX

December 20, 1955

My sister and I sat in the Singh drawing room, painting henna on the hands of girls from the finest Jaipur families, smart in their English dresses, chatting about the latest film they had seen and the clothes their favorite actresses were wearing. Some watched me work; others danced to *Rock Around the Clock*, next to the gramophone; several were glued to Parvati's *Life* magazine, admiring the photos of the glamorous film star Madhubala.

Sheela Sharma had grown up with most of these girls, having attended the same schools, the same parties. She held court on Parvati's sofa. Radiant in a champagne silk frock and matching heels, she was clearly the most beautiful girl at the holiday henna party. It was easy to imagine her as the future doyenne of Jaipur society. I allowed myself a private smile, knowing I'd proposed an excellent match.

Radha and I were seated next to one another on footstools, an armchair in front of each of us. One by one, the girls sat in front of Radha so she could prepare their hands, then moved to my station for their henna application.

"Has anyone seen Ravi?" Sheela asked the group. "He should at least come to his own party."

Next to the gramophone where she was showing another girl how to do the swing, a girl said, "He'd better be here. I heard he's performing tonight," she said.

"Performing what?"

"Didn't you know? Mrs. Singh hired the Shakespeare theater troupe and Ravi is playing Othello."

"Sheela, you're next," I said, patting the chair in front of Radha's stool.

Sheela moved to take her place in front of my sister. We had rehearsed this moment, Radha and I. I had dressed my sister differently so Sheela would not be able to recognize her from the *mandala* fiasco. Instead of a *salwaar-kameez*, Radha wore one of my saris, a fine cotton in pale blue with white embroidery. With her hair up—topped with a sprig of jasmine—she looked older, like a miniature version of me.

As I'd suggested, Radha avoided looking at Sheela's face. She concentrated on oiling her hands.

Having taken no notice of Radha, Sheela was addressing the room. "I'm singing tonight, too."

"Onstage?" a girl asked.

"I wanted to sing *Na Bole Na Bole* from *Azaad*—"

"I *adored* that movie!"

Sheela shrugged her graceful shoulders. "*Yar.* But Pandey Sahib is so old-fashioned. He tells me only a *gazal* will do for the maharaja." As if she sang daily for His Highness.

I stole a sideways glance at Radha, who liked our neighbor Mr. Pandey and wouldn't take kindly to criticism about him. The color rose in her face, but she kept her eyes focused on her task.

One of the girls at the gramophone, now playing an Elvis Presley hit, said, "Pandey Sahib is brilliant. He's really improved my singing this past year."

Sheela smirked. "Is that what you call it, Neeta? Singing?"

The other girls burst into giggles while Neeta's cheeks turned pink.

"You idiot! You're hurting me."

With a start, I looked to my right. Sheela was glaring at Radha. Radha looked up briefly, mumbled an apology for pressing too hard on Sheela's hand and dropped her eyes again. Sheela blinked, as if wondering where she had seen Radha before. My pulse quickened.

"Sheela." I patted the armchair in front of my stool. "Come sit. You're the star tonight so I have a special henna design planned for you."

A chorus of "Lucky you, Sheela!" and *"Waa! Waa!"* went up.

Her attention diverted, Sheela hopped off the armchair with a smug smile, upsetting the bottle of clove oil Radha was capping. Did she do it on purpose? Radha managed to catch it in time, and looked at me, her eyes filled with fear. The velvet armchair could have been ruined!

I gave Radha a comforting smile and, with a tilt of my head, indicated that she had other girls to attend.

My sister had behaved admirably. In less than two months in Jaipur, she had learned a lot that was new to her. I felt the beginnings of a small hope: everything would be fine from here on out. Ravi Singh and Sheela Sharma would be married. Samir would make sure I was introduced to the palace. Hari would give me a divorce. I would pay off the builder and he would finish my house. We would move out of our rented room. And my life of true independence would begin.

Comforted by these thoughts, I finished Sheela's hands with a design of large roses and perfumed them with pure rose oil to arouse feelings of the heart. I usually reserved the precious oil for wedding henna, but tonight I wanted Ravi to be drawn to Sheela as a bee to *chameli*.

After Radha and I finished with the girls, they joined their parents and other party guests on the lawn, while we gathered our tiffins. As we walked down the long hallway to the kitchen, we could see the back terrace, half a level below us, through the floor-to-ceiling windows. Torches glowed along the edges of the velvety lawn beyond. Bearers in red turbans and white coats offered drinks and hors d'oeuvres to guests on silver trays. Gold rings flashed on the gentlemen's fingers as they raised glasses filled with ice and *sharab*. The women's *pallus*, threaded with gold and silver, fell like shimmering streams from their shoulders.

Radha slowed to admire the glamour. While I had been to such occasions before, it occurred to me that this was the most elegant party she had ever attended. It wouldn't hurt to let her enjoy it a little. I set down my tiffins, and motioned to her to do the same. Putting an arm around her shoulders, I led her closer to the windows and pointed my chin at the gentlemen directly below us.

"See that fellow with the glasses? Recognize him?"

"Yes! From the photo. Kanta Auntie's husband?"

I nodded. Manu Agarwal, in a smart suit and tie, chatted with a gray-haired man in a Nehru cap and a wool vest over his *kurta*, common attire at this party. It was a mild night and the windows were open; we could hear their conversation.

The older man waved his glass of Scotch. "Only, you have to talk to my friend Mr. Ismail at the Transportation Ministry. He will give you all the permits and licenses for the bus routes you want. Without delay."

Kanta's husband adjusted his glasses. "The maharaja will be pleased."

"*Zaroor.* I only have to ask and it will happen. That is..." Nehru Cap smoothed his mustache over his lip. "Perhaps the maharaja would consider extending his bus route to Udaipur? A beautiful city—if you've never been. An investment of, say, half a *lakh* would pave the way for your project, so to speak." He took a sip from his crystal tumbler, observing Manu over the rim.

I murmured in my sister's ear, "Bribes. This is how roads, petrol pumps, bridges—even cinema houses—get built. Before independence, that man was a cobbler. He's illiterate, but he knows his numbers."

She smiled. "Jiji, why isn't Kanta Auntie here with her husband?"

I'd noticed, too, that Kanta wasn't at the party. "Maybe she preferred her *saas*'s company tonight."

Radha chuckled.

We moved to the next window. Two plump matrons in bright silks, both clients of mine, huddled with Parvati, whose pink satin sari must have cost more than I paid for my yearly lodging. The ladies talked excitedly, gesturing with their hands, their earrings dancing with every nod and shake of the head. Every now and then, they looked around to make sure they weren't being overheard.

"The maharaja's driver went to your friend's house and just left His Highness's Rolls there?" Parvati was asking, incredulous.

The woman in the beaded shawl nodded. "But my friend didn't ask to borrow the car. Didn't need to. He owns four cinemas in Jodhpur—so much money he's making!"

The third woman cut in. "That's because His Highness wasn't *loaning* the car. The palace was sending a message: *pay up.*"

"What did your friend do?" Parvati asked.

"He paid the Maharaja of Bikaner ten thousand rupees."

"Hai Ram!" Parvati exclaimed.

"The maharajas are all broke, I tell you. All the money they spent on polo ponies, tiger hunts, fancy cars!"

Parvati, who came from tiger-shooting, polo-playing gentry, raised her chin.

"The Maharaja of Bharatpur is the only one who really went crazy. Buying twenty-two Rolls Royces. He uses most of them to haul municipal garbage. Which is a good thing, don't you agree?" she said.

The matron with the shawl sniffed. "I just hope I won't be seeing *our* maharaja's car at my gate anytime soon."

Parvati chuckled. "I'm sure His Highness is smart enough to avoid bankruptcy." Her lips twitched. "Either that or he'll run for Parliament."

The ladies burst into laughter.

Radha glanced at me, a question in her eyes.

"Politics and real estate. The two favorite career options of royalty," I said.

I guided Radha to the next window. Her breath caught. It looked like a meeting of the royals. The Maharaja of Jaipur was easy to identify from the photo at Kanta's house—the long brocaded coat, white leggings, ornamented headdress. He carried himself like the sportsman he was—chest thrust out, legs planted firmly on the ground, strong calves—taking up more physical space than his companions, including two *nawabs*, their Muslim headdresses and elaborately jeweled coats rivaling the maharaja's. Samir stood in this group, too, gesturing animatedly with a glass of Scotch in his hand, telling a story by the look of it. As he finished, the group exploded into laughter.

The maharaja addressed Samir and I saw him turn toward the stage on the lawn, beckoning to someone. We watched as Ravi, dressed as Othello in a yellow silk *dhoti* and gold crown, jogged into view. His face, neck and naked torso were covered in dark blue greasepaint. The muscles of his chest rippled as he ran.

"Who is he?" Radha whispered, pointing at Ravi.

I pulled her finger down gently. "That's Parvati and Samir's son, Ravi. A handsome Othello, don't you think?"

She looked happy. "That was Pitaji's favorite play."

I hadn't remembered that. *"Accha?"*

"That and *The Taming of the Shrew.* He'd have me read them aloud. Over and over. Till I knew them by heart…almost."

"Did you enjoy it?"

She grinned wickedly. "I *adored* it!" she sing-sang in British English, imitating the girls from the henna party.

I laughed along with her, and at that moment, Samir and Ravi looked up at our window. I pulled Radha back into the hallway. "Time for us to clean these tiffins."

As we rounded the corner, Samir entered from the veranda, "I thought I saw you up there!"

I smiled and introduced Radha, who set her load down to *namaste* him. "Good evening, Sahib. You have a lovely home."

If he remembered her from that awful night with Joyce Harris, he didn't let on. Samir placed a hand over his chest, the sides of his mouth creasing in a warm welcome. "Have you come to break my heart?"

I raised an eyebrow, surprised that Samir would flirt with such a young girl. "Pay no attention to him, Radha."

Samir pretended to be offended. "I get Lakshmi an audience with the palace, and this is how she treats me?"

I blinked, not sure I'd heard correctly. *"Kya?"*

"You have a meeting with the maharani tomorrow."

Radha turned to me, cupping her mouth with her hands. "Oh, Jiji! A maharani! We'll get to see the palace!"

I put a hand on her shoulder, as much to steady myself as her. *It's finally happening!*

Samir laughed and pointed to the ceiling. "Take your dinner plates up to the roof. You can see tonight's performance from there and tell me how good of an actor my son is. He fancies himself a thespian."

"Oh, Jiji! Can we? It's *Othello*!" Radha asked me, her face full of hope.

I hadn't planned on staying, but she had been on such good behavior today. I smiled at her. "First the kitchen, then the play."

She excused herself politely and continued down the corridor with the tiffins, trying not to run. I knew she couldn't wait to share the news with Malik. They talked about anything and everything.

Samir followed Radha with his eyes. "Pretty girl."

He gestured to the open door of the library and followed me inside.

This room, with its built-in bookshelves, crammed with English, Hindi and Latin tomes, and red leather armchairs, was Samir's favorite. The hearth had been lit for the evening.

"More good news. Gupta has agreed to hire Naraya, and Naraya has approved an extension on your invoice. Happy?"

I was excited enough to throw my arms around him and kiss his feet, but I settled for a generous smile. "Thank you, Samir. This means a lot to me."

"Good." The reflection of the hearth fire flickered in his eyes. "I'm looking forward to seeing how you'll handle the palace commission."

"Any idea what's troubling the young queen?"

"All I know is she needs cheering up. You'll sort it out. I have faith in you." He reached into his suit coat pocket. "In the meanwhile…"

Samir took my hand and laid a gold pocket watch on my palm. It was a beautiful thing, the size of a betel nut—much smaller and more delicate than the other Victoriana watches in his collection. On the cover, an engraved hand held a lotus flower, similar to the one the goddess Lakshmi carried.

"Open it," he said, crossing his arms.

The false cover masked the scene of an Indian woman holding the hands of another. When the timepiece moved, one of the woman's hands moved up and down. That's when I noticed she was holding a tiny stick.

I gasped. "A henna artist?"

"*Hahn.* A lovely one. Like you." He sprang open the next layer to reveal the watch face. "White enamel dial. Gold hands. Nineteen-jewel lever movement with gold escutcheons."

"It's exquisite." I gave the watch back to him.

"I had it made." He turned it over, so I could see the seed pearls on the back forming a cursive *L*. He placed the watch in my hand again, folded my fingers over it and clasped my hand with both of his. "For you."

No one had ever given me anything this fine. In fact, I couldn't remember the last gift I had received. I cleared my throat to thank him but couldn't find my voice. A gift from Samir. What would Parvati say if she found out?

I heard a rustle and, from the corner of my eye, a bright swish of pink satin. The door to the Singh library was ajar. Has someone been crossing the hallway or had they been standing in the opening, watching us?

I tried to extract my hand from his. "I wouldn't know what to do with it."

"Do what others do. Tell time." He let go of my hand. "The Maharani Indira is expecting you tomorrow morning at ten sharp."

"It's lovely, but—"

"Hide it in your petticoat, along with the Singh silver."

At intermission, Sheela Sharma sang a ballad in a high, clear voice about a woman's devotion to love. It could have been

Desdemona's swan song. From the rooftop, where I sat with Radha and Malik and the household staff, I had a good view of the admiring audience below, and despite what Mr. Pandey had said about the challenges of teaching Sheela, I could see that his work had been rewarded. Her performance was flawless. For his part, Ravi turned out to be a convincing Othello.

My mind, however, was distracted, planning for my meeting with the dowager maharani. I thought about the supplies I would need. What would I say? What would I wear? Were any of my garments appropriate for a palace visit? Resisting the impulse to check my notebook (how could I see anything on the dark rooftop, anyway?), I tried to remember which appointments I would have to reschedule tomorrow to accommodate Her Highness. My stomach felt so jittery that I barely touched the crisp *aloo tikki* or the creamy spinach and *paneer* curry on my plate.

When the final curtain came down, Ravi, who looked larger than life in his blue-dark body, the greasepaint shimmering in the stage lights, delivered a pretty speech. He thanked the maharaja and the *nawabs* for gracing the holiday gathering with their presence, bowing a *namaste* to His Highness and cupping a *salaam* to each of the *nawabs*. Ravi appeared perfectly at ease addressing the royals, who tilted their heads in acknowledgment.

I signaled to Radha and Malik to take our plates to the washing area and gather our supplies for leave-taking.

I went to the kitchen to ask after Lala. I'd been on the lookout for Parvati's servant all evening to see what she'd wanted to talk to me about the last time I was here, but I hadn't seen her.

The head cook told me Lala and her niece no longer worked for the Singhs.

I was packing the last of our supplies in the Singh drawing room when Malik drew up beside me.

"Auntie-Boss, MemSahib wants to see you in the library."

I smiled. Of course! Parvati wanted to thank me for the henna work. She'd been so busy with her guests that I'd barely crossed paths with her all evening.

I arrived at the library where I'd met with Samir a few hours earlier. Parvati was pacing in front of the hearth like a restless lioness. With every turn, her satin sari swished angrily, the *pallu* threatening to catch fire. Her back was ruler-straight, her generous bosom thrust forward.

When she saw me, her dark eyes flashed. "How can I trust you to arrange a good marriage for Ravi when your own sister is playing with him behind my back?" The bright red *bindi* on her forehead flashed accusingly at me.

"What— H-how? My *sister*?" With Ravi? What nonsense was this? Radha doesn't even know the boy!

Parvati crooked a finger and Radha came out of the shadows. Her face was flushed, her mouth pinched in anger. Were those welts on her cheek? On closer inspection, they appeared to be slashes of blue paint. Her arm had the same streaks. My heart hammered in my chest. "Radha, what happened?"

"I won't allow my family to be touched by scandal. I have my son's future to think of." Parvati resumed her pacing.

I waited for Radha to say something, anything. But her eyes were focused on some spot far away, not in this room, the way they had in the Sharmas' courtyard. It was as if her mind were somewhere else.

Parvati hissed, "She was covered in Ravi's greasepaint. What am I to believe but the obvious?"

Greasepaint? The evening flashed before me: Radha and me with the girls in the drawing room, she and I standing together at the back windows, having dinner on the roof, watching the play. I looked more closely at the blue marks on my sister. When did she have time to be with Ravi? Surely there had to be some other explanation?

"What did Ravi say about all this?"

Parvati hesitated. "He doesn't have to say anything."

My breath tightened. "Did you ask him?"

She pointed her forefinger at me. "You know as well as I do men can't control themselves. It is up to women to stay out of their way. If your sister had been brought up properly, she might know that."

Nudging my sister's arm, I said quietly, "Go. Clean your face."

Radha glared at me for an instant, then went out the door, slamming it behind her.

I swallowed, gave myself time to think. "Parvati-*ji*. Please. Sit down," I said. "I'm sure there's been a misunderstanding. Radha is only thirteen. Much too young to..."

Parvati slowed her pacing.

"Your Ravi, such a mature boy—indeed, young man—can't be interested in a girl like my sister. He is completely taken with Sheela. Did you see how perfect they looked together onstage? What a handsome couple they'll make when they're married." I indicated the sofa. "Please, *Ji*."

Abruptly, she sat down on the leather couch with a heavy sigh. "If my late father were with us today, he'd know what to do. Everyone listened to him. But I can't get Samir to—" Her voice cracked. She looked at me with moist eyes. "What were you and Samir doing in the library earlier?"

Parvati *had* been at the library door.

I folded my hands together. "He was telling me how generous you had been in recommending me to the palace. I'm truly in your debt. If not for your relation to the royal family..." I let the implication hang.

She looked away. I was lying and she knew I was lying, but no matter. The truth was less important than saving face. If she'd kept her end of the bargain and spoken to the palace on my behalf, I wouldn't have had to ask Samir to intervene.

She could no more admit that she hadn't fulfilled her promise of a palace introduction than I could admit that I had asked Samir for help.

She pouted, straightening a pillow on the sofa, smoothing the tiny beads embroidered on the silk. "I've seen you two talking, before—on the veranda. What could you and Samir have in common?" Slowly, she raised her eyes to meet mine. I saw something I'd never seen before: trepidation. As if she wondered what secrets her husband kept from her. And possibly, what secrets I kept from her. All she knew about me was that I had come highly recommended by the wives of Samir's business associates in Agra.

I held my palms open, showing I had nothing to hide. "He likes to ask what I painted on you and where. I always tell him that's for him to find out."

She allowed herself a hint of a smile, perhaps recollecting a lusty afternoon with her husband. She touched the diamonds on her earlobe. "How did I not know you had a sister?" The same question Kanta and my seamstress had asked.

I sighed. "Parvati-*ji*, why would I bore my clients with the petty details of my life? But since you ask. Both my parents died recently, and I've taken Radha into my home. She's working with me now, but she will attend the government school this coming term."

Parvati picked at a loose thread on the pillow. If she kept pulling it, hundreds of beads no larger than poppy seeds would scatter across the floor.

I smiled with more confidence than I felt. "I'm certain nothing untoward has happened, but I'll talk to Radha." By degrees, I could see Parvati's anger cooling, reluctantly, although she still looked peeved. It was time to press my credentials. "Have I ever let you down in the past ten years? And what about your miracle? Your Govind?"

Parvati's face brightened at her son's name.

"It's important that I win back your trust, *Ji.* You've done so much for me over the years. Introduced me to the best of society."

She closed her eyes and pressed her fingertips against her lids. To save face, she needed to deliver the parting shot. "If I catch them together, ever again, it will be the last time you and I have anything to do with one another." In her indirect way, I knew she was also warning me: *stay away from my husband.*

Blood pounded on my temples and my stomach felt queasy, but I tipped my chin serenely to indicate that there would never be a need for her to carry out her threat.

Regal once again, she rose, threw her *pallu* over her shoulder and walked out. Alone in the library, I let myself collapse onto the sofa. Perspiration had soaked my blouse. I used a corner of my sari to dab my forehead and neck. I had seen Parvati angry before, but never more so than today, and never had her anger been directed at me. I found it hard to believe that a simple village girl like Radha, not in the same league as Sheela Sharma, could have attracted Ravi's attention. If, in fact, that was what had happened.

My reputation relied on Parvati Singh's word. Without her approval, I would get no work for henna, *mandala* designs or marriage commissions; my income would come only from the contraceptive sachets I provided Samir—and even those had been jeopardized now.

My insides were in knots. I had to get out of here—now.

Radha and Malik were waiting for me on the front veranda. Malik looked troubled, Radha nervous. I rushed past them, gulping the cool night air, skipping down the front steps to the garden gates.

"Jiji," Radha said behind me, running to keep up. "I did nothing. Malik and I were coming out of the kitchen when Ravi started talking to me. Ask Malik. He'll tell you."

I stopped so abruptly that Malik, who was behind me, tripped on my sari. "Is it true?"

He nodded. "Ravi Sahib saw us when went to the kitchen to put down our dinner plates. He asked if we enjoyed ourselves. We said his performance was first rate. Then Radha—" Malik stopped.

"I told him Othello was a general, not a king, and he'd do better to get rid of the crown."

"Radha!"

Her peacock eyes were defiant. "Well, it's the truth. In any case, he didn't seem to mind. He laughed."

"He did laugh, Auntie-Boss. He told her he would do anything as long as she would be his—what was it?"

"Desdemona."

"Then he—" Malik looked uncertainly at Radha.

"Go on."

"He touched her." Malik pointed at Radha's arm.

"And my face," Radha added.

So, not an accident, then—worse than I imagined. How could I be sure she hadn't encouraged Ravi with a look or a smile? But then, I'd never seen Radha flirt with anyone. She and Malik teased each other, but as a sister and brother would.

A headache knocked at my temples. "We'll talk later."

Radha's brows rose, as if she couldn't believe I was taking it so well. She shot a look at Malik.

Frankly, I didn't know what to do. I'd never known Malik to lie, but would he lie for Radha? If he and Radha were telling me the truth, my sister was innocent. And if she was innocent, how could Parvati have jumped to such a ridiculous conclusion? It was laughable.

On the other hand, there were so many things Radha clearly didn't know. Like how to keep boys like Ravi—confident, worldly, a little arrogant—at a distance. All she had to do was to drop her gaze, clamp her mouth shut and walk away.

When we stopped to let Malik off at Jhori Bazaar, I told him to meet me early the next morning for our appointment at the palace. The news that would have had him spinning like a top a few weeks ago now only elicited a tip of the head. He squeezed Radha's hand before heading off.

The rest of the way home, Radha hugged her stomach with both hands, suppressing her moans. When we arrived at Mrs. Iyengar's, I filled a pan halfway with milk and took it down to the outdoor hearth, puzzling over tonight's events. After the milk boiled, I returned upstairs to find Radha sitting on the cot, doubled over. I stirred turmeric into the warm milk and added a little sugar.

Radha, her arms wrapped around her belly, rocked back and forth. "Jiji, please say something. Anything. I did nothing bad. I don't want to be the Bad Luck Girl anymore." She hiccupped. "I can't help it if he talked to me, or touched my face. I swear on the holy waters of the Ganga it wasn't my fault."

"Shh," I said, handing her the glass. "You've had too much rich food tonight. This will settle your stomach." She sipped the milk, cupping her belly with her free arm.

Delicately, so as not to jostle the glass of milk in her hand, I sat down next to her.

"I've never had a client speak to me the way Parvati Singh spoke to me tonight. If Parvati removes her support, I stand to lose everything—*we* stand to lose everything. Do you understand what I'm saying? She's the one all the ladies follow. If I lose Parvati, we can say goodbye to the roof over our heads, the *atta* in our bellies, the fine cotton sari you wore tonight."

I lifted the empty glass out of Radha's hand, and set it on the floor. I took her hands in mine. "I shouldn't have accepted Samir's offer to stay and watch the show tonight. We didn't belong there. We should have done our job and left."

Her face fell. "You're not listening! Jiji, *he* grabbed my arm! *He* started talking to *me*!"

I continued, as if she hadn't spoken. I rubbed her back, moving my hand in tiny circles. "You had no one to teach you things that a girl your age should be taught. By the time you were old enough, Pitaji was not really there, was he? And Maa was too upset about me to pay attention to you. You were on your own. And that wasn't good. You're my sister, Radha, but I don't know you that well—"

"Ask me anything! I'll tell you. *Anything!* You've never asked me the month I was born. October. What's my favorite food? *Gajar ka halwa.* I love saris that have mirrors sewn into them. And I love *kajal* on babies. My favorite color is the green of mango leaves. And I like the taste of guavas just before they're ripe, when the flesh is tart enough to make my mouth water."

She was right, and it stung. I hadn't tried to get to know her. Not really. To be close to her made me feel my guilt more acutely, and I hadn't wanted that. I didn't want to be reminded of the terror she must have felt with a father who was defeated—or worse, a drunk—and a mother who seemed either resentful or indifferent. My sister had grown up alone in Ajar because of my transgression. Since her arrival in Jaipur, I'd buried myself in work, my steadfast companion. I was good at my work; it welcomed me, and I shined in its embrace. Radha, who was smart but naive, courageous but foolhardy, helpful but thoughtless, was far less manageable.

I let out a long sigh. "It's not that easy, Radha. I can't trust you. Not yet. Not in the houses of the women I've worked so hard to win over. Not when I have so much debt to pay off. We're so close, Radha, to having it all."

"You're taking their side again! You think I'm the Bad Luck Girl just like—"

"No, I don't. I believe you. I don't think you did anything wrong. That's not the point." I wiped her cheeks with my thumbs and smoothed her brows. "But I can't let you go to the palace with us tomorrow. I can't take a chance that something like what happened tonight won't happen there." As I said this, I felt relief wash over me. Ever since that first episode at the Sharmas', I'd been tense at every client appointment for fear that Radha might say or do something inappropriate. If she stopped coming with me, I could stop being so anxious.

"But, Jiji, Malik gets to go—"

"He's been with me a long time, Radha." I rubbed her slender arm, and trailed my fingers through her thick hair. "Tomorrow, you'll go to Kanta's house and tell her why we have to reschedule. She'll understand. After that, you'll come straight home, *accha*? I'll have a list of chores for you."

"Nooo!" She turned away from me, sobbing. I knew what it was to be young and powerless. At fifteen, when Maa told me I had to marry Hari, she had been sure—just as I was now—that she was doing the right thing. She had wanted to wait until I was eighteen, the age when she'd been married, but Hari's offer of marriage had come at the right time: there was no money to feed two, much less three people at Pitaji's house. I'd cried and cried, begged her to let me stay. I promised to eat less, to work as a servant in someone's home. She'd cried, too. She said there was no choice; it was more honorable to marry than to be a servant. So I did as my parents instructed, and look how miserable it had made me. Was I making Radha that miserable?

I rubbed my forehead, which felt as if it were in a vise. "In a few weeks you'll start school and you'll forget all this. You'll be too busy with your studies. You'll see."

She moved her arm out of my reach.

PART TWO

SEVEN

Jaipur, State of Rajasthan, India
December 21, 1955

The next morning, we set out for the palace. It was a crisp December day, and Radha, Malik and I, huddled in woolen shawls, sat in a *tonga* loaded with our supplies. As much as I had wanted to be rested and refreshed for my first meeting with a royal personage, I hadn't slept a wink, getting up every few minutes to add yet another item to our carriers. I hadn't a clue about what was ailing the younger queen, so I had packed almost every lotion and precious item in my repertoire, including the Kaffir lime leaves I'd ordered from Thailand. So much depended on making a good impression on the elder maharani, the gatekeeper for the ladies of the palace.

The Pink City of Jaipur was a beehive this morning. Our carriage trotted past a basket weaver braiding flattened grass. A turbaned cobbler, who was shaping crude iron into a hammer, looked up as we passed. I watched a woman on the side of the road as she expertly threaded marigolds into cheerful *malas*.

A woman in a gaudy lime green sari caught my eye. Her color was off, an unhealthy yellow. Her head was uncovered, her hair oily. I had seen enough poor prostitutes in Agra to recognize them by sight. This woman's cheap sari was a give-away. The man next to her had his arm around her shoulders. He seemed to be guiding her—or was he forcing her?—along the road.

My heart skipped a beat.

It was Hari.

His clothes were cleaner than the night he'd delivered Radha to me, but there was no mistaking him.

Was the prostitute Hari's new meal ticket? Was he now managing pleasure girls to pay for his food and lodging? Disgusted, I turned away and willed myself to focus on my task at the palace. Nothing else mattered.

When we arrived at the palace gates, I instructed the *tonga-walla* to take Radha to Kanta's address. My sister looked small and frightened in the carriage. Her eyes were swollen—whether from crying or from rising at dawn to help me with our preparations for this morning, or both, I wasn't sure. Last night, I'd listened to her sniffles and to her attempts to stifle them. She was still angry with me, but she had let me hold her. I'd rubbed her back, and eventually she had fallen asleep.

When the *tonga* left, Malik and I stood for a moment to take in the maharanis' palace. Compared to the maharaja's palace, with its long, winding entrance lined with *peepal* trees and giant hibiscus, the maharanis' residence, adjacent to the Pink City, was surprisingly modest. The tall iron gates were flanked by stone elephants, their trunks raised. Behind the gates was a circular driveway, barely large enough for three cars. Today, only one flag was displayed at the guard station, which meant the maharaja was away from the city. When His Highness was in Jaipur, an additional quarter-size flag hung at each of the palaces; he alone was considered to be a man and a quarter.

Clutching our heavy tiffins, we proceeded to the guard station. Malik winked at me—*Enjoy this, Auntie-Boss!* I smiled nervously at him while going through a mental checklist of my supplies yet again: jasmine and clove oil, the *bawchi*-coconut hair tonic, *neem* and geranium lotions, mustard oil, henna paste with extra lemon juice, a *khus-khus* fan, which I'd soaked overnight (to dry the henna quickly and perfume the air), a tea made from *tulsi* leaves, white paste from ground sandalwood (to apply to her forehead in case she had a headache), fresh reeds, cool water perfumed with jasmine and a number of sweet and salty edibles designed to elevate the maharani's mood or increase her desire.

A guard in a red turban and pristine white waistcoat clasped with gold buttons sat behind a barred window. His long gray mustache danced from side to side as he asked me what my business with the palace was. When I told him we had an appointment with the maharani, he frowned and gazed past me, sizing up Malik. "Elder or younger?"

I took a deep breath. "Elder. Maharani Indira." My voice shook. If she approved of me, I'd be hired to take care of the maharaja's wife. If I did not please the elder Highness, we could take our supplies home without having opened one tiffin.

The guard asked us to wait. For the tenth time, I checked the pocket watch Samir had given me—I didn't want to be late. After some minutes, another attendant appeared. He led us through an arched door and down a series of hallways lined with Persian carpets, tables made of silver and displays of Rajput spears, shields and swords. Our guide moved briskly, and we struggled to keep up with him, weighed down as we were with our supplies. I was out of breath, both from hurrying after our attendant and from the anxiety of meeting a maharani for the first time. We entered a colonnade flanked by lush gardens. Topiary elephants frolicked on the lawns. Live peacocks pranced around circular fountains. Stone urns sprouted honeysuckle, jasmine and sweet pea. We walked through a breezeway fronting a three-story building that, I assumed, was the ladies' quarters. The younger queen, Maharani Latika, had attempted to abolish *purdah*, but the centuries-old tradition had proved hard to overturn, and the palace females continued to live separately from the males.

We passed under a scalloped arch painted in blue, green and red enamel and outlined in gold—a peacock in courtship display. How Radha would love all this! I felt a pang of guilt for making her stay home. I glanced at Malik, who I knew was also thinking of her. His eyes were darting left, right, up, down, like a badminton birdie. He was storing details to share with her later.

Now we entered what looked like a waiting room. I recognized the elegant lines of the French chaise-longue from my ladies' homes. Opposite was a row of damask chairs, the arms of which ended in gold tassels. On the center table, which was almost as wide as my one-room house, were marigold roses in a cut-glass vase. Chandeliers glittered from the ceiling. And on the walls, Rajput history: portraits of former maharanis in ermine capes or in riding gear, ready for a hunt.

The attendant gestured for us to sit. He knocked on double doors three times his height, each door ornately carved with a scene from Rajasthani life: shepherding, farming, shoemaking.

Malik raised his eyebrows at me, mouthing, *"Pallu."* Taking the hint, I draped the embroidered end of my best silk sari, the cream one I'd worn last night at the Singhs' holiday party, over my hair.

Our guide disappeared briefly through the door, then returned and held the door open. Earlier, we had agreed that Malik would wait with our supplies in the waiting room while I met with the maharani privately. Now, he grinned and wagged his head from side to side in approval, giving me courage.

I walked through the door. It closed behind me with the barest of clicks.

I found myself in a beautifully appointed sitting room. The ceiling, high above us, depicted the courtship of Ram and Sita. Facing me were three damask sofas, the middle one occupied by a stout woman of about fifty in emerald green silk. Her blouse was stamped in a gold *boteh* motif. She was playing patience, the cards spread in front of her on a polished mahogany table. Dense salt-and-pepper hair, cut into a pageboy, grazed her shoulders and her diamond *kundan* necklace.

It was the first time I'd stood in front of royalty, and I felt a tickle in my throat. Was I going to cough in front of the maharani? I swallowed, fought the urge to clear my throat. With trembling hands, I adjusted my sari to cover more of my hair and walked toward her, my hands clasped in a *namaste*. When I reached the sofa, I bent to touch first her feet and then my own forehead. She waved me away with a flick of her bejeweled fingers.

She had just extracted a card from the deck and was looking for a place to put it, deciding finally to lay it facedown on the table.

"You see," she said, "I'm always looking for the king, but he eludes me." Her voice was deep and husky.

A high-pitched whistle made me stand straighter. From an elaborate silver cage behind the sofa, a bright green parakeet turned its head to fix, first, one eye on me, then the other. The door to the cage was open.

The maharani, who had yet to look directly at me, made a careless gesture at the cage. "Meet," she said, "Madho Singh."

The bird said, "*Namaste! Bonjour!* Welcome!" and whistled again, rolling a black tongue in his red beak. His neck was ringed iridescent black and bright pink, as if he were wearing a necklace like the maharani. His top feathers were the color of a summer sky.

I had heard of talking Alexandrine parakeets but never seen one myself. He was beautiful. "Your Highness has named the parakeet after the late maharaja?"

She fixed her dark eyes on mine for the first time and arched an eyebrow. "Regrettably, the two never met. My husband died thirty-three years ago, and little Madho Singh is only fifteen." She regarded me coolly, from head to toe. "Please sit."

I did so on the adjacent sofa, smoothing my sari over my knees to calm myself.

Yet another attendant, who must have been standing just inside the door, came forward quietly.

"Tea," the maharani said.

He bowed and left the room. She pulled another card from the deck. "You've been to the Elephant Festival?"

"I've not had the pleasure, Your Highness."

"Great fun it used to be. Rajputs came from all over to play polo on their gorgeous elephants. Everything was painted: tusks, trunks, feet. They would even paint the nails." She swept an arm around the room to indicate how vast the decorations had been. "Before Maharani Latika married my stepson, I used to give the prize for the best decorated elephant. One year, as a gesture of appreciation, they presented me with little Madho Singh."

The parakeet whistled again and screeched, "*Namaste! Bonjour!* Welcome!"

The maharani looked at the doorway. There, peeking around the open door, was Malik. I stiffened. How many times had I told him to wait outside? Hadn't I made it clear how critical the elder queen was to our future?

She beckoned him with a hooked forefinger, and he stepped gingerly into the room, looking for the source of the sound. I was thankful that I'd bought the long-sleeved yellow shirt and white pants for him the day Parvati had first mentioned a palace appointment. This morning after he arrived at Mrs. Iyengar's, I'd washed and oiled his hair and scrubbed his neck and ears until they turned red. Today, he was even wearing sandals that fit.

The maharani was studying him curiously while he examined the bird, taking no note of her at all. "Would you like to say hello to my precious?"

Madho Singh flew off his perch and landed on the back of the maharani's sofa. "Precious," the parakeet repeated prettily.

Malik *salaamed* the bird with his graceful hand. "Good morning," he said in his best English, not once taking his eyes off the parakeet.

The bird repeated, "*Namaste! Bonjour!* Welcome!"

Malik smiled. "Smart bird."

"Smart bird," repeated Madho Singh.

The maharani, who'd been watching Malik all the while with interest, asked, "How old are you?"

He seemed to give the matter some thought. First, he looked up at the ceiling, then back down to the maharani. "I prefer to be eight."

The corners of her lipsticked mouth quivered, then gave way to a generous smile. "How perfectly charming." Her laughter began in her chest and bubbled up to her throat, jangling her bracelets and rustling the folds of her sari. She looked from Malik to me. "Yours?"

I shook my head.

She turned to Malik. "Young man, what's your favorite sweet?"

The bird mimicked, "What's your favorite sweet?"

Malik scrunched up his face and looked again at the ceiling. *"Rabri,"* he said.

"Marvelous! We must tell Chef," the maharani said, "to make you *rabri* at once."

My face grew warm and I lurched forward to the sofa's edge. "Your Highness. We've come to do your bidding, not for you to do ours." Making *rabri* was tedious and time-consuming, requiring constant attention while the milk cooked and the water evaporated over a low flame for two hours, leaving only the cream. It was impertinent to ask the palace for it!

The maharani opened her eyes wider. "But it would give Madho Singh the greatest pleasure. Would it not?"

The bird blinked. "I love sweets."

Malik darted his eyes at me, the slightest smile on his lips, as if asking what game we were playing, and if he might be allowed to join.

I protested. "Your Highness, *rabri* takes so long to make—"

"Precisely." She turned to the door and another attendant came forward. She instructed him to take Malik to the kitchen and not to return until the boy had had his fill of *rabri*. "Make sure Chef doesn't send the boy off to one of the other kitchens. And take Madho Singh with you." To me, she said, "He loves sweets."

Malik's eyes were huge as he turned to look at me. I lifted one shoulder slightly. Who was I to argue with a maharani? As if he had understood the maharani perfectly, the parakeet flew off of the divan and settled on the white-coated shoulder of the attendant.

"I love sweets," Madho Singh repeated as Malik followed bird and attendant out the door.

I turned back to the elder queen, who was trying, and failing, to suppress a laugh. "Chef is odious," she said. "He never flavors food the way I like. He was my late husband's favorite and now resents the fact that he must serve *me*. It will annoy him to slave over a hot stove to feed yet another mouth."

My shoulders relaxed. Like my ladies, the maharanis had devised their own rules of gamesmanship.

The maharani turned over a six of diamonds and placed it on a seven of clubs. "So...you know Parvati Singh. Her father and my mother were cousins." She looked at me with a becoming smile. "It's her husband I find irresistible. Perhaps because Samir sends the most fitting presents. Did you know?"

Puzzled, I replied, "No, Your Highness."

"You should," she said, her expression cagey. "I believe you're his supplier."

The sachets? Impossible!

"My hair has never been thicker." She shook her head; her hair flowed gracefully from side to side. Samir bought a case of my *bawchi* hair oil every month, but I'd assumed it was for his mistresses.

I smiled. "It's beautiful, Your Highness."

"So when Samir says you work miracles, I believe him." She threw a shrewd glance in my direction. "Do *you* believe you perform miracles?"

"I have that reputation."

"Let me see your head."

I hesitated, surprised by her request. But when she gestured with a finger for me to remove the *pallu*, I uncovered my head. Her dark eyes took in my hair (freshly washed and oiled), the sprig of jasmine at the top of my bun, my naked earlobes. She twirled her finger and I turned my head around so she could see the back of it. When I faced her again, she nodded, once.

"I like a well-shaped head," she said.

A bearer entered with a silver tea service. The porcelain was decorated in a pattern similar to Parvati's. On a plate rimmed in gold were paper-thin tea biscuits, their centers embedded with slivers of pistachios and spikes of lavender. The bearer poured the tea. With a tap of her manicured fingernail, the maharani indicated that her tea should be placed next to her cards. She did not, however, pick up her cup.

"My late husband was very fond of tea. I knew him to take five, six cups a day with heaps of sugar. All that sugar should have made him a sweet man." She paused. "It didn't."

Her Highness's bluntness was unexpected, but curiously, I found it agreeable. Perhaps all royals were eccentric, I reasoned, and, for once, allowed my back to rest against the sofa cushion. I took a leisurely sip of tea, which was creamy, sweet and scented with cardamom and cinnamon.

"He was selfish to the end," Her Highness continued. "To his concubines he gave sixty-five children because, well, who cares about the illegitimate? To his five wives, myself included, he took great care to give none. Do you know why?" She was holding a card between her forefinger and middle finger in midair the way a man held a cigarette, waiting for a response.

I inclined my head politely.

"His astrologer advised him not to trust his blood heirs. So instead of having a legitimate son, he adopted a boy from a Rajput family, who is now our maharaja." She slapped her card on the table, facedown. "I live in a palace with a maharaja who is not my natural son and a maharani who is my *step*daughter-in-law."

It wasn't the first time I had heard of an Indian palace adopting a crown prince on the advice of an astrologer. In some royal families, it was common practice.

She palmed her teacup briefly, but left it on the table. "The current maharaja loves his third wife. Latika is beautifully turned out, expensively educated, smart. The son she gave him *should* have been the crown prince."

She covered a queen with the jack she'd taken from the deck.

"The only problem was that *he* also heeded the advice of *his* astrologer, who warned that his natural son would overthrow him. So the maharaja sent his son to England, to boarding school, without telling his wife. He left that to his chief adviser. Maharani Latika hasn't eaten or slept since her son was taken away. She will not talk. She has not gotten out of bed."

Shaking her head, she said, "Her boy is only eight, the same age your assistant prefers to be. But she is not allowed to see him."

I understood the trauma mothers suffered when they lost their children to fever or malnutrition. I'd seen it often enough working with my *saas*. But to have a child taken away without your knowledge must have been another kind of torture.

Maharani Indira had reached the bottom of her deck. "The citizens of Jaipur may think we maharanis have power, but that couldn't be farther from the truth."

She picked up the pile of rejected cards and began to turn them over one by one.

"Now we come to you, Lakshmi Shastri. While the young queen is not my natural daughter-in-law, she is my responsibility. Her spirits must be restored so she can resume her royal functions. And she needs to be a fit wife for the maharaja once again." She lifted an eyebrow. "She has no choice but to accept her fate and that of her son. *Que sera, sera.*" The Maharani Indira stilled her hands. "At least she has experienced motherhood."

The woman sitting in front of me had known grief, too. If it hadn't been improper, I would have offered her the cashew nut sweet in my carrier, which I'd prepared this morning with cardamom to ease sadness.

I waited a moment. "How can I be of service, Your Highness?"

"Make the Maharani Latika whole again. Lift her sorrow, which Samir all but guarantees you can do."

Samir's confidence in me was heartening. But the thought of failing with a noblewoman—such a public figure—sent a shiver through me.

I wet my lips. "Your Highness, healing takes time. As do my applications. I will need to see the Maharani Latika first to determine how I might help and how long it might take. I'm honored Mr. Singh has such faith in me, but please allow me to assess the situation first."

She studied me, her look stern. I met her gaze, waited.

After a few minutes, she gathered the cards from the table, as if coming to a decision. "Assess away," she commanded, her voice brisk again. "And come see me when you're done."

I was relieved that my task here was to soothe a troubled woman, as I had done many times before. Success would be sweet, would spread my reputation beyond the city walls. Defeat, however, would be fatal. My business would never recover from such a humiliation. I would need to use every herb from my *saas*'s repertoire to heal the young queen.

Despite the rich tea, my mouth was dry. "It will be my pleasure, Your Highness."

Satisfied, she nodded once. She looked at the attendant, who came forward. "Take Mrs. Shastri to Her Highness." Then she touched her teacup again and said to him, "And tell Chef never to serve me cold tea again! How dare he do that to a maharani?"

I rose from the couch, my legs unsteady, and bent to touch her feet.

When I was a girl and my father was too hungover to teach school, my mother would worry aloud: *What will we eat when he loses his job? Books?* I sought refuge from her anxieties at old man Munchi's hut, painting on his *peepal* leaf skeletons. I could lose myself—drawing the pattern of a milkmaid's *chunni* or the tiny feathers of a myna bird. It calmed me. Later, when Hari berated me for not giving him children, I would retreat once again into my art, but I would draw in my mind, imagining the paintbrush in my hand, even as he punched my stomach or kicked my back. Concentrating on details, like the ladybug crawling up my arm or the paisley pattern of my sari, and ignoring everything else, crowded out anxiety, pain and worry.

Now, as I was led to the rooms of the young maharani, I busied my mind studying the enameled patterns around the doorways, the latticework framing the windows, the mosaics decorating the marble floors and walls, the stories woven into the silk carpets. Centuries ago, the princes of Jaipur had invited the best stone carvers, dyers, jewelers, painters and weavers from foreign lands—Persia, Egypt, Africa, Turkey—to showcase their talents. By the time I arrived at Her Highness Latika's bedroom, my anxieties had lessened; my mind was calmer.

To the left of the door, a guru sat cross-legged on a padded mat, rocking back and forth, rolling a strand of beads through his fingers. An orange *bindi* made from turmeric powder ran from his brow to his hairline. The folds of his white tunic pooled around his substantial stomach. In front of him, smoke from an incense cone curled lazily toward the ceiling.

The Maharani Latika rested against cream satin pillows on a four-poster bed. She was not a widow, yet she wore a white sari of fine muslin and a white blouse. Three court ladies, dressed in silk saris, attended to her. The one combing the queen's hair was obviously her dresser. Another lady fanned her, while the third read aloud from a poetry book. I recognized the poem as Tagore's. *Dark? However dark she be, I have seen her dark gazelle-eyes.* The court women looked up when I entered the room but continued with their tasks. I folded my hands in *namaste* and walked up to the bed, touching the air above the maharani's feet and pulling any jealous energy up to my forehead. But her listless eyes stared straight ahead, as if she hadn't seen me. I greeted the ladies with my hands, and they cocked their heads in acknowledgment.

Whether by design or purpose, the room was dark, so I asked the bearer to set my carriers near the window where I could see more clearly. I looked around for a low stool and the bearer brought me an upholstered one. I unpacked the items I would need, then rinsed my hands in the cool jasmine water from one of my containers. After that, I oiled them. Carefully, I lifted the queen's hand. Her skin was dry and cool. She stirred. From the corner of my eye, I saw her head turn toward me, and although I had avoided looking her in the eye, I did so now. I'd heard about her beauty, which had captivated the maharaja at first sight. Her eyes, round and luminous, with mahogany centers, appeared naked, unable to hide her immense sadness. The tender skin around the lids was darker than the rest of her complexion, as if it had been seared. Her Highness wore no jewelry. The red vermillion powder snaking through the part in her hair was her only ornament. One of her attendants must have put it there.

Her gaze dropped to her hand, the one I was holding. She fanned her fingers and examined them as if she'd never seen them before. The tips of her nails were well cared for, having been trimmed into a rounded shape, the cuticles pushed back. She released a long sigh and retreated, again, into her personal reverie. I could go to work now.

One morning after I had gone to live with Hari and his mother, I saw three purple-pink eggs near where I was washing clothes along the riverbank. I heard a shrill, *Kink-a-joo! Kink-a-joo!* and saw, under a bush, a red-whiskered *bulbul* watching me, tilting her head—first this way, then that. She was leaning to one side, dragging a wing on the ground. I ran back home to get my *saas*, who said the bird must have been hurt before she could fly up to her nest to lay her eggs. At home, my mother-in-law made a poultice to immobilize the wing. Two weeks went by before the wing healed, after which *saas* told me to let the bird go where I'd found her. When I did, the *bulbul* looked in vain for her eggs, which had long since disappeared. I hadn't been able to save her eggs; neither could I bring Maharani Latika's son home, but, with time, I could help heal her wound.

I started by gently massaging her hands and feet so she could get used to my touch. I had worked with my ladies a long time, and they trusted me, but the Maharani Latika didn't know me, hadn't even acknowledged me, so it was difficult for her to relax the way she could relax in the hands of her dresser. With the mixture I'd created this morning—sesame and coconut oils and extracts from *brahmi* and thyme leaves—I stroked the area between her thumb and forefinger. I rubbed the pulse point of her wrist. Likewise, I worked on the arch of her feet, pressing the crevice between her middle and big toes to release tension. The noblewoman who was reading from the book of poetry set the pace with her hypnotic rhythm.

After a while, I felt the maharani's bones begin to soften and heard her breath reach deeper into her lungs. I continued massaging up her arms and legs and back down to her hands and feet with my oils for the next hour. I stretched her tendons, loosened her limbs, opened her meridians. If her muscles resisted, I directed my attention on pressure points to release the tension. As I worked, I kept my mind focused on transferring my energy to her. Everything else fell away.

When I felt her arms go limp, I hazarded a look at Her Highness. She had fallen asleep. It wouldn't last, but, for the first visit, this was as much as she could handle.

When I'd gathered my supplies, an attendant escorted me through another set of hallways to a room made of glass and filled entirely with orchids. The air was humid here, the temperature much warmer than the air-conditioned palace. I felt a fine layer of sweat gathering above my upper lip.

With a tiny pair of silver scissors, the elder maharani was trimming dead leaves from a plant. Half-moons of sweat stained the underarms of her silk blouse.

Without turning, the Maharani Indira said, "The sooner Latika recovers, the sooner I can get back to my babies." From a nearby table, she picked up a glass filled with ice and a clear liquid and jiggled it. "Gin and tonic. Care for one, Mrs. Shastri?"

I was tempted, but had never taken alcohol before. "Thank you. No."

She looked at me, smiling. "Are you sure? The British left us some lovely things, and this one is, by far, the loveliest." She took a sip. "More so because it keeps malaria at bay."

She moved to the next plant, and began turning over the leaves to inspect them. Satisfied, she took a large swallow of her cocktail. "Come meet my darlings."

I moved closer.

She pointed to a yellow flower with green stripes and an outstretched wing on either side of its body. The wings were dotted in black. "That is a lost lady's slipper. But I call her *titli* because she looks like a butterfly. And this blue vanda over here, I've named Sita." She tenderly caressed a petal with her finger. The hothouse appeared to be the maharani's nursery in more ways than one. "Rumor has it that Lady Sita used to twist blue orchids into her hair during her exile. A rare species she is."

Maharani Indira crossed the room and brushed her fingers against tiny pink flowers—about twenty in all—emerging from a single stalk. "Now this was a gift from the Princess of Thailand. I'd wanted to name him after my late husband until the princess told me she hadn't been able to get the stalk to grow, and I thought, that hardly sounded like my husband!" Delighted with her bawdy joke, she delivered a deep and throaty laugh. The dowager maharani seemed to have found a sanctuary within her narrow confines. The poor weren't the only ones imprisoned by their caste.

"I have a secret to make anything grow." She poured a few drops of her drink around the base of a plant. Her lips curved in a conspiratorial smile as she glanced sideways at me. *"Chup-chup."*

I laughed, unable to help myself.

She sipped from her glass. "So, Mrs. Shastri, tell me when can I return full-time to my orchids?"

I'd thought about this while attending to the younger queen. "Your Highness, if you please. Before my work can truly help her, the Maharani Latika needs to trust me. Were I to work with her every day at the same time for two, three weeks, I believe we would make progress."

"And did you make any progress today?"

"I believe so. I've started preparations for a henna pattern that I'll add to every day. By the time it's complete, I believe Her Highness will be feeling much better."

She nodded, pursing her lips. "What's the cost of this resuscitation?"

I clasped my hands in front of my sari. "Whatever you deem appropriate, Your Highness."

The older maharani looked me over. "Every morning, when you finish with Her Highness, I'd like you to give me a report. If you see progress, we'll continue. If not, we'll try something else. On your way out today, give the bursar this." She passed me a slip of paper. "He is to pay you five hundred rupees every day you come."

I felt as if I might faint. In one hour I had earned the amount I made during a busy week of henna appointments. Two weeks would amount to seven thousand rupees! The humidity was stifling and my forehead was slick with perspiration. I needed to get out of there.

"Thank you, Your Highness."

She dismissed me with a nod, and turned to inspect the plant in front of her. As I left the room, I heard her say, "Drooping again, Winston? Am I not giving you enough attention, pet?"

Malik was waiting for me at the palace gates. He rushed forward to relieve me of my tiffins.

"You're smiling, Auntie-Boss. Success?"

"You could say that." I smiled. "And the palace chef? Did you enjoy your time with him?"

"To tell the truth, Auntie-Boss, except for tamarind candy, I'm not much for sweets. But Madho Singh is. That bird ate most of my *rabri*. He might be sick tonight." He swung the tiffins by their handles as we walked to the next street to flag an ordinary rickshaw. I shook my head. What good would it do to admonish him?

"So what did you do while you were with the chef?"

"I didn't stick around. I ran my errands, took orders, made deliveries."

I stopped in my tracks. "Malik! You deliberately disobeyed Her Highness's orders?"

Malik turned to face me. He was grinning. "No bother, Auntie-Boss. When the attendant told him to make *rabri* for me, Chef looked like he wanted to slice me in two with his knife." He whistled for a rickshaw. "So I thought, how can I make him as happy as I make Auntie-Boss every day?" He laughed when he saw me raise my eyebrows. "I asked him how much the palace paid for cooking oil. When he told me, I said, '*Baap re baap!* You're being robbed.'"

I closed my eyes. What was Malik up to now?

"Auntie-Boss, relax." He gestured with his hand as if he were screwing in a lightbulb. *No harm done.* "I'll get him oil for a lot less than the buggers overcharging the palace and Chef will pocket the difference." He pointed to one of the carriers in his hand. "He's so pleased he promised to make me a special treat every day whether I ask for it or not. Today it was *puris* and *choles*. Tomorrow, *bhaji*! You and Radha won't ever have to cook again."

He ran ahead to put our belongings in the waiting rickshaw and I followed, amazed and a bit in awe of my little friend.

Word of my visits to the palace spread like *ghee* on a hot *chapatti*. All it took was for the mango vendor to spot us at the palace gates and tell his wife, who told her neighbor, who told his brother-in-law, who told his doctor, who told his washerwoman, who dropped off the ironing at the house of one of my ladies. Before long, my services were being requested by new clients for every celebration and ceremony: engagement, seventh month of pregnancy, baby's birth, baby eats his first solid food, baby gets his first haircut, boy comes of age, first entry into a newly built house, birth of Hanuman, fire worship for Goddess Durga, the Great Night of Shiva, job promotion, acceptance to university, a safe journey ceremony, a safe arrival ceremony. In India, there was no shortage of rites and rituals, and the three of us were busy from morning to late evening. Radha prepared the henna paste and helped me cook the savories. I attended to the Maharani Latika in the mornings and to my ladies in the afternoons and evenings. Malik crisscrossed the city, delivering my creams, oils and lotions, sales of which had tripled. It was a good time for us; I should have enjoyed it more, but I couldn't—not until the Maharani Latika could resume her royal duties.

Many of our new clients were eager for gossip.

Is the Maharani Latika as beautiful as one hears?

Tell us about the sofas that seat ten people!

Is it true that the silver urns at the palace are as tall as a man?

Do they serve meat in the dining room?

Even the ladies I had attended for years couldn't help sneaking in a query or two: *Are all the maharani's saris from Paris? What does her georgette pattern look like?*

My favorite ladies, like Mrs. Patel, who were not impressed by wealth or title, remained incurious. A sixtysomething matron, quiet and placid, who kept the books for her husband's hotel, Mrs. Patel said, "I hope you are taking rest, Lakshmi. Times like these can be very disquieting," before lapsing into companionable silence.

Malik remained discreet. I'd advised him how to answer questions from gatemen, servants and *tonga-wallas*. He could describe the paintings of maharanis on royal hunts to Rajput families but not to Brahmins (vegetarians). He could talk about the scented gardens, but not the details of European plumbing in the royal loo (too vulgar). He could say that the palace band employed forty musicians but not reveal that each of the three chefs—Bengali, Rajasthani and English—had a separate kitchen and his own assistants (too showy).

Radha went about her tasks with barely a word. Once she'd finished, she went to Kanta's. Since the new school term hadn't yet begun, Kanta had suggested that my sister read to her in the afternoons. I thought it a splendid idea. By the time I arrived at our lodgings late in the evenings, I assumed she'd be eager to share her day—in fact, I looked forward to it—but she would just lay on the cot, her back to me, reading a book Kanta had lent her.

I would ask what she was reading. Her answers were curt. "A book." If I asked which book, she would say, "You wouldn't know it." I would reply, "Try me," to which she might say, "A novel by one of the Brontës."

She knew perfectly well that I was familiar with all three. Hadn't we been raised by the same father who taught us to read English aloud by the age of three? We may only have been able to sound out words without knowing their meaning, but his methods started us reading literature from an early age.

I couldn't believe she was still mad at me about not being able to go to the palace. It was infuriating. I was the older sister, the provider. I set the rules, and she should obey them without question, like a good younger sister should. But I buried my anger. With time, she would get over it. With time, she would learn to accept what she couldn't change.

Look at me: despite my repeated objections, I hadn't been able to change my fate; I'd ended up married to Hari.

During my next appointment with Mrs. Sharma, she congratulated me on the palace commission. Emboldened, I said I wanted to discuss the marriage I had proposed between Sheela and Ravi. (Samir had already started discussing a joint bid arrangement for the Rambagh Palace contract with Mr. Sharma, so my bringing up the subject was only natural.) Mrs. Sharma met me halfway, unable to hide the smile that was pushing the mole up the side of her cheek, and played her own hand. In lieu of giving a dowry, the Sharma family wanted to build a house for Sheela and Ravi, provided the marriage went forward. Sheela preferred not to live with her future husband's family, as per custom. Mrs. Sharma said, "One family opposed this request, and we had to reject their offer."

I could see why Jaipur families found Sheela's request untenable; joint family compounds were the norm. Even Kanta and Manu, who were modern and Westernized, lived with Manu's widowed mother. Parvati would fight like a tiger to have her firstborn son live with her. She would argue that there was plenty of room in the Singh mansion; Ravi and Sheela could have their own wing.

If I wanted the marriage commission—and I did—it was up to me to find a solution to suit both parties. An irritant, to be sure, but I was close to sealing this agreement. I wasn't about to give up now. With less wealthy families, the value of the dowry was usually the sticking point: how much money, how much gold, how many silk saris. But the Singhs and Sharmas weren't going to haggle over money; satisfying their demands required finesse, creativity and more than a little luck.

A week after I'd begun my daily visits to the palace, I went to Kanta's for our regular appointment. Radha was already there, seated in an armchair, her finger marking the page in the book they must have been reading together.

Kanta jumped up from the sofa, breathless with her news. "Lakshmi, I've been dying to tell you!" Her eyes flickered with joy. "I'm pregnant!" She wrapped her arms around me. "And it's all thanks to you and your magic henna and your keen designs and I'm sure you must be slipping something naughty in those sweets of yours."

I smiled. "Kanta, that's wonderful!" I turned to Radha, "Did you hear?"

Radha raised her eyebrows. She said with a superior air, "Auntie already told me."

"Saasuji knew before I did," Kanta said. "I started getting nauseous whenever I opened a book. She said it was like that when she was carrying Manu. Imagine! My mother-in-law and I finally have something in common besides my husband!" She chuckled.

Her happiness was infectious; I found myself laughing, too.

Kanta put an arm around Radha's shoulders. "That's why it's been so wonderful having Radha read to me. I can't do it for myself anymore!" she cackled.

We walked to Kanta's bedroom where she took off her sari. "Saasuji thinks the baby can see what I wear. If it makes her happy to see me in saris, fine." She lay down on her divan. "Let's do another baby *mandala* on my tummy to ensure a good-looking boy like Manu."

My sister had followed us into the bedroom and sat on the bed, as if she lived there.

"Radha, please keep reading while Lakshmi works her magic."

Happier to do Kanta's bidding than mine, Radha smiled smugly and opened the book she'd been carrying to the page where they had left off. I looked at the cover. *Daisy Miller.* I hadn't read it, but my ladies had talked about it. The novel was about a teenage American girl on a European tour. How generous of Kanta to help Radha improve her English—and her knowledge of the world. I was grateful that she had time for my sister when I didn't. My days were so busy that it was a relief to have Radha taken off my hands.

"Oh, Lakshmi! Tomorrow I'm taking Radha to that American film I told you about. *Some Like It Hot.* Starring Miss Marilyn Monroe!" Kanta rattled on cheerfully like a purple-rumped sunbird. "And next month, *Mr. and Mrs. 55* is coming back for another run—it was so popular the first time! We'll go see that, too. You don't mind, do you, Lakshmi?"

How could I deny her when she was so generously chaperoning my sister? I glanced at Radha, who I knew was eagerly waiting for my answer even as she feigned indifference. I felt a vague sense of unease, but said, "Of course not. It's very good of you, Kanta."

Radha offered me a small smile.

My sister needed a friend, and so did Kanta. Allowing them to spend more time together was my way of asking Radha to forgive me for spending so little time with her. Or so I told myself.

EIGHT

January 5, 1956

During my second week of daily visits with the Maharani Latika, I sensed a shift. When I arrived, the young queen looked directly in my eyes. The dark color around her lids had lightened and she looked alert. Her eyes were no longer bloodshot. I touched her feet, inquired after her health. She didn't respond but continued to study me with her large eyes.

"Her Highness slept a full six hours last night!" said the noblewoman who read aloud to the young queen.

I couldn't conceal my excitement. I opened a tiffin with the lemon slices I had candied the night before. "Perhaps a celebration is in order?" I asked. My *saas* had taught me that women who had suffered a deep loss needed remedies rich in fruit and essences of flowers. Lemon promoted energy and gastric fire; the candied fruit would increase Her Highness's appetite. "If you will permit me, Your Highness?"

Maharani Latika raised her eyebrows and looked to her ladies for guidance.

The first lady-in-waiting instructed one of the bearers to take the tiffin down to the kitchen. Food prepared outside the palace was suspect and one of the cook's assistants would have to sample it before the maharani did. If all went well today, in a few days I could serve her creamy *rasmalai*, homemade curds with sugar, cardamom and rose petals. The maharani's cheeks had become hollow; for weeks, she had refused everything but a *dal* as thin as drinking water. By feeding her foods that stimulated hunger in her belly, I was hoping to correct the *vata* imbalance in her body. When we could switch to heavier textures like curds and spices like cardamom, her depression would lift more quickly.

Today, Her Highness took an interest in the henna and watched while I drew. Each day I added to the pattern from the day before. First, I had painted her nails, the tips of her fingers and her wrists with solid henna paste. I did the same thing to her toes and the soles of her feet. Another day, I drew intertwining branches down each finger, thumb and toe. The day after: a complex pattern of leaves on the backs of both hands and the tops of her feet. Now, I surrounded each leaf with tiny dots around the edges. My goal was to cover every inch of the skin on her hands and feet with henna; the more henna I applied, the more the calming properties of the paste would relax her mind and body, and allow Her Highness to rest.

When the bearer returned with the candied lemons, now arranged on an imperial blue china plate, the lady-in-waiting took it from him. She offered the plate to the young queen. Her Highness hesitated before taking a lemon slice. All eyes were on her. Even the guru looked up from his prayer with pursed lips as if he were about to suck the candy.

The maharani took a tiny bite, chewed and swallowed. She closed her eyes and took another bite. The tension in the room eased; shoulders were lowered as everyone breathed a collective sigh.

The lady-in-waiting resumed her reading. "'When storm-clouds rumble in the sky and June showers come down, the moist east wind comes marching over the heath to blow its bagpipes amongst the bamboos. The crowds of flowers come out of a sudden, from nobody knows where, and dance upon the grass in wild glee.'"

The following day, Her Highness was dressed in an eggplant silk sari. Her ladies had placed a matching purple *bindi* on her forehead. The borders of her blouse were hand-embroidered in gold and green flowers. Her hair gleamed with the *bawchi*-coconut oil I'd left with her dresser the day before. At the last minute, I'd added a drop of peppermint, which now perfumed the air along with the guru's sandalwood incense.

I exchanged smiles with the ladies.

"Good morning."

We all turned to stare at Her Highness, who had uttered this greeting. It came out as a croak; she hadn't spoken in a month. She cleared her throat, and one of her attendants rushed over with a glass of water.

After taking a few sips, Maharani Latika tried again. "Good morning."

Her voice was scratchy. Her Highness put her hand to her chest and closed her eyes. I thought she was about to cry. Then a shy smile spread slowly across her face. She opened her eyes and patted her chest. She was attempting a laugh, as if the sound of her hoarse voice amused her.

"*Hai* Bhagwan. It *is* a very good morning, Your Highness," the guru said.

That evening, after using the privy in the Iyengar's backyard, I was climbing the steps to our lodgings when I overheard Radha and Malik in our room. The door to the room was ajar. Since Radha rarely spoke to me at any length these days, conversations between the two of them were the only way I knew what was going on in her life. I stopped on the landing to listen.

"Marilyn Monroe is so different from Indian women, Malik." Radha sounded dreamy. "Her skin is white like the petals of the *champa* flower, and her hair is fluffy—like the cotton candy they sell at the theater."

"Gopal says her clothes are so tight he can't help staring at her breasts. They look like mountains on the cinema screen," Malik said.

"Your friend is a cheeky boy."

The more time my sister spent with Kanta, the haughtier Radha sounded, as if she were trying on city sophistication for size. It was hard to believe she was the same girl with the dusty petticoat, dirty nails and unkempt hair I'd met just three months ago. It made me a little nervous, how quickly she was changing. Was she growing up too fast? On the other hand, when I caught sight of her in a smart *salwar-kameez* with her hair glistening in a neat bun, didn't it make me glow with pride? My very own Pygmalion sculpture?

"Was the movie funny?" Malik asked.

"I guess so. Kanta Auntie explained to me the bits I didn't understand. Miss Monroe has the best smile." A pause. "Do you think Americans have more teeth than we do?"

"I don't know. Maybe they just smile more."

"Hmm. They certainly have better teeth than the *Angreji*."

"Everybody has better teeth than the English!"

They laughed.

After a pause, Radha said, "That's the first film I've seen in color."

"I thought you told me it was your first film ever."

"*Arré!* You don't have to remember everything I tell you."

Malik chuckled.

"Although," Radha mused, "maybe her teeth look whiter because her lips are so red."

For a moment I heard only the jangle of stainless steel plates. Then: "Radha, does lipstick have a taste?"

"How should I know?"

"I saw you. When I was doing errands. You were standing at the polo grounds of the Jaipur Club. You had lipstick on."

"You were spying on me?" Radha's voice was sharp.

"Ow!" She must have pinched his earlobe. "No! I'm too busy to spy on you!"

After a pause, Radha said, "Kanta Auntie wanted me to try it on. She often has me try on her things."

I felt my chest tighten. Kanta was encouraging my thirteen-year-old sister to put on lipstick?

"You know what Gopal says about lipstick, Radha? The girls in Bombay are born wearing it. Saves time when they become film stars."

I heard Malik's throaty chuckle and Radha's deep laugh. She sounded happy.

The Jaipur Club was where the elite played polo and tennis and sipped cocktails on the veranda. It wasn't the kind of place I had ever been invited. Kanta and Manu belonged to the club, but they hardly ever went there because Manu didn't play tennis or polo. If Kanta had taken my sister, surely she would have mentioned it. I didn't want to confront Kanta about indulging Radha too much; I would appear ungrateful and petty. It would seem as if I were jealous of the joy Kanta was bringing to my sister's life.

But I didn't want Radha to become obsessed only with superficial things. I wanted her to have the higher education I never had. It was too much to hope she could study abroad like Kanta, but it was within my reach to hire tutors to supplement her studies at a government school and pass the difficult exams for a local college.

I took a deep breath; school was starting in another week and Radha's head would be filled with math equations and scientific theories instead of what brand of toothpaste Marilyn Monroe used.

After two weeks of treatment, Maharani Latika had begun to get the bloom back in her cheeks. Today, her dresser had chosen a red georgette sari shot with fine silver threads. The ruby shade of Her Highness's lipstick complemented her black hair, which had been teased in the manner of a film star. A silver *maang tikka* in the center part of her hair ended in a teardrop ruby. The transformation was breathtaking. Bearing no resemblance to the queen in low spirits I had first encountered, this woman radiated good health and well-being. The treats I'd been feeding her, as well as the oils I massaged her with, had done wonders for her mood.

It was time to put the finishing touch on my henna design. In the center of her left palm, I drew her name in Hindi: *Latika.* On the right palm, I wrote her son's name in henna: *Madhup.* When I lifted her hands so she could see what I had done, she gasped.

"When you think of your son, Your Highness, you need only bring your palms together to be close to him." It was a risk, I knew. Reminding her of what she'd lost could backfire, trigger another depression. But as I'd tended her body these past few weeks, I'd sensed the steel of her muscles, the resolve in her tendons, the strength of the current in her veins. She was a woman who would always look forward despite setbacks, and I'd set in motion the healing she needed to guide her there.

Her eyes filled and a tear trickled down her cheek. One of her ladies dabbed her face with an embroidered handkerchief.

"Lakshmi," she said. Since she had started talking again, her voice had become stronger.

I wasn't aware that she knew my name. "Your Highness?"

"Thank you."

The heat I felt behind my eyes was relief—and pride—for summoning every skill I'd developed to soothe her ravaged soul. I didn't trust myself to speak. I lowered my eyes and tipped my head slightly to acknowledge her gratitude.

"Maharani Indira tells me you have a younger sister."

Surprised that the two queens talked, much less knew, about my private life, I nodded. "Yes. Radha. She's thirteen."

"Does she go to school?"

"In another week, she'll start at the government school near our lodgings."

The maharani looked at me and cleared her throat. "Would you consider having her attend my school?"

For a moment I forgot my manners and stared. The Maharani School for Girls was the most prestigious in the state of Rajasthan. Marahani Latika had founded it to train young ladies in the arts of grace and self-sufficiency. My clients could afford to send their daughters there, but even with the increase in my business, I could never have earned enough to pay the tuition.

As if she had read my mind, Her Highness waved a hand and said, "No need to worry about the fees."

I continued to stare at her. A place at the maharani's school meant Radha would have a future far better than any I could have imagined for her. It meant she might be able to study abroad—just like Kanta—and see the larger world, something I'd only dreamed of doing. Yesterday, I hadn't even thought it was possible!

The queen looked down at her open palms, sighed and brought them together in a *namaste*, stopping just short of smudging the wet henna. "I'm grateful for what you have done for me."

I was overcome with emotion. And relief. What had seemed an overwhelming task had come, finally, to fruition. I lowered my head and returned her *namaste*.

When I could control my voice, I said, "May you always wear red, Your Highness."

I did not complete the traditional blessing: *And may your sons carry on your husband's name.* Her only son, Madhup, would never be crown prince, and at this point, it would have been kinder to wish that she would never be a widow.

I was summoned by the dowager queen for my daily status report. An assistant led me to the salon where she had first interviewed me, only this time she was sitting at a card table with three other elegant and bejeweled ladies. A bridge game was in progress. I brought my hands into a *namaste* for Her Highness first, then her companions.

Madho Singh whistled and squawked, "*Namaste! Bonjour!* Welcome!" He flew from his cage to the top of his mistress's chair.

Maharani Indira said to the woman across the table, "Nalani, you met Helen Keller in Bombay a few months ago, but the real miracle worker is standing to your right."

The woman called Nalani scrutinized me over her half-moon lenses. "Is that right?"

Her Highness studied her cards. "Ladies, meet Lakshmi Shastri, who has brought our young maharani back from the depths of gloom."

I smiled. "I'm pleased to be of service, Your Highness."

"I believe, Gori, that you're hosting the French Minister of Finance next month. What a treat it would be for his wife to have Lakshmi henna her hands! And, Anu, aren't you welcoming your third grandchild soon? Lakshmi is just the woman to design your *mandala*. She'll work her magic, and before you can blink, you'll have a grand*son*."

"Now that *would* be a miracle," said Anu, chuckling.

The maharani smiled benevolently at me. I acknowledged her praise by touching a hand to my forehead.

She returned her attention to her cards. "I'd like you to continue seeing Latika several times a week for the next month. She's sure to relapse when the maharaja permits her to speak to her son again, and she'll welcome your assistance." Then Her Highness dismissed me with a nod.

As I walked to the door, I heard her say, "Just my luck, ladies, I'm to open the ceremonies for the Desert Festival next week. Gori, you must accompany me this time. Why should I always be the one to judge the mustache competition?"

"You know what they say—the longer the mustache, the longer the *lingam*."

Their laughter followed me out the door and down the corridor.

Malik and I were on a *tonga*, headed to our next appointment. I was telling him about the new work we'd be taking on for the Maharani Indira's friends when the carriage lurched to a stop. The horse reared and whinnied. I grabbed Malik's arm with one hand and the rickshaw awning with the other to keep us from falling out. What had we hit? Pothole? Rock? Stray dog? Then I saw Hari. Off to our right, gripping the wooden pole he had just jammed into the wheel of our carriage. The driver was gesturing wildly and shouting insults at him. The motorists behind us honked. People turned to stare. Even the white calf by the roadside stopped munching on discarded potato peels to look up.

Malik tugged my arm. "Let's get off."

He grabbed our tiffins and jumped off, but I couldn't move. Malik tossed several rupees at the driver, dragged me off the carriage, gathered the tiffins and pulled me into an alley. My limbs felt heavy, as if I were swimming through oil. *Would I truly be tied to Hari for seven lifetimes?*

When we were safely out of view, Malik turned and released the tiffins but still held on to my arm.

Hari approached, dropping the pole on the bare dirt.

Malik spat on the ground. "You can't make an appointment like everyone else?"

Ignoring him, Hari said to me, "You're never home. I need you."

"Money?"

"Yes, but—"

"I thought you'd found someone else to help you with that."

He frowned, looking confused.

"That *nautch* girl. Have you spent all her money, too?"

He waved a hand. "Oh, her. She—" He stopped and shook his head. "Look. I need your help with this." He stepped aside. Behind him was a girl, smaller and younger than Malik. She had on a ragged, unwashed frock. No shoes. Her nose was running. Hari turned her, gently. I saw a gash on her right calf, oozing yellow pus.

"I put Maa's poultice on it, but the infection only got worse," he said.

I looked at the wound more closely but didn't move nearer. "Who is she?" Then I glanced at Hari, surprised. "And what do *you* know about poultices?"

He sighed. "After you left, Maa needed help. At first, I didn't want to help her, but when she got sick, she begged me to attend to the women who came to her. She taught me the same as she taught you." He licked his cracked lips. "Here, in Jaipur, people also need help." With care, he pulled the girl's thumb out of her mouth. "She's the daughter of one of the *nautch* girls."

Thirteen years ago, I'd known Hari to be a man who would do anything, say anything, to get what he wanted. There was a time, in the first year of our marriage, when I believed everything he told me. Hari would bring shepherd's purse he'd gathered by the riverbank ("Look, Lakshmi. Heart-shaped, just for you."). And one time, dried *rudraksha* seeds. ("What a fine necklace they'll make!"). At times like those, my heart would soften. Later, I learned the shepherd's purse had come from *saas*'s supplies (she used it to treat malaria), and the guru passing through our village had left his prayer beads (made from the coveted blue seeds) behind. I would not be made a fool of again.

"How much this time, Hari?"

"Can't you see? She needs—"

"How much?"

"She's a child, Lakshmi."

"I already gave you hundreds of rupees. Do you know how long I had to work for that? How much?"

He moved his jaw from side to side. His grip on the girl's shoulders tightened, and she turned her head to look up at him. He shook his head at me, as if I had disappointed him.

I felt a pang of guilt then. If he was telling the truth, I was wrong not to help the girl. She looked like she needed it. Even if I found it hard to believe that Hari had changed enough to carry on Saasuji's work, I owed it to the girl to do something. I knew my mother-in-law would have helped her.

I looked at Malik, and he let go of my arm. I went to the girl and squatted down to inspect the wound. The gash was deep. The skin around the wound was mottled red and pink and purple. I'd watched Hari's mother use a disinfected thread and a superfine needle to close the skin, but I'd never done it myself. I suppose I could have tried to do the same for this little girl, but I felt unsure. I didn't want the wound to get worse; I worried she might lose her leg.

"She needs stitches," I said. "And disinfectant. And you must cover the wound after."

Hari chuckled, a sound without joy. "Now that you're working for the palace, you're too good to help her yourself?"

I felt my face grow warm. For a decade, I had been healing the rich, only, for their minor, more emotional troubles. If I'd stayed with Hari, no doubt Saasuji would have gotten around to teaching me the more complex procedures only she practiced. I shivered as I imagined my mother-in-law regarding me with as much dismay as Hari was now.

He knew he'd touched a tender spot. "Even Radha travels in such fine circles now." Before I could ask him what he meant, he said, "How much did the palace bursar give you?"

I looked again at the poor girl. A blameless child. It wasn't her fault she was poor. I took a thousand rupees from the bursar's payment and held them out to Hari. "You need to take her to the hospital right away. And get medicine."

When he reached for the money, I drew my hand back. "A divorce, Hari. That's my price."

He squinted his eyes, then shrugged, as if it were all the same to him. I let him take the money from my hand and watched him pocket it.

"I'll send Malik with the papers," I said.

We looked at each other for a long moment. Finally, he nodded.

He took the girl's hand and walked out of the alley. The girl turned her head around to stare at me as they turned the corner.

"Hai Ram," I said. I hadn't even had the money long enough for it to feel real. Now I had even less to pay the builder.

"Goonda!" Malik said.

Maybe he was a bad man. Maybe not. I'd known the Hari of long ago. Was he different now? I was skeptical.

I put my hands on Malik's shoulders, forcing him to look at me. "Tell me you will *never* become a thug. Promise me."

Malik didn't answer. He picked up the tiffins and walked away.

I arrived home earlier than usual. Seeing Hari had rattled me, but I was trying not to think about it. I focused instead on the news I wanted to share with Radha. The Maharani School for Girls. How excited she would be to read Shakespeare alongside the elite young ladies of Jaipur!

From Mrs. Iyengar's gate, I watched Radha at the outdoor hearth, pouring graham flour from a sack onto a steel plate. Her hands worked quickly, sifting through the powder, removing the pebbles. She was still brusque, dismissing me with a toss of her head. Or she ignored me completely and buried her head in one of Kanta's novels. But things would be different now. Especially now that I could offer her what neither of us had anticipated—something even better than Kanta could offer.

I approached Radha, bade her good evening.

She flicked her eyes at me but said nothing. She poured flour from the plate in a pan of melted *ghee.* The rich smell of warm butter and flour filled the air.

I squatted next to her. For the first time, it occurred to me that she'd never had her earlobes pierced as a baby. Maa and Pitaji probably couldn't afford gold for the earrings. I would get them pierced with small gold hoops.

"The next time I go to the palace, Radha, I'd like to take you with me."

My sister blinked in surprise, but continued stirring the flour. I waited for a response. None came.

"You've been so diligent with your work. You grind henna finer than I ever could—"

"I can't."

"Can't what?"

"Go to the palace with you."

"Of course you can. Kanta would excuse you for an afternoon—"

"She's cooped up in her house all day," she said flatly. "And her *saas* is difficult." She began pouring a sack of sugar into the hot pan. "She needs me." I heard what she didn't say: *You don't.*

I was stung. How could this girl, who had cried all night two weeks ago when I wouldn't let her go to the palace with Malik and me, now act as if it made no difference to her? Perhaps I chose the wrong time to tell her? I should have waited until she finished cooking. Since the fire at Mrs. Iyengar's hearth when she first arrived, she had tried to be especially careful.

I lifted the bowl of crushed cardamom, intending to pour it into the sugar mixture.

Radha grabbed my wrist. "Not yet."

I set the bowl down, embarrassed. I shouldn't have interfered. Her *laddus* turned out far better than mine.

She turned over a spatula-full of flour. It was browning nicely.

The silence between us lengthened.

"I have a surprise for you. The Maharani Latika has offered you a scholarship at her school. Just think, Radha! Instead of a government school, you'll be going to a private one. Where all the girls from Parvati's holiday party go. Starting next week."

She kept stirring the flour.

"Radha?"

"I'll tell Auntie tomorrow when I see her. She'll be pleased."

Perhaps she was too tired to take it in. Had I been working her too hard?

"You'll have to take an entrance exam, but I know you'll

pass easily. You know so much already about books, Radha, and your English is so good—"

"I'll go, if that's what you want."

"I'd thought you'd be pleased—"

She lifted her eyes and looked at me steadily. "You'd like me to thank you? All right. Thank you. Now I need to finish these treats or you'll be upset with me for not finishing my chores."

I blinked. My sister, who had looked up to me, called me "Jiji" for the first time just three months ago, acted as if she no longer cared what I said or did for her. Should I have been glad she was detaching herself from me, becoming independent, making her own decisions? But I wasn't. I missed the other Radha, the one who had clung to me on our cot, cried helplessly and told me about Maa and Pitaji and her life in Ajar.

I rose carefully to standing and smoothed my sari. I watched her add ground cloves to the mixture. When I could speak without a tremor in my voice, I said, "If you change your mind about coming to the palace—"

"I won't. Leave the tiffins. I'll wash them before coming up," she said, reaching for the cardamom, the clipped edges of her words cutting off any further discussion.

NINE

February 12, 1956

The Maharani School for Girls consisted of three horizontal buildings, each two stories tall. I stood across the street from the school, watching a line of cars go through the gates, down a paved driveway, around the circular courtyard and back out into the street. Drivers in khaki shirts and pleated knickers held back doors open for young MemSahibs who were going home for lunch. A few day scholars were walking to local food stalls for their meal. The boarders ate at the school cafeteria.

The younger girls, eight to twelve years old, wore light blue skirts and half-sleeve shirts with a red sash. Students Radha's age and older wore a blue *kameez*, white *salwaar* and a maroon *chunni*. Every girl had a maroon cardigan on—Jaipur in February was chilly. I'd heard that the maharani had been involved in every detail of her school—from the uniform, the selection of Miss Genevieve as principal (she'd been Her Highness's tutor at her Swiss boarding school) to the lunch menu (no fried foods, plenty of vegetables and fruits, no sugar).

It was Radha's first week at the Maharani School, and I wanted to take her to lunch. With everything going on, I'd barely seen her to ask how she liked it and what her classes were like. My heart grew full as I watched her skip down the front steps of the main building. Her complexion was rosy. Her uniform smart and neat. (This morning when I offered her a lift in the rickshaw with Malik and me, she'd wrinkled her nose. She said she didn't want to smell the sweat of the rickshaw-*walla* or wrinkle her clothes.)

As Radha came down the last step, Sheela Sharma cut in front of her, bringing my sister to an abrupt halt. Without apologizing, Sheela dove into the back seat of her family's sedan. Radha's mouth tightened.

I held my breath.

To my relief, Radha resumed her walk to the guard's station to check herself out for lunch. The gateman took his time looking for Radha's name on his clipboard. She seemed nervous, glancing up the street, chewing on her lip.

I called to her. She turned, startled. She didn't look pleased to see me, which, by now, I was learning to take in stride. I was carrying no tiffins, no carriers—only a handbag.

She took another look up the street. Her shoulders slumped.

"How smart you look in your uniform!" I said brightly.

She looked down at her clothes, self-conscious, as if I'd spotted a stain on it.

Hooking one of her slim arms in mine, I guided her to the *chaat* shops at the other end of the street. "I thought I'd take you to lunch." I stopped to rearrange the long *chunni* so it fell evenly across her shoulders. "How are you enjoying school?"

"Fine."

"Come now." I took her arm again and resumed strolling. "This is your first big-city school—not like Pitaji's little shack. There must be some surprises? Have you met anyone you'd like to have as a friend?"

She wagged her head from side to side and shrugged. *Yes. No. Perhaps.*

Two girls in uniforms identical to Radha's overtook us and turned to smile at my sister, but she was too distracted to return the greeting.

I squeezed her arm. "It must be wonderful. So many new experiences." With a practiced eye, I judged the wares of each *chaat* vendor we passed: *samosas, choles, pakoras, dal batti.*

"How about some *sev puri*? *Puris* take so long to make at home, and here we can order them fresh off the stove." I looked to her for confirmation.

She raised her brows. "You don't approve of street food."

She was right, but I said I wanted to make an exception. She managed a slight nod. We sat at a small table in front of the food stand.

"Tell me about your teachers."

Tracing a finger along a groove in the wooden table, she sighed. "The Hindi teacher is small and thin and has dandruff in her hair. You would not like the way she cleans her neck."

"Radha! Is that any way to speak about those who teach you reading-writing?"

She met my eye as if to ask, *Have you come all this way to scold me?*

I put my hand over hers. "Pitaji would be so proud of you."

"He would have been happy with the government school."

It was true that our father had supported free education for all castes. But a chance at the Maharani School—the girls she would get to know, the opportunities! Even he would have been excited.

Our tea arrived in small glass tumblers, the potato-and-chutney *puri* wrapped in newspaper. She must have been hungry because she took a large bite. Automatically, I laid a hand on her forearm to remind her to eat like a lady. She checked to see if any girls from her class had seen me correcting her, making me wish I hadn't.

I sipped my tea. "How about your other teachers?"

"For History we have Mrs. Channa. She's mean. A girl in my class was talking to her friend. Mrs. Channa didn't like it, so Sonia had to squat with her arms under her knees and pull at her ears. Like a rooster."

Some school punishments never changed. My lips twitched. "Looks like Mrs. Channa was trying to set an example."

Radha lifted her shoulders, as if she didn't care either way. I thought of how happy my sister always seemed around Malik and Kanta. Why couldn't she be the same way with me?

I pulled a slim kidskin case from my handbag. "Since you like to read so much, I thought you might want to try your hand at writing. This should come in handy."

She looked at the case for a moment, then at me. It occurred to me that she might never have received a gift before. She pulled out her school handkerchief and wiped the grease from her hands. Slowly, she opened the case and lifted the marbled orange fountain pen carefully from its blue velvet bed, as if she were afraid to break it. She slid her fingers over the smooth barrel and unscrewed the cap. She examined the engraving on the gold nib: *Wilson 1st Quality Fine.*

Radha's lips were halfway to a smile. Then, suddenly, she blinked. She slipped the pen back in its case, snapping it shut. "You shouldn't have."

Stunned, I said, "Don't you like it?"

"If I lose it, you'll be angry." Another rebuke.

She took another large mouthful of *puri* and potatoes, defying me to correct her table manners.

I pressed my lips together. I pushed the case closer to her. "It's yours, *choti behen.*" The words *little sister* just slipped out. I hadn't planned them. I was used to Malik calling her *choti behen* because he felt protective of her, as if he were the older sibling. This was the first time I'd called her that.

She stopped chewing. With difficulty, she swallowed. "Thank you, Jiji."

She quickly finished the remainder of her puri and said she had to get back to catch up on her reading before her next class. "I could have finished it this morning but I had to grind the henna for you."

"Radha, if your schoolwork is suffering, you don't have to make the henna paste anymore. I can manage."

"Can we go now?" She sounded impatient and got off her stool.

When we arrived at the school gates, she checked in with the guard and walked across the courtyard and up the steps, disappearing into the main building. She hadn't even said goodbye.

I crossed the street, lost in thought. She hadn't wanted to go the Maharani School in the first place, but now she was anxious to return early from lunch so she could do well in her studies. What an unpredictable girl she was.

"I wish I could send *my* daughter to a school like that."

I jumped. My builder, Naraya, had come up behind me. He was standing a little too close, cleaning his teeth with a toothpick. He was a hefty man, with a bulging belly, and the *kurta* he wore was voluminous, making him appear even larger.

I took a step away from him. "You scared me, Mr. Naraya."

"Did I? Apologies, Mrs. Shastri." Although he was gazing at me calmly, there was a hint of menace in his voice. "Did you notice that we put in that fancy Western plumbing you like? Unfortunately, we ran out of money for a privy. And the shutters for the windows." He took a piece of paper from his *kurta* and moved closer to me to again. "You haven't paid the invoice." I smelled the cheap *beedis* and the curry he'd had for lunch.

I was about to take the sheet from him, but he pulled it back. "Of course, I had to double it."

What? Samir had secured a two-month extension for me. I snatched the invoice out of his hands and scanned it. "Ten thousand rupees? What about—"

"Your extension? Two months was up—" he scratched his neck "—two days ago. The amount doubles if you miss a payment. It's in the contract."

I'd been so preoccupied with the palace and our new bookings, getting Radha ready for school and, of course, working, working, working that I'd forgotten to mark it in my notebook.

"I already gave you two extra months." He picked his teeth. "If I don't get the money today, I can take possession. That's also in the contract. And my daughter and her new husband need a house."

Hai Ram! I still didn't have his money. Most of my palace earnings had gone toward a combination of the Maharani Latika's supplies (Parvati had yet to pay me for the marriage commission), to Radha's uniform and books, the increased rent Mrs. Iyengar was charging for my sister and, of course, to Hari. Naraya had deliberately held back the installation of the toilet. Without a proper privy, I couldn't move in.

I attempted a smile, but it came out as a grimace. "I need a little more time."

His face with its Buddha-cheeks looked pleasant enough, but his voice was grim. "My daughter's dowry can't wait. Else she will deliver *before* the wedding."

I raised my eyebrows. "She's pregnant?"

He bared his stained teeth, as if we had just shared a joke. "I kicked her out once. But my sister begged me to take her back. Finally, I found an old fool to take her off my hands. But she'll start showing soon."

"The groom doesn't know?"

Mr. Naraya laughed so hard his belly rippled under the *kurta*. "Am I crazy?"

I backed away.

"You don't look well, Mrs. Shastri. Why don't I drive you to wherever it is you keep your money?"

I clutched my handbag tightly, as if the money were in

there. "No. I'll meet you at 3:00 p.m. Just outside the Jhori Bazaar gate. With your money."

He pointed his toothpick at me. "See how easy that was?"

I had no choice but to ask Samir. He had offered me a loan before, and I knew he could spare it, but I hated to ask. As fiercely committed as I was to having a house of my own—my dream of an independent life—debts were abhorrent to me, more so if they came from friends. Especially if they came from Samir. Our arrangement was based strictly on the sachets; after Parvati's holiday party, I wanted to avoid any other personal entanglements with him.

I checked my pocket watch: 1:30 p.m. At this time of day, unless he was taking a client to lunch, Samir would most likely be at his office.

I hailed a rickshaw.

When I arrived at the office building with the tall white colonnades, I almost lost my nerve. My hands felt clammy. I wanted to turn around. But where else would I get the money? Banks? When had they ever loaned money to a woman without a husband?

Then, a chilling thought: How was I different from Hari, begging for money, begging for time?

I stepped out of the rickshaw before I changed my mind.

"Well, this is a surprise," Samir said. He indicated the chair in front of his desk. His office, enclosed in glass, was on one side of a large open space where five draftsmen were busy at their desks. "Tea?"

I shook my head. "It's urgent. I wouldn't have come here otherwise." I wet my lips. "The builder's invoice. I've passed the deadline."

He didn't hesitate. "How much?"

I handed him the receipt. "I'll pay you back with interest."

Samir whistled when he read the receipt, then looked at

me. He walked to the office safe behind him, opened it with the combination and took out a bundle of bills. He inserted them in an envelope, handed the envelope to me and sat down again.

I wanted to apologize. *I'm sorry, Samir. I thought I could do it on my own.* I sat in my chair a moment longer. "Do you want a…receipt?"

His eyes crinkled at the corners and he fought back a smile. He stood.

Time for me to go, I thought. I nodded my thanks, then hurried through the office doors, the fat envelope in my hand. I allowed myself a sigh of relief. Samir had made the asking so easy.

Coming out of the building, I almost crashed into Parvati.

I froze. For once I couldn't come up with any small talk. Couldn't think of a lie to explain what I was doing here.

Last December, at the holiday party, she had all but warned me to stay away from her husband. Yet here I was, at his office door. I felt my cheeks redden. *It's not what you think*, I wanted to say. *It's not how it looks.* Isn't that what Radha had said when Parvati found blue greasepaint on her skin?

Parvati's gaze landed on the envelope in my hand. Her eyebrows shot up.

I put my hands together, one still holding the envelope, to greet her. I sputtered, "Samir Sahib…ordered—I delivered… they're for his clients."

It was partially true. He did buy my hair tonic for the Maharani Indira once a month. Just not today. In my harried state, I couldn't think of anything else to say.

I had to meet my builder in half an hour. I couldn't afford to lose my house! Flustered, I rushed past her to flag down a rickshaw.

The day after, Parvati sent a note canceling her next appointment.

PART THREE

TEN

Jaipur, State of Rajasthan, India
March 15, 1956

By March, our henna business had grown so much that I had to put new clients on a waiting list. The three of us were busy around the clock. Radha mixed henna paste before she left for the Maharani School. Malik and I packed the tiffins and traveled across Jaipur to our appointments. After school, Radha went to Kanta's. When she returned to Mrs. Iyengar's in the evening, she helped me cook delicacies for the ladies. All of us were so exhausted by day's end that we only spoke when necessary.

Did you get the limes we needed for the hair tonic?

How is your math homework coming?

Did we get reimbursed for the stale bawchi *oil?*

I was also finishing up the Rajnagar house. Using Samir's

loan, I had paid off Narayan and hired another builder to complete the privy. There was still no electricity, but we could manage with lanterns. We were almost ready to move in.

One fine morning, when the temperature had not yet begun to rise, I was bringing a few tiffins down the stairs for our first appointment of the day. Radha and Malik had gone down before me. When I got to the courtyard doors, I heard them talking outside.

"No, it *was* you. I saw you as clearly as I see you now in front of me." Malik sounded as if he were talking to someone much younger, who needed explaining.

"What if it *were* me? I don't owe you any explanations, Malik."

"Who said you did? Just be careful, *accha*?"

Lately, they had been bickering like tetchy siblings. I put it down to too much work and not enough sleep.

I stepped through the gates. "Careful about what?"

Radha shot a hot glance at Malik before she walked away, headed for school.

He wouldn't meet my eyes. Instead, he said, "Be right back. I forgot the *khus-khus* fans."

I attended to Maharani Latika once a week now, more as a way for her to relax than recuperate. The young queen's mourning period was all but over. She was becoming more involved in the day-to-day workings of her school.

One day as Malik and I arrived at the palace, a sleek black Bentley was just coming out of the gates.

Maharani Latika leaned out of the driver's window. She was wearing dark sunglasses and a white chiffon scarf. Her lady-in-waiting sat in the passenger seat.

"I was hoping to catch you!" Her lips widened in a brilliant smile. "I regret I must cancel today, but the bursar will

Radha said impatiently, "She didn't rob me. She hit me with her elbow when we were dancing the fox trot."

"Fox trot?" Saasuji said in heavily accented English. Her tone implied that Western dance was a worse offense, to her, than robbery. "You see what kind of thing that school is teaching? These foreign customs—not at all suitable for Rajasthani girls." She sniffed.

"Baap re baap, Saasuji!" Kanta turned to Radha. "This happened at school? It was an accident?" Kanta asked.

"Yes. No." Radha looked down at the carpet. "I know she meant to do it."

"Why?"

"She doesn't like me." My sister hesitated. "The maharani paired us up for the dance—Sheela and me. Sheela kept telling me I would never learn how to dance—my feet were too big. Then she hit me in the eye with her elbow and said, *'Kala kaloota baingan loota.'" You're as dark as an eggplant.*

Kanta looked at me. "We should call Mrs. Sharma."

Radha slapped her free hand on the arm of her chair, making us all jump. "No! I'm not a tattletale. It's just—I didn't grow up in a big fancy house like her. I don't fit in with any of them. I'm clumsy. I don't wear the right clothes. I don't have the right shoes. I'm different and they know it."

She flicked a nervous glance at me, caught my startled expression. She'd never told me that she felt left out. It never occurred to me that more privileged girls might pick on her.

Kanta frowned. "That's the reason Sheela did this? Because you're not like them?"

Radha eyed me from the corner of her eye. In a small voice, she said, "Maybe she remembers that I tried to throw rocks at her once."

Kanta looked to me for confirmation.

I shook my head. "It was just silly nonsense. No one was hurt."

"It's jolly well no one was hurt! Young women shouldn't be throwing rocks at one another," Kanta said.

"My head." Radha pressed her forehead with her free hand.

Kanta's *saas* glared at Baju, who was hovering by the door. "Why are you still here, you fool? Go get aspirin and water."

Baju's mustache twitched as it did when he was offended as he left the room.

"Well, there's an easy fix to this." Kanta turned to the table beside the sofa and picked up the phone. Before I could stop her, she was chatting with her tailor, informing him that she would bring Radha the next afternoon to get measured for English dresses. Then she called her hairdresser and made an appointment to have Radha's hair cut in a smart pageboy.

When she put the phone down, she was smiling. She looked at Radha, then at me. "Now, don't scold me, Lakshmi. It's important for a modern girl to look, well, modern."

Radha jumped up and threw her arms around Kanta's neck.

I turned away. Kanta always knew just what to say and do to make my sister happy when I seemed to have no clue.

ELEVEN

April 20, 1956

I wasn't keen on having a move-in ceremony for my new house. But Malik kept asking, and I finally relented. Malik's fondness for rituals like the Hindu *Griha Pravesh* wasn't surprising. Many Muslims, the majority of whom had lived in India for centuries and decided to stay after Partition, observed Hindu customs as well as their own. After all, celebrations were happy occasions and no one was excluded.

At the entrance of my new Rajnagar house, Malik erected two bamboo poles and strung a garland of mango leaves between them. They were fertility symbols, per custom, but since I was a woman who didn't see children in my future given my circumstances, they made me slightly uneasy. Still, I *was* excited about finally being able to call this house my home. Perhaps that's what Malik, who knew me almost as well as I knew myself, wanted to help me celebrate. The walls belonged to me. The windows, the mosaic floor, the dirt in the courtyard. I even felt entitled to the stars above my roof.

Malik had also lobbied for a *pandit* to purify the house for the *Griha Pravesh* ceremony. Unless we transferred all our belongings on the auspicious date chosen by the priest (which, as it turned out, was to be April 20), we'd be inviting bad luck.

"I'll find a *pandit* for us, cheap-cheap, Auntie-Boss," he promised.

"And I'll cook the food," Radha added. She was eager for us to leave Mrs. Iyengar's house. Six months ago, when she first arrived in Jaipur, she'd been happy to sleep on the stone floor of my room, but the more time she spent at Kanta's and the Maharani School, the less enchanted she became with our humble lodgings.

Radha and Malik packed our belongings into two metal trunks and a great number of vinyl and cloth bags. They scrubbed the windows of our new house with newspapers, dusted the built-in shelves, polished the terrazzo floor until it gleamed and swept the courtyard. Over the packed dirt in the courtyard, they laid sheets and blankets for our guests to sit on. No one was allowed to enter the house now until it had been purified.

True to his word, Malik found a twenty-rupee priest, a tiny man with a bald head whose scrawny arms and legs protruded from his saffron robes like shoots on a potato. He wore eyeglasses as thick as the bottles of colored water sold at street stalls. (Did all priests look like Gandhi-*ji*, I wondered, or was it Gandhi-*ji* who started to resemble all *pandits*?) Because I still couldn't afford shutters on the windows (a requirement for *Griha Pravesh*), the *pandit* was uncomfortable agreeing to the ceremony until Malik sweetened the pot with another five rupees.

The priest's assistants began unloading their supplies for the ceremony: a statuette of Ganesh, several silver plates, three silver bowls, sandalwood incense, freshly cut flowers (red, of course, for good luck, and picked, I was sure, from a park along the way, as many women did on their way to temple in the mornings), leaves of the camphor laurel tree, a red candle, red cotton thread, sesame seeds, whole wheat grain, a clay pot of red vermillion and water paste, a silver pot of *ghee*, bells and a wooden rosary tied with red thread.

Malik added the fresh sweets he'd bought this morning from the corner shop.

First, the *pandit* built an altar to Lord Ganesh. From time to time, he consulted a well-thumbed book of incantations, although he seemed to know the words by heart. "'The tusk he holds represents service; the goad prods us along our path; the noose reminds us of that which binds us; to his favored he grants all boons.'"

Guests began arriving. Since it was tradition to invite every neighbor to ceremonies with a box of sweets (whether you knew them or not), Malik had dropped off boxes at everyone's doorstep. They were the first to arrive, curious to meet us and to get a firsthand glimpse of the new house on the street.

Radha and I were both delighted to welcome Mr. and Mrs. Pandey from our former lodgings at Mrs. Iyengar's. I suspected that, like me, Radha had a small crush on Sheela Sharma's handsome music teacher.

Mr. and Mrs. Iyengar came, too. My former landlady made a show of examining the premises and wrinkled her snub nose. "The courtyard certainly makes such a small house more tolerable."

I smiled at the rebuke. Nothing was going to spoil my mood today.

I had not mentioned this celebration to my ladies. It would not have been fitting for me to invite them to my home—so much more humble than theirs. But Radha must have let it slip to Kanta because I saw my sister leap up to greet Kanta and Manu and usher them into the courtyard. With a stab of envy, I thought Radha never showed such enthusiasm when I came into a room. It reminded me that the gap between us had widened since she started attending the Maharani School a few months ago.

Kanta appeared cheerful even though the hollows under her eyes were dark. Manu helped ease her onto a blanket. I asked Kanta how she was feeling as it had been several weeks since I had seen her. She hadn't felt well enough to keep our appointments.

"Except for reading and riding in moving vehicles, both of which I like to do very, very fast, all's well. Oh, and also sleeping and eating are an issue!" she cackled.

As guests made themselves comfortable and soft-voiced conversations continued, the priest began dropping laurel leaves into the clay pot of *ghee*. He then lit them with a match, and prodded the flame. Without skipping a beat in his repetitions of *Om Ganapati Namah*, he pointed to the virgin incense stub, and one of his assistants hurried to light it. The unexpected combination of scorching camphor, *ghee* and sandalwood was musky, sweet, bitter and rich at the same time—the scents of past ceremonies, long forgotten.

I thought of my marriage years ago, the hasty ritual, the *pandit* complaining that he could barely afford the *ghee* with the fee he was being offered. No *chura* ceremony for my uncles to slide bangles on my arm and give me money, for I had no uncles. Pitaji struggling to stay upright, the yellows of his eyes red-veined from drink. Maa shooing flies from the meager platters of *pilao, samosas, subjis* and sweets.

With my red wedding sari shielding my face, I'd cried and cried, amazed I still had tears left after arguing with Maa for five straight days: *Did Maa not need me to help to teach the school when Pitaji was absent? Was fifteen so very old to still be at home?*

Who would roast and grind the gram after I left? Who would bring water from the well?

Maa was gentle, but firm. She was brought up to obey her parents and her husband, not to defy, question or contradict. She told me Pitaji's books had filled my head with too many silly ideas. They had given me the useless notion that I could make my own decisions. As a daughter, my job was to marry the man my parents chose for me, as she had. She was as powerless to change that age-old tradition as I was. Besides, there was no money to keep me at home.

I glanced at Maa's neck, where her gold chain used to hang and where the groove it had carved would always be a reminder of what she had sacrificed, and knew that to be true.

But I also knew that as soon as I married, I would become *jaaya*—my husband taking birth in my womb in the form of future children. And once there were children, there would be no more *I* or *me*, only *we* and *them*. So often I'd begged my namesake, the goddess Lakshmi, to hear my pleas—*I'm hungry for the knowledge of three Swaraswatis! Let me see the wider world before shutting me inside a small life.* But, as always, she'd held up her delicate hands in apology: *It's the way it has always been.*

It would have been so much sweeter to share today's ceremony with my parents. I would have seated them in the place of pride—in the front of the *pandit*—and introduced them to my guests, fed them rich *burfi* with my own hands, cooled their faces with *khus-khus* fans—

The rustling beside me brought me back to the ceremony. Radha was holding a *chunni* to her nose as if the fragrance of the altar was too strong. She rose, weaving toward the privy. It was the third time in an hour she had done so.

Malik met her as she came out, whispered in her ear, then ran to the *mutki* to get her a drink of water. It was only April, but she was fanning her face as if the heat were unbearable. Malik handed her the tumbler. She took a sip and blanched.

I blamed myself. The packing and cleaning of the last few days, school, the chores for our henna business—it had been too much for her.

When she returned to her seat, I noticed she'd rinsed her face—the tendrils on her forehead were damp and her cheeks pink. She looked so different from the dusty, hollow-cheeked girl I'd first met just six months ago. Now, her face looked as ripe as a mango in June. She even carried herself differently—shoulders back, neck long. She walked with a surer step. The pageboy suited her oval face. Her village diction was less noticeable; she'd dropped double words like *small-small* and *far-far*. The other day she used a word—what was it? *Antediluvian*?—and *I* had to ask *her* the definition. It made me proud—how easily she picked things up.

Pandit-*ji* poured sesame seeds, whole wheat and red paste into the small fire, dousing it. Smoke curled up into the open sky. He wrapped banana leaves around the warm pot, and turned to hand it to me. But I nodded at Radha. I knew she would enjoy being the bearer. She bit her lower lip and smiled shyly as she lifted the pot to her head. Then she rose carefully and went into the empty house to disinfect and purify it.

She was wearing one of the frocks Kanta had ordered for her, a lighter-than-a-feather chiffon with a slim-fitting bodice. Kanta said, "It's an exact copy of what Madhubala wore in *Mr. and Mrs. 55*. I had the tailor weave gold chains into the waist, just like the dress in the movie."

Radha's breasts were straining against the fabric. She grimaced now and then, as if the binding were too tight. Her hips, which had been slim as a boy's when I first met her, swayed as she walked. I watched the faces of the guests and was shocked to see the men taking notice, their eyes following the movement of her buttocks. She was only thirteen! But when I turned to look at her, I had to admit she seemed far older.

I watched the holy assistants circle the main room and the courtyard three times with red thread, starting from the east, while the *pandit* sprinkled holy water around the area. Then he lowered a clay container filled with grain and red flowers into the pit Malik had dug in the southeast corner of the courtyard. Now that we had fed the gods and asked them to watch over the house and protect us from evil intentions, the house, and its inhabitants, were safe from harm.

Until a move-in ceremony was finished, the house had to be free of all our possessions, so the driver of the camel cart had waited patiently with our carriers and trunks in front of the house. After the guests left, Malik's friends (who had also been invited to the move-in festivities) carried everything inside the house. I told Malik he looked tired and should go home; Radha and I would clean up. Pleased that the ceremony had been such a success (the *pandit* stayed three hours), Malik left with his pals (and the leftover sweets).

Eager to settle in, I began unpacking the first trunk and stacking our clothes on the built-in shelves. I asked Radha to organize our kitchen. She bent over the other trunk, turned and bolted out of the room. I could hear her retching in the privy. When she returned, I asked if she'd eaten something that didn't agree with her.

She shook her head and headed for the *charpoy*. "If I can just lie down for a few minutes..." Within seconds, she was asleep.

Poor thing. Her days were so full now that she often nodded off at dinner. I decided to finish arranging our clothes. When that was done, I started to set up the kitchen, pulling out pots, stainless steel plates, cups and glasses from the trunk. The carriers stuffed with odds and ends would have to wait until tomorrow. Satisfied, I glanced around the room.

Radha still had not stirred. I walked to the cot in the corner of the room to admire my sleeping sister. The Madhubala dress stretched across her rounded hips. Her hair gleamed with coconut oil. Her skin glowed. She didn't look sick; she looked peaceful, content. Perhaps I should make her some ginger and honey water. It always worked wonders for women who suffered from nausea early in their pregnancy.

The word started as a tingling in my ear, slid down my throat and snaked into my spine. Radha was nauseous. Her breasts were tender. She was always tired. I remembered her telling me she had already started her menses. Could she be *pregnant*?

Whom had she been with? She went to a *girl's* school—she didn't know any boys. Malik was too young. There was Manu, Kanta's husband, but I couldn't imagine he would take advantage of her. Mr. Iyengar? Baju? Who?

The answer landed on my heart like a thousand-pound Brahma bull.

I reached the Pink City Bazaar. The air reeked of stale cooking oil, rotting vegetables, diesel exhaust.

I found Malik sitting on a low wall across from his favorite *chaat* stall, sharing a Red and White with his friends (English cigarettes were more expensive than Indian *beedis*, and ever since he'd started going to the palace, Malik's tastes had become more refined).

He was describing to his friends some dish Chef had prepared for him the last time he was at the maharinis' palace. When he noticed me, he stopped midsentence.

I must have resembled a cheetah on the prowl—wild, dangerous. One side of my hair had come loose from my bun. My sari was wrinkled from unpacking, bending, squatting, rearranging. My eyes blazed with anger.

Malik jumped off the wall and gave the almost-finished Red and White to another urchin. "Auntie-Boss?" he said.

"Can you take me to Hari?"

★ ★ ★

We zigzagged down narrow streets, Malik stopping at a tea stall or a *paan* stand to ask the proprietors if they had seen Hari. The chai-*wallas* and their customers stared at me. I stared back. We rushed past a woman in the Refugee Market who'd set up shop at the edge of the street. She was sitting on a piece of cotton cloth, her shoe repair tools lined up neatly. She eyed my sandals and said, "*Ji*, your straps are coming loose."

We came to a nondescript building that, like the others, had been decorated decades earlier in pink plaster. Shops took up the bottom floor. In one, a man patched a large inner tube. In another, a tailor haggled with a customer while his two male assistants, bent over tiny sewing machines, worked in the faint light of a bare bulb. Next came a busy *lassi* vendor. Men loitered in front of his shop, talking and laughing, carelessly discarding their empty clay tumblers in the ditch by the road.

Malik turned into a dark passageway. I followed. We climbed a flight of stairs to a dimly lit, narrow landing. Malik moved quietly, peering inside the door of each room. At last, he turned and nodded at me.

In the room, two young men played cards on the wooden floor. They looked up when I entered. There was no window, and the air was fetid. The walls were uneven where chunks of plaster had fallen off. The only furniture in the room was a *charpoy*, on which a third man was sleeping. *Hari.* The strings of the cot were so stretched his body hung only an inch or two above the rough wood floor.

I felt a sharp pain in my chest just before I lunged at him. Out came the anger I hadn't been able to summon the first time I'd encountered him in Jaipur. I punched his arms. I slapped his ears. I pounded his shoulders. If I could have broken his skull with my bare hands, I would have.

Hari put his arms around his head to protect himself, turned over on his back and cried, *"Arré!"*

"Maderchod!" I screamed. *"Salla kutta!"* Obscenities I'd only heard men use.

The other men had frozen in midplay. Malik yelled at them to leave, waving his arms at them, as if shooing away pigeons. They got to their feet and went through the open door, leaving their cards behind. They turned to gawk, but Malik rushed at them. He followed them out and pulled the door closed behind him.

Hari managed to roll over and sit up. He tried to grab my arms, but my anger had given me the strength of Shiva. I freed one arm from his grasp and slapped his head again and again with the flat of my hand.

I was shouting as loudly as my lungs would allow; I didn't care what the neighbors or the *lassi* drinkers thought. "She's a child! She's like your sister! You would do that to your *sister*? Bastard! Donkey's ass! Worthless piece of shit!"

Hari scrabbled out of bed and lost his balance, upsetting the cot. He crab-walked backward to the wall. I followed, kicking, smacking, pummeling. I felt a dull throbbing in my hands and scanned the room to see if there was something else I could hit him with. In that instant, Hari stood and grabbed me, pinning me against the wall.

"Stop!" he shouted as he held my arms against my sides. "Have you gone mad?"

I saw terror in his eyes.

"What's got into you?" His forehead was bleeding and red welts were rising on his forehead and cheeks.

He was holding me so tightly I couldn't free my arms no matter how hard I tried. We panted like dogs fighting over a piece of meat. I spat at him before he saw it coming, and spittle dribbled down his cheek.

He slapped me with such force a tooth snagged the inside of my cheek and I tasted blood.

"Buss!" he growled. *Enough!*

I couldn't stand the thought of Radha's flesh against his skin, the sweaty stench of him on her. Radha, thirteen. Still a child, barely old enough to know what men expected from a woman. *I* was responsible. If I'd stayed with him, as a good wife would have, Hari would have never claimed Radha for himself. He wouldn't have soiled her. Now she was carrying his child.

I let myself slide down the wall. I pulled my knees to my chin, hugged them with my arms, rocked back and forth. I shut my eyes. I wailed. What a mess I'd made of my life, my parents' life, my sister's! If I hadn't been so selfish, this would not have happened. My sister would not have been sullied. My mother-in-law would not have died without me to comfort her. My parents would not have been humiliated. And for what? So I could live a life of my own? How self-centered I had been!

Malik opened the door and stood, small and frightened. "Auntie-Boss?"

When I didn't answer, he came to me and shook my shoulders. "Auntie-Boss. It's me." He said it over and over until I opened my eyes and saw how terrified he was. His swagger was gone, his shoulders hunched in fear. Why had I brought him to this miserable place?

"Please," I said, "go home."

His eyes became hard, and he shook his head no. Then he left the room, closing the door behind him. I should have known he wouldn't leave me as easily as I had left my family. He would stay with me all night if he had to.

Hari picked up the *charpoy*, straightened it and sat, all the while keeping a wary eye on me. "Why are you here?"

His forehead was bleeding. His hair had grown long, hanging unevenly around his ears. He'd let his beard grow, too, a sparse, patchy growth that make him look like a Kashmiri nomad. His clothes were cheap but clean, his sandals new.

Which of us deserved more blame for what I was about to ask? "How long have you been lying down with Radha?"

He sat up straighter. His bug eyes widened. "Why would you think *that*?"

"How long?"

"I would never—she's a child!"

"I believed you when I saw you with that little girl. I thought you were helping the women here. But you were lying then, and you're lying still!"

"I never touched your sister!" He looked away, then rubbed his hands together. "She offered herself, but—"

"*Offered* herself?"

Hari's lower lip was turning purple; he touched it gently with his tongue. "When she came to me, in my village, she said she would give me money if I took her to you. I didn't believe her. So she said she'd let me do what I wanted with her." He stuck out his chin, defiant. "I *could* have—but I *didn't.* I *wouldn't.*"

"*How* did she get pregnant, then?"

His mouth fell open in disbelief.

"She'll start showing soon enough."

He shook his head. "No!"

"Yes!"

He got up and came to me, squatted, gripped my arms. "Lakshmi, it wasn't me." If he were lying, he'd be covering the scar on his chin.

I searched my memory: Radha when I first saw her with her messy pigtail; Radha welcoming me home with *dal batti* and *subji*; Radha in the yard, watering the camellias and jasmine, as she'd promised Mrs. Iyengar she'd do; Radha and Malik playing fivestones on the floor of our room.

My memories grew hazy about the time I started working at the palace; since that day I'd seen Radha less, and only for brief periods. If she wasn't at school, or at Kanta's house, where *had* she been?

I frowned. "She had bruises when she first arrived here."

Hari returned to the *charpoy*, and sat. He put a finger to his forehead, which now was weeping blood. He winced. "We didn't take the train. I used your money to pay debts. We rode on lorries, farm wagons." He swallowed. "One night, we were on a truck carrying sheep. When the driver stopped to relieve himself, I did the same. When I returned to the truck, he was trying to—" Hari glanced at me, quickly, before looking away. "But I stopped him. Nothing happened. Radha was safe."

I covered my eyes with my hand. *All my fault.* I could hear men chatting, laughing, outside.

For a long moment, neither of us said a word.

Then: "Will you take her child? Like you took ours?" he asked.

I took my hand away and looked at him. *"What?"*

"You took our children away. Why?" His lips trembled.

I swallowed hard. "What children?"

Tears filled his eyes. "Maa knew all along what you were doing." He pressed his palms together. "How could you?"

"You're talking foolishness."

"Our children were gifts from Bhagwan."

I fought to keep from shouting. *Gifts from God?*

During the day, I would take the tonics, broths, seeds and concoctions that *saas* fed me to increase fertility. But while she and my husband slept, I'd prepare the brew that kept me childless for the two years of our marriage. The moment my breasts felt tender and I couldn't keep food down, I would drink my *saas*'s cotton root bark tea. Relief came only after the bleeding started—when I knew my pregnancy was over.

His mother was the one who had opened my eyes. How could I explain that to him?

Day after day, I worked alongside her to heal women—most were children still, twenty years old or younger, bodies weak from too many births, too many of them rough. Their days were filled with worry about how to feed their brood; at night they prayed their husbands would come home from labor too tired to add to their troubles. One day Saasuji taught me to prepare the contraceptive tea. And I realized that cotton root bark could change a woman's life: she could choose for herself.

That was what *I* wanted: a life that could fulfill me in a way that children wouldn't. From that day, I hoarded all the knowledge my mother-in-law could give me. *Let her be the rolling pin that shapes a ball of* chappati. Almost overnight, my world grew large with possibility.

Hari stood, began pacing. "I thought you'd left me for another man. I thought...all kinds of things. I worried you'd been hurt. You might be lying in a ditch. You might be sick, or injured. I looked everywhere for you. I couldn't sleep. I couldn't work. And Maa." He looked at me, his eyes filled with pain. "She was never the same. Not after you left."

I closed my eyes. I could imagine my mother-in-law as if she were standing in the room with us, neat and trim in her widow's sari and her round eyeglasses. Always gentle, always kind. *I'm sorry, Saasuji.*

I wiped roughly at my eyes, my nose. "You didn't deserve your mother," I said to Hari.

All at once, his eyes were aflame. "My mother always took *your* side. When we realized you were gone for good, she went to her jar and found you'd taken all the money and her herb pot. I thought she'd be angry, but she said, *'Shabash.'* She thought I hadn't heard her congratulating you, but I had. My Maa chose *you*!"

His tears were real; he wiped them with his palms.

It had never occurred to me that his mother had *hoped* I'd

use the money. We never spoke about the beatings Hari gave me for being barren. Rarely had Hari hit me in the face, and my sari covered the bruises on my body. Only now was I remembering that when she treated women with a swollen face, she'd insist I prepare the poultice. Had she been showing me how to heal myself?

"You left me huddled on the floor with bruises every time you learned that my menses had come." I could still remember how frightened I'd felt. "One day, I figured you'd go too far."

He winced. "I've—I've tried to make amends."

Well, this was a surprise. "How? By following me around town and taking my money?"

He started to speak, then stopped. Gingerly, he touched his forehead, feeling the bump there. "I help women who need help."

"The pleasure girls?"

He heard the skepticism in my voice and shook his head. "You don't believe me. That's fine. I wouldn't have believed me either ten years ago. Except...Maa taught me what she taught you, after you left. And I understood, at last, why those women sought her out. She was their last hope."

He must have seen the shock on my face. He sighed.

"See, I knew about her sachets. It made me angry that men were being deprived of their children. Then you started helping her. And one night—you didn't know—but I saw you drinking her tea. I was so...angry...and ashamed that *you* didn't want *my* children. Then you...left, and Maa got ill."

He stopped, passed a hand over his eyes. "A woman came to her for help. She was...bleeding from her womb." He looked away. "Her husband had thrust a—a broom handle there because she had laughed at another man's joke. She had lost so much blood...she was half-dead. Maa told me what to do, where to harvest the herbs we needed, how to relieve the woman's pain."

My breathing had become shallow. I could see the scene that Hari described so clearly before me. I'd seen similar ones while working with his mother. The urgency. The plaintive cries of the women. Their brutal wounds.

Hari rubbed his hands together. "She revived. But then came the infection. I did everything as Maa instructed. But the woman died, anyway." He swallowed. "She was only sixteen, Lakshmi. I thought of you then. I didn't want to, but I thought of how I had hurt you. How many times… And I was…ashamed. Little by little, I began helping Maa. The women. The children. I saw so much—pain, misery, hunger." He ran his hand through his hair.

I leaned my head against the wall. I didn't want to believe him. I closed my eyes so I could hear the truth in his words.

"When I first came here, I did go to the Pleasure District. I was lonely. Especially after I realized Radha had lied to me about what was in your letter."

I opened my eyes, puzzled.

"When I refused to help Radha get to Jaipur, she showed me your letter, saying you had written that you wanted to see me again. It made me so happy."

My eyebrows shot up, both at the absurdity of the claim and at Radha's impudence. She must have tricked Hari into a scheme to find me. She gambled on the odds that Hari was illiterate.

"She finally found an angle that got me to do her bidding." He shook his head, as if he couldn't believe he'd been duped by a young girl. "In any event, once I got to know the Pleasure District here, I found women who needed help—Maa's kind of help. *My* kind of help now. I've used your money to do what I can. But I need more—real medicine. For injuries that herbs can no longer heal." He sounded earnest now. "Some have been hurt by the men they…service. Broken bones. Some have recurring infections in their…private regions."

"Why didn't you tell me this before?"

"I tried. But you wouldn't believe me, and..." He looked down at the floor. "I didn't blame you. I—" He rubbed his hands together. "I understand many things now I didn't before."

My chest felt tight. Hari was trying. He was righting his wrongs. He was carrying on his mother's work in a way I had failed to. She would have approved. I could not forgive the younger Hari, the one who had felt he owned me, who left me with lasting scars. I had changed, grown stronger. Was it so hard to believe Hari had changed, too, and grown softer? Couldn't I could begin to make peace with this Hari, the one his mother would have blessed? I thought of the little girl with the gash in her leg and how I'd wanted Hari to make her go away. Saasuji would have been far less proud of me for that.

"The little girl—how is her leg?" I asked him now.

"Good. They stitched her at the hospital."

I nodded.

I put my palms against the wall to brace myself and stood. My bones felt tender, as if I'd been walking for days or even weeks.

Hari watched as I tucked my hair behind my ears. He smiled.

"I had my eye on you long before we were married."

I stared at him.

"I'd walk miles to the river from my village to watch the women washing clothes, listening to their gossip. My father was long dead and my Maa was busy tending to her women. I'd see you sometimes, on the opposite bank, headed to the village oven to roast peas. You always looked as if you'd been entrusted with an important mission. So young. So serious." He smiled. "I told my mother, when it was time, I would have only you. She went with me to the river once. We watched you from a distance. Eventually, she took my hand and patted it. 'Yes, *bheta*, yes,' she said."

Too little, I thought, shaking my head. Too late.

"I mean to keep my promise, Lakshmi. The one I made to Maa. I'm doing good here. If only..." He started to pace. "We need medicine for the children's fevers. And several of the younger *nautch* women will deliver soon."

What he was telling me was true—I'd seen it with my own eyes. But my purse was not bottomless. I, too, had debts to pay.

The door opened. Malik came into the room. His ear was red from being pressed against the door.

"Auntie-Boss," he said, "I know a way to help him."

The streetlight was shining inside my Rajnagar house. I saw Radha's body curled on the cot, our metal trunks, a jumble of carriers, filled with odds and ends. I fumbled in the dark, not caring how much noise I made, rummaging through our belongings, wishing I'd had the money to put in electricity.

"Jiji?"

"Matches. Where did you put them?"

I upended a sack, spilling its contents. Herbs wrapped in newspaper packets, spoons, toothpicks. *The Tales of Krishna* that Radha had brought with her.

Radha raised her body on one elbow. "What time is it?"

"Matches! Did I forget to put them on Malik's list last week?"

She pushed herself off the cot and reached inside the vinyl bag by the door. "Here." She yawned.

I grabbed the matchbox from her hand. My fingers were shaking as I lit a match. I emptied the contents of another carrier on the ground, examining the labels on the bottles and packets.

"Now what are you looking for?" She rubbed her eyes.

I broke off my search to glare at her.

She blinked, awake now.

My bun had come loose. My tangled hair fell across my face. My sari was damp, and smelled of vomit; I'd retched a half dozen times on the way home.

My finger began to sting. I shook the match to put out the flame. "I've seen Hari."

In the dark, the white orbs of Radha's eyes shone brighter. "Why?"

"Radha, I didn't know—"

I was afraid I might cry again. I'd been crouching on the floor. Now, I stood up and reached for her hands. She flinched, retreating in the dark.

"Sit down." I indicated the cot. "Please."

She settled on the edge of the *charpoy*, gingerly. Her hands fidgeted in her lap. I knelt on the floor in front of her.

"Radha, whoever did this to you, you're not at fault! If I'd known—that Maa had another child after me, that I had a sister, that you were alone—I wouldn't have left. I would have..."

I wasn't sure what I would have done.

Her brows knitted.

"To think that you *offered* yourself to Hari—it's appalling. It's my fault. Please forgive me."

I sat down next to her.

She shifted, away from me, afraid.

"I was supposed to protect you. I didn't. I let it happen. He—"

"Jiji, you're scaring me." She looked as if she was about to cry. "What are you talking about?"

My eyes dropped to her stomach. She followed my gaze down the length of her wrinkled dress, frowning, and looked up again. *She didn't know?* Of course she didn't! She was a child!

"Your breasts are tender?"

Her eyebrows rose.

"You're making water all the time? You're nauseous?"

Her mouth went slack.

"How long since your last menses?"

She looked past me, at the floor, breathing through her mouth. She glanced at her stomach. Then her eyes softened, as if recalling a memory, a pleasant one.

"Leave it to me, Radha. If you're no more than four months along, it's safe. Help me look for the cotton root bark." I gathered my hair and wound it into a knot at my neck, getting up off the floor. "Remember Mrs. Harris? She drank my tea?"

She made a face.

"But she's fine now! You will be, too. Whoever did this—tell me it wasn't Mr. Pandey?"

She shook her head and flattened the rumpled chiffon over her thighs.

I couldn't read her face; she must be in shock.

"Try to remember where we put the cotton root bark."

"Jiji."

"Maybe the plaid carryall?" I hurried to the bag and emptied it on the cluttered floor.

"Jiji."

I needed more light. Where had the matches gone now? I dropped to all fours searching through the mess. I pushed aside a bundle of books. A spool of thread clattered to the floor.

"What if I keep the baby?"

I stared at the thread unraveling across the terrazzo. *What did she just say?*

I don't know how much time passed before I could move again. Slowly, I turned to look at her.

She was biting her lip, avoiding my eyes.

"You don't *have* to keep it," I said. "Haven't you learned anything from me?"

She lowered her chin, looked down at her lap. I could feel the slippery edges of her guilt. *She had been willing. She had let a man touch her, there, perhaps more than once. She had wanted it.*

While I worked. While she lived in my house. What a fool I'd been!

I had felt sympathy for her. Told myself she needed time to forgive me. She'd come around. She would appreciate what I was making possible: a home, enough *chapatti* so she'd never go hungry, the Maharani School and the possibility of a life better than either of us could have imagined.

I stood up, reached for her. Without thinking, I grabbed the skirt of her dress. She ducked, tried to run. I snatched her bun and clawed at her hair. She screamed. I slapped her. She stumbled and fell.

My heart thudded against my ribs. I watched her cough and sputter. She lay sprawled on the floor amid the contents of the carriers, her legs tucked to one side. Her lip was bleeding, her face contorted in pain.

I towered over her. "What did he do, this *Devdas* of yours? Promise to love you forever?"

"Stop!"

"Give you gifts?"

"It wasn't like that!"

"Or did you *offer* yourself in return for something—like you did with Hari?"

Red splotches appeared on her cheeks. "What choice did I have? I had to get to you and I couldn't do it alone. So what if I used him to get to Jaipur? You chose one way to escape and I chose another! I haven't blamed you, so why blame me?"

"Whatever your boyfriend said to you, it isn't true. And if you think he'll claim it—"

"He will!"

"Oh, how could you be so stupid? Listen to me, Radha. This child has no future!"

"He does!"

"I know the world, Radha. You don't. If you think the father will marry you, you're dreaming!"

She lowered her head. She was crying now. "He loves me."

I wiped my hands on my sari and walked to the Primus stove where a pan filled with water lay ready for tomorrow's tea. Looking around, I spied a stray match on the floor. I picked it up and struck the tip against the stone countertop, then held it to the burner. The blue flame lit up the room.

"Come help me, Radha," I coaxed, forcing my voice to be gentle, as I had done a thousand times to put my ladies in good humor. I gripped the handle of the pot with both hands so she couldn't see how badly I was shaking. "Tomorrow, everything can be the way it was. Back to normal." My jittery voice belied my words.

"You worry what your ladies will think."

I stiffened.

"Your respectable MemSahibs who don't know what you do outside their drawing rooms," she sneered. "How you make babies disappear." She sounded so different, this Radha, whose words had a dagger's edge.

I turned to face her.

"What would they say if they knew you had gotten rid of your own babies?"

She must have seen the stricken look on my face. "Hari told me. Then, after Joyce Harris, I figured it out. What you'd done to stop from having your own."

I was finding it hard to breathe. "This isn't about me! This—this is about you. You're thirteen! A girl with a chance to do more, be more—"

"You're talking about yourself, not me! I'm not *you*."

I pressed a hand against my chest. "No, we're talking about you—a girl with a child and no husband," I wheezed.

She thrust her chin. "We'll get married."

She was overwrought. Delusional. I gripped the edges of the countertop to keep myself upright. "By this time tomorrow, Radha, you won't even remember you drank the tea. You'll be whole again, and clean. Tomorrow, we'll start over."

"You're not listening. You never do! I'll tell the father, and we'll marry. We'll keep the baby."

"And what if he refuses, Radha? Then what will you do? Think about it. Who will dress your child and give him *dal* to eat when you go back to school?"

Her eyes grew huge in her face, Maa's face. Even now, incredibly, she hadn't thought of this. "I won't go back to school. I'll work. Like you."

I shook my head. "You think it's that easy? This house took thirteen years of hard work and *Yes, Ji* and *No, Ji* and *Whatever you say, Ji*. You'll never have to do that if you go to that school. You have many years in which to have a child, after you've finished school. Listen to me, Radha. Please. The Maharani School is a prize—few get in—and you go there for free. You can be something better than a henna artist. Better than me. You can have a meaningful life." The water was almost boiling. "Just—please help me find the cotton root bark."

Her voice trembled. "He said I was just another cheap pair of hands to you. Your business only took off after I arrived. You told me yourself you book more appointments now because of my henna. If that's true, then why can't you trust me to think for myself?"

She moved to stand in front of me, her face inches from mine. The blood on her lip was glistening. "You didn't trust me at the holiday party and you don't trust me now," she said. "It doesn't matter how hard I work, how much I do. You'll never have faith in me!"

More than her words, the tone of her voice, its bitterness, was worse than any insult I'd ever endured from my ladies. What had I ever done for this girl but house her, feed her, clothe her! My heart closed in on itself, curled into a ball.

I pointed a finger at her chest. "You're going to drink every drop of this before dawn arrives."

"I won't. I'll prove you wrong!"

She took flight as swiftly as a hummingbird. As she ran past me, her chiffon skirt brushed the hair on my arm. I tried to grab her, but I felt as if I were moving through water, and I only managed to rip the delicate fabric off her dress. I heard the slap of her bare feet in the courtyard and then she was gone.

I watched the flicker of blue on the Primus stove, heard the water boiling. I wouldn't need it now. I turned the burner off.

I crossed the room and fell onto the *charpoy*. It must have been after three o'clock in the morning.

This was a day that should have ended in celebration, full of hope for the future. Instead, I felt a void as wide and as deep as the river Ganga.

Without my parents to witness the long road I had traveled to get here, the struggle to build my house seemed pointless. In their place, I'd been sent Radha to look after, and I'd ruined her future, as well.

Where would she go at this time of night? Not to her lover surely? Who was he? If not the milkman, Mr. Iyengar or Mr. Pandey, who?

The teachers at the Maharani School were women. It couldn't have been the toothless old gateman? Impossible!

With a start, I thought: *Samir?* He had admired her beauty. But...no. Radha didn't fit his pattern; she wasn't a widow, and she was far too young, wasn't she?

Wherever Radha was going, she would have to walk. Everyone, including the *tonga-wallas* and the rickshaw-*wallas*, was in bed. Radha had no money to take a train or even a bus. Would she sleep in the street as she and Hari had done when they first came to Jaipur? She couldn't be going to Hari, surely?

Kanta would know. I should phone her. But how? At my lodgings I had used Mrs. Iyengar's telephone with her permission, but I couldn't afford a phone line here. The post office, where I sometimes paid a princely sum to use the phone, was closed.

If Radha didn't return by morning, I would send Malik to Kanta's with a note. I sighed. Another embarrassment. Girls from good families didn't run away from home. Which is probably what the gossip-eaters had said about me thirteen years ago.

The next morning, there was still no sign of Radha. I hadn't slept all night. I kept picturing her out in the streets, alone. I saw myself at Radha's age, too shy to look at boys or men, much less talk to them. Maa had made sure of it: *Men will eat even unripe fruit if it's placed in front of them.* When had my sister stopped heeding such warnings? Or had Maa been too dispirited by my desertion to teach Radha the same things she taught me? She might have felt that since her advice hadn't kept me dutiful, it wouldn't work on my sister, either.

I tried to imagine a past where I stayed with Hari, allowed myself to have children, watched Radha grow up with them. Would it really have been so bad? Radha would have been safe. She wouldn't have ended up in this unfamiliar city, lecherous men at every corner.

When Malik showed up at dawn to work, I sent him immediately to Kanta's. I kept myself busy, packing the tiffins we'd need for the day. In less than an hour, I heard a car outside. I ran to the window. A large gray sedan had stopped in front of my house. Baju was at the wheel. He got out and opened the back door. Malik stepped out and turned to help Kanta out of the car.

Within seconds, I was out my door and through my gate. When she saw me, Kanta cried, "Lakshmi!" Her face was ashen.

My heart hammered in my chest. *Oh, Bhagwan, let Radha be safe! Don't let anything happen to her!*

"She's at my house. She's fine. But I'm the worst kind of auntie! How could I not have known or at least—"

As soon as I heard her say *fine*, my body relaxed. Radha was all right.

Kanta was speaking loudly enough to draw the attention of my neighbor, who had come out of her house and was pretending to water a scrawny lemon sapling in her yard.

"Kanta!" I said sharply. "Come inside for tea."

Chastened, Kanta shut her mouth and allowed Malik and me to usher her inside. Baju returned to the car.

No sooner had I closed the door behind us than Kanta started to wail, her arms hugging her belly. "If I'd only known what it was doing to her! But I thought exposing her to Western ways would prepare her better—you know, for modern life, womanhood. I thought of it as an education! I was so impressed with my own forward thinking! Thought you'd be pleased, too. I never— I didn't realize—"

I lit the kerosene lamp with shaky fingers. "What did Radha tell you?"

"Everything." Kanta started to breathe in ragged gasps, as if the air had suddenly become too thin. "It's terrible."

I saw now she had been crying for some time. The skin around her eyes was swollen. Her skin was sallow. Guiding her by the shoulders, I eased her onto the *charpoy* and sat next to her.

Malik poured a glass of water from the *mutki* and handed it to Kanta. Then he went to the Primus and lit the stove for tea.

The air in the room was stale with scents from the move-in ceremony the day before, but I dared not open the windows in case my neighbors overheard us. Kanta brought with her a scent even more oppressive—fear.

"She— I— Oh, Bhagwan! Where do I begin?" She put

her hand to her forehead. "Those novels of mine, the English ones she reads to me. I was thinking, 'These will help her with English. They'll teach her things about the larger world. And she can best those snobs at her school.' And the films I took her to! Oh, God! I didn't know she would confuse a story in a book or film with her own life."

I closed my eyes. Radha's imagination, shut tight six months ago, had been pried open. Without parents to quash her dreams of romance, her imagination had allowed her to turn fiction to fact.

Kanta was older than Radha and should have known better, but I was, after all, the one responsible for my sister. What kind of steward had I been?

Kanta was still railing. "All that talk of love and romance. Fine for English girls, but not for Indian ones." She sounded like her *saas*. "I should have realized how young she is, how impressionable. She takes everything to heart, absorbs it like a sponge! And she learns so quickly—it flattered me that I was her teacher. We were having fun…"

I turned away from Kanta; I couldn't let her see me fall apart. I looked down at the map of my life on the terrazzo as my tears blurred my vision. The pattern mutated. The shapes shifted into something I no longer recognized.

Kanta choked back another sob. "Oh, Lakshmi! I can't believe our Radha is carrying a child! She hasn't told me who the father is. She wants you to be there when she does."

Radha wanted to confess in public. Like the monsoon rains, so fierce they eroded our temple friezes, my sister was about to destroy the fortress I had built. No question about it: my life, as I'd designed it, was about to change. Plans, meticulously plotted, were about to unravel. The room spun. I lost my balance, gripped the window ledge to prevent myself from falling.

Malik ran to catch me, but Kanta got there first. She eased me to the floor.

"I filled her head with *bukwas*! Me and my books and my films and my magazines and my ideas. My pregnancy has made me starkers! That's the only way I can explain it. I thought it was all a good thing. And it's Radha who will pay the price. And you, Lakshmi."

She cried harder, and distractedly, I wondered if my neighbors would assume there had been a death in the family.

"I'm sorry," she said. "I'm so sorry."

She wound her arms around my neck, wetting my chest with her hot tears, but my body felt limp, wrung out. I couldn't comfort her.

TWELVE

April 21, 1956

Kanta and I sat side by side on her drawing room sofa. Radha stood in front of us as if she were facing a British inquisition. She wore a frock borrowed from Kanta; the Madhubala dress was ruined.

My sister glanced nervously at the carpet, then at us, then at the photos of Gandhi-*ji* and Kanta's newfound goddess, Swaraswati, on the wall.

"Go on, *bheti*," Kanta said encouragingly.

Radha licked the cut on her lip, the wound I'd given her last night. "I used to pass by the Jaipur Club every day on my way to Auntie's house from school. You know, the polo grounds, at the edge of the road?"

I started to speak, but Kanta put a hand on my arm to stop me.

Radha bit her cheek. "I would see him playing polo during the holidays, and one day, he saw me. He was walking his horse to the stables. He stopped and we started talking. He told me that he was working on a Shakespeare play at his school. And asked could I rehearse it with him? So that's what we would do. Sometimes for a half hour, sometimes an hour."

I clawed the piping on the sofa, trying to rein in my impatience.

"And one day he told me that I looked just like Madhubala." She blushed and looked away. "He said he had never met a prettier girl and he wished he could spend all his time with me. He thought about nothing but me all day." My sister flicked a glance at me, then back at the floor. "It was just like the movies."

Kanta groaned. My heart pounded.

Radha folded her hands in front of her. "I liked him. He apologized for the holiday party. The way his mother had talked to me. I told him I had gotten into so much trouble with you about it, Jiji."

The room was closing in. My vision narrowed.

"He said you were jealous of me." She eyed me from lowered lids. "Because you had no one in your life, and I did."

A cold sensation spread throughout my body. Radha's voice sounded faint, faraway.

She was talking about Ravi Singh.

When I come to, my head was in Kanta's lap and she was pressing the end of my sari to my forehead. It felt cold. I realized why: she had wrapped ice in it. Radha sat in the armchair opposite, rubbing her hands nervously on the upholstery.

I tried to sit up, but my head spun. Kanta guided my shoulder back down. I watched the slow *tak-tak-tak* of the ceiling fan. My brain was still reeling from the news that Ravi Singh was the father of my sister's baby.

"Of all the people in the world… *Parvati's son*?"

Radha looked frightened yet defiant. She looked to Kanta for support. "This is why I needed you here, Auntie. I knew she wouldn't understand, but you do, don't you?"

Kanta's forehead creased with worry. She opened her mouth to speak but nothing came out. She looked away.

My sister pleaded. "Make her understand, Auntie. He loves me. He cares for me. He wants this baby as much as I do—"

Hai Ram! Until now, I'd been hoping we could keep the pregnancy a secret if I could just convince her to use my sachets. "He knows about the baby? Already?"

As if she were talking to a child, Radha explained, "He doesn't know...yet. But when I tell him, he will be so excited. He told me I'm the only girl he's ever cared for."

"That's ridiculous! He's seventeen! You're thirteen!" I said.

Radha narrowed her eyes. "You told me that when I started my menses I became a woman."

"I didn't mean you were *ready* to have children!"

"Girls in our village have children at thirteen. Why can't I? They have whole families before they're twenty. I never had a family. Not really. With Maa sad all day. Pitaji drunk. And you—you ran away from Hari and only God knew where you were until I found you!"

At the mention of Hari's name, I looked helplessly at Kanta. When Kanta came to me this morning, I had told her about my past—Hari, the beatings, all of it. I told her more than I'd ever told anyone in my life. Although it had unsettled her, she had accepted it without judgment.

Radha hiccupped. "Ravi and I will be married as soon as he learns about his child. This is *his* baby!"

"Lakshmi," Kanta whispered, bringing a hand to her mouth. "What will happen when Parvati finds out?"

It was exactly what I'd been wondering.

Radha looked from me to Kanta. "Why would you be

worried about his mother? Ravi is the father. He's the only one who matters!"

I had not fully grasped how naive Radha was, how much of a secret fantasy life she had. How little I understood her feelings. How little I *wanted* to understand them.

I didn't *want* to have to talk to her about the things she must have wondered about. Like love. How did you know when you were in love? What did it feel like? What did *I* know of love? I'd never experienced it. I hated to admit that I couldn't have answered her questions. I'd hoped Kanta was doing that.

Carefully, I sat up on the sofa. Pain shot up my temples. "Radha, I'm sorry. It's my fault. I should have talked to you more... But listen to me now. You cannot marry Ravi Singh."

"No, no, no. I won't listen!" She was crying now, her mouth a grimace. "First you tell me I can't go to the palace. Then you put me in a school where they make fun of my hair, my accent, what I wear. What did I ever do to you? Why do *you* get to do everything you want in your life, but *I* have to do everything you tell me to?"

I knew she was angry about being kept from the palace, but I thought we'd moved beyond that. She had Bombay-style dresses now. A sleek haircut. She was learning Western dances and how to prepare an English tea party for eight—things I wouldn't even have known to teach her.

Perhaps it was the bewilderment on my face that made Radha jump out of her armchair and plop down next to me. She grasped my hands. Hers were wet from wiping her tears.

"Jiji, isn't Ravi everything you want in a husband for me? He's as handsome as a film star. He's educated. He's talented." It sounded like the list I'd made when I first proposed a girl for Ravi.

Oh, you foolish girl, I wanted to scream. Instead, I kept my voice low. "Radha, Parvati Singh will never let her son marry you. She won't let him be married at all until he graduates from university."

She tightened her grip on my hands. "Auntie says love blossoms in the most unexpected places." She appealed to Kanta. "Didn't Mr. Rochester love Jane Eyre, Auntie, even though she had no money? And Lady Chatterley! Despite all her wealth, she loved a poor gamesman. And you, Auntie, you married Manu for love, not money. Why is it impossible for you to believe that Ravi and I can make a love match?"

Kanta cringed, closing her eyes. *"Hai Ram!"*

I sighed. "Because Parvati Singh will not allow a love match."

Radha flung my hands aside. Her voice bubbled with fury. "You don't care about *my* feelings. Or Ravi's."

I'd heard enough. "Kanta, tell her."

"If I'd known—"

"Tell her!"

Kanta's mouth twisted with sadness. She looked at Radha.

"Bheti," she said, "I would do anything to spare you. But when Sheela Sharma turns eighteen, she will be married to Ravi Singh. The Sharmas announced it at a celebration dinner two nights ago."

My sister looked stunned. She reached behind her, found the armchair and sat down.

Kanta said, "Manu and I were there. So was Ravi."

"But...he told me his parents would never arrange his marriage without his consent!"

"They did ask," Kanta said, "and he agreed."

Radha's eyes filled with tears.

"*Bheti*, did he actually say he would marry you?" Kanta asked, her voice kind.

My sister had retreated into herself. She looked so lost that I wanted to comfort her, but I knew she wouldn't let me.

"Ravi isn't who you think he is." I said it as gently as I could.

"You're just saying things to hurt me. You always do. Just like you never wanted me to find you. Never wanted me to live with you." She turned her red-rimmed eyes toward Kanta. "That's why I want a family, Auntie! She's not my family. Not really. Not in the way that counts! You and Uncle are more of a family to me than she is!"

Her words felt like a hammer blow. Kanta looked at me sympathetically.

No one said anything for a while. Finally, Kanta released a long sigh and stood. She went to sit on the arm of Radha's chair and lifted her chin with two fingers. "Listen to Lakshmi. She is your *jiji*. She has done everything she can to make sure you have a good future—the best. You cannot talk to her like that. Not in my house."

I looked at Kanta with gratitude. She had spoken up for me the way no one ever had. I turned to my sister. "Radha, I arranged this marriage. I did it so—"

"*You* did this to me?"

"I didn't *do* anything to you. I didn't even know you were—"

Radha blinked. "Wait! Ravi's marriage is years away! So much can change! And the way your ladies listen to you—perhaps if *you* talked to Ravi's mother, Jiji..." She was desperate to change her future, as I'd been at fifteen.

I shook my head. "Parvati had her son's future mapped out before he cut his first tooth. It was the same with her and Samir and with all generations of Singhs."

Kanta gasped. "What if—if he doesn't claim the baby—"

"Radha doesn't have to have it."

"No! I will not do anything to harm this baby! You may do that to other women, but you won't do it to me!"

The shock on Kanta's face told me another secret was out.

I turned to face her. "Kanta, don't tell me you haven't

known women who had abortions. Who fell in love and didn't take heed of the consequences. What about at university? In England?"

Kanta covered her mouth with her hand, staring first at me, then at the floor.

Radha waited, her eyes imploring my friend to side with her. In the silence, the whirring of the ceiling fan grew louder. After a pause, Kanta squeezed my sister's shoulder gently and nodded. "They went on to marry later, often someone else. And have other children."

Radha just shook her head. "No!"

"Lakshmi is doing the right thing."

But that wasn't what Radha wanted to hear. She squeezed her eyes shut. I could guess what she was thinking: *What has Jiji ever done but scold me and keep me from having what I want?*

Kanta put a palm on Radha's wet cheek. "Don't make that face. You're far too pretty. Lakshmi told me that she didn't know you existed until six months ago. She was shocked when you showed up, but it never occurred to her to turn you away.

"Look at me, Radha. Your sister has a very strong sense of responsibility, which I admire. You may be upset with her, but she has taken you under her roof. She has put you in an excellent school. You've become so sophisticated it's easy to forget you're only thirteen." Kanta tugged at Radha's frock. "Lakshmi hasn't had an easy life." Kanta glanced in my direction. "I understand why she left her husband. I also want you to know I don't judge you or your sister for what's happened. She has tried to teach you how the world works. She's tough—I've seen her with you. But that's her duty as your older sister. Whereas—" and here, she sighed "—*I* have been a very naughty auntie."

Radha sat up straighter and balled her fists. "But I've loved having you for an auntie! No one could have been better!"

"I'm very fond of you," she said. "But I'm not a responsible *jiji*. I had you read those books to me when you weren't ready for them." She grimaced. "I still can't believe how thoughtless that was. I was bored and I wanted company, and you were splendid company."

"I love those books!" Radha protested. "Where else would I have had the chance to read them?" She cut her eyes at me. "She never spends time with me. All she does is work!"

Each of Radha's accusations felt like a slap on my cheek.

"She has to support herself." Kanta took Radha's hand in hers. "And you. And Malik. She's brave, and she's very fierce. You two are a lot alike, you know."

Alike? I'd never thought Radha and I shared anything but the watercolors of our eyes.

"I'm lucky, Radha," Kanta continued. "I've never had to support myself. Never had to worry about money. Even now my father helps us out when Manu's civil salary falls short of our expenses. My situation is very different from yours." She sighed. "As much as I would like it to be different for you, it's not. You must think about money—how to pay rent, how to afford a new pair of shoes, food. As your sister has always done. I accept responsibility for what I've done, Radha. Your sister's not to blame. And neither are you."

Radha let go of Kanta's hand. "First Jiji arranges Ravi's marriage to someone else! Then you tell me to kill my baby?"

Kanta sat back. "I want you to have a good life, Radha." With a gentle motion, Kanta rubbed my sister's back. "*All* of us are on your side. But you're too young to be a mother. Your life has barely started, *bheti*. You can do so much more. More and more women—"

"Stop!" Radha sobbed. She squeezed her eyes, causing more tears to fall. Her cheeks turned pink.

Wearily, Kanta stood. "Let's leave it for now, Lakshmi."

The ceiling fan slowed, then stopped turning altogether.

Kanta grunted. "*Baap re baap!* Three times today already,

the electricity has quit. Only April and it's started to boil." She wiped the perspiration on her neck with her sari. "We will think of something. But for now we must keep our own counsel—you, me, Radha and Manu." She looked at me. "Radha can stay with us until we sort this out." She didn't look at either of us when she said this, probably to save us the embarrassment of acknowledging the wide breach between us.

Kanta pulled her *pallu* over her shoulders and tucked it into her petticoat. "Perhaps some tea will cool us all down?"

I thought back to the holiday party on the Singh estate where it had all started. Where Ravi and Radha had met. Where Samir had told me about the palace commission. At the beginning of that evening, I had felt hopeful; Radha and I would come to an understanding, as sisters. She was learning the ways of the city. I was helping her. But that night had ended altogether differently, in recriminations and hurt feelings.

I didn't need tea. I needed to clear my head. I made my excuses and left, noticing the relief on Kanta's face.

THIRTEEN

I'd asked Malik to cancel our appointments for the day. I had nowhere I had to be. So after leaving Kanta's house, I walked. For hours. Without a destination. I thought and thought. About my failures. I'd failed as a wife to Hari. Failed as a daughter to my parents. Failed as a sister to Radha. Failed, even, to finish my house. The courtyard was bare dirt; the back fence, incomplete. The fraying cot was still fraying. All I had ever wanted was work that sustained me. What would happen to that now?

I imagined the fallout from Radha's pregnancy. The whispers behind my back. Rumors that started first with servants, then spread like wildfire to my ladies. The nervous glances, the barely disguised scorn, the outright scoldings. I wouldn't be able to hold my head up anywhere. Even shopkeepers in the Refugee Market might refuse to cater to me. I grew more hopeless by the hour, wondering how I would pay Samir back for my loan if my ladies abandoned me.

By dinnertime, I found myself in GulabNagar, the Pleasure District. As in Agra, there was a house here to satisfy every taste, and every purse. First came the tumbledown shacks. Prostitutes with untidy hair and homemade petticoats leaned against the walls, or sat on chairs in open doorways: village girls of ten or twelve, runaways and orphans both, two to three rupees for the asking. Perhaps this was where Hari was spending his days. Helping these girls in a way I had failed to.

Past the shacks stood dignified bungalows, crumbling from age and neglect. Here, women were slightly older, kohl-eyed, hardened. They charged twenty to thirty rupees a night. As I passed, they stared—at my clothing, my hair, my sandals—and turned away. Another do-gooder sent to save them or their children from a fallen life.

Hardly, I was thinking, when I saw a young girl, heavily made up, in front of a red bungalow. Her cheap orange sari couldn't hide her swollen belly. As I came closer, she turned into a doorway. Was it—*it couldn't be*—Lala's niece? I was seeing things. But it made me wonder what had happened to the two servants Parvati had dismissed.

Soon enough, I came to the far end of the district, to the estates of wealthy courtesans—many of them Muslim. Like my old friends Hazi and Nasreen, these women were trained in the ancient arts of music, poetry and dance. They catered only to *nawab*s, royals and successful businessmen. They never opened their houses until evening and never to the public. A single night with them could cost a thousand rupees. They wouldn't have needed someone like Hari to help them; they could afford doctors, specialists. They could also afford to buy my hair oils, skin-lightening creams and, of course, my herb sachets—which Malik delivered monthly.

I kept walking. Half an hour later, I came upon the European

District, so-called because the French, Germans and Scandinavians lived here alongside well-to-do Indians. If not at his office or the Jaipur Club, Samir could be found here. Perhaps this had been my unwitting destination all along.

I looked for the trim, white bungalow. It was too small a property to employ a gatekeeper. I let myself into a tiny courtyard bordered by magenta roses. Their heady scent was strongest at this time of the evening.

The steps leading to the veranda were wide and graceful. When I knocked, I heard one of the upstairs shutters open. I stepped back and looked up. A handsome young woman in a georgette sari opened the second-floor window. I smiled and brought my hands together in greeting.

She hesitated. "I'll come down."

Soon enough, she was at the door: Samir's mistress, Geeta.

All of Samir's women had the same things in common. They were widows of a certain age, neatly coiffed, trim. Women who powdered their faces.

Samir would have thought a garden with only a single variety of flower dull, and his women differed in height, breast size, the shape of their noses, the curve of their lips. Geeta, a widow in her early thirties, was blessed with eyes as large as areca nuts. Her small nose and delicate mouth, pretty but unexceptional, drew even more attention to her eyes. She was holding a book in one hand.

I said, "I'm sorry to disturb you at this hour."

She looked beyond me to the street, glancing in both directions. "Come in," she said, opening the door wider to let me in.

"I need to speak to Samir Sahib," I told her.

"Leave it with me."

She thought I'd brought sachets.

"I haven't come for that." I smiled. "I need to talk to him."

There was a pause. "He's not here."

"Is he expected?"

Another pause. "Later."

"May I wait?"

She set the book on a table in the entryway. Did I detect a sigh? "Of course. Please." She indicated the drawing room.

The moment I stepped into the room, I felt as if I might faint. Blood rushed to my head. My legs ached. I leaned against the doorframe to steady myself.

Geeta grabbed my arm. *"Hai Ram!"* She looked worried. "Are you quite all right?"

I realized I hadn't eaten all day and that I had fainted at Kanta's house. I touched the bump on my forehead. "Perhaps I will take some juice. *Nimbu pani*, if you have it." I eased myself into a French bergère chair.

"Of course."

I smiled my thanks, and rested my head against the back of the armchair.

On the fireplace mantel, a clock ticked, then trilled, delicately. It was decorated in an emerald green enamel, and it was much finer than the heavy English clocks many of my ladies favored.

"It's French," said Geeta, setting a glass of sugared limewater on the table next to me. "My late husband was a Francophile. The English were never good enough for Jitesh. In the end, he was proved right." She smiled, revealing charming dimples, and I could see why Samir was drawn to her. She took a seat on the sofa.

I took one sip of my drink, then gulped down the rest; I hadn't realized I was so thirsty.

"Another?" She stood, but I shook my head.

"Thank you, no. I'm feeling a little... If it's not too much... perhaps I could lie down, *Ji*?"

"Are you ill?" She took the glass from my hand. "I can send for someone if you wish."

"*Nahee-nahee.* I work too much...and forget to eat."

I could see she wasn't happy about it, but she led me upstairs, into a room that must have been guest quarters. There were no photos in it, no paintings or books. The walls were painted a pale yellow. The furnishings, a narrow bed with an ornate headboard and a dressing table, were French Empire. I lay down on the bed and closed my eyes. Unlike the hard jute of my cot, the feathered mattress gave way, and I slept.

I was awakened by a sharp click. I opened my eyes to see Samir closing the door. He sat next to me on the bed and placed a hand on my arm. His brows were drawn. "What's happened? Are you hurt?"

I didn't know where I was or how I'd ended up here. The room was dark. Was I dreaming?

"What time is it?" I was groggy with sleep and shut my eyes again.

He turned on the bedside lamp and checked his pocket watch. "A quarter past twelve."

I sighed.

"What's the emergency?"

Reluctantly, I opened my eyes. He brushed the hair away from my forehead to examine the swelling. His face was inches from mine. I could see the copper rim of his irises, their olive centers. How long his eyelashes were! And the feathered lines at the corners of his eyes—deeper now that he was frowning. I reached up to smooth them with my fingers and let my hand linger there. I caressed his cheek, the skin soft but the whiskers rough against my fingertips. I trailed my thumb across his lower lip.

He watched me with a puzzled smile.

I smiled back. He always made me feel safe. He was my comfort, made the big problems go away. Like when the owner of the Rajnagar land didn't want to sell to a woman,

Samir had stepped in and talked him into it. And when he loaned me money for herbs when I first arrived in Jaipur. He was on my side, always.

I parted his lips with my thumb and felt the wet flesh inside. Still looking into my eyes, he licked my thumb with his tongue. When my breath caught, his lips closed around it and he sucked. My belly tightened. I flattened my hand against his chest, feeling the *thaka-thaka-thaka* rhythm of his heart. The top two buttons of his chest were open. I slid my fingers through the opening and trailed my fingernails on his chest, felt his heart beat faster.

He leaned closer and brushed his lips along the low neckline of my blouse. My breasts swelled. My back arched. My skin grew warm.

I kissed him. He kissed me back.

I pulled his shirt out of his trousers and dug my nails into the muscles of his back. He undid my blouse, snaking a finger along the elastic of my bra until he found the hooks in the back.

His tongue was warm and wet on my nipples, sending an electric charge between my legs. My entire body hummed—the soft flesh under my armpit, my belly button, the tender place inside my thigh. I pushed Samir to sitting. I lifted the shirt over his head and kissed his nipples. He groaned. *So this is how it feels. This is what* she *feels.*

We rolled over on the sheets and I straddled him. Pulling down the zipper of his pants, I stroked him. He moaned and sought my lips. He kissed me hard, and kept on kissing me, his tongue exploring my mouth, my tongue, my neck, the underside of my breasts. He loosened the drawstring of my petticoat so the pleats fell out and my sari unwound around us. Out came my notebook and my pouch, my pocket watch. Samir swept them off the bed. He took off his trousers. His thighs squeezed mine. I pulled on his mouth with my teeth, inhaled his cardamom breath. He turned me on my side and flattened himself behind me, his stomach pressing my buttocks, his lips on my earlobe, my shoulder, his hand stroking the warm skin between my legs, rocking me back and forth, back and forth, like water lapping the riverbank. As he entered me, I could no longer think, only feel pleasure. I no longer felt bound to my body, or to the bed. I felt everything and nothing at once.

I awoke with a start, unaware I had fallen asleep again. Samir was getting dressed.

For the past hour, I had shut everything out except desire. I hadn't told him what I'd come here to say.

When he saw me watching him, he smiled and pulled me to standing. He helped me into my petticoat and bra. He hooked the eyes on the front of my blouse.

What I was about to say could change everything between us. Where should I start?

He pulled my sari, wrinkled now, off the bed, gathered it and began tucking it into my petticoat. His movements were sure, exact, as if he had done this a thousand times—no doubt he had. He straightened the *pallu* across my shoulder and took a step back to inspect his work.

He smiled, leaned in for a kiss.

I put my hand on his chest to stop him. "Samir."

He cocked his head, bemused.

"There's something..."

He raised his eyebrows.

When I failed to say anything, he felt for the cigarette case in his trouser pocket, lit a Red and White. I watched as he took a drag and blew out a stream of smoke. Then he sat on the bed and spread his hands in a gesture that said he was listening.

I cleared my throat. "Your son and my sister...have been..."

I glanced at the scrambled sheets on the bed and he followed my gaze. "Spending time—together…like this."

He looked at the bed, then narrowed his eyes at me. He smiled tentatively; he thought I was joking.

"They met at the holiday party." I pressed my lips together. "She's pregnant."

"What? Who?"

"My sister, Radha, is pregnant."

"Pregnant?"

"Radha is pregnant. Ravi is the father."

"Your sister's only…"

"Thirteen."

"But—how do you know it's Ravi's?"

It was a reasonable question, though it was maddening to have Samir ask it.

Radha had been so secretive that I, too, had asked myself the same thing. But I saw the way her face glowed when she talked about Ravi; it was answer enough. Still. It was one thing for me to doubt my sister and another for Samir to do so.

"I believe her. But you should ask your son."

"No, no, no, no, no!" He stood, shook his head and pointed his lit cigarette at me. "We've had trouble with servant girls before."

Servant girls. The words hung in the air. Is this how Samir thought of Radha? Of me?

We've had trouble with servant girls before. This wasn't the first time?

I felt the words in my mouth before I could give them a voice. "Is that why Parvati got rid of Lala's niece? *And* Lala?"

He shot me a furtive glance before looking away.

Hai Ram! My body shook with anger. "Is this how you take care of your problems? Remove them from sight? While your son continues to—to— I didn't believe Radha at first! But she was telling the truth. I—"

"*You're* the one who let it happen." He frowned. "She's *your* sister."

"And your son? Who's responsible for him?"

He turned away, studied the carpet, smoked. "Can't you get rid of it? I mean, isn't that what we pay you for? To take care of this kind of thing?"

Just an hour ago I'd imagined Samir coming to my aid. I'd pictured us working through this together. More fool, me! Of course I'd already suggested terminating the pregnancy. But coming from Samir, it sounded heartless. Is this how I'd sounded to my sister?

I looked down at my hands, rubbed them together. "I offered my sachets, but she said no. She thinks Ravi is going to marry her."

"Rubbish! He knows better than that."

"Does he?" I frowned at him. *"As is the king so are his subjects?"* As soon as I said the proverb, I knew it was true. There had been servant girls in Samir's past, too.

He avoided my eyes. Ash from his cigarette fell on his shirt, but he didn't notice. He pointed to the bed. "So that's what all this was about?"

"This?"

"What we just did!"

"No!" I massaged my temples. "You think I'd come to the home of your mistress to—for this…so you would—what? Make Ravi marry my sister? Give me money to keep quiet?"

He dropped his eyes and released a strangled breath. "Lakshmi, this is all such a shock. I… Marriage is out of the question."

That's what I'd said to Radha. I lowered myself, slowly, on the stool in front of the dressing table.

"Have you talked to Ravi?"

I looked up at him. "I think that's for you to do."

Samir scratched his neck. "Where's your sister now?"

"With friends."

Some of the tension drained from his face. He stabbed his cigarette in the crystal ashtray on the bedside table. "The Sharmas..."

"The Sharmas." How ironic. I'd finalized the match between Sheela and Ravi by suggesting a solution everyone found agreeable: Samir would design a house, separate from the main residence, on the Singh estate for Sheela and Ravi. Mr. Sharma would build it. Yet, all the while I was plotting and planning, Ravi and my sister had been— How could I fault Samir for blaming me when I blamed myself?

Samir lit another cigarette and inhaled deeply. He sat on the bed once more, facing me. "All right. What do you suggest we do now?"

"Radha won't agree to an abortion, but she might agree to an adoption. An orphanage is out of the question. You and I know those places are little better than a prison."

Few Indian families ever adopted; the majority of children stayed in care homes until they came of age. It might have been different if couples didn't think it was so shameful to admit they couldn't conceive. "But there is *one* family for whom adoption is a way of saving face, not losing it." I pressed my hands together, brought them to my lips. "The palace is looking for a new crown prince to adopt."

"You mean—"

"The maharaja banished his natural son to England because his astrologer told him to *adopt* the future ruler. Radha's baby will be a perfect candidate for adoption because Ravi's son will have royal blood from Parvati's side. He'll be cared for, sent to the best schools, given everything. An orphanage can give him nothing. Don't you want that life, and not the other, for your son's child?"

He made a face.

"The Maharani Indira is very fond of you, Samir. She trusts

you. A word in her ear is better, even, than speaking to the maharaja. She'll make it seem as if the idea came from her."

"Ravi is my son. What you're asking me to do will expose him—"

"He is the *father* of Radha's baby." I glared at him. I hadn't meant to raise my voice.

Samir's nostrils flared in anger, whether at me, Ravi or the truth, I wasn't sure.

"I, too, want the matter to be kept private, Samir. But we need a blood test from Ravi to prove paternity and bloodline. That way, you'll also know Radha is telling the truth."

I turned around on my stool. I watched him as I plaited my hair in the dressing table mirror. I knew he was thinking of the Sharmas—whether he could keep the secret from them, how the Singh name would be tarnished if he couldn't.

And the Rambagh Palace contract? If his clients found out about an illegitimate baby—or if members of the Jaipur Club did—it could jeopardize his livelihood and his very place in society. For a decade, Samir had been my friend and business partner. Always easygoing, jolly. Lifted my mood whenever I saw him. Yet, I doubted now how well I really knew him. Was I looking at the real Samir in the mirror, the one who cared more about his social status than the lessons he was teaching—*or not teaching*—his son?

He cleared his throat. "If she won't agree to an abortion, what makes you think she'll agree to an adoption?"

"She may not." I shrugged. "But as her legal guardian, I can force the issue." I met his eyes in the mirror. "And I will."

I wound my hair into a bun on top of my head and began inserting the pins to hold it in place.

He smoked. "They're very careful with these royal adoptions. All legal guardians are required to sign the contract. I'll have to tell Parvati."

At the mention of her name, the hairpin I was holding

slipped and scratched my scalp. I cleared my throat. "Do what you must."

He spread his palms wide. "Because of the bab—" I could tell by the twist of his mouth that the very word was distasteful to him. "We'll have to send Ravi to England sooner than we'd planned. The farther away he is from scandal, the better. It would be all too easy for this one mistake to taint the rest of his life."

"And Radha's reputation?" I shot back. "Won't this taint the rest of her life?" The blood in my veins boiled. I was disgusted with *this* Samir, the one who gave no regard to my sister's future.

He was immediately contrite. He wanted the women in his life to love him, adore him, look up to him. "Lakshmi, I—I'm sorry. This has come as such a shock. I had no idea they were… Of course, she's young, your sister—"

He put a hand on my arm—to console me? I flung it off, furious. His mouth hung open. The look on his face was one of surprise, as if I'd slapped him.

I rose from the bench, consumed with loathing for him and for myself. What light work I had made of infidelity, for him and his friends to cheat on their wives for ten years! I'd helped them discard their mistresses' pregnancies as easily as they discarded the lint in their trouser pockets. I had justified it by treating it as a business transaction. To me, each sale had been nothing more than another coat of plaster or another section of terrazzo for my house. At least when I made sachets for the courtesans, I had done so for women who had been raised to be prostitutes, who needed to make a living from their bodies without the interruption of pregnancies.

My skin felt prickly. I remembered all the places Samir had touched me, kissed me, caressed me, and I shuddered. All at once, I wanted to get as far away from him as possible.

I looked for my notebook and pouch and slipped them into my petticoat.

"Look, I know I was wrong to— Lakshmi, please don't leave like this..."

I would never be able to look at Samir again without feeling disgust and shame. I could barely stand to be in my own skin. I walked to the door.

He followed me. "What if—what if the baby is a girl?"

I didn't have an answer. I kept walking.

I doubted he would agonize too much about what had happened. He would shake his head, and his life would go on, as before. On his next visit to the elder maharani, she would welcome him with a smile, and he would charm her with a joke and a gift of *bwachi* hair oil. His son, Ravi, who already showed signs of growing up to be just like him, would continue to bed young girls too innocent to know he did not care enough.

When I stepped out of the room, Geeta moved out of the shadows, startling me. I'd forgotten about her and about the sheets Samir and I had soiled in her house. She was standing so close I could see her eyelashes, wet and clumped.

When she spoke, her voice trembled. "You will not come again." It was not a request.

"No," I said. I went around her, down the hall and out into the night.

FOURTEEN

April 28, 1956

I knew Kanta objected to my business with the cotton root bark and, in her heart, she wanted Radha to give birth. Moreover, she felt responsible for Radha's predicament and wanted to help by taking her away from Jaipur to have the baby.

So I didn't protest when Kanta asked to take Radha with her to Shimla, where she went every summer to escape the Jaipur heat and dust. This year, she decided to leave at the beginning of May, a lot earlier than planned.

Two letters arrived the following week.

May 2, 1956

Lakshmi,

The Maharani Indira will meet with you. I have broached the possibility of a royal adoption with her, but I will leave the details to you. If she agrees to it, the palace will require a royal physician to monitor the progress of the pregnancy and to see to it that the mother's health is not compromised in any way. You told me that Mrs. Kanta Agarwal is taking Radha to Shimla to have her baby, and I was thinking of asking Kumar to serve as proxy for the royal physician there. Would that be agreeable to you? The royal physician has drawn Ravi's blood. The baby's has to match.

I made some calls on Ravi's behalf. This week, he leaves for England. He'll complete his studies at Eton.

Samir

The second letter was from Hari. It was the divorce decree I had sent to him. He had signed it. I showed it to Malik.

"He'll never bother you again, Auntie-Boss." Malik grinned. "I've taken care of it."

He refused to tell me more.

At the doors of the Maharani Indira's salon, Malik pointed to my sari to remind me to cover my head. Then he pinched my cheeks, startling me. "For color," he said. He knew I was anxious about my meeting with Her Highness, and he was trying, in his way, to boost my courage. I knew my eyes were puffy, and there were gray half-moons underneath them. I'd spent a week of restless nights, sick with worry about what the maharani would decide about Radha's baby. My hair had gone a week without being oiled and the flyaway strands would not be tamed.

For the tenth time, I reached in my petticoat to check my pocket watch before remembering that I hadn't been able to find it at home.

The attendant beckoned me inside. The Maharani Indira

was sitting on the same sofa, in the same position, as the first time I met her. The younger maharani had made a complete recovery and my services were no longer required at the palace. I had not seen either maharani for several weeks.

Now, as then, Her Highness was playing patience, her cards arranged in rows on the low mahogany table. Today, she wore a sari in marigold yellow silk and a matching blouse patterned with taupe leaves, large and small. Her neck was adorned with five strands of pearls clasped in the middle with the largest amethyst I'd seen.

Madho Singh was in his cage, making quiet noises that sounded very much like grumbling. His door was open.

I greeted Her Highness with a *namaste* and reached for her feet. She gestured to the adjacent sofa. She was faring better with her cards today. Most lay faceup, in orderly rows, a good sign.

"Madho Singh has been very naughty today," she said. "He was stealing cards during our bridge game." She turned to glare at him. *"Badmash."*

The parakeet paced nervously on his swing with his head down. "Naughty bird." He sounded miserable, stretching out each syllable as if to emphasize the depth of his regret.

The maharani looked at me but tilted her chin at the bird. "He's as peculiar as his namesake. For King Edward's coronation, my late husband insisted on taking water from the Ganga to avoid bathing in 'filthy English water,' as he put it." She laid a ten of clubs on a jack. "To make matters worse, he carried the water in those preposterous silver urns. I knew the English would make fun of him, but did he listen?" She turned a baleful eye on the parakeet.

"Naughty bird," Madho Singh repeated, as if he had been responsible for that idiocy, as well.

She turned her gaze to me. "You look unwell, my dear,"

she said with what seemed like genuine sympathy. "You must take better care of yourself."

"I'm fine, Your Highness. Only a little tired."

There was a crystal bowl filled with salted pistachios on the table to the right of her card game. The maharani selected a few and rolled them in her palm. Throwing her head back, she tossed a nut in her mouth, expertly, and chewed, studying me. She, at least, looked rested and refreshed. I heard she had recently returned from Paris.

"You've pulled off an amazing feat in a very short period of time, Mrs. Shastri. The maharaja is impressed. Latika has recovered, again, full of energy and purpose. Almost every day she leaves the palace to officiate at functions, or kiss babies, or cut ribbons. She's been inaugurating government centers for the unfortunate. And I—" she tossed a second pistachio in her mouth and chewed "—am free as a *oiseau*." She chuckled.

"I'm pleased to be of service."

"Before Samir suggested your work with the maharani, His Highness was thinking of sending Latika to Austria to see a specialist. What an embarrassment that would have been! I believe you would agree that a family's dirty laundry is best cleaned by its own?"

Bilkul, I thought, but said nothing.

An attendant brought the tea service and poured. During my previous visits, she had waited to drink until the tea had cooled, but today Her Highness took a sip right away. I had eaten nothing, and my body welcomed the chai, infused with hints of vanilla and saffron.

"And so we come to another bit of dirty laundry. Samir Singh tells me there is a baby, due in October, out of wedlock. A baby of royal blood. Whom we might consider adopting as the crown prince."

She waited a few moments before resuming.

"How could we be sure of his lineage? A blood test will

prove it, he assures me. When I ask for more details, he says I must talk to you, my dear. Now why would Samir continue to intercede on behalf of a woman we know only as a henna artist?"

I felt my neck flush with heat.

The maharani continued. "I begin to think your talents may extend beyond your art." Her gaze dropped, pointedly, to my stomach.

I set my cup and saucer on the table. "The baby is not mine, Your Highness. It's my younger sister's, who is underage. I am her legal guardian. Because of my negligence, she spent unsupervised time with the Singhs' elder son, Ravi."

"Ah."

"The baby will be of Rajput blood and fine features, Your Highness. All the guardians involved are in agreement."

From the recesses of her sari, the maharani produced a fine linen handkerchief, and brushed the pistachio salt off her fingers. That accomplished, the handkerchief disappeared once again in the folds of her sari.

"I see," she said. She picked up her teacup.

"You know the Singhs well. You know their past, and pedigree, Your Highness," I said. "The Shastris are Brahmin. My sister, Radha, attends the Maharani School for Girls thanks to a generous scholarship from Maharani Latika."

"And how is she doing?"

"First in her class, Your Highness."

She sighed. "Pity."

I wasn't sure what she meant. "Your Highness?"

"I'd rather hoped it was yours." She grinned, then shrugged charmingly. "Very well. I have already spoken to His Highness. As Samir is a favorite, the maharaja has consulted his advisers and has approved the agreement—pending this interview and paternity tests, of course."

I exhaled a long, slow breath.

She pushed her saucer and cup to the side and beckoned the attendant who had been waiting discreetly. He laid a silver tray in front of her. In addition to a sheaf of papers and a fountain pen, the tray held a silver bowl filled with red-gold liquid, a small silver spoon and two cloth napkins.

The maharani reached into her bosom for a pair of half-moon spectacles. She put them on, and instantly looked more severe, which, I think, was her intention. Before handing the papers to me, she scanned them briefly, although I knew she must have scrutinized them, line by line, earlier.

I had never seen royal adoption papers, nor had I ever expected to. The contract contained phrases such as "the child's legal relationships," "permanent transfer of parental responsibility" and "forbidden access to birth family." A clause on page three specified the required physical attributes: birth weight, height and length, pulse rate and, of course, the baby's gender, which had to be male. Samir had asked, aloud, what would happen if Radha gave birth to a girl. I didn't know that he had an answer to that question any more than I did, but I refused to think about it. This may have been shortsighted on my part, but I knew Samir didn't want to consider the possibility, either, because he had let the matter drop.

There was a long clause specifying the royal physician's role. In particular, he needed to certify that the baby's sexual organs were healthy, and that his genital identity was unambiguous. This last, I realized, was to prevent a future *hijra* or intersex child in the royal family.

Page four made clear that if any of the aforementioned conditions were not met to the palace's satisfaction, the contract would be declared null and void, and the Jaipur royal family would be held harmless, and released from any monetary obligations, which obligations were specified on page six.

In addition to the cost of the labor and delivery, the birth mother or guardian was to receive thirty thousand rupees.

The numbers swam before my eyes. *Thirty thousand rupees.* Not once had it occurred to me that compensation might be offered. Thirty thousand rupees was enough to pay for a university education for Radha; she could study abroad. I read further: if the contract were canceled, for any reason, I, as her legal guardian, would be responsible for the hospital bills. I bit my lip. I would not entertain that possibility either because I simply could not afford it.

"I must ask, Mrs. Shastri." Her Highness's spectacles had slipped halfway down her nose. With her chin, she indicated the papers in my hand. "Do you not trust us to present a fair contract?"

My forehead felt clammy but I resisted swiping it with my sari. I was doing what was best for Radha, but this formal document made the relinquishing of her baby much more real than just talking about it.

"If it pleases Your Highness," I said with all the humility I could muster, "I've never before been given the responsibility of signing such important papers. I hope it won't offend you if I give the details their due."

"As you wish."

She began laying out a fresh hand of patience as I continued reading.

By the time I finished, the Maharani Indira had started on her third card game. I straightened the papers in a stack and set them on the coffee table, aligning them as perfectly as possible with the table's edges. The tea things had long been cleared. The maharani gathered her cards onto a single deck.

"Satisfied?" She smiled.

"Yes, thank you."

She adjusted her spectacles, uncapped the fountain pen and signed the papers quickly in the three places designated. Then she handed the pen to me. My first two signatures flowed with ease, as if I were doing nothing more than drawing with henna—nothing that would change, forever, who this child would become, what kind of life he would lead and how his destiny would be shaped.

Above the last signature line, however, my hand, so used to skating over skin, hovered. Instead of the relief I'd thought I would feel, I was seized by anxiety: I was giving away a life—a living, breathing person—as randomly as I had given my old saris to the beggar women in Choti Chuppar.

I was sending Radha's baby away, forever. He would not know his mother. He would be raised in a royal household with no blood relatives. Radha's son—*my nephew*—would be attended by two queens, each with her own reason to resent him. Maharani Latika would never forgive him for displacing her son, and Maharani Indira would be forced, once again, to accept a child into her family who was not her blood. When this baby awakened from a nightmare, his mother would not soothe him back to sleep with caresses, would not whisper sweetly in his ear, would not sing him lullabies as my father had done.

When this baby tried to take his first steps and failed, his real mother would not smother him with a hundred kisses, or stroke his cheek. The only substitutes for a mother's love would be devoted wet nurses, nannies and governesses. We could hope, but there were no guarantees.

How could this have seemed so logical a solution only a week ago?

The room was cool; I could hear the low hum of the air-conditioning. Yet, I was perspiring. The faint glimmer of a headache at my temples would soon explode into a throbbing pain. When I ran my tongue across my mouth, my lips were as rough as sand.

"May I have some water, Your Highness?" It was impertinent to ask, but I couldn't continue otherwise.

Her Highness looked at me curiously but gave the order. The bearer poured water from a crystal pitcher and handed the glass to me. For whatever reason, as I drank, I thought of Samir the night I'd told him about Radha's baby. The look of terror, anger and shame on his face. I thought of orphanages and boys and girls with lonely eyes and pinched mouths. A palace upbringing was surely preferable to that. There was no other choice available to me or Samir or Ravi or Radha. Before I could reconsider, I scrawled my name, and pushed the stack of papers far away from me.

The maharani removed her glasses and patted the cushion next to her. "Come, now, Mrs. Shastri. We will seal the contract." She turned her head slightly to include the parakeet. "You may join us."

Her tone signaled that Madho Singh had been forgiven. He flew out of his cage and landed on the tea table.

Her Highness spooned the red-gold liquid into her right palm, lifted the hand to her lips and sucked, expertly. Madho Singh crooked his neck to watch. He was expectant, nervous, hopping from one foot to the other. I assumed he'd been present at many such ceremonies.

The maharani wiped her hand on a clean napkin, poured another spoonful of liquid into her palm, and held it out to me. "Drink," she commanded.

I obeyed, slurping inelegantly from her hand. The liquid was odorless and slightly sweet. I raised my brows, not daring to ask.

"Liquid opium." She smiled, her eyes twinkling. "If it's good enough for the maharajas to seal a treaty, it's good enough for us."

Another, much smaller spoonful, she gave to Madho Singh, who licked with his black tongue until it was all gone. He fluttered his wings and squawked, "*Namaste! Bonjour!* Welcome!"

A strange calm descended over me. My headache began to recede.

"One more matter," Her Highness said, settling back against the cushions.

"Yes?"

"A man called Hari Shastri."

My heart sped up, and not, I was sure, because of the opium.

"Chef told me about a cousin-brother of his—named Shastri—a do-gooder, I gather. He's been helping the women of GulabNagar—a relief since we can't find doctors to attend to them. At Chef's request—pleading, really—I have agreed to finance Mr. Shastri's efforts. Everyone has a right to make a living, *n'est-ce pas*?" She grinned. "And Chef learned—almost overnight—to season my food just the way I like it. A jolly trade!"

So this was what Malik had been so cagey about. He'd bribed the palace chef (with promises of cheap cooking supplies, I supposed) into persuading the maharani to help Hari so he would stop asking me for money.

The maharani puckered her lips. "Shastri is not a name you come across often in Rajasthan. He wouldn't, by any chance, be a relation of yours?"

When I looked her in the eye, I didn't blink. "No, Your Highness."

She considered me a long moment before speaking. "As I thought."

FIFTEEN

May 6, 1956

We decided Kanta would be the one to tell Radha that we had an adoption contract. I'd been relieved to learn that Radha had been agreeable when Kanta brought it up. If I had brought it up with my sister, I doubt she would have listened to what I had to say. Kanta and I also agreed not to tell Radha that the Jaipur Palace was adopting her child. If she knew, I worried that upon her return to Jaipur, she might take to loitering outside the palace gates for a glimpse of her baby. (Samir had told me that before Radha left for Shimla, she had often been spotted outside the Singh compound, hoping to speak to Ravi.)

May 6, 1956

Dear Dr. Kumar,

Once again, we seem to be cooperating under difficult cir-

cumstances. Perhaps you'll recall our conversation from last December—in another strained situation—when you questioned whether my herbs had any medicinal benefit. Now it appears that my sister is more in need of your sort of medicine than mine.

Mr. Singh tells me you'll be acting as the proxy physician in Shimla on behalf of the Jaipur Palace, monitoring Radha's pregnancy and dispatching regular progress reports to the royal family. I only wish I could talk to you in person instead of by letter, but I hope to be present for the birth. I know you can appreciate how delicate her situation is and the need for secrecy—even, or especially, from Radha. I prefer not to tell her who is adopting the baby until—or unless—it's absolutely necessary.

Radha is thirteen years old. She has never had smallpox, measles or mumps. She is not allergic to any medicines or herbs, but she is partial to fried foods (perhaps you can persuade her that the baby may not be partial to them). She's a dedicated sleeper, and you can be assured she'll get adequate rest during her pregnancy. Her personality is generally cheerful, and she has a restless and curious mind. She loves to read, a habit that has both developed her imagination and given her some (very) worldly ideas.

You'll be in receipt of this letter by the time Radha arrives in Shimla. She is accompanied by my dear friend Kanta Agarwal, who is looking forward to meeting you and also being treated under your excellent care. Kanta's baby is due a month before my sister's, a happy circumstance, and the two of them are very close, which is a comfort to me. Kanta is familiar with the Himalaya foothills and with Shimla—her family has vacationed in the cooler mountain air before, when the summer dust of Jaipur triggers her asthma. Manu Agarwal, Kanta's husband, will be coming up for a visit every few weeks.

I shall be grateful to you, Dr. Kumar, for treating Radha as if she were your own sister. I place myself in your debt.

Until we meet again, please feel free to ask me any questions via post or through Mr. Singh by telephone.

Respectfully yours,
Lakshmi Shastri

SIXTEEN

July 23, 1956

I sifted through the mail. Another letter from Kanta. One from Dr. Kumar, whose letters were getting longer and arriving more frequently. Still nothing from Radha—although I never gave up hope. To my surprise, I missed her. Missed seeing her, sitting on the cot, cross-legged, frowning in concentration, absorbed in *Jane Eyre*. Or cooking *laddus* at the hearth, chatting happily with Malik. I wanted to tell her things. *Mrs. Patel has a new Alsatian puppy. Mrs. Pandey found a job selling sewing machines.*

The irony was that Radha penned Kanta's weekly letters; words on a page still made Kanta's head spin. So when I read Kanta's letters, I could imagine my friend dictating rapid-fire from a divan, chuckling, while Radha's pen raced to keep up. Then I could almost make myself believe the letter was from Radha.

July 18, 1956

Dear Lakshmi,

I would take Radha down to the Shimla Mall more often but she would just spend my money! I want her to appreciate the beautiful Tudor architecture around us, but she's drawn to baby trinkets like a rabbit to grass. Yesterday she brought home Himachali topas—the size is so big the cap will be wearing the baby instead of the other way around. (She's laughing!)

Thank Bhagwan my dust allergy has calmed down, as it always does when I come to Shimla. If I'd stayed in Jaipur for the summer, I wouldn't have been able to breathe. The doctor at Lady Bradley Hospital, Dr. Kumar (splendid fellow—just as you'd promised), says I must take it easy because I'm still spotting. So while Radha is climbing hills like a mountain goat, I must stay put on the sofa like a Himalayan bear. (I'm beginning to look like one, too, with all the rose milk I've had to consume!)

You'd be happy to see the pink in your sister's cheeks (she's blushing as I dictate this). Even her complexion is lighter. Last week, Dr. Kumar said her baby is an all-rounder—he'll be good at batting and bowling on the cricket field. Radha thought that explained what he's doing in her tummy all night, not letting her sleep. (I hope I did right by bringing Gray's Anatomy *with me so she could see how the babies are developing inside us. If you disagree, I'll put it away.) Every few days, Radha brings back an armload of books from the Shimla library—most are books the British left behind. By now her English is quite good, and I think your prediction that Radha may become a writer or a teacher someday seems more likely than ever (she's shaking her head).*

Well, Uma has just brought us our rose milk (don't tell my saas *that I've actually grown fond of the stuff) so it's off to bed for me. Radha says goodbye, too.*

Affectionately,
Kanta

P.S. Baju went to a letter writer and dictated a note, begging me to send him a passage to Shimla. He's threatening to quit because Saasuji is making him raving mad. See? I'm not the only one who wants to escape her clutches!

I passed the letter to Malik and opened the other envelope.

July 17, 1956

My Dear Mrs. Shastri,

In your letters you've mentioned how much Radha likes to read. You did not exaggerate! Last Tuesday, I ran into her as she was leaving the Shimla library—lugging half its contents in her carrier, which she was eager to share with me. If I remember correctly, there was a book of poems by Elizabeth Barrett Browning, The Canterbury Tales, *Shelley's* Frankenstein *and Thurber's* Fables. *I marvel at her eclectic tastes! I realize that I'm merely a doctor-for-hire, a temporary caretaker for your sister, not qualified to offer recommendations outside the medical realm, but I hope you will permit me one suggestion: private tutoring. Radha shows an unusual ability to grasp literary concepts and she can discuss Elizabethan poets with the best of them. It would be a travesty to let her fall behind in her studies because of her unfortunate situation.*

As I've repeatedly stated in my letters, I'm most interested in learning about the herbal therapies with which you've had so much experience. (Perhaps a belated apology is not entirely out of order—I refer to the cotton root bark.) It's worrisome that the hill people of the Himalayas rely solely on folk remedies when they could come to Lady Bradley for medical treatment. Yesterday, I saw a little Gaddi boy along the Mall with severe dermatitis, which his mother told me she'd been treating with tulsi *powder. Obviously, it wasn't helping. She refused to try the antiseptic ointment I suggested, even after I volunteered to bring it for her the next day. Perhaps you have an herbal recommendation that might prove useful? Your thoughts on the matter would be most welcome.*

Rest assured that your sister's pregnancy is progressing nicely. She's extremely healthy, enjoys robust exercise and eats well. It's a pleasure looking after her. I look forward to your next letter and your suggestions for bridging the gap between old world and new world medicine.

Your friend,
Jay Kumar, M.D.

P.S. Thank you for sending the mustard poultice. My cough is greatly reduced. However, my chest looked as if it had been dipped in batter and was ready for the fryer!

I made a note to tell him in my next letter to mix *neem* powder with rose water, resulting in a sweet-smelling antiseptic, a cure the Himalayan women would prefer to an ointment with a medicinal odor.

As I slipped the letter back inside the envelope, I said a prayer for the safe arrival of both babies—Kanta's and Radha's. Despite my skepticism, I had gained a little confidence in the gods, after all.

Outside, I heard the ring of a bicycle bell. At the front gate, the Singhs' messenger boy handed me a small parcel wrapped in brown paper.

The package was from Samir. My heart sank. Samir had tried several times to see me. He sent me notes. He even came to my house. I wouldn't let him in, so he talked to me from the other side of the door, apologizing for his words that night at Geeta's. He wanted everything to go back to the way it was. Maybe he wanted me in his bed again. Or he wanted to trade proverbs and hear me laugh again. Or maybe he simply wanted more sachets. I no longer cared to find out.

I untied the string on the package. It was a pen case, identical to the one I'd given Radha on her first week of school. Inside was the same orange marbled fountain pen I'd gifted her. *Wilson 1st Quality Fine.*

How had Samir ended up with Radha's pen?

I looked through the package, but found no note.

Radha's tepid response to my gift had hurt. *If I lose it, you'll be angry.* Had she lost it, after all? And, somehow, Samir had found it?

Then I knew.

She must have given the pen to Ravi, as a gift, when they were still meeting in secret. If so, why had he returned it? Or had Parvati made him do so?

Or maybe after she found out she was pregnant, Radha asked the Singh *chowkidar* to give it to Ravi, hoping he would meet with her. And Samir had returned it without showing it to Ravi.

Either way, Ravi's rejection must have seared my sister's tender feelings. The ache in my heart grew. "Oh, Radha," I whispered.

The following week, I erased Mrs. Gupta's name from my notebook.

Malik was standing in front of my herb table, in my

Rajnagar house, rolling a marble in his palm. "She said she's become allergic to henna," he said.

I stared at him in disbelief. "What? Mrs. Gupta has been a loyal client for six years! I did the bridal henna for her daughter—and she delivered a baby boy!" I frowned. "No one has ever become allergic to my henna."

Malik shrugged. He had grown six inches in the past six months, and the top of his head was level with my chin. He no longer looked to be eight, as he had told the Maharani Indira. I would have guessed ten. Since he didn't know, either, we pretended he was now nine. In any case, I needed to get him a haircut and new clothes.

"What about Mrs. Abdul? Her daughter has a birthday coming up."

"She sent regrets." He sent the marble shooting across the floor and ran to pick it up.

"Why?"

"She didn't say." He chewed the inside of his cheek. "Oh, and Mrs. Chandralal is going to Europe for the whole summer, so no appointments for her."

"The whole summer?" I sighed. "That makes five cancellations this week."

Henna appointments usually fell off in June and July, when many of my ladies fled the scorching desert for the mountains up north or to relatives abroad. But we were coming up on August. Where were the appointments for the Rakhi ceremonies when women wanted their hands to be decorated as they tied shiny bracelets on their brothers' wrists? In the fall I was usually busy with Dhussera and Bagapanchaka festivals for *mandalas*, but so far only two ladies had made an appointment. And there were no takers for Diwali, the festival of a thousand lights, when I was usually booked for two weeks solid.

Losing Parvati's business had come as no surprise. I hadn't heard from her since the day I ran into her outside Samir's office. Now that Samir had told her about Radha and Ravi, I knew I would never see her name again in my appointment book. Still, I could trust her to be discreet; with her political connections, she stood to lose a lot more than me if word got out.

But why were clients of long standing, who competed for the few empty spots in my notebook, canceling, or failing to book, their usual appointments? The curiosity-seekers, who wanted news of the Maharani Latika, didn't count. I'd always known they would stop asking for me when the novelty wore off; I was an expensive luxury.

I looked at Malik, bewildered.

He threw the marble in the air and caught it. "I'll see what I can find out."

Mrs. Patel remained loyal. She kept all her appointments. Arthritis had disfigured her hands, and she relied on me to disguise them with my henna. It was her only vanity. She also loved the *moong* bean *laddus* and cabbage *pakoras* I fed her to ease the pain in her joints.

Today, I was drawing a lotus flower in the center of her palm when she cleared her throat. "Is everything quite all right, Lakshmi?"

"Yes, *Ji*. Thank you for asking."

"There's no...money trouble?"

Aside from my dwindling income? Clients canceling daily with flimsy excuses? The fact that I now owed Samir ten thousand rupees—twice what I originally owed? And Parvati had yet to pay me the marriage commission? I almost laughed, but held back, realizing I might sound insane.

"Why do you ask?"

"One—well, one hears things." She sounded embarrassed and looked at the Alsatian who lay at her feet, the dog I had wanted to tell Radha about.

My heart picked up its pace. I drew *tulsi* leaves around her fingers. "Things?"

"Gossip is easy to spread."

My senses were on alert now. "What is it you've heard, *Ji*?" I asked as I drew third eyes for safety on the backs of her hands.

Her voice dropped to a whisper so the servants couldn't hear. "You have been accused of stealing."

I straightened my back, gazing at her with more calm than I felt. "By whom?"

"I've heard it from my cook, so the information may not be reliable. People say gold bangles have gone missing from Mrs. Prasad's. So has an embroidered sari—with silver work."

Who would spread such rumors? None of it was true, but that hardly mattered where rumormongers were concerned.

"A necklace vanished after you had been to Mrs. Chandralal's. That's what my *chowkidar* heard."

I frowned. "I've served those women for a decade. Why, suddenly, would I start robbing them? I don't need to steal—I have my own house."

She dropped her chin, looked at her hands. "Well..."

"Please."

"There's talk... How could you afford a house unless you were taking from others?" She put her hand, the one I hadn't started on yet, over mine. Her touch was cool. Either that, or my skin was on fire. I pulled away. "Lakshmi, I want you to know I don't believe a word of it. But I thought you should know what's being said."

If Mrs. Patel had heard these rumors from her servants, my other ladies had heard them, too. How long had they been circulating?

Deep in my gut, I felt fear. The Alsatian sensed it, and turned his head to look at me. "Why? Why're they telling lies?"

"Mrs. Sharma knows more than I, I'm sure. She always

does. I'm not at the club as often as she is." Her eyes were full of compassion.

I reached for her hand, the one I had almost finished painting. I tried, but failed, to hold the reed steady.

"That's enough for today," Mrs. Patel said quietly. "Go see Mrs. Sharma." She withdrew fifty rupees from the knot in her sari and held them out to me.

"But we're not done."

"There's always next time. Call it an advance payment."

She meant it kindly, but the charity angered me, nonetheless. I quickly packed my supplies. The dog got up off the floor.

"Next time," I said, avoiding her eyes, "will be my treat for not finishing the job today."

I didn't take the money. I wasn't even sure I said goodbye before leaving.

The Alsatian barked, once, as if in farewell.

The Sharmas' *chowkidar* was an ex-army man, smart in a khaki blazer and white *dhoti*. He greeted me politely at the gate. When I told him I'd to come discuss arrangements for the Teej Festival with Mrs. Sharma, he brushed both sides of his mustache with his forefinger, as if he were deciding whether to let me in. In the end, he nodded.

Mrs. Sharma had many daughters-in-law and nieces who looked forward to the Teej festival every August. It was a women's celebration, commemorating the reunion of Shiva and his wife after a hundred years apart. Teej was supposed to ensure wedded bliss. Given my experience, I remained skeptical of that promise, but I did enjoy the festival because it came at the start of the monsoon season, when the plants I depended on gorged themselves and gathered enough strength to produce the healing properties for my lotions and creams. And Mrs. Sharma's annual Teej party—a high-spirited affair where all the women in the family told stories, laughed, teased, sang and danced, while I applied henna to their hands—was always a joyous affair. Mrs. Sharma gifted each woman a silk sari and matching glass bangles. Every year, her cook outdid herself, creating more exotic and demanding delicacies than the year before.

With the festival only three weeks away, I'd been surprised, but not too concerned, that Mrs. Sharma hadn't made her usual appointment. Knowing she had a large household to manage and had been busy with Sheela's engagement celebration, I had penciled it in. Now, after what Mrs. Patel told me, I wondered if there was another reason for her delay.

As I mounted the steps of the veranda, goose bumps rose on my arms even though the summer sun was unbearable. My scalp felt as if it were on fire.

At the front door, the servant girl, who usually greeted me with a smile, raised her brows up to her hairline. It was clear that she, too, had heard the gossip. She asked me to wait—unusual in itself—and scuttled down the hall. I heard their murmurs—hers and Mrs. Sharma's—before the girl emerged and indicated the drawing room with a tilt of her head.

Mrs. Sharma was seated at her writing table, a sturdy lowboy with built-in drawers and brass pulls. She glanced at me when she heard me enter. Her gold-framed spectacles flashed, reflecting sunlight from the window.

"Ah, Lakshmi. I'm glad you've come. I just need a moment to finish this letter to my son." She turned back to her writing. "He says London is expensive and he needs more funds. Who knows where he spends it all?" She folded the thin blue aerogram. "Unless I reply urgently, he will fret that he is missing out on Coca-Colas with his friends."

She flicked her tongue on the edge of the aerogram to seal it. Then she removed her glasses, draping them on the silver belt around her waist, which also held keys to *almirahs*, jewelry boxes, the pantry and the exterior doors.

I took a handkerchief from my petticoat to dab the sweat on my forehead; I had practically run here from Mrs. Patel's with my heart in my throat. Just as I was wishing for something cool to drink, the servant girl brought in a tray with two tall glasses of *aam panna*. She left the mango drinks on the tea table and closed the door behind her.

Mrs. Sharma joined me on the sofa and offered me a glass. "It's one of our hottest summers yet, don't you think?"

She tilted her head back and, in one long swallow, gulped the whole of her sweet and sour drink. She was wearing another *khadi* sari and she mopped perspiration from her upper lip with the stiff *pallu*. The overhead fan was pushing hot air down, carrying the aromas of her talcum powder and sweat toward me. How a builder-contractor like Mr. Sharma could neglect the comforts of his own family, when every other wealthy household had long installed air-conditioning, was a mystery.

As if she had read my mind, Mrs. Sharma smiled, showing me her large, crooked teeth. "It's necessary for the body to perspire, Mr. Sharma always says. Helps rid the body of toxins."

I smiled politely and sipped my drink, wondering how to begin the conversation, and frightened of doing so.

"Even so," she said, mopping her neck, "I look forward to the monsoons."

"Yes." I realized she was giving me a way in. "Almost time for Teej."

Mrs. Sharma smiled. She wiped her mouth with her fingers and looked at the three porcelain dogs, chained to one another with gold links, on the tea table. The largest, obviously the mother, with painted eyelashes and red lips, gazed coquettishly at Mrs. Sharma, while the pups looked at their mother.

Mrs. Sharma spoke, still regarding the tableau. "Teej is a good time for us. With all my nephews married. And Sheela's marriage arranged, thanks to you."

There was always a moment before I placed the final dot of henna on a woman's skin that felt significant somehow. Never again would I repeat that particular design, and after a few weeks, it would disappear entirely. This moment with Mrs. Sharma felt final, and ephemeral, in the same way.

I shivered and set my drink on the table, afraid my teeth would chatter against the glass.

"What would you say," Mrs. Sharma began, "if I told you that the *mandala* you created for Sheela's *sangeet* party wasn't up to snuff?"

It was hard to conceal my surprise. While I decorated the hands of Mrs. Sharma's sisters-in-law, several of them told me they found the pattern both original and beautiful. "Might I ask what, specifically, was unsatisfactory?"

"It might not have been traditional enough. There should have been more colored powder used." She shrugged her broad shoulders, as if the reasons were inconsequential.

Was she asking me to criticize my own work? "But, Mrs. Sharma, you asked for something similar to my henna designs. You said, very particularly, that you wanted a different kind of *mandala*."

She puckered her lips and swiped her damp neck with the sari. "So I did. What if I told you that the henna was second-rate?"

I thought back to that evening. Had my paste been clumpy? No, I had used Radha's batch, the one with a consistently silky texture. All the products I used were first-rate and blended by my own hand or Radha's. Could Malik have said, or done, something to disturb the guests? (He'd never done anything untoward before.) But I remembered: he had barely begun working on the *mandala* before Sheela demanded that he leave.

Someone must have seen Radha trying to throw rocks at Sheela. But that had happened almost eight months ago; I would have heard about it through the servant network long before this.

I began carefully. "As you know, I inspect my work carefully, Mrs. Sharma. I have exacting standards. Did—did one of the ladies complain?"

Mrs. Sharma sighed. She pressed her palms on her thighs, arms akimbo, as if she were about to get up. "You've said exactly what I thought you might say, Lakshmi. And why should you say anything else? You are not at fault here. And I'm no good at telling lies. If I tried to make something up you would see right through it."

She hoisted herself off the sofa and walked purposefully to the writing table, where she unlocked a compartment with a key from her cord-cum-belt. She returned to stand in front of me, and held out an envelope that bulged at one end. I heard the tinkling of coins.

"Yours," she said. "Please take it." When I did, she lumbered back to her sofa and sat, heavily. "Parvati didn't have time to give you this before she went abroad for the summer. I've been lax getting it to you." No doubt Parvati had gone to England to keep Ravi from coming back to Jaipur.

The name and address of Singh Architects was printed on the upper left corner of the envelope. There was no addressee.

"She requested that I witness you opening it." Mrs. Sharma now looked sheepish. She focused her attention on the porcelain dogs again. "It's the marriage commission."

I broke the seal. Inside were one-rupee coins. I counted them. *Ten rupees?* I had a wild urge to turn the envelope upside down, to shake it, make sure there was nothing else inside. I tore it open wider.

It was empty.

I lowered my chin to my chest and closed my eyes to stop

the buzzing in my head. Parvati's aim had been to disgrace me in front of Mrs. Sharma. She knew the insult would be a thousand times more shameful.

Mrs. Sharma said, "Parvati asked me for one other thing..." Her voice trailed off. She lifted her glass to take another sip before remembering it was empty. Reluctantly, she set it down and looked at me. Her gaze was not unkind.

"I'm sorry to lose you, Lakshmi. Artists like you are hard to come by and you have served my family well."

She wanted to offer comfort; I heard it in her voice. Even the mole on her cheek climbed higher, as if trying to give me strength. "But Parvati claims you've been stealing. And while I do not believe her—would never consider such a thing—I must stand by her. You understand, I'm sure. When Sheela and Ravi are married, the Singhs will become part of our family. And whether I agree with Parvati or not, my hands are now tied to hers."

Parvati! I'd served her. Pampered her. Fawned over her. I'd handled Radha's pregnancy as delicately as possible for the benefit of her family and mine. I hadn't created a scene. I hadn't demanded money. After all that, *she* was telling lies about me? In retaliation for my sister's—and Ravi's, don't forget!—folly! Her son was as much to blame—*more*, since he was older. But Parvati was taking it out on *me*.

It was so unfair! I tried to hold back my tears, but I failed. *I've worked so hard*, I wanted to tell Mrs. Sharma. *I followed their rules. Swallowed their insults. Ignored their slights. Dodged their husbands' wandering hands. Haven't I been punished enough?* At this moment, sitting in front of this good, sensible woman, I wanted the thing I hated most in this world: sympathy. Even more, I hated that I wanted it. Hated myself for my weakness, as distasteful to me as Joyce Harris's self-pity the day I'd given her the sachets.

Oh, if not for Radha! Nothing in my life had been the

same since her arrival. She had been my personal monsoon, wrecking years of trust the ladies had invested in me, destroying a reputation it had taken so long to build. If not for Radha, I would never have had to grovel, in silence, in front of Mrs. Sharma. But I deserved it. I had committed the first sin, deserting the husband I should have stayed with for seven lifetimes.

Mrs. Sharma was eyeing me with concern. I needed to leave before I stained her sofa with my tears.

I cleared my throat and pressed my fingertips against my eyelids. As I stood to take my leave, I managed to say only, "Well."

Her last words to me were, "Go with luck, *bheti*."

SEVENTEEN

August 31, 1956

The month of August—scorching, blistering, unrelenting—dragged on. I opened my appointment book and flipped through the empty pages. August 15, the day of our nation's independence, had come and gone without a single booking.

With each passing week, I received more cancellations than appointments. Where I used to serve six or seven ladies a day, I now served one (and was lucky to do so). These days, the few clients I still had paid me less, without asking, and I took their reduced fees without complaint.

I had tucked Dr. Kumar's last letter in the notebook. I pulled it out and, for the third time, tried to finish reading it.

August 17, 1956

My Dear Mrs. Shastri,

I respect your wishes vis-à-vis Radha; I have not let her know the palace is adopting her baby, but I would like to discuss the matter with you further, realizing that the opportunity may not present itself until the baby's birth.

Radha will be kept under observation at the hospital for a week after the delivery. However, keeping her from the baby for that period of time may prove difficult. She's grown very attached to the life within her and talks about the baby constantly. I'm not sure she's fully reconciled to the idea that the baby is to be adopted. She understands the situation intellectually, but emotionally I feel she hasn't accepted it.

Your friend Mrs. Agarwal has assured me that Radha does understand the situation, and she believes it's only hormones that account for Radha's strong attachment to the baby. I have no better explanation, so for the moment I will rely on hers...

At this point in the letter, I always stopped reading. Radha had agreed to the adoption; I would not permit myself to think otherwise. The palace would raise her baby. We would be paid thirty thousand rupees, which would save us and pay for Radha's education. The baby would be healthy; it would be a boy. It would, because I did not want to talk to Dr. Kumar about any other possibility.

The monsoon rains, which came in early September, usually brought with them a feeling of relief. *Wash away the old; welcome the new.* This year, when the rains came, I felt only dread. With nowhere to go, my house became my prison, and all around me, I saw evidence of my failures. Water pooled on the bare dirt of the courtyard where I had planned to grow my herb garden. It bounced off the dried thatch that was to have sheltered my young plants. It dripped off the stacks of bricks I'd bought to build my back fence. I no longer cared to chase away the neighbor's pigs that rooted in my yard.

More often than not, I stood at my countertop for hours, mixing oils and lotions no one was going to use. The rhythm of the pestle was hypnotic and, like the constant rains, it soothed me. I stirred and thought about what I should have done differently. I should have kept a closer eye on Radha, whom I was supposed to protect. I should have refrained from sleeping with a man like Samir, who used women as callously as his son did. I should have demanded Parvati pay me up front for a marriage arrangement far more brilliant than the average matchmaker could have devised.

After leaving Mrs. Sharma's house, I had briefly considered confronting Parvati. For a decade I'd been in her thrall, circumnavigating her moods, inferior to her superior. The thought of challenging her face-to-face seemed a herculean task. I had a glimpse then of my father, how demoralized and inadequate he had felt when forced to confront the British Raj. The British always had the upper hand, and at some point Pitaji hadn't the energy to fight back anymore. He had chosen the coward's way out: a bottle of *sharab* every night, then eventually two or three per day.

I was taking the coward's way out, too: instead of confronting her in person, I talked to Parvati in my head. *It's your responsibility—not mine—to control your son! Look at the brilliant match I arranged for your family! And you repaid me by destroying everything I've worked so hard to achieve!*

My only other option was to retaliate by telling all of Jaipur that her son seduced my thirteen-year-old sister, but it wouldn't have helped. I would have come out worse, like a petty, vindictive crook. Even if the ladies believed me, they would be compelled to side with Parvati, one of their own. If their sons found themselves in similar straits (not that unlikely), they would need her support.

Malik visited me daily, even if we didn't have appointments, to make sure I was eating. Today, he wafted a tiffin full of curried dumplings under my nose.

"Won't you even try the *kofta*? Chef seasoned it with extra *jeera*." His lucrative side business, selling supplies to the palace kitchen at cut rates, still earned him five-star meals from the palace chef.

I said nothing. I wiped perspiration from my neck with my old sari and kept grinding.

"Auntie-Boss, please."

I told Malik I had no appetite.

He shook my shoulder. I shrugged it off.

"I told you! I don't feel like eating."

"Auntie-Boss?"

I turned to him, annoyed.

He tilted his chin at the door.

I followed his gaze.

Parvati Singh was standing at my threshold, a handbag slung over one arm, a dripping umbrella at her side. I had never, even in my dreams, expected to see her in my home. I released the pestle. It revolved around the inside of the bowl until it came to rest.

"May I come in?" she asked, her voice cool.

I watched Malik walk to the door and stand in front of Parvati, as if he meant to knock her down. She was forced to step back, in the corridor, to make room for him.

"Your shoes," he said.

I thought she was going to argue, but she bent to remove her wet sandals.

Just outside the door, he stepped into his *chappals* and, with his head held high, walked out into the street. He had no umbrella; the warm rains never bothered him.

Parvati took a moment. Then she walked through the entry, majestic once more, as if it were her house and not mine. She closed the door, and stood. I watched as she inspected the room: the scarred table where I mixed the lotions, my sagging cot, the battered carriers, the folded, fading blankets, the *almirah* with the uneven doors I had bought from a neighbor. I cringed, seeing my possessions through her eyes.

"Hmm," she said, "I'd expected..." She let the sentence hang.

She took a step toward me.

Instinctively, I took a step back.

She stopped.

Parvati set her handbag on the countertop and picked up a box of matches next to my lantern. "I had expected *you* to come to *me*," she said as she lit the lantern and turned up the flame.

Until then, I hadn't realized how dark it had grown inside. I stood still, unsure of myself.

"Always before you relied on me. Remember?" She blew the match out. "When you first came to Jaipur and you wanted to be introduced to society. Then to the palace. You're an ambitious woman. I don't hold that against you, you know."

I looked at her. It was hard to tell whether she was smiling or frowning.

"Now that your business is failing, I thought at least you'd ask me to—"

I couldn't believe what I was hearing! My hands curled into fists, and anger flared in my breast. "My business is failing because of *you*. And you want me to *beg* you to stop spreading lies about me?"

Her eyes narrowed and her mouth twisted, much as Sheela Sharma's did, in displeasure. "Did you for one moment consider," she said, "that those rumors didn't start with me?"

My surprise must have shown in my face.

"Not that I wasn't happy to fan the flames," she continued. "I had thought at least a portion of your clientele would think the accusations too ridiculous to believe. I was wrong.

People are more gullible, and less compassionate, than any of us want to believe, don't you agree?"

She reached into her handbag. When she pulled out her hand, her fingers were curled around an object. She slid her hand on the countertop toward me until her arm was stretched flat. Then she removed her hand.

The pocket watch Samir had given me lay between us.

Reflexively, I felt in my petticoat. It wasn't there, of course. I hadn't seen it for ages—hadn't needed to be anywhere on time. Images came unbidden to my mind—Samir's lips, his hands, our bare chests—from that night at Geeta's. I hadn't remembered picking up the watch when I left.

My courage evaporated—*poof!*—and my face flushed with heat.

Parvati shook her head in disappointment. "Geeta came to see me several months ago. Samir's latest." Her smile turned into a grimace. "Just how humiliating would it be for *you* to have your husband's *mistress* come to you for comfort, to complain he'd been unfaithful, not to you, but to *her*?"

I shut my eyes. I wanted to forget that night ever happened.

She began pacing the room, restlessly, the way she had paced in front of her hearth at the holiday party. She was rubbing the knuckles of one hand against the other. She stopped suddenly to study the terrazzo floor, tilting her head. "Hmm." She turned to me, nodded her head once, as if acknowledging my design.

She resumed pacing. "Samir needs to be loved. To be worshipped. Men of his type do. I understand. I accommodate him."

Was she trying to convince me, or herself?

"What does matter is that *you* betrayed me, Lakshmi. I trusted you. In my home. And with my husband. You assured me there was nothing between you."

It was only one night. I held out for ten years. I have no intention of repeating it. Nothing I said would have made any difference.

Parvati came to a stop in front of her handbag. She took out a heavy pouch and set it on the countertop. It tinkled, a sound that confirmed it was filled with coins.

"Here's what we'll do," she said, looking at the pouch. "I will give you the marriage commission. In silver, no less." She hesitated. "You earned it." She wasn't about to thank me.

When I didn't reach for the money, she said, "Ten thousand rupees. More than we agreed on." She smiled at me, and for the briefest of moments, I imagined she was offering me something more: apology, forgiveness, understanding, respect. I was surprised, and confused, by how much I wanted to be in her good graces again. I thought of Pitaji and of my fellow Indians, how they felt about the British after independence. Accustomed to subservience, they were more comfortable reverting to that role, however humiliating, as I seemed to be now.

"And?" My voice was faint.

"And I will tell everyone that the rumors were a mistake. I'll even hire you back for regular engagements. I'll help you arrange more marriage commissions. That's what you want, isn't it?"

I coughed; it was too good to be true. "What's the price?"

"You will stay away from Samir. Geeta told me about the business you roped him into—those sachets. Really, Lakshmi." She shuddered.

I tasted bile, bitter and hot, in my mouth. She thought *I'd* talked *Samir* into selling those sachets. She had no idea he'd lured me to Jaipur to sell them.

I kept my voice soft. "You talked to Samir, then?"

She cleared her throat, as if it hurt her to do so. *She hadn't.*

I looked at the pouch—enough money to pay back Samir's loan. I could agree to her conditions, and soon enough my notebook would be filled with the names of former clients. The privileged and the powerful would welcome me, once again, into their grand homes, invite me to sit on their divans and drink their creamy tea.

I heard my mother's voice: *a reputation once lost is seldom retrieved*. She was right. After his British employers labeled him as a troublemaker for his part in the independence movement, my father never recovered his reputation. He was branded for life.

My standing as a popular henna artist was soiled forever, too. Even if Parvati made good on her promise, the thieving scandal would follow me like a bad odor. When I came to their homes, the ladies would watch my every move, quick to blame me the moment a bracelet had been mislaid or money was missing from MemSahib's purse. And then what would I do? Go begging to Parvati—every time it happened—to convince them otherwise.

I realized, now, that as long as I remained in her debt, Parvati owned me, which was exactly where she wanted me to be.

I could say yes and keep my business intact—tarnished, but intact. Just like Pitaji, whose job as a schoolteacher had remained intact—albeit in the tiny, forgotten village of Ajar.

How demeaned he must have felt every second of every day, making do with outdated textbooks, no school supplies and no chance of escape.

I straightened my shoulders and slid the pouch back in her direction. "Keep your money. In return, *I* won't tell the ladies of Jaipur how many of your husband's bastards I've kept from this world."

Her face contorted. In a flash, she raised her arm and flattened her hand. Before she could slap my face, I seized her forearm. Our eyes locked. I saw her then, all of her, red-faced, eyes wet and frenzied. It must have taken every fiber of her being to stay in control this last half hour.

"You might want to save a few sachets for your sons," I said. "My sister wasn't the first, and I doubt she'll be the last." I thrust her forearm away from me.

She struggled to stay upright. Her eyes blazed with hate—and shame. Black eyeliner streaked down her cheeks along with her tears. Her nose was running. There was a pink lipstick smudge on one side of her mouth. She rubbed her arm where my hand had left an imprint.

I thought she had more to say, but she was quiet. We listened to the rain pounding the roof. I watched her pick up the pouch of silver coins and drop it in her handbag. For the briefest of seconds—and absurdly—I thought about grabbing it from her (it was ten thousand rupees!).

Then Parvati did something I'd never seen her do; she wiped her face with her *pallu*, not caring that she was smearing her makeup or ruining her fine sari. Her face was stained black, red and pink. Her gaze fell on the pocket watch, still on the counter. She turned away.

At the door, she steadied herself against the frame as she slipped into her sandals. Before she left, she looked out at the rain and said, "He does tire of all of you, eventually."

I waited, every muscle in my body tense. After a moment, I walked to the window. She was standing in the middle of the street, drenched. She'd forgotten her umbrella. Her sari, completely soaked, clung to her curvy frame, revealing every bulge, every bump. Her bun had collapsed into a mass of wet coils down her back. She didn't notice. Neither did she hear the *tonga-walla*, who stopped to offer her a ride. The part of me that was used to serving, to pleasing and appeasing, wanted to run after her with the umbrella. I held myself back. Watched as she staggered and slipped her way down the street, until she disappeared from view.

I stood at the window for a long time. Thought about what I had just given up for a few minutes of righteous anger. I'd slept with her husband. I'd made contraceptive sachets for him. I had no right to the high moral ground.

From the corner of my eye, I saw a postman walking to my house from the other end of the street. He was coming for me, like a homing pigeon.

I ran to my front gate, heedless of the rain. Before he could tell me I had a telegram, I snatched it from him and tore it open.

It was from Radha.

All it said was, Come. Now. Auntie needs you.

PART FOUR

EIGHTEEN

Shimla, Himalaya Foothills, India
September 2, 1956

"When I close my eyes, all I see is Auntie's sari dripping blood." Radha sobbed into my neck. "Dr. Kumar said her baby had stopped breathing. Days ago. Her body was trying to get rid of it, but she tried to stop it from happening."

I stroked my sister's arm as we sat on a hospital bed opposite Kanta's. Radha had filled out, and not just around her middle. Her arms were plumper. Her face was heavier. How different she looked from the girl who had showed up in Jaipur last November!

"You did the right thing to call Dr. Kumar right away. She might have died of blood poisoning," I whispered into her hair.

Tubes ran from Kanta's arm to bottles hanging upside down

above her bed. The bulging belly I'd expected to see—she'd been in her ninth month—was gone. Huddled under the blankets, Kanta looked small and frail. Manu was sleeping in another room, on an empty bed. He had driven all night to get us to Shimla.

Radha hiccupped. I handed her my handkerchief and she blew her nose.

When I first arrived, she'd cried out, like a child. "Jiji!"

Without hesitating, I'd wrapped my arms around her, as tightly as her pregnant belly would allow. She was shaking. "It's all right. It's going to be fine," I'd said. Dr. Kumar, who had led me to my sister, told me he had given her something for the shock when she had brought Kanta in the night before.

"This place frightens me," my sister was saying. "All these nurses with serious faces and starched caps who call each other 'Sister,' even though they're not. My baby must think the whole world smells like the bottom of a medicine bottle." She sniffed. "I prayed to Krishna every day at Jakhu Temple, Jiji. Prayed that our babies would have their naming ceremonies together. Eat their first cooked rice at the same party. Share their toys. I know I wasn't supposed to, but I couldn't help imagining the babies growing up together." Radha nestled into my neck, her tears wetting my sari.

This was what Dr. Kumar had been talking about in his letters. Radha's baby had become real to her; their separation would be unbearable. But I held my tongue. I couldn't remember the last time Radha had needed me like this. I didn't want her to let go.

She made a choking sound, and I pulled away to see what was wrong. She was staring at me in astonishment. Her mouth opened but no words came out. She clutched her belly and let out a deafening scream.

As he had the first time I'd met him, Dr. Kumar's eyes studied several objects in the waiting room—the metal table, the leather chairs, the faded photograph of Lady Bradley—before coming to rest on me. "Seven pounds, give or take an ounce. He's small but perfectly healthy. A boy. Radha is doing fine. She'll need time to recover from the stitches."

I covered my mouth with cupped hands, sighing in relief. *She was fine! My little sister was fine!* I fought the urge to hug Dr. Kumar. To my surprise, I felt a burst of pride and wonder: *Radha has a son!* No sooner had I thought it than I tamped it down, deep. What was I thinking? That baby was now the property of the palace!

I dropped my hands. "Where is he now?"

"The nurses are cleaning him. After that, as you instructed, they will put him in the nursery."

I nodded. "And Kanta? How is she?"

His eyes shifted to the batik print of an elephant and rider on the wall behind me. "Her organs weren't compromised. And we're taking care of the infection. There's a— I didn't want to tell her, but Mrs. Agarwal insisted." Dr. Kumar looked at his hands. "She will not be able to have children. Her body has undergone a major trauma."

Oh, Kanta. I put a hand on my chest to steady my heartbeat. "Perhaps your medicine is better, after all, Dr. Kumar. None of my herbs helped her keep the baby."

"I doubt she could have conceived without your help."

A nurse entered the room and handed the doctor a cup of tea. He offered it to me and asked the nurse for another. "Take it, Mrs. Shastri. Please. You look as if you haven't slept."

I took the cup gratefully. "The altitude doesn't agree with me. And that winding road up the Himalayas. Now I know why people take the train."

"I'm glad you made it," he said, looking at his shoes. "Safely."

The nurse brought another steaming cup, which he accepted. The skin under his eyes was puffy; he'd been up all night, too.

"I want to show you something," Dr. Kumar said. He led

me down the hall and out the double doors to a garden. We were closer to the sun here, in the Himalayas; the light was so bright it hurt my eyes. I had to wait a moment for them to adjust, and then I managed, just, to squint, taking in the pink roses, blue hibiscus and orange bougainvillea surrounding us.

On this early September morning, several patients, wrapped tightly in shawls, were strolling along the paths, aided by family members or nurses.

He gestured with his teacup. "What do you think?"

After the events of the past twenty-four hours, I could barely stand straight. But the sight of the flourishing garden revived me a little. "It's lovely."

"It does the patients good, but I think it can do much, much more."

A cool breeze blew over us, chilling my arms and legs. I sipped the tea for warmth. Dr. Kumar set his cup down on a bench, removed his white coat and draped it over my shoulders. It was still warm from his body, and smelled of spearmint, antiseptic and limes.

"As I've been saying in my letters to you… I've begun to see that the herbal remedies of the Himalayan people have a place in modern medicine. If their homemade poultices and potions didn't work…well, they wouldn't still be using them." He spoke as if thoughts came to him in short, staccato bursts. "I'm convinced that we must learn from their methods. *And* practice our medicine. Both. I've… I'd like to test my theory." He ducked his chin. "I was hoping you could help."

"Me?"

"You could tell us what to plant, what herbs and shrubs—here, in this garden. That *neem* powder. It worked so well on my young patient. Absolutely cleared his skin… Why couldn't we grow plants like those here?" Excitement flashed in his gray eyes like lightning.

"You're serious?"

"Frightfully so."

The teacup rattled in my hand, though I didn't know if it was because of nerves, fatigue or excitement. For ages, I had dreamed of growing a large-scale herb garden where I could plant *tulsi* and *neem* and almond trees and geranium and bitter melon and crocus. It wasn't long ago that the means to make it happen had been within my grasp, in my own courtyard, and then—suddenly—had vanished.

"Surely you've noticed I live in Jaipur," I said with a smile.

"We'll consult by correspondence, as we're doing now. Look, I saw the way you…helped Mrs. Harris. She received more benefit from your herbal compress than she did from my injection. I simply haven't been able to get that out of my mind. And the mustard poultice that eased my cough…amazing!"

He shifted his feet on the cobblestones. "I'm thinking that the new India, well, she may not be quite ready to give up her old ways. And that might be for the best." He looked at my shoulder. "Think about it, anyway." He glanced at his teacup. "I confess I'll be very disappointed if you…if you say no."

A tight-lipped nurse in a white wimple called his name. She was at the double doors, pointing at the watch pinned to her habit.

"Patients." He grinned shyly. "Perhaps we could continue after my rounds—"

"I'll be here."

"I could have a cot set up for you in Radha's room. You must be tired."

I thanked him.

He nodded and walked to the waiting nurse, then swiveled on his heel. He pointed to his coat. He was blushing.

"Um, could I?" he said. "Unless, that is, you're planning to do surgery."

I laughed and handed his coat back to him. The scent of

him was on my sari now, and as I resumed my walk, I imagined him by my side, explaining his plans for the garden.

Radha was asleep in her hospital bed. I wondered at the miracle of this girl, at once familiar and alien, who had come to me less than a year ago. I felt as if I'd known her all my life, and yet, as if I didn't know her at all.

As before, Kanta lay in the bed opposite Radha's. She was awake now, staring dully at the ceiling.

I looked for the bottle of lavender-peppermint oil in my carrier and took it to Kanta's bed. I lifted her free hand (the other had an IV tube attached to it), kissed the back of it and hugged it to my chest. She had aged years in five short months. Her skin was gray and the lines around her mouth were more prominent. Her hair lacked luster, as if it, too, had been sapped of life.

I put my forehead to hers, and left it there.

Her hollowed eyes filled. "I took such care," she said, struggling to get the words out.

I placed a drop of lavender-peppermint oil on my forefinger and traced the skin above her brows and down her temples to calm her. "I know you did," I said.

There was nothing else to say. There would be no more chances for Kanta.

"I would have welcomed a girl. Why couldn't it have been a girl? Maybe, then, it would have lived."

I wasn't sure why she thought this, if she really did, but she was grieving. She would have loved to rewrite the story of the last two days, toward a different ending. All of us would have liked that.

"I know," I said. "Look how good you've been with Radha."

She allowed herself a small smile. "My record there is not exactly perfect. She strayed on my watch."

"And mine. But she loves you as much as ever."

"She loves you, too, you know."

I cocked my head. "Not a single letter in five months. Not one."

"You never came to see her."

"She's too stubborn."

"So are you, my friend," she said.

I straightened my spine. She was right; I could have made the first move.

I looked out the window. "I saw Manu out in the garden earlier."

"I sent him there. No good both of us being sad together." Her eyes sought mine. "He was so looking forward to meeting his child."

"Shh." I massaged the space between her brows.

"Manu told me Radha had a boy."

We regarded each other in silence.

"He must be beautiful."

I didn't want to talk about him now. Kanta was in too much pain. Instead, I did something quite unlike me. I gathered a few tendrils of her hair in my hand and pulled them across my mouth like a mustache, exaggerating the pucker of my lips the way her servant, Baju, did.

"Madam," I said, doing my best to imitate his village accent. "I escaped! I stole money from your *saas*'s purse to join you. Please not to tell her. She will most definitely jail me."

She managed to smile through her tears, and put a hand on my head to bless me, a gesture usually reserved for elders and holy men.

After Kanta fell asleep, I went to the baby nursery.

Radha's boy had all his fingers and toes, two legs, two arms. He was a beautiful baby. His skin was a delicious color: tea with cream. He even had a full head of wispy black hair. I stroked his silky cheek, ran a finger across his chubby ankles.

I felt a magnetic pull to him. We shared blood. We shared eyes the color of the sea. We might even have shared family in a previous life.

"How is it that you don't have children of your own?"

I turned to look at Dr. Kumar, who had just come into the room. I wasn't sure how to answer his question.

He was looking at the *pallu* of my sari, worry lines crossing his forehead. "I'm sorry. It's impertinent of me to ask."

I looked down at the sleeping baby. Under his pink lids, his eyes made tiny, rapid-fire movements. He had only been in this world for one hour. I couldn't imagine what he was dreaming about. One tiny fist opened, then closed, as if he were squeezing pulp from a mango.

"I have no husband, Doctor."

"So you aren't—forgive me—I thought it was Mrs. Shastri."

I am divorced. It was official now, but the words wouldn't leave my mouth.

"I *was* married," I said. "Long ago."

I wondered if Jay Kumar knew about Samir and me. But when I looked at his face, the eyes tilting down at the corners, I thought not. His question had been innocent enough.

I smiled. "Surely you must have a family."

"I did. That is, when I was a very small child." He put a hand out, palm facing the floor, to indicate how small. "Parents. No siblings. My parents, well, both of them died—car accident—when I was young…" His starched coat rustled as he removed the stethoscope from around his neck, and wound the tubing around the metal carefully.

"I'm sorry."

"Oh, it's been ages. I was still in knickers. My late aunt raised me. Paid my way through all my schooling."

A nurse came to check up on her tiny charges. Radha's son rested in a corner crib, apart from the other newborns. Unlike the other cribs, his lacked the small card giving his family name. But his bed was clean, his cheeks rosy, his sleep restful. He was obviously getting excellent care.

"How did you end up in Shimla, Doctor?"

"Boarding school. The Bishop Cotton School for Boys. Then Oxford—where I met Samir."

I realized I'd forgotten to send Samir a telegram about the baby. "You've informed the palace?"

"I'll take care of it," he said. "Haven't found the time, so far, to complete their forms. Ten, twenty pages—down to the smallest detail. We must measure each fingernail. And every other body part." He chuckled, glancing slyly at me.

I laughed.

He checked his watch against the wall clock. "It's time for my clinic. Will you join me? There are some people I'd like you to meet."

"Now?"

"No time like the present. Radha will sleep a few more hours."

Radha's son attempted a halfhearted croak and kicked. We turned to look at him.

"We're still agreed that Radha is to have no contact with the child?"

He held his hands up in surrender. "The Sisters know. They have their orders."

The tiny clinic was on the hospital's first floor. The walls were painted toothpaste green. Half the chairs were occupied by local residents: women in dazzling blouses, petticoats the color of Himalayan wildflowers, headscarves adorned with orchids; the men in woolen tunics and drab suitcoats, their heads warmed by Pahari *topas*.

Dr. Kumar approached the pretty nurse behind the reception. "How many today, Sister?"

"Fourteen."

He grinned, his chin dimpling. "Twice what we used to get."

Ushering me into a cramped office, he indicated a chair for me. "My surgery," he said. "Such as it is."

His desk was littered with stacks of paperwork, prescription pads, an inkwell. An open medical textbook sat on top of the latest issue of *Time* magazine. On the wall: a photo of Gandhi-*ji* surrounded by leaders of the India National Congress. The scenery behind the Mahatma was familiar: Shimla in bloom.

Dr. Kumar sat down behind his desk. His eyes were restless once again. "We started this clinic a year ago. To serve the mountain tribes. Patients come from miles around to be cured at Lady Bradley. Well-heeled ones like Mrs. Agarwal. And, of course, like Radha, whose expenses are being borne by the palace. But no one—absolutely no one—was serving the people who have lived here…for centuries." Hazarding a bashful glance at me, he said, "It's your skin remedy for the little boy. That started bringing these new patients in. Today, we have more patients than ever."

I smiled. "You give me too much credit."

His expression became serious. "Actually," he said, "I don't think I've given you enough."

A nurse poked her head around the door. "We're ready, Doctor."

He stood. "Let me show you what I mean."

A drab burlap curtain separated the waiting room from the examination room. There, a nurse was helping a pregnant woman onto the table. Dr. Kumar introduced me as his herbal consultant and asked his patient questions in a mix of Hindi and the local dialect. He shared his diagnosis of her case with me, and when I didn't understand the medical terminology, he explained it in layman's terms. I had questions of my own, which he translated. We did this through five more appointments. In four out of five cases, I was able to recommend an herbal substitute for Western medicine.

For the pregnant woman suffering from severe indigestion, I suggested bitter melon cooked in garlic. *Neem* oil for a grandmother with hands gnarled from arthritis; asafetida—available from any vegetable vendor—mixed in water to calm a colicky baby; turnip greens and strawberries for a sheepherder who preferred my dietary recommendations to having his goiter removed.

The wall clock struck eleven.

Dr. Kumar checked his watch. "Radha must be awake now."

How quickly the last hour had passed! I had been so occupied with the patients that I hadn't thought of Radha. Or the baby. Or Kanta. I felt no hunger or thirst.

The doctor chuckled. "You enjoyed it, didn't you? I was watching. Please say you'll work with us! Mrs. Agarwal told me the work would come at a good time..." He stopped when he saw the look on my face.

Kanta had been telling him my problems! How I'd lost my business. That I didn't have two *annas* to rub together. Did he pity me? Is that why he'd gone to all this trouble?

I set my jaw. "Doctor, I'm not looking for sympathy."

"No, I meant— I'm only suggesting... What I'm trying to say is...your knowledge is worth a great deal to us. You see our need. No one else can do this work as well as you. I've looked. I need you." He combed his fingers through his hair. When he let go, the curls fell in all directions, haphazardly.

"But I only know the herbs of Rajasthan and Uttar Pradesh. I have no knowledge of the plants that grow here—at this altitude and in this cool climate."

His eyes scanned my face. "I'm bungling it, Mrs. Shastri. Medicine doesn't pay handsomely but...there will be remuneration. We're applying for funds. I'm asking you for professional advice. Think of all the people you could help."

It was true that the patients at the clinic had been relieved to learn they would not have to take foul-smelling medications. The pregnant woman had touched my wrist as a gesture of thanks before leaving. Counting the time with my *saas*, I had fifteen years of knowledge about herbs and natural substances that I'd refined and improved upon. It could prove useful to people other than my ladies. (*My ladies!* As if there were enough of them left.)

Still, I wasn't ready to make a decision. I needed to consider my options. Money would be coming from the palace after the baby's birth, which gave me time.

"May I think about it?"

"Only if the answer is yes." He smiled, the dimple on his chin deepening.

NINETEEN

September 3, 1956

The baby was a day old. Radha had pleaded with me for hours before I agreed to let her see him.

"We must at least cover him in sandalwood paste to guarantee his health, Jiji," she had argued.

I had said no.

"A new birth calls for a blessing by the *pandit*. How about an ash *tikka* on his forehead?"

I had said no.

Now, Radha sat in her hospital bed holding the baby I had tried desperately to keep her from. We were alone; Manu and Kanta were taking a stroll in the garden.

Radha sniffed the baby's head, perfumed with Godrej talcum powder. She tapped each of his fingertips. They were the size of peppercorns. His lips were the smooth texture of marigold petals, parting greedily as she slid her finger across them. She kissed his bare soles, tinted a dusky rose, and studied the crisscrosses on them. It was as if he had walked miles to get here.

"Can't I at least feed him?"

I looked away. I knew her breasts were swollen. If I hadn't been in the room with her, she would put him to her breast and let him drain her.

"He should get used to the bottle. That's what his adoptive family will give him," I replied.

Just then, the baby opened his eyes and tried to keep them open, but they rolled back in their sockets and closed again. Radha looked at me, her watercolor eyes round as marbles.

"Jiji, they're blue! His eyes are blue! Like yours. Like Maa's. He has *us* in him!"

I turned my head and cleared my throat. "You're sure about the *kajal*?"

It was the only concession I had made: we could apply the black eye paste to ward off the evil eye. It was an old superstition, but Radha firmly believed it, and I suppose I had, too, at one time.

"Of course! He needs protection from *burri nazar*."

I opened the tiffin I'd brought with me and reached for the tin of *kajal*. I had mixed soot with sandalwood and castor oils to make the smooth paste that many women wore as eyeliner. I dipped my little finger in the paste. While she held the baby steady, I gently pulled his bottom eyelids away from the sockets and drew a thin black line across the rims. Then I placed three tiny dots at both his temples and another three dots on the sole of each foot.

"It will come off when the nurses bathe him," I said, screwing the lid on the tin.

"But the gods have seen us do it. Which means he'll be

safe." Her baby's fat fingers were curled around her thumb. "Would you like to hold him?"

I was wiping my hands on a towel, pretending I hadn't heard. Through the window of the hospital room, I saw the sky: its silver cast, the clouds hovering above, a smoky green horizon of cedars, pines, rhododendrons.

"Jiji?"

"He's healthy. His new family will be pleased."

Her mouth became a thin line; my answer had irritated her.

The baby made sucking motions against her finger.

"You've barely looked at him."

She wanted me to admit I loved him, too. That I saw us in him. If I did that, I wouldn't be able to ask her to give him up. "I see him."

"Then look at him with me."

"No." I set my jaw.

We stared at one another in silence.

"I'm not giving him up, you know."

What?

"I only said I would because I thought you'd change your mind once he was born—"

"Change my mind? We can't—"

"I've changed mine," she said. "He's *my* baby."

My heart was beating so rapidly I thought it would burst out of my ribs. We'd sorted this ages ago! Kanta had assured me that Radha was willing to let the baby be adopted.

"Radha, he belongs to someone else—legally. That was the agreement."

"He's *my* son. He's one of us. Could you really give up your own family?"

I already had. "He's a baby someone else is expecting to raise!"

The baby yawned, exposing soft pink gums. She moved him to her other arm. Her eyes narrowed. "Why don't you admit you hate babies?"

I blinked. "What?"

"I've seen you with little children—at your ladies'. You're always polite and full of compliments. *'What a pretty child, Mrs. Seth; she looks just like you. You've got a real Einstein on your hands, Mrs. Khanna.'* But then you turn to your work without another glance. You never look at the mothers pushing prams around the bazaar—I do. I want to see if it's a girl or a boy. If the hair is straight or curly. You walk right past them.

"And the beggar children along the road. You hand them coins without a glance, as if they're ghosts. I see them. I talk to them. They're people, Jiji. *This* baby is a person. He's *our* people. Look at his eyes. They're Maa's. Those ears are Pitaji's. Doesn't that mean anything to you?"

The baby fussed.

"*Hai Ram!* And family means so much to you that you'd destroy the only family you have left?" I said. The vein on my temple flared. "*I'm* family, Radha. I'm blood, too. What about me? I took care of you. Made it possible for you to go to the best school. And you repaid me by getting pregnant!"

"I didn't do it to hurt you!"

"I spent thirteen years building a life. Now my appointment book is empty. Page after page—nothing."

The baby was squirming now and clenching and unclenching his fists.

"But I loved him— I love Ravi," she said, as if that made it all right.

My voice rose. "Love? This isn't one of your American films where the heroine does as she pleases. And you're not Marilyn Monroe." I couldn't stop. "How many times do I have to tell you that we don't have the means to give this baby what he deserves? We're not part of the polo set or the ladies' auxiliary, no matter how much you wish it. We can't afford to take a day off work while they book European tours for a month. Tailors, vegetable-*wallas*, cobblers—they go to *their* houses, not to *ours*. I wish it were different. But it's not. It never will be." I was in too deep. "You say you don't want to be the Bad Luck Girl? Well, parade this baby around the city and you will be the Bad Luck Girl forever! No one will want to come near you or him."

Radha's eyes glittered, like the marbles Malik shot across the dirt. "I *hate* you! Get away from me!" she screamed.

The baby let out a loud wail. Radha rocked him from side to side, but her arms were shaking, which only frightened him more. His face had turned red.

The door opened. Dr. Kumar entered, followed by the sour-faced nurse with the brooch watch.

His eyes wandered from me, to Radha, to the baby, back to me. "Everything all right?"

I wiped the corner of my mouth where a little spit had formed. I couldn't look at him because I was filled with shame. What I'd said to my sister about the Bad Luck Girl was a cruelty I hadn't known I was capable of. I cleared my throat. "Please take the baby away."

"No!" she shouted. "I want to feed him!"

The baby's cries were deafening.

With an effort, I shifted to the smooth voice I always used with my ladies. "Doctor, please."

He sighed. Slowly, he turned to the nurse and nodded. Glaring her disapproval, the nurse took the screaming baby from Radha's arms, and walked quickly out of the room.

The doctor rubbed his eyes. "Radha—"

"Dr. Kumar, I beg of you. Please. Let me keep my baby."

It embarrassed me to hear her plead like a beggar.

"It's not my decision," he said.

"I'll take care of him, I promise! I'll find a way."

"Your sister is your legal guardian until you come of age. You must follow her wishes."

Radha covered her ears with her hands, shaking her head. "It's *my* baby! Don't I have a say?"

I looked at Dr. Kumar, who was rubbing his jaw, his eyes troubled.

He took a step toward me and touched my shoulder, leaving his hand there for the briefest of moments. It was soothing, as if he were telling me to be brave; that all would be well in the end. Then he was gone, quietly shutting the door behind him.

Her face wet and flushed with anger, Radha exploded. "You control everything! Whether I can feed my own baby. Who I spend time with. How I talk. What I eat. Will it always be like this? When will *you* stop running my life? I managed by myself for thirteen years! Thirteen years! I may as well have been alone. Pitaji drunk. Maa barely there. I found a way to get to you hundreds of miles away! Do you know how hard that was?"

She looked down at her hospital gown, now damp from her leaking breasts. "I want a family, Jiji. It's all I've ever wanted. It's why I traveled so far to find you. This baby is my family. He wants my milk. Did you see the way he looked at me? I talked to him the whole time he was in my belly. He knows my voice. He knows *me*. I *know* he needs me."

Of course he knew her. He'd had her to himself for eight months. I understood that. And yes, my feelings toward him were so tender, so strong, it surprised me. Which is why I wanted the best for them both. Didn't she realize that? How could I not manage one sentence that would help my sister understand that everything I did was for her own good? She exasperated me and sometimes intimidated me, but I would do anything to make her life better, easier.

She crossed her arms over her chest but instantly regretted it; her breasts hurt.

They were filled with milk because I hadn't let her feed

the baby. It was as if she needed him as much as he needed her. But I'd seen what Radha hadn't: desperate women begging my *saas* to rid them of their burdens. Where she saw joy, I saw hardship. Where she saw love, I saw responsibility, obligation. Could they be two sides of the same coin? Hadn't I experienced both love and duty, delight and exasperation, since she entered my life?

I stood up. "I brought something for you." I removed two thermoses from my carrier, unscrewed the cup from one and poured the steaming liquid into it.

"Drink this. It's bitter, but it will help with the soreness in your breasts."

She wrinkled her nose.

"Please."

"What's in it?" She took the cup from me and sniffed it.

"Burdock root. Mullein leaves. A little dandelion root. It will make the swelling go down."

As she sipped, she watched me pour hot liquid from the other thermos into a cup. I dipped two strips of flannel in the liquid, one at a time, wetting them thoroughly. "Open your gown."

She set her cup on the side table and wiped her eyes with the backs of her hands. She unbuttoned her gown, exposing her breasts. Her nipples were twice as large as they had been when she first came to Jaipur. Her face flushed in embarrassment, but I pretended not to notice. Tenderly, I placed a warm compress on each breast.

Radha let out a sigh and closed her eyes. "Ginger?"

"Chamomile oil, too. And calendula flower."

Her face relaxed. She took a deep breath.

This was how my *saas* had taught me to show my love. Not with words or touch but through healing.

Outside, a green warbler tweeted, and we turned to see it fly past the window.

"Auntie's breasts are filled with milk, too."

I sighed. "I offered her the compresses, but she doesn't want them. She wants to feel the pain. I think it's her way of saying goodbye to her baby. Her breasts will be hard and sore for a while, but her milk will eventually dry up."

Fresh tears sprang to her eyes. "I feel so guilty because my baby is alive."

"That's not your fault."

"She came to Shimla because of me—so far from her husband. And look what happened."

"Lady Bradley is far better equipped than the hospital in Jaipur. The air here is better for her asthma. Besides, she *wanted* to be here with you."

The warbler returned with its mate; both landed on a rhododendron near the window. He stood guard while she scratched under her feathers with her beak.

"She can try again, can't she?"

Someone had to tell her. "Dr. Kumar doesn't think it likely."

"Oh."

We watched as the female warbler turned toward us. She was either gazing at us or admiring her reflection in the window.

"I wanted Auntie to replace you as my *jiji*, you know."

It hurt to hear her say it, but it didn't surprise me.

"But the day I sent the telegram I'd never been more glad that you were my sister."

I met her eyes. She didn't look away.

"I knew you'd make everything all right."

Something hard inside me yielded. She depended on me to be there for her, even when she was angry and told me she hated me. I smoothed her coverlet, scratchy from too many washings and ironings. Her hand lay on her lap, and I clasped it. She let me.

"How's Malik?" she asked.

"Busy. Delivers a few orders—hair tonic, that sort of thing. He's always coming around. Thinks I need the company."

"Do you?"

I shrugged. I replaced the warm compresses on her breasts with cooler ones. I could tell by her exhalations that the ache had lessened, and, with it, the urge to breastfeed.

"You said the ladies aren't coming to you for henna anymore?"

I thought Kanta had told her. "They don't trust me. They think I steal."

She raised her brows. "That's ridiculous! Why would they think such a thing?"

"Gossip-eaters." *Crocodile lies.*

I removed the cool compresses. Radha buttoned her gown, lost in thought.

I looked past the bed, out the window. Dark clouds breezed past the sun, blotting out the light. I could see my reflection. There were purple bruises under my eyes and lines at the corners of my mouth. The fluorescent lights overhead caught a few strands of silver in my hair and the groove of a wrinkle on my forehead. There was a slight stoop to my spine. I was getting older. I looked at my hands. No longer smooth, the skin was like a rutted path, grooved and bumpy with veins.

Dr. Kumar walked in. He stood, uncertain, as if he might have intruded on a private moment.

"All is well?" He looked at my sister. "Radha, how are you feeling?"

"Better." She told him about my herb compresses.

"You're a woman of many talents, Mrs. Shastri," he said.

When he realized he was staring at me, he turned his attention to Radha, to Kanta's empty bed, then to the stack of paper in his hands. "I need your signature."

Ah. The official forms, certifying the birth of the new

crown prince. I stood to take them, but my legs felt unsteady, and I sat down again.

"If you'll just give us a moment, Doctor."

He nodded and left the room.

Radha smiled.

"What's so funny?"

"He is." She lifted her chin to indicate Dr. Kumar. "He was always saying my baby would be an all-rounder, and he does have sturdy little legs."

Of course Radha had given thought to her baby's future. He would be a cricketeer. A star bowler. Would he ask for *kicheri* or *aloo tikki* at breakfast? His hair might grow straight, like hers, or curly like his father's.

"Jiji?" she asked shyly. "Could we see the baby again? I promise not to make another scene."

I started to rise from the bed, but Radha grabbed my hand with a strength that surprised me. She squeezed my fingers. Her hand was warm and slightly damp. I sat back down.

"Jiji, I know I took you by surprise. I must have been four or five—I was stirring the boiling milk for yogurt when the postman delivered one of your letters. Maa took one look at the envelope and threw it in the cooking fire. I asked why she didn't open it, and she just shrugged and said, 'Someone who died in my heart a long time ago.'

"I wondered who she was talking about. After that, I started listening, more closely, to the gossip-eaters, and realized Maa was talking about you. I thought how brave you must be—how very strong—to leave everything behind. And then I met you. You were everything I'd imagined. Smart. Beautiful. Funny. I was proud. You could do so much. I loved you from the moment I laid eyes on you. See, I'd had time to get used to the idea of you."

My eyes filled. No one had ever said they loved me. Oh, I knew Maa and Pitaji loved me, but it wasn't something they said aloud. In his own way, Hari had loved me, or thought he had, but his hadn't been a selfless love. He'd wanted to own me, make me a part of him. And Samir didn't love me; he wanted me in bed.

"I want children. I want to be tired at the end of the day because I've had to boil milk for their *kheer* and play hopscotch with them and put turmeric on their hurts and listen to the stories they make up and teach them how to read *Ramayana* and catch fireflies. And it makes me sadder than you can imagine to think I'll never be able to do that with this baby."

Her persistence was wearing me down. Was I being too narrow-minded? Maybe she and I could raise that beautiful baby together. Radha could go to school while I took care of the boy. No, I couldn't. I'd have to keep working to pay off Samir's debt. And now that I thought about it, no school in Jaipur would take a girl who'd had a baby. She wouldn't be able to complete her education. With an illegitimate baby in tow, we'd be pariahs, shunned from society, any and all celebrations, weddings and funerals, even a way to make a living. No one would want me to do their henna or their *mandala* or arrange their marriage. We wouldn't be able to feed ourselves! No matter how I looked at it, it just wasn't possible for us to take Radha's baby home.

I looked out the window. Outside, sunlight was peeking through the clouds. Scarlet minivets bathed in the garden fountain, with nervous little movements of their heads, a furtive splash of feathers.

I watched Kanta and Manu as they sat on a bench in the Lady Bradley garden, a wool blanket covering their knees. Kanta had her head on her husband's shoulder. Her eyes were closed.

Kanta had wanted to be a mother so desperately. And she would have been such a wonderful one. She was good-natured, funny, generous. She had Manu, her mother-in-law and Baju to help her at home. And she could afford to hire an *ayah* for the baby. If only *she* could take Radha's baby home. She would love that little boy as if it were hers.

I felt my pulse quicken.

She and Manu had the means, the time and the energy to give the baby a good home.

It was absurd to think such a thing! I had signed a contract.

Unless…

Sweat beaded along my hairline.

"Radha," I whispered. If I said it, I could never take it back.

I turned to face her.

I told myself that I knew what I was doing. If I went ahead with this and the royal family discovered the truth, I risked a legal breach of contract, hefty fines and even imprisonment.

She must have seen the excitement in my face. "Yes?"

I was giving up *thirty thousand rupees* and a secure future for Radha! But the baby would have a far more loving home.

I pointed at the window with my chin. Kanta and Manu had risen from the bench. They were walking to the far side of the hospital, where the nursery was.

"Kanta never got to hold her baby. That's why she loves going to the nursery to hold yours."

Radha lifted her eyebrows and looked out the window.

"She sings to him. He seems to like it," I said.

Radha smiled. "She made up all kinds of silly songs when the babies were in our bellies. Just like Pitaji used to."

"If Kanta were raising your baby…" I looked at Radha. My heart beat fast in my ribs. "Would she read Shakespeare or the *Tales of Krishna* to him?"

Her eyes flickered.

I took her hands in mine. "Would she feed him sweets or savories?"

Radha's lips parted. "She loves my *laddus*." Her voice was a whisper.

"Would her *saas* feed him rose milk, too?"

Her eyes were full of wonder and hope. "Till he turned pink."

I smiled and touched my forehead to hers. "Wouldn't Kanta just love him to pieces?"

My *choti behen* nodded slowly. She gripped my hands. "But, Jiji, what about the family who wanted to adopt the baby?"

"Leave that to me."

Kanta was looking at some point beyond me, as if I'd become transparent. I wondered, for a moment, if she'd heard me. Then she said, "But, Lakshmi, what about the contract with the pala—"

"I'll handle it." Radha still didn't know that the palace was the adoptive party. Now, I would never tell her.

I watched the struggle on Kanta's face: she wanted it to be true, but should she believe her luck?

Manu, looking dazed, said to Radha, "Are you sure?"

"You'll treat him as your own." Radha meant it. Only I noticed how her hands clutched the bedsheets, how white her knuckles were. Until this moment, others had made choices for her; now she had made one of her own, the hardest decision of her young life.

"You were right, Auntie. I can't take care of him—not in Jaipur, not in Ajar, not in Shimla. But you can, Auntie. You can, Uncle."

In their excitement, Kanta and Manu couldn't conceal their joy; they answered at the same time, speaking over one another. I clasped my hands in front of my lips, happy for them.

"We will take the *best* care—"

"—already, he's one of the family—"

"—I know he favors salted cashews—"

"Of course, we'll wait until he has teeth…"

If I had known what Kanta was going to say next, I would have stopped her, told her that it was rash—the sort of gesture made by the heart, not the head. But Radha nodded excitedly, accepting the offer: Radha wouldn't be going back to school. She would stay with Kanta to be the baby's *ayah*.

Kanta and Manu rushed to embrace Radha, the three of them laughing and crying at the same time, wiping the tears from each other's cheeks.

Dr. Kumar was seated at his desk, pen in hand, when I walked into his office.

"I've thought about your offer. I will consult with you on a professional basis, Doctor."

He dropped his pen and tried, unsuccessfully, to keep from looking overjoyed. "That's smashing! Absolutely…"

"But there's been a change in plans."

"Change?"

I braced myself for his reaction. "Mr. and Mrs. Agarwal will adopt Radha's baby."

Now he looked confused. "I—I don't understand. The palace—"

"I was hoping you could… The papers you're submitting to them…"

He put both hands to his temples and looked down at his desk. "Mrs. Shastri? May I ask, what are you—"

"I need to know reasons why the palace would reject the baby. Medical reasons." I knew the contract by heart, but he would know the proper terminology.

His hands slid from his temples to his cheeks. He left them there, his skin stretched clownishly. Abruptly, he got up and went around the desk to check his office door, though I'd made sure to pull it closed behind me.

"You realize you're asking me to do—"

"The proper thing."

He took his seat again, behind his desk, and folded his hands together. He picked up the fountain pen and capped it, tapped it lightly on the piece of paper in front of him, smudging his hand and whatever he'd been writing.

"Radha has made this decision?"

"Yes."

His gaze landed on the bookshelf behind me. "I told you

something like this might happen. Before the baby arrived, we could have canceled the contract. It's too late now."

"Haven't you discovered, Dr. Kumar, that the wrong course can, at times, turn out to be the right one? The baby is better off with a woman who loves him than with a palace full of strangers. The royal family can adopt another baby from the Kshatriya caste with the right bloodline."

It was difficult to read Jay Kumar's expression. His eyes were gray pearls, the outer rim luminescent. He chewed his lower lip, pushed his lanky frame out of the chair and started to pace, rubbing his jaw with his ink-stained hand.

"Dr. Kumar," I said. "Please."

He sat again, picked up the letter he was writing and noticed the smudge. He blew out a breath, tore the page in half. Then he searched through the stack of papers to his left and pulled out a sheet; I saw that it was a form, embossed with the royal seal. He uncapped the fountain pen, threw a hasty glance in my direction and carefully amended a number on the form.

"A newborn's heartbeat generally ranges from a hundred to a hundred and twenty beats per minute," he said. "However, when the heart is enlarged, the heart rate is much slower."

He tore a clean sheet from his writing tablet. His pen glided across the paper and filled the page in less than two minutes. He lifted the finished letter in his hands, blew on it to dry the ink, then handed it to me.

September 3, 1956

My Dear Dr. Ram,

At 6:20 a.m., September 2, 1956, the patient you had entrusted in my care delivered a baby boy weighing six pounds, fifteen ounces. While there were no apparent physical defects, the vital statistics revealed a heartbeat of 84 bpm. As you are well aware, hypertrophic obstructive cardiomyopathy or asym-

metric septal hypertrophy are indicated in cases such as these—if not now, then in the future when the myocardium has been compromised.

I attribute the complication to an early birth, as the baby was three weeks premature. I wish I had better news for you. Mrs. Shastri will be in touch regarding contract closure.

Please convey my sincerest condolences to the palace. A thousand thanks to you for entrusting me with such a privileged and providential task.

Respectfully,
Jay Kumar, M.D.

I read it twice. No one would lose face: the royal family, Dr. Kumar or the Singhs. But who would pay Radha's medical bills now? Hastily, I pushed the thought aside. One thing at a time.

I read the letter a third time. Only then did it occur to me that Jay Kumar was passing up his opportunity for fame. He would have been the doctor who delivered the new Crown Prince of Jaipur.

I looked up at him. "I'm sorry."

He returned my gaze.

"Mrs. Agarwal," he said, "will make a fine mother. Very fine indeed."

He pushed the letter and the form across the desk. All that was missing was my signature. He passed me the fountain pen.

TWENTY

Jaipur, State of Rajistan, India
October 15, 1956

I stayed two weeks in Shimla. On my return to Jaipur in late September, I felt happier, lighter, than I had in a long time. In Shimla, I had worked with people who needed me, who valued what I had to offer. The Himalayan people had welcomed my suggestions eagerly, the way parched soil welcomes rain. A few had arrived at Dr. Kumar's clinic, bearing gifts of wildflowers and home-cooked treats, to thank me. Not since my time with my *saas* had I experienced such joy in healing others.

Seeing Kanta and Manu with Radha's baby had lifted my spirits, too. They were doting parents, eager to take care of their first, and now only, child. I had watched Radha for signs of jealousy, but she seemed content to share her baby with her auntie and uncle. They would all be coming back to Jaipur in a week, and Radha would live with them.

It only took a few days back in Jaipur, however, to bring me back to the reality of my life. After thirteen years of hard work, I was right back where I started, as poor now as I had been at seventeen. We would no longer be getting thirty thousand rupees from the adoption agreement. I'd refused Parvati's tainted marriage commission. I had no money to pay back Samir's loan or the Lady Bradley medical bills. My saris had faded from too many washings; there was no money for new clothes. I walked to my few appointments (ladies like Mrs. Patel had remained steadfast) to save money on rickshaws.

I could have asked Kanta and Manu for money, but that would have been like requesting compensation for the baby my friends had adopted. The very thought of it repulsed me.

I had other debts. The *neem* oil vendor to whom I owed several hundred rupees came knocking at my door. Six months ago, I would have told him to go through Malik. Yesterday, I merely showed him my empty hands. He had a lean, hawkish face with eyes set too close together. He scanned my property, my tattered belongings, my threadbare blouse. I could tell he was surprised at how far I'd come down in the world.

His small eyes studied me, lingering on my chest, until I felt the need to cross my arms over my breasts.

He snorted and swallowed phlegm. "You henna women, don't you?"

I nodded.

"You can henna my wife in exchange for what you owe."

When I arrived at his house, the vendor said his wife was waiting in the bedroom. As I walked toward it, he grabbed my arm.

I stiffened.

"I want you to henna her breasts."

I stared at him. Not since my time in Agra with the courtesans had I been asked to henna anything other than hands or feet, with the exception of Kanta's stomach, which had been my idea.

I could hardly refuse him. I had no other way to repay what I owed. I stepped inside the bedroom, closing the door behind me. The vendor's wife, a thin woman as dark as a coconut husk, waited for me on the floor, her hair covered with her *pallu*. Since we were alone, I suggested she might be more comfortable uncovering her head; she smiled shyly and refused, hiding even more of her face with her sari.

She surprised me by saying, "You're thinner." She had seen me in better days, when I had shopped at her husband's store with Malik.

I had stopped giving reasons for my diminishing weight. When someone asked, or noticed, I simply shrugged. Almost daily, Malik brought treats the palace chef had prepared, but I only took a few bites before my appetite left me.

I asked her to remove her blouse. She had breastfed three children, and her chest sagged. I used the henna design to hide as many of her stretch marks as I could. I had finished decorating one breast only when I heard the bedroom door creak. I lifted the reed and turned to see the oil vendor standing in the doorway, working a toothpick between his lower teeth.

I raised an eyebrow to ask what he wanted.

"Continue," he said, stepping inside the room. He closed the door. His wife retreated farther behind her sari.

"My work with the ladies is private. You can see it soon enough after I leave."

"You're the one with the debts, remember?"

I dropped my gaze and turned back to his wife.

"Could you paint a face? On her breasts?"

I ignored him, dipping the reed in the henna. "I'm painting a spiral of new buds, an infinite blessing of good fortune on your house."

"Other images might do the same." His voice softened in a way that chilled me. I could imagine the leer on his face.

"Such as?"

"Your face."

The impudence! He knew how desperate I was, or he wouldn't have dared. The insult wasn't just aimed at me, but at the mother of his children. That he might disgrace or shame her was of no concern to him; she was his property. I felt disgust, as I'd felt at the home of the *kulfi-walla* earlier this week, when he asked me to henna his hair. Of course I had refused. The drawing skill I was so proud of wasn't worth anything to people like him.

"Well?"

I wanted to throw something at him to shut him up, but the reed was too light, my henna pot too precious. I met his eyes. "No. The agreement was to paint her breasts."

He chewed his toothpick. After a moment, he said, "Very well."

But he didn't leave. He settled on the floor, behind me. I moved my body so I didn't have to look at him, even from the corner of my eye. I continued patterning leaves that spiraled outward and upward from her nipple, to make her breasts appear lifted.

After a few minutes, I heard him rustling. I knew by a slight shift of her head that his wife had heard, as well. A wave of nausea swept over me as I realized his hands were fumbling with his *dhoti*. I felt her shame, and something else. Her resentment. At *me*, not him.

I dropped the reed on the floor and jumped up. Hurriedly, I began loading my supplies into my carryall.

He gripped my arm. His hand was warm from pleasuring himself; I wrenched it loose. "Don't touch me!"

I reached for the henna pot.

"You haven't finished!"

I grit my teeth. "I would sooner clean latrines than step into this house again."

He tore the henna pot out of my hands and threw it at the wall. "You're *cheating* me?" The paste splattered the floor and walls. His wife jerked the sari off her face and, for a moment, all three of us stared at the wreckage.

Saasuji's bowl, my precious henna pot, was nothing now but shards. I could buy another for a few rupees in the Pink Bazaar, but this bowl had made me feel close to her even as I moved a thousand miles away.

Furious, I elbowed the vendor's ribs and pushed him up against the door with all my weight. His shoulder hit the doorframe, and he fell to the floor. I'd knocked the wind out of him. Before he could catch his breath, I grabbed as many of the clay shards as I could, dumped them in my carryall and ran out of the house.

I burst into a run, crossed the road and turned into the first alley. A rat scampered down one side, in the murky, fetid water. I braced myself against the crumbling wall, bent over and vomited. Milky tea swirled in the tobacco-colored cesspool.

A memory of an alley similar to this one came to me. Me, at sixteen. Back in my village. Running from an angry, violent Hari. Spewing my guts out.

Here I was at thirty, still looking for an escape. But where was there to go?

"*Ji?* Are you all right?"

I whirled around.

Lala, Parvati's former servant, was looking at me with concern. She led me away from the sewage, then used the end of her sari to wipe a corner of my mouth.

I put my hand on her wrist to stop her, using my own *pallu* to wipe my mouth.

"It's a hard habit to break," she said, smiling, "after raising MemSahib's boys all those years."

Her dark face was leaner than I remembered, the cheeks sunken. I took in her patched sari.

"Where did you go after…?" I couldn't complete the question. I already knew why she and her niece had been fired from the Singhs'. Samir had confirmed it.

The woman ran a tongue over her teeth. "To my brother's at first. He's a big man, a builder, and he has means. But he refused because she was with child. Finally, he arranged a marriage for her."

I remembered that Naraya had been arranging a hasty marriage for his pregnant daughter. "Your brother—is he called Naraya?"

Her eyes welled with tears. *"Hahn."* She wiped them with her sari. "A harder man you will not find. Called his own daughter a whore, a she-dog."

I already knew the answer but I had to ask, "And Master Ravi—"

"I raised him, but I spoiled him, too. We all did. Such a beautiful boy he was. I told my niece he wasn't for her, but she wouldn't listen."

"Where is she now?"

Tears rolled down the old woman's wrinkled cheeks. "Her new husband locked her out of the house when he found out she was already pregnant. She sat in the courtyard, *Ji*, and put herself on fire. They both died—her and the baby."

My legs gave way. I would have fallen if Lala hadn't supported me.

"I had heard about your sachets. They could have helped her." That day, a year ago, at Parvati's. I remembered Lala standing on the veranda. I had a sense that she wanted to talk, but she seemed to lose her nerve. I should have sought her out and asked what she needed. It's the kind of thing my *saas* would have done. How far I'd come from everything my mother-in-law stood for!

I looked at Lala. Here I'd been feeling sorry for myself, when this woman had given everything—even her livelihood—to take care of her niece.

"And you, Lala? How…?"

"I tried other ladies, but MemSahib made sure they wouldn't hire me. I clean houses now. Here, in this neighborhood."

Parvati had ruined Lala, too, to protect her son from scandal.

I stood up, leaning on Lala for support, dizzy from the effort. "I wish— I'm so sorry—"

"We are powerless against God's will, *Ji*."

She rubbed my back, as she might have comforted a child.

My *saas* wouldn't have scolded me for my actions, or lack thereof, either; she would have patted my arm pityingly, as Lala was doing now, which was worse. I wanted to shed my skin and start over.

I mumbled another apology before turning toward home.

Malik caught up with me a mile from Rajnagar. He stank of cigarettes.

I edged away. I stank, too, of sick and shame.

I was holding a piece of my henna pot in one hand. He looked at it.

"I'll take you home," he said.

"I have no money for a rickshaw."

"*I* do."

"I don't want your money," I said, regretting now how harshly I'd spoken. "I have two legs."

"So do I. We'll walk together."

Malik had been my helper, and my friend, for a long time. He'd followed me around Jaipur for a while before I noticed him. When I did, I saw a skinny child, bedraggled, shoeless, watching me with eyes alert and clear. I knew that if I waited long enough, he would come to me. When he did, to ask if he could carry my tiffins, he spoke respectfully, but also with a confidence that belied his youth and frail body. I handed my tiffins over to him, as I handed my carrier to him now.

I didn't deserve his loyalty, just as I hadn't deserved the comfort Lala had tried to give me.

"Auntie-Boss."

"I'm not your boss anymore."

"You'll always be my boss," he said with the smile that came so easily to him. "Because you're smarter than Chef." He started walking backward so he could face me. "I told him I could get the sweetest raw cashews from the Pathans—better than the ones he puts on his lamb curry—for less than he's paying now. And the fool turned me down. You know why?"

I said nothing.

"He won't do business with a Muslim—except for me, of course! But you're a better businessman. You would have gone for the better deal."

I stopped walking. "If I'm so smart, why don't I have two stones to rub together?"

"*Arré!* That was my fault! When you were in Shimla, I bragged about your henna to the *kulfi-walla*." Malik spat. "He put henna on his hair and told everyone *you* had done it! Now all of Jaipur thinks you've touched his unclean head."

That explained why the tailor and the vegetable seller crossed the street when they saw me coming. And why the *doodh-walla* had stopped delivering my milk. When I went to ask the milkman if he'd forgotten, he said he wouldn't take money from a fallen Brahmin. Now I scurried weekly to a shop twenty minutes from my home, hiding my face in my *pallu*, trying not to call attention to myself, like a petty criminal.

Malik picked up a stone and threw it, casting a sideways glance at me. "You can't go on like this."

Something in the way he spoke ripped apart whatever was

holding me together. I stopped and covered my mouth with my sari, let out a sob.

Malik put an arm around my shoulders. I allowed it.

"Auntie-Boss, I know you've worked hard. But weren't you happier before you built that house? Your business was good. You had money in the bank. You were free to do as you pleased."

"I was never free, Malik. No more than I am now."

"Move away."

"Where? To do what?"

"Same thing you were doing here. Maybe in Delhi or Bombay. I'll go with you."

"You're doing fine here."

"Didn't I just say I don't like working for fools, Madam?"

Dear Malik. How much I had missed him.

I let out a long sigh. "Starting over isn't easy."

Malik looked as if he'd been as patient with me as he could; it was time for tougher medicine.

"When have you let that stop you, Auntie-Boss? You must move from Jaipur—there is no other way. Unless you've thought of something better."

My belly and breasts were raw from scrubbing. Shreds of coconut husks and slivers of charcoal pricked my underarms, the insides of my thighs and my scalp. I sloughed the debris off my skin with my palms, wincing from the pain, praying the punishment would make me feel less polluted. But no matter how hard I rubbed, I could still feel the *neem* oil vendor's hand on my arm this afternoon, his breath on my back. And I would start the cleansing all over again.

When I was too tired to go on, I rubbed lavender oil into my raw skin. I put on a clean sari, the hem of which was frayed. As I combed through my tangles, my eyes landed on the hole in my cot I'd meant to fix—a year ago already?—when the jute had started to fray. Now it had completely come apart. As I slept, sometimes my foot went right through the hole.

A *sadhu* called from the street to beg for food. I put the comb down and wrapped newspaper around the *chapattis* Malik had brought yesterday. I ran out the door to give him the food. The holy man, covered in a faded saffron cloth, was waiting, leaning on a cane. He had renounced his home and material comforts, and freed himself of ego, something I didn't have the courage to do.

When I held out my offering, he said a blessing for me in a dialect I didn't understand. But he didn't take my gift. He stood looking at me.

In the pupils of his eyes, I saw what he saw: a sapling of a woman, wet strands of hair dangling like snakes around her shoulders, the thin sari. Neck and arms scratched and bleeding. I realized that I seemed so pitiful to him that *he*, who had so little, was refusing the food I offered.

I thrust the *chapattis* in his hand, roughly, and ran back inside, slamming the door. I leaned against it and closed my eyes, my heart hopping wildly in my chest.

When my breathing returned to normal I moved to the worktable.

With shaking hands, I unfolded the letter that had arrived yesterday.

October 10, 1956

My Dear Mrs. Shastri,

Our current situation is best described by Mr. Dickens: it was the season of Light, it was the season of Darkness. Alas, the migration of the hill tribes and their herds to southern climes has brought our local clinic to an abrupt halt—and, with it, our consultation agree-

ment (at least until the season changes). There is, however, light in the darkness: the opportunity to begin planning the herb garden.

Were you to commit to an extended stay in Shimla, you could study our climate, soil conditions and the indigenous herbs here, talk to the city's residents (you'll even find herbal enthusiasts among our staff) and draw up a plan for developing the Lady Bradley Healing Garden.

Say you will consider my proposal and help me minister to the people of Shimla. Of course, I intend to do everything in my power to persuade you to settle in our fair city once you're here. Are our environs not beautiful enough? Our people not adequately hospitable?

Undeniably, you have a valuable service to provide the ladies of Jaipur, but if I am to believe Mrs. Agarwal, some untoward and unjust accusations have been leveled at you. Let me speak plainly here. Pride should not get in the way of sharing your gift with a larger public. (Mrs. Agarwal should be held blameless for sharing your plight with me; when she paid your sister's medical bill, I was compelled to ask her how you were. If she hadn't told me, I might have lacked the courage to write to you with this request.)

You have much to teach us. Your work could help—and has helped—save more than a few lives and given our patients comfort. The hill people have not forgotten you. (Our pregnant patient from the Gaddi tribe whom you helped can't stop raving about your bitter melon recipe. Her baby is due any day now!)

I, for one, hope you will consider, and accept, this invitation. I eagerly await your arrival, both as a keen and willing student and as your devoted friend.

With great respect and anticipation,
Jay Kumar

Kanta's generosity brought tears to my eyes. She'd known that if she had told me what she was going to do, I would have stopped her. Radha's medical bills were one less worry now.

I thought about what Malik had said. Not for the first time, he suggested I move away from Jaipur.

Jay Kumar was offering me a chance to heal, to work with people who wanted what I had to offer. Who believed my knowledge was sacred. It was a chance to do the work my *saas* taught me. She lived in me, still. I could make her proud once more. Be proud of myself again.

But…my house! I had dreamed it, worked hard for it, built it. I'd loved knowing that all the decisions were mine. Moving meant I would have to leave it behind.

Yet, what had the house brought me but debt, anxiety, sleepless nights? Did I need it to announce my arrival in the world of the successful, as I once had? Success was ephemeral—and fluid—as I'd found out the hard way. It came. It went. It changed you from the outside, but not from the inside. Inside, I was still the same girl who dreamed of a destiny greater than she was allowed. Did I really need the house to prove I had skill, talent, ambition, intelligence? What if—

All at once I felt lighter. It was the same weightlessness I had felt in Shimla. I breathed deeply. As if I could already smell the bracing air of the blue Himalayan mountains.

Before I lost my courage, I tore a fresh sheet from my notebook.

October 15, 1956

Samir,

It is with great regret that I must leave the city I have called my home for eleven years. Rest assured, I will not leave without settling my debts. In order to repay your loan, however, I must sell my house. Estate agents are loath to represent female owners, so I must ask you to do this for me. If you are amenable, I would appreciate your subtracting my loan from the sales price and forwarding the remainder to the address below.

Had circumstances been different, our association might have continued. But as they say: What is the use of crying when the birds have eaten the whole farm?

I leave for Shimla in a month. Please let me know your decision in the coming week.

Lakshmi Shastri
c/o Lady Bradley Hospital
Harrington Estate
Shimla, Himachal Pradesh

I read it over several times. Satisfied, I tore off another sheet and wrote to Jay Kumar. Then I blew out the lamp and slept for twelve straight hours.

Two days later, a messenger arrived at my door. I opened the lavender-scented envelope.

Lakshmi,

You asked Samir to sell your home. It's not important how I found out; I just did. However, would it surprise you to learn that I'd rather keep your patterned floor than sell it? Enclosed is the money for your house, less your loan (yes, I know about that, too). I am not buying your favor (we are even on that score), merely acknowledging that we may never again have someone with your hand making our hands a wonder to hold.

Parvati

Not quite forgiveness. Nor an apology. But it unwound something in me: a coil of resentment, a long-held grudge. I sat with the note in my hand for a long time.

TWENTY-ONE

October 20, 1956

I had money now. There was no excuse to put off the inevitable.

I took a rickshaw to Kanta's house.

I'd been avoiding Kanta, Radha and the baby since their return from Shimla a few weeks ago. I missed them. But I wanted them to have time as a family. And I didn't want Radha to feel that I was underfoot, trying to manage her life.

"Lakshmi! What a nice surprise!" Kanta gathered me in a hug. She looked happy, refreshed. Gone were the hollows under her eyes. Her cheekbones had filled out.

"Radha's in the nursery. Go on in. I must sit with Saasuji for her prayers and then I'll join you."

Kanta's mother-in-law had accepted the baby as her grandson. If she guessed the truth about his birth or noted his resemblance to Radha, she said nothing; she had the grandchild she wanted.

I stopped just outside the nursery door, which was ajar. If the baby was sleeping, I didn't want to wake him. I heard Radha's voice from inside the room. "'How dare you taunt me with your presence?' roared the evil King Kansa. So many times he had tried to destroy Lord Krishna and so many times he had failed.'"

Quietly, I stepped inside. Her back to me, Radha was swaying to and fro in the rocking chair. The baby was cradled in her arms, and she was reading to him from her *Tales of Krishna* book, now so worn that the pages had been cellotaped to the spine.

Kanta and Manu had named the baby Nikhil. At the naming ceremony, Kanta purified the baby's forehead with water before handing him to her *saas* for the ritual blessing. Given the date and time of his birth, the *pandit* had declared that the baby's name should start with *N*. With his blue eyes, Neel would have been the natural choice for a name, but Manu whispered Nikhil four times in the baby's ear, deciding the issue.

The baby gurgled.

Radha cooed, "Why, that's exactly what Krishna said!" She bent her head to kiss his cheek. "Aren't you clever?"

"He's certainly as handsome as Krishna."

The rocking chair jerked to a stop, and Radha turned to look at me. "Jiji! Don't sneak up on me like that!" She was frowning.

In one hand she held the bottle that must have popped out of the baby's mouth. He reached for it with his plump little fingers, wanting it back, but she dropped the almost empty bottle in her baby bag.

Was that guilt on her face or was I imagining things?

"I'm sorry. I didn't want to wake him if he was sleeping."

I took one of the baby's chubby hands in mine and jiggled it. He stared at our joined fingers. He looked well-fed, happy. He wore a baby gown in cream linen.

"Auntie didn't tell me you were coming." There was accusation in her voice. As I feared, she thought I was checking up on her.

Radha lifted the baby on her shoulder, where she had a clean towel at the ready, to burp him. I still marveled at how she knew these things, instinctively, as if she'd raised many babies.

"She didn't know. Malik and I have big news—"

Kanta rushed into the room. "*Puja* is over! Okay, let me feed him."

"He's almost asleep." Radha rose from the chair, patting the baby's back.

Kanta stood uncertainly in the middle of the nursery. "But...it's been hours since he ate. Do you think he's all right? He's not sick, is he?"

Radha tilted her head to one side, as if she were the adult and Kanta a child. "He's fine, Auntie. You worry too much."

Kanta's eyes landed on the burping cloth. "You didn't just give him a bottle, did you?"

Radha glanced at me before responding. "Only a little. He was fussing."

Behind Kanta, I frowned. The bottle had been nearly empty when I entered the room. Why had Radha lied?

"But, Radha, if you give him the bottle too often, my milk will dry up." Kanta smiled weakly at me. "It's just... I want to keep feeding him until he's a year old—longer if he wishes." She looked at Radha. "It makes me feel closer to him. Like I'm his mother."

It was as if she were apologizing to Radha for *wanting* to feed the baby.

My sister caught my expression. Her cheeks turned pink

and she looked away. She placed Niki awkwardly in the crook of Kanta's arm. "I need to wash the diapers." She picked up a basket of soiled nappies and left the room.

Kanta sat in the rocking chair and undid the buttons of her blouse. She pulled out a small breast and pointed it toward the baby's mouth, but he turned his head away. She tried again and again, but he was not interested, having had his fill of the bottle. Her face fell. She raised the baby to her shoulder and patted his back as tears filled her eyes.

"Kanta, what is it?"

All at once, she looked haggard. "I don't know how to be a mother. I want to—I really do, but…Radha seems to know so much more. Like how to feed him, when to feed him. When to lay him down for a nap. It's like she is a better mother because, well, she gave birth to him."

She tried a laugh, but it came out as a croak. "Listen to me! I'm so lucky to have this lovely baby to look after." She kissed his plump arm. "I'm just being silly."

"Do you feel—" I began carefully. "Is Radha's presence…?"

Kanta shook her head vigorously. "*Nahee-nahee.* I'm sure it's— I'm such a goose! I've seen it happen to women after motherhood. Emotions running high."

She got up from the chair and gently laid the baby, now asleep, in his crib. She affected a false brightness as she buttoned her blouse. "Shall we have some tea?"

We eased out of the room.

Over biscuits and chai, I told Kanta and Manu about Shimla. Kanta clapped her hands. Manu congratulated me. I answered their questions about what I would be doing for Lady Bradley Hospital and Dr. Kumar's clinic, and they responded with assurances about my future success. If not for Kanta, I told them, I would never have experienced Shimla and fallen in love with its majestic mountain range and its welcoming people.

After an hour, I excused myself to tell Radha the news. I had the feeling she was deliberately avoiding me. I found her in the back courtyard, hanging diapers on the clothesline.

When I told her Malik and I were leaving for Shimla in two weeks and that Parvati Singh had bought the Rajnagar house, she looked stunned. Her arms, which were about to pin a wet diaper on the clothesline, froze in midair.

Her reaction surprised me; I thought she'd be pleased to have me move so far away.

"You know it's time for me to leave Jaipur," I said gently. "I can no longer be a henna artist here, and I'm ready to try something different."

"But…will I ever see you again?"

It occurred to me that after everything that had happened—Pitaji's drowning, Maa's death and Ravi's betrayal—she might be thinking I was abandoning her, too. I squeezed her arm and smiled. "Anytime you want. I'll send you a ticket. Come as often as you like. Of course, Malik will be busy at school, so you might be a little lonely."

Radha eyed me warily. "Malik? In school?"

"He's missed so much of it, but I'm not going to let him get away with it anymore. He'll go to the Bishop Cotton School for Boys." I dropped my voice to a mock-whisper. "He's been practicing wearing shoes."

I'd thought we would share a laugh, but she was lost in thought. I looked inside the basket of washed diapers and pulled one out. "It must be hard to see Niki every day and know that Kanta wants so much to feel like she's his mother."

There was a bag full of wooden clothespins hanging on the line. I pulled out two. "Losing a baby has been so hard for her. She had two miscarriages before this. She seems a lot less sure of herself. Not like the bubbly Kanta she used to be."

I pinned the diaper to the line. "She probably worries that Niki loves you more. And you're so good with him, so natural. If you weren't here—of course, you *are* here, but if you weren't—do you think the baby could get used to just being with Kanta?"

I glanced at my sister. She was chewing on her lower lip. With Radha I could only guide and suggest. She was strong-willed and preferred her own counsel. I had learned that much.

I reached for another diaper. "I know of a wonderful *ayah* who needs a job. She used to be with another family, but they don't need her anymore. Lala is kind. She loves children. She would love Niki as if he were her own." I paused. "That is, of course, if you decide to come with us to Shimla." I touched her shoulder. "It's up to you."

She glanced at me and something flickered in her eyes.

I kept talking. "Malik would be over the moon, of course. He's going to need help with his homework. If you were going to school there, you could help him. And, of course, Dr. Kumar would love it, too." I laughed. "He misses chatting with you about poetry."

Radha was quiet. But I could tell by the way she pursed her mouth that she was thinking about it.

Two weeks later, the Rajnagar house was empty. The movers had taken our heavy trunks for transport to Shimla. Malik had given my sagging cot to one of his friends whose father worked with jute. We were left with only the three vinyl carriers we would take on the train.

Tomorrow morning, Malik would pick me up in a *tonga* to take us to the station. But tonight, I wanted to say good-bye to my house. I lit lamps along the edges of the walls so I could admire the mosaic on my floor one last time. I circled the room, thought of the hours I spent planning the design.

The saffron flowers, for my childlessness. The Ashoka lion: the mark of India's ambition and my own. My name, in script, hidden in a basket of herbs. And my *saas*'s name, for everything she had taught me.

I felt my spirits lift. I would leave the map of my life here, in Jaipur. I would leave behind a hundred thousand henna strokes. I would no longer call myself a henna artist but tell anyone who asked: I healed, I soothed. I made whole. I would leave behind the useless apologies for my disobedience. I would leave behind the yearning to rewrite my past.

My skills, my eagerness to learn, my desire for a life I could call my own—these were things I would take with me. They were a part of me the way my blood, my breath, my bones were.

I took a second, then a third round of the room, moving faster. I heard the *kathak* beat in my head, *Dha-dhin—Dha-dha-dhin*, the ancient rhythms of a dance that celebrated the slaying of the demon Tripuraasur.

Dha-dha-dhin—Ta-tin—Dha-dha-dhin.

I danced, cupping my hands in the shape of a lotus flower and waving my arms like floating fishes, as I'd seen Hazi and Nasreen do in Agra. What would they say if they could see me now? I pictured them, one clapping her hands with gusto, rolling her plump hips, the other chuckling. "Better leave the dancing to us *nautch* girls, Lakshmi!"

I laughed.

Dha-dhin—Dha-dha-dhin.

My feet slapped the terrazzo floor, dancing to the *tabla* drums only I could hear. If not for my *saas*, I would not have been able to fend for myself, would never have chanced the move to Agra, would never have built my house.

Dha-dhin—Dha-dha-dhin.

A feeling of floating on air, of watching clouds race against the endless Jaipur sky, filled me. I twirled faster. My heart raced.

Dha-dhin—Dha-dha-dhin.

A hundred times I spun—toward an ending and a rebirth.

Dha-dhin—Dha-dha-dhin.

My door flung open and gust of cool air rushed in.

I stopped, out of breath, chest heaving, sweat pooling in the hollow of my throat.

My sister stood in the doorway, cradling a bundle in her arms. It was the quilt I had made for Nikhil.

"Radha?"

She lifted the bundle to her shoulder. Her mouth quivered. "I know Auntie loves Niki. I know she does." She patted the quilt. Her breath was ragged. "But I don't want her to. I know she's good to him, but every time she gets close to him, I want to push her away. I want to tell her, 'He's mine!'" She gasped for air—she'd been speaking too fast.

"Radha—"

"I'm grateful to her for keeping me near my baby. But… I want to stop him from loving her. I know that sounds horrible. But it's true. Why should *she* be allowed to raise my baby when I'm forbidden to?"

Blood pounded at my temples. "What have you done?"

She was rocking back and forth now, squeezing the quilt—too tightly. "I *hate* her for it. I don't want to, but I do." She let out a painful groan. "And I want Niki to hate her, too. I know how awful that sounds. I know I'm selfish. But I can't help it!"

Her arms went slack. The bundle slipped from her hands, dropping to the floor.

"No!" I cried. I lunged forward to catch it.

The quilt unfurled. A pair of yellow booties landed at my feet.

Nikhil's silver rattle skidded across the marble and bounced off the wall.

The book Radha had brought with her from Ajar, *The Tales of Krishna*, split in two as it hit the terrazzo.

Nothing else.

Radha squeezed her eyes shut. "Jiji." It was difficult for her to get the words out. "I have to leave my baby." Her mouth gaped. She released the sobs she'd been holding back.

I ran to her. My sister clung to me, and I felt the full force of her heartbreak. I rocked her, as she had rocked her baby.

"I've been so ungrateful. All I've done is cause trouble." She hiccupped. "The gossip-eaters were right. I'll always be the Bad Luck Girl."

I pulled my head back to look at her. I lifted her chin. "No, Radha, you won't. You never were. You never will be. I'm sorry I ever said that of you. You've brought so much good luck into my life, into our lives. If it hadn't been for you, do you think I'd be going to Shimla? Building my own healing garden? Working with Dr. Kumar? How would I have done any of that without you?"

She blinked her wet lashes.

"For years, I've been serving women who only needed me to make them *feel* better. In Shimla, I'll be serving people who want me to *make* them better. Because they're truly suffering. Those are the people *saas* trained me to work with. They *need* me. And I *want* to be with them."

I smoothed her hair.

"And look how you've helped me create a family. Malik. Kanta and Manu. And Nikhil. And, of course, you. *You*, Radha, Krishna's wise *gopi*."

What a miracle that she had found me, and I, her.

"So, *Rundo Rani, burri sayani*...are you coming to Shimla with us?"

Radha looked up at me. After a while, she nodded.

In the pause that followed, I heard a dog yelp, a *tonga* clop, crows flutter in the trees.

When, at last, she relaxed her hold on me, I kissed the top of her head.

"We'll get your things in the morning from Kanta's." I wiped her face with my sari. "Come. I have *aloo gobi subji* waiting. I don't know why it always tastes much better at night."

The next morning, while I swept the Rajnagar house, Malik and Radha loaded our carriers onto the waiting *tonga*. We would stop at Kanta's and say our goodbyes en route to the railway.

I took one last round of the room. Touched the walls. Trailed my fingers across the mosaic.

My life as a henna artist was over. I would never again paint the hands of the ladies of Jaipur.

I pulled the pocket watch from my petticoat, ran my thumb over the smooth white pearls that made up the initial *L*.

I set the watch on the countertop, stepped outside and closed the door behind me.

TWENTY-TWO

Jaipur Railway Station
November 4, 1956

The platforms of the Jaipur railway station were teeming with passengers, spiced peanut vendors, shoe shiners, toothless beggars and stray dogs sniffing for discarded morsels. Even after a train started moving, people continued to board, asking for a hand up, their luggage loaded by helpful passengers who themselves were hanging by handrails on both sides of the cars. It was a wonder any trains managed to take off at all.

Our train was scheduled to depart in ten minutes. With the money from the sale of my house, I had splurged on a first-class private cabin for all of us. Inside the cabin, Malik and Radha chatted excitedly.

I stood in the passageway just outside our compartment, along the row of windows facing the platform, where porters swathed in mufflers were hauling bags on and off the trains. Important-looking husbands in wool vests, trailed by wives and children, shouted at the baggage handlers to be careful. Families with first-class tickets walked to our part of the train. Most headed to second-class seats. Those who couldn't afford porters were stuffing their mismatched carriers into the third-class cars, yelling at everyone to make room. The chai-*wallas* strolled up and down the platform, selling glasses of tea through the car windows. Keeping one eye on the departure schedules, men hurriedly consumed *chappati* and curried *subjis* in tiffins prepared by their wives, mothers, sisters, aunts and friends.

I thought back to the first time I laid eyes on Jaipur at the age of twenty—my first ride on a train. How exciting it had all been! The promise of a new life. The worry about whether it would all work out. And it had. I had come to this city with nothing but a skill for drawing and the lessons my mother-in-law had taught me. I had helped women fulfill their desires—whether in the pursuit of something or in the pursuit of its absence—so they could move on with their lives. Now, Jay Kumar was giving me a chance to reinvent myself, to use my knowledge to heal the old and young, sick and infirm, poor and in need of solace.

So many people had helped me in my journey. My *saas*. Hazi and Nasreen. Samir. Kanta. The Maharanis Indira and Latika. Mrs. Sharma. And even Parvati.

I wouldn't miss Jaipur—every city had its charm—but would I miss Samir?

To be honest, I thought about him still.

How companionably we had managed our business, the times we had laughed together, moments when our bond had felt true, strong, that one night of lust.

There were things I no longer admired about him, as I once had, but he had been a part of my life for so long. To quash those memories would have been like pretending that a third of my life didn't exist.

If I hadn't met him, I might still be in Agra, working with the courtesans, hidden away in their pleasure houses. Without his connections, who knows if I could have created a business as a henna artist? If he hadn't introduced me to Parvati, I might never have been invited to the maharanis' palace. Been served tea by Her Highness.

My attention was diverted by a commotion on the platform as the sea of travelers parted for a substantial man in a palace uniform. He wore the red cummerbund and headdress of the maharanis' attendants. He was carrying a large container draped in satin. A thin roll of carpet was wedged under his left arm. Oblivious to the stares and hushed voices of people on the platform, the man was consulting a piece of paper and looking up at each car he passed.

I called Malik to the window and pointed at the platform with my chin.

Malik craned his neck to look out the window. He grinned and waved. "Chef!"

The palace chef turned toward Malik's voice. His face relaxed into a warm smile. Malik ran to the door of our car to greet him. I watched them exchange greetings, a *salaam* from Malik and a *namaste* from Chef. The big man handed Malik the parcels and an envelope from his jacket pocket. They talked for a few more minutes before Chef waved goodbye.

Laden with his packages, Malik came down the passageway of our carriage, beaming. He gave me a heavy cream envelope with my name on it. I broke the palace seal, unfolded the stationery and read aloud.

"My Dear Mrs. Shastri,

"Your young friend has stolen Madho Singh's heart. All that bird can talk about is rabri *and Malik, Malik and* rabri. *He has started asking for Red and Whites, which leads me to be-*

*lieve that he has also taken up smoking. This I cannot abide. Furthermore, he refuses to learn any more French (*bonjour *and* bon voyage *are the extent of his repertoire), and as I'm spending all my time in Paris now, this presents a problem. So I must bid adieu to my lovely bird and ask if you will be so kind as to present him to Malik. I'm sure Madho Singh will be happier with him than in the tomb that is my sitting room at the palace.*

"The two of them are quite a pair, don't you agree?

"Your friend and admirer,
"Maharani Indira Man Singh

"P.S. The carpet is a favorite of Madho Singh's. He would be homesick without it."

Inside our compartment, Malik lifted the satin cover of the cage. Madho Singh hopped from side to side on his perch. He said, "*Namaste! Bonjour!* Welcome!" and whistled. Malik whistled back. Radha, who was meeting Madho Singh for the first time, let out a delighted chuckle.

I smiled at my family.

The shrill whistle of the train pierced my ears, announcing our departure. I took one last look out the window. In the middle of the platform where people scurried about like ants, one man stood as still as a statue.

His eyes were on me. He wore a spotless white shirt and *dhoti*. He had shaven his face. He had cut his hair. He looked… handsome.

I had lived with Hari for only two years, but he had lived in my mind for half my life. By turns, I had feared him, been indifferent, felt contemptuous, full of hate or pity. Not once had I believed him capable of change. But if I could change, why couldn't he?

Slowly, the engine began to pull its heavy load. Its wheels

chugged and heaved, heaved and chugged. Last-minute passengers threw themselves and their cargo onto the cars. Chai-*wallas* collected empty glasses from passengers.

Hari put his hands together in a *namaste* and raised them in front of his face. His smile was without reproach or anger. For the first time since I'd known him, he appeared content.

I returned his *namaste.*

The train picked up speed. He opened his mouth and his lips moved, but I could hear nothing over the screech of the wheels.

EPILOGUE

Shimla, Himalaya Foothills, India
November 5, 1956

"That was the last tunnel, Auntie-Boss!"

Malik had been poring over a railway map and he was counting every one of the hundred tunnels our toy train entered. We had taken the regular train from Jaipur to Kalka and then the toy train to Shimla.

He pointed at our location on the map. "Just a few more minutes and we'll be at the Shimla railway station!" He grinned. "Did you hear that, Madho Singh?" On the seat next to him, the parakeet was grumbling under the satin cover of his cage.

Radha had fallen asleep with her head in my lap, but now she sat up and rubbed her eyes. She looked out the window of the train, where deodar cedars and Himalayan pines dotted the rocky mountains across the valley. The first snows had fallen, leaving the treetops decorated with bluish-white icing.

"Is there always snow here, Radha?" Malik asked. He had only ever lived in the Rajasthani desert.

She smiled. "Only in the winter. But wait another month. The ground will be completely covered in snow. Then we will build a snow-woman who looks like Mrs. Iyengar!"

They laughed. Even *I* found the image of a stout snowman in a sari amusing. I hid my smile behind the letter I was rereading.

Dr. Kumar had been sending me letters every few days since I accepted his offer to come work with him. This one had arrived just before we left for Shimla.

November 1, 1956

Dear Lakshmi,

I have found a three-bedroom house in Shimla for your family. Radha and Malik will each have their own room! It is close to Lady Bradley, so you can walk. Or, if you prefer, I can arrange a car and driver.

I've also taken the liberty of arranging a few appointments for you when you first arrive. Already I feel I must apologize for putting you to work so quickly. You'll be sprinting the moment you step off the train!

Mrs. Sethi, the headmistress of the Auckland House School, looks forward to meeting with you regarding Radha's enrollment. I would be happy to accompany you and Malik to Bishop Cotton, my alma mater, for his first day. Unless, of course, you'd rather reserve that pleasure for yourself. (My old headmaster is still there, but don't believe any of the stories he tells about me!)

Samir Singh had offered to pay for Radha's education. His note to me had come as a surprise. He said he hoped my sister would continue studying Shakespeare. I accepted that for the meager apology it was, though Radha deserved better. I had asked that he pay her fees anonymously; I wanted no further contact with him. Nor did I want Radha to have any reason to communicate with the Singhs.

Jay Kumar knew about this financial arrangement but not the history, and when I explained it to him, he had not asked any questions. He seemed focused only on our shared future. In his letters (which came frequently), he told me what he was learning about the hill people and their age-old medicinal cures.

> *A part of the rhododendron bush, they tell me, is used as a cure for swollen ankles. Have you heard of this? Yesterday, an old Gaddi woman brought a bowl of* sik *(made from the dried fruit of the* neem *tree) for one of our cleaners who is pregnant. She says it ensures a healthy body before and after delivery. Out of curiosity, I tasted it—much to the delight of both women!*

The thought of Jay Kumar eating a bowl of porridge meant for a pregnant woman made me smile.

> *Every day the people ask me when you're arriving. Many remember you from the clinic. You left an impression on them—a good one—judging from the way they talk about you. They, and I, look forward to welcoming you back.*
>
> *Till we meet,*
> *Jay*

The train's whistle brought me back to my present surroundings.

"We're here!" Malik was out of his seat before the train had even stopped.

I returned the letter to my handbag. Radha and Malik gathered our things. The train slowed, and as we came around the curve of the mountain, I saw the Shimla railway station.

Jay Kumar was the tallest man on the platform. He was wearing his white coat over a green turtleneck sweater; he'd probably come directly from the hospital. The Himalayan wind was blowing his curls about. Funny how I'd forgotten the streaks of gray in his hair. Or the way he stood with his head tilted to one side, as if he were listening for something important.

When he spotted me at the window, his eyes locked on mine, and his expression changed—a slow smile of recognition. I noticed, too, the gray of his eyes, and, for once, he did not look away.

I felt myself blushing, the heat on my neck like fire.

Radha tapped my arm. "Jiji, look!"

Now I noticed the crowd of people assembled beside him, their bright wool skirts, embroidered *topas*, colorful blouses. There was the woman to whom I had recommended bitter melon and garlic when her pregnancy had given her severe indigestion. She was holding her new baby, proudly, in the crook of her arm.

To her right was the grandmother who suffered from arthritis, smiling with her toothless gums, holding the reins of her mule.

And over there—the sheepherder! Jay had written me that the diet I'd suggested had saved the shepherd from having his goiter removed. He held up a hand in greeting, his eyes crinkling in pleasure.

A thousand miles from the tiny village where I'd started, I was finally home.

Behind us, from his cage, Madho Singh called out again: "*Namaste! Bonjour!* Welcome!"

★ ★ ★ ★ ★

ACKNOWLEDGMENTS

I wrote this novel for my mother.

Sudha Latika Joshi had an arranged marriage at eighteen and three children by the age of twenty-two. She never had the opportunity to choose whom to marry, when to marry, whether to have children, whether or not to continue her studies or what she would do with her life. But she made sure that I could make all those choices for myself.

In the novel, I reimagine her existence—as Lakshmi, the henna artist who creates a life of her own. Every day, I thank my remarkable mother for her fierce love, her tenacity and her utter devotion to my brothers and me. Without her, this book could never have been written.

My father, Ramesh Chandra Joshi, whose remarkable journey from humble villager to globe-trotting engineer never ceases to amaze me, was enthusiastic about this novel from the start. He shared with me the India of his youth following the British Raj and the part he played in rebuilding the new India. His memories helped me better understand the post-independence enthusiasm I wove into the story. Dad read early versions of the novel and sought out Indian friends to review the drafts and share their own experiences. Any mistakes in the telling are mine.

I owe a thousand thanks also to Emma Sweeney of Emma Sweeney Literary Agency, who fell in love with this book so many years ago and stayed with it until it was ready to be brought out into the world. And another thousand thanks go to MIRA Books senior acquisitions editor Kathy Sagan, and to the extraordinary HarperCollins team: Loriana Sacilotto, Nicole Brebner, Leo MacDonald, Heather Connor, Heather Foy, Margaret Marbury, Amy Jones, Randy Chan, Ashley MacDonald, Erin Craig, Karen Ma, Irina Pintea, Kaitlyn Vincent, Roxanne Jones and Laura Gianino. You guys rock!

To Anita Amirrezvani, the mentor whose novels inspired me to write a story set in another time, place and culture, I extend heartfelt gratitude.

Early readers who helped make this book sing are Tom Barbash, Janis Cooke Newman, Aimee Phan, Lanny Udell, Sandra Scofield, Robert Friedman, Samm Owens, Bonnie Ayers Namkung, Ritika Kumar, Shail Kumar, Grant Dukeshire, AJ Bunuan, Mary Severance and my fellow CCA MFA workshop participants.

My brothers, Madhup Joshi and Piyush Joshi, read drafts of the novel and cheered me on. My mother and I traveled several times to Jaipur after 2008, where we stayed in Piyush's condo. While in Jaipur, I interviewed Rajput families, shopkeepers in the Pink City, women my age and their daughters, teachers at the Maharani Gayatri Devi Girls' School, Ayurvedic doctors and, of course, henna artists. I spoke at schools and colleges, danced at glorious weddings and drank copious cups of chai.

I also researched India's medicinal plants, Ayurvedic and

aromatherapy remedies and the history of henna—how it's made and why it's so important in Indian culture. I pored over the history of the British in Rajasthan, the education of girls in that era, the caste system and how it affected the lives of those defined by it.

For inspiration, I read authors whose works recall an India of times past and present: Kamala Markandaya, Ruth Prawer Jhabwala, R. K. Narayan, Anita Desai, V. S. Naipaul, Rohintin Mistry, Amitav Ghosh, Manil Suri, Chitra Banerjee Divakurani, Thrity Umrigar, Shobha Rao, Akhil Sharma and Madhuri Vijay. I also read brilliant postcolonial works by authors such as Jamaica Kincaid, Chinua Achebe, Khaled Hosseini, Chimamanda Ngozi Adichie and Edwidge Danticat.

Finally—and always—I thank my husband, Bradley Jay Owens, who told me I married a writer because I secretly wanted to be one. If he hadn't given me that encouragement in 1997, I might never have taken a writing workshop, never earned my MFA, never had the chance to immortalize my mother in the way she deserved. You have my heart, love.

I love hearing from readers, so if you'd like to get in touch, you'll find me at www.thehennaartist.com or visit me on Facebook (alkajoshi2019) and Instagram (@thealkajoshi).

ABOUT THE AUTHOR

Alka Joshi was born in India and raised in the United States since the age of nine, she has a BA from Stanford University and an MFA from California College of the Arts. She lives in Pacific Grove, California, with her husband. *The Henna Artist* is her first novel. *The Secret-Keeper of Jaipur* is the sequel to *The Henna Artist*.

What inspired you to write *The Henna Artist*?

I have my mother to thank for my first novel.

When I was fifteen, my mother and I went shopping for school clothes. We'd been living in the States—in the Midwest—for six years by then, but she still wore saris. As we passed the dresses, she plucked one with a plunging halter top off the rack and asked me to try it on. An American girl might have thought her mother hip, but I was embarrassed.

For my sixteenth birthday, my mother made an appointment at Merle Norman Cosmetics so I could learn to wear makeup, something she knew nothing about but felt I needed to learn.

At eighteen, when I told her I wanted to sleep with my first boyfriend, she immediately took me to get birth control pills and urged me to experiment—she who had had an arranged marriage at the age of eighteen and still stumbled over her English.

It took me years to understand that what my mother wanted was a life for me that she herself had been denied. She wanted me to experience the freedom of choice.

At some point, I began imagining a different start to my mother's life. What if her father hadn't made her marry at such a tender age? What if she hadn't had three children in rapid succession? What would a creative, fierce, smart woman like her have done to survive on her own if she had defied her father and refused to marry?

Lakshmi, the henna artist, embodies the alternative life I imagined for my mother. The frenetic period following India's independence from the British, when India was building new universities, government and cultural institutions, and roads, dams and bridges at an unprecedented rate, was an ideal setting for Lakshmi to start a new life for herself. Like my mother, Lakshmi wanted to make her own decisions about what she wanted to do, who she wanted to be with and where she went. She rejected convention even when she knew the cost would be steep, not only for her but also for her family.

Yet, like the citizens of a newly independent nation, Lakshmi finds that progress takes time. While Lakshmi is recognized for her talents publicly the way my mother was not, the cultural norms she grew up with will not easily bend to accommodate a clever, headstrong young woman. Ultimately, she is forced to create a new path that will satisfy her ambitions and society's expectations of her.

My mother is no longer with us, but she lives in every breath Lakshmi takes and every word she utters. Through Lakshmi, my mother revels in the freedom she never had in real life.

Are you working on another novel?

Yes, I am exploring what the future will look like down the road for a few of the characters central to The Henna Artist. *The year is 1967. The younger characters are now the new generation of progressive Indians moving the country forward.*

**Note: Alka Joshi's second novel* The Secret-Keeper of Jaipur *was published in 2021.*

ALSO BY ALKA JOSHI

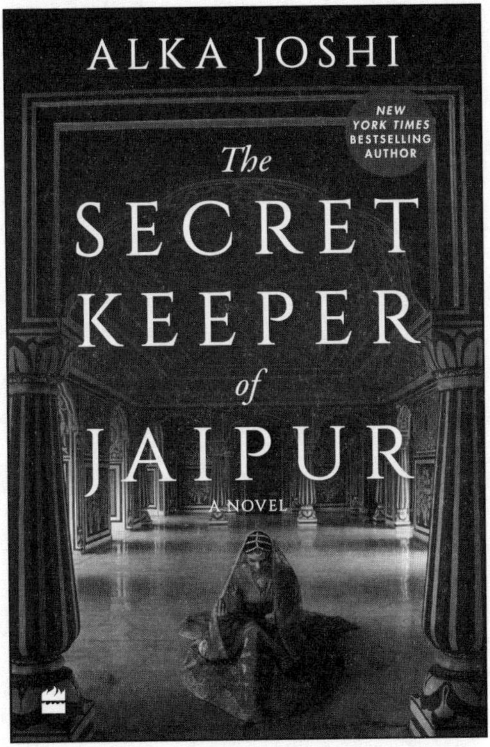

Praise for *The Secret-Keeper of Jaipur*

"Alka Joshi is a master storyteller."

—Christy Lefteri, author, *The Beekeeper of Aleppo* and *Songbirds*

"An applause-worthy encore."

—*Booklist*

"An engaging and powerful story."

—Pam Jenoff, author, *The Lost Girls of Paris*